I0634818

The Germans on Venus
And Other French Scientific Romances

also by Brian Stableford:
* The New Faust at the Tragicomique
* The Shadow of Frankenstein
* Sherlock Holmes and the Vampires of Eternity
* The Stones of Camelot
* The Wayward Muse

also translated and introduced by Brian Stableford:
* News from the Moon (*anthology*)
* *by Félix Bodin*: The Novel of the Future
* *by Charles Derennes*: The People of the Pole
* *by Paul Féval*: Anne of the Isles and Other Legends of
Brittany – The Black Coats: 'Salem Street – The Black
Coats: The Invisible Weapon – The Black Coats: The
Parisian Jungle – The Black Coats: The Companions of
the Treasure – John Devil – Knightshade – Revenants –
Vampire City – The Vampire Countess – The Wandering Jew's Daughter
* *by Paul Féval*, fils: Felifax, the Tiger-Man
* *by Octave Joncquel & Théo Varlet*: The Martian Epic
* *by Jean de La Hire*: The Nyctalope vs. Lucifer – The
Nyctalope on Mars
* *by Gustave Le Rouge*: The Vampires of Mars
* *by Marie Nizet*: Captain Vampire
* *by Henri de Parville*: An Inhabitant of the Planet Mars
* *by Pierre-Alexis Ponson du Terrail*: The Vampire and
the Devil's Son
* *by Albert Robida*: The Clock of the Centuries
* *by Villiers de l'Isle-Adam*: The Scaffold and Other
Cruel Tales – The Vampire Soul and Other Sardonic
Tales

The Germans on Venus
And Other French Scientific Romances

translated, annotated and introduced by
Brian Stableford

A Black Coat Press Book

English adaptation and introduction Copyright © 2009 by
Brian Stableford.
Cover illustration Copyright © 2007 by Gil Formosa.

Visit our website at www.blackcoatpress.com

ISBN 978-1-934543-56-6. First Printing. March 2009. Published by Black Coat Press, an imprint of Hollywood Com-
ics.com, LLC, P.O. Box 17270, Encino, CA 91416. All rights
reserved.
Except for review purposes, no part of this book may
be reproduced or transmitted in any form or by any means,
electronic or mechanical, including photocopying, recording,
or by any information storage and retrieval system, without
permission in writing from the publisher. The stories and characters depicted in this anthology are entirely fictional.
Printed
in the United States of America.

Table of Contents

Introduction

This is the second anthology of French scientific romances that I have compiled for Black Coat Press, following *News from the Moon and Other French Scientific Romances.*[1] The introduction to the first volume defined the genre and offered some comments on the fundamental pattern of its development, which there is no need to repeat here. I shall introduce each story individually, so all that remains to be done in this general introduction is to offer a few observations about the tenor of this particular showcase.

I have attempted to provide a representative cross-section of texts spanning the entire period in which the genre of scientific romance thrived, before it went into a decline and eventually gave way to "science fiction" imitative of the work produced under that American label. Any such cross-section confined to a single volume is bound to be highly selective and therefore somewhat distorted; although it was not my initial intention, this one is somewhat biased in favor of the humorous, not so much because I wanted to emphasize the comical aspects of the genre as because I wanted to emphasize stories that had uncommon imaginative range. It is when writers forearm themselves against charges of absurdity by a deliberate intention to be absurd that they are most likely to let their imagination run free—and, indeed, to push it all the way to its apparent limits.

This narrative strategy works backwards as well as forwards; even when writers set out to write dramas or melodramas, they tend to excuse the more extravagant reaches of their imagination by adding in an apologetic note of irony. For this

---

[1] ISBN 978-1-932983-89-0.

reason, even an earnest and calculatedly propagandistic work like André Mas' "The Germans on Venus"—an early attempt to use scientific romance as propaganda for the feasibility of space travel—finds it politic to adopt an uneven gloss of satirical comedy, and a heartfelt plaint like Marcel Schwob's "The Future Terror" cannot help acquiring a taint of the kind of *grand guignol* grotesquerie that is more carefully cultivated in such *contes cruels* as Rémy de Gourmont's "The Automaton."

Another consequence of reaching for the limits of the imagination is that it poses acute challenges in terms of narrative format. The general history of literature during the period covered by this anthology—the 1780s to the 1920s—was one of the steady sophistication of techniques of narrative realism: the development of better ways to give a reader to enter into a story as if it were a lived experience, often by "identifying" with the characters. The result of that methodical evolution was the gradual development of the standard features of the modern novel—a process that was perhaps more conscious and studied in France than anywhere else. Although it is not strictly necessary for techniques of narrative realism to be applied to mundane content—the development of modern horror fiction has largely been a matter of their careful application to supernatural materials—problems inevitably arise when the intention is to deal with matters of scientific speculation, futuristic extrapolation and cosmic visions.

An early discussion of such problems is found in and exemplified by Félix Bodin's *Le Roman de l'avenir* (1834; tr. in a Black Coat Press edition as *The Novel of the Future* [2]). Bodin wrote that book in order to stake his claim to the idea of using novelistic techniques in a story set in the future, but his attempt to practice what he preached soon ran into problems that he had not anticipated, and became a kind of tortured commentary on its own frustrated ambitions. Before starting out on his exemplar, Bodin had observed that previous literary works dealing with the future mostly fell into the categories of

[2] ISBN 978-1-934543-44-3.

"utopias" and "apocalypses," both of which were species of visionary fantasy. Such works inevitable resemble expository non-fiction more closely than novels, usually having ideological axes to grind with relentless intensity. As soon as he started to write his own futuristic fantasy, however, Bodin found it impossible to put away, or even to blunt, his own ideological axe as a committed believer in and (in his capacity as an elected deputé in Louis-Philippe's government) a would-be activator of social progress.

Not only did Bodin's narrative voice and characters alike find it difficult to adopt any topics of conversation but issues relating to past and future progress, but they could not help acting out a plot whose motive threads were orientated towards an apocalyptic climactic battle, which would presumably have settled for good and all the question of whether the perfectibility of human society—which is to say, the establishment of an Earthly utopia—was feasible. Somewhat to the author's horror, as expressed by a slightly panic-stricken narrative voice, he found that the simple fact of adopting the conventions of the novel—which meant, in that era, the conventions of the Romantic novel—revealed a fundamental contradiction between the assumptions of that kind of fiction and the ambitions of progress, to the remarkable extent that the narrative voice began to deplore and mourn the fact that his readers (especially the female ones) were likely to find his satanic arch-villain more attractive than his intrinsically-reasonable hero, and root for the insanely evil Anti-Prosaic organization against the thoroughly sane Association for Civilization.

The fact that the cause of social progress had its enemies was, of course, as indisputable in post-Revolutionary France as it had been in pre-Revolutionary France, but the series of upheavals that had taken France through the 1789 Revolution, the Terror, the Empire, the Restoration and the July Revolution of 1830 before Bodin set pen to paper had already made the most diehard champions of progress deeply anxious as to the viability of their cause, and their opponents—who, as Bodin reluctantly concluded and admitted, included a clear and perhaps unassailable majority of Romantic writers and artists—lost no opportunity to feed that paranoia. The situation got no better, of course, as France proceeded its political drunkard's walk through the Revolution of 1848, the *coup d'état* of 1851, the Second Empire, the disastrous Franco-Prussian war of 1870 and the consequent Paris Commune, a new Republic and, ultimately, the Great War of 1914-18.

Against that historical backcloth, it required unusual ideological heroism to maintain any sort of faith in the probability of future sociopolitical progress, and a pair of rose-colored glasses to confirm the believe that much more than a smidgen had recently been accomplished. On the other hand, there was not an atom of doubt that vast strides had been accomplished in scientific and technological progress, and it began to require a perversely stubborn lack of imagination to cling to the conviction that progress of that sort would soon run out of steam—or, eventually, electricity.

The early philosophers of progress—Anne-Robert Turgot, the Encyclopedists and the Marquis de Condorcet—had taken it for granted that social progress towards liberty, equality and fraternity would go hand-in-hand with scientific and technological progress, each facilitating the other in a healthy feedback loop, but their successors not only began to doubt that it was so but also began to wonder whether the feedback might be negative rather than positive, and that further scientific and technological progress might actually be inimical to the utopian causes of liberty, equality and fraternity. Not long after Bodin's heroic failure to write a novel of the future—and, incidentally, to plot a course for the future development of the novel—the utopian mode of optimistic speculative thought that he had identified was confused by the emergence of its pessimistic opposite, rapidly christened (probably by John Stuart Mill) "dystopian."

This combination of ideological conflict and anxiety was the fertile ground in which scientific romance sprouted and eventually flourished, and it is clearly reflected in this anthology, not merely by the stories themselves, which use the conflict and anxiety as dramatic fuel, but also by their writers, who include among their number a crop of ideological malcontents as rich as one could ever hope to find, even in a country as fecund in the production and proliferation of ideological malcontentment as France. Restif de la Bretonne, Charles Nodier, X. B. Saintine, Louis Ulbach, Jules Lermina, Rémy de Gourmont, André Mas and Théo Varlet cannot be said to constitute any kind of uniform group—politically and philosophically, they are scattered about a broad spectrum—but they were all, in their different ways, deeply discontented with the world as they found it, and even those who had little or no faith in their capacity to make a difference to it were determined not to let it rest easy without hurling a little vitriol in its face. The writers featured in these pages that I left out of the above list were generally less flamboyant in their manner than those cited, but the difference was one of degree rather than kind.

The early philosophers of progress also took it for granted, of course, that scientific and technological progress went hand-in-hand as a matter of logical necessity, given that the former was the parent, or at least the midwife of the latter. This assumption too came under stress, as it became increasingly fashionable to distinguish between the abstract and philosophical enlightenments of science and the brutal pragmatic effects of industrial technology and "mechanization." Both kinds of progress had their reactionary opponents, who were often allied if not identical, but the grounds of their opposition were often quite distinct and sometimes wildly divergent.

The ideological opposition to the main plot-threads in the narrative development of science was religious, consisting of the digging of trenches in defense of divine creation and all its corollaries, and to inhibit the advance of materialist theories of life and all their corollaries. The ideological opposition to the development of technology was, on the one hand, more straightforwardly and primitively paranoid, and, on the other, more mundanely pragmatic; in the former instance, the fear was that our inventions would get out of hand and run amok;

in the latter, it was simply that they would throw us all out of work and make us redundant.

As all the stories in this collection, without exception, illustrate clearly and rather strikingly, the war between inherited faith and empirical revelation was not one a simple one in which battle-lines were drawn up between Biblical "fundamentalists" and geologically-inspired evolutionists, although the import of *Genesis* was a key pivot of controversy. The question of how life originated, on a cosmic scale, and what the implications of different theories of origin might be for its extraterrestrial distribution and manifestation, was far more complicated than a simple matter of the exact point, or points, in time and space at which God or some automatic process of spontaneous generation had imparted, or was still imparting, the vital spark. Old theological quarrels regarding the plurality of worlds, and more recent theological speculations regarding the possibility of cosmic palingenesis—the interplanetary transmigration of souls—were very much alive in late 18th century France, and they remained significant throughout the history of French scientific romance, making a substantial contribution of its distinctive flavor.

Because fiction trades so heavily in conflict and fear—those being essential components of drama, especially the strategic exaggerations of melodrama—scientific romance inevitably draws very heavily on paranoid objections to technological development. The 20th century science fiction writer Isaac Asimov called attention to the prevalence of what he called "the Frankenstein complex:" a neurotic anxiety that any new technology, however useful or benevolent it might seem, is bound to have disastrous consequences. He objected strenuously to the prevalence of this complex in speculative fiction, and declared his own intention to resist it with all his might—which turned out, in practice to be slightly less mighty than he might have supposed or hoped.

Despite its extreme convenience in enabling the construction of sturdy story-arcs, the Frankenstein complex is only given full-blooded expression in three of the stories in this anthology,[3] but its haunting presence is tangible in the background of a further three,[4] and it is arguable that those phantom manifestations are more interesting than more flamboyant displays. The more pragmatic aspect of anti-technological sentiment is far less visible here, precisely because its essential mundanity made it less attractive to the editorial sieve, but it lurks in the background of at least two of the stories,[5] more like a shabby tramp than a hungry ghost, but by no means devoid of menace.

Like Félix Bodin and Isaac Asimov, most all of the writers represented here believed themselves to be on the side of progress, and the minority who stood up against it damned the idea of social perfectibility because it was impracticable, not because it was undesirable. Charles Nodier, for instance, was absolutely convinced of the impossibility of perfectibility, but he was not delighted by that impossibility—indeed, the main reason why he took the trouble to put the boot into it with such febrile determination was that he was venting his sense of anger and disappointment regarding the tragedy of its impossibility.

The underlying story told by the collection—which does have an underlying narrative of sorts, despite its carefully-contrived variety—is the story of the problem discovered and mourned by Félix Bodin: that the covert fundamental assumptions of Progress and Romance are at odds, and that anyone who sets out to amalgamate or alloy the two, no matter how well-intentioned or ingenious he might be, will eventually find his work racked and tormented by contradictions, pulling in different directions. From a literary point of view, however, that is not entirely a bad thing, and perhaps not a bad thing at all, because fiction—especially Romantic fiction—is, at the

---

[3] Those by Robert, Lermina and Schwob.

[4] Those by Ulbach, Mullem and Allais, although a case could be made out for adding Nodier to the list.

[5] Those by Ulbach and Robert, although a case could be made for adding Lermina and Mas.

end of the day, and whether we like it or not, the purest and most defiant celebration of our cherished imperfections that we possess.

Brian Stableford

Restif de la Bretonne: *Posthumous Correspondence*
(Excerpts)
(1796)

Nicolas-Edmé Restif de La Bretonne (1734-1806) was the son of a farmer named Edmé Rétif; he elaborated his name in imitation of aristocratic nomenclature, mainly by adding that of the farm his father had taken over in 1742. After receiving an education of sorts from Jansenist clergymen before the order was suppressed he was apprenticed to a printer in Auxerre, acquiring skills that he allegedly later put to use when he became a writer, sometimes allegedly composing straight to type without bothering with an intermediary manuscript. That allegation would help to account for the eccentric typography of some of his works, but might be somewhat exaggerated, as many tales about him were—especially those he told himself in his autobiography, *Monsieur Nicolas* (1794-97), which was supposedly intended to "lay his heart bare."

Restif went to Paris in 1755 after completing his apprenticeship and lived a hectic and somewhat dissolute life there, prowling the city by night—he nicknamed himself *le hibou* [the owl] and apparently helping to pioneer the dubious art of graffiti. He published his first novel, *La famille vertueuse*, in 1767 and produced prose of a prolific scale thereafter, much of which was regarded as disreputable because of his obsessive interest in sex and the necessity of social reforms that would better accommodate the sexual urge. When his friend and fellow "Rousseau du ruisseau" [gutter Rousseau], Louis-Sébastien Mercier, supported by Jacques-Henri Bernardin de Saint-Pierre, suggested nominating him for the Académie to the president Jean-François de La Harpe, the latter vetoed the nomination on the grounds that Restif "had genius but lacked taste;" Mercier is said to have replied, modestly but undiplomatically, "Ah, but which of us has genius?" Restif was certainly a great admirer of Rousseau, more for the latter's determinedly oppositional mentality than his actual philosophical convictions, but La Harpe might have been closer to the mark in cruelly labeling him "the chambermaids' Voltaire." Subsequent generations were more inclined to lump him in with the Marquis de Sade, and his erotic fascinations are certainly reminiscent of Sade without the sadism, but both men were well aware of the possibility of confusion, and affected to loathe one another.

Unfortunately, Restif's reputed "lack of taste" minimized his literary reputation long after his death as well as during his life, until champions of his unique combination of erotic frankness and philosophical adventurism began to emerge in the mid-19th century, including Gérard de Nerval and Charles Baudelaire. It was, however, too late to recover much of his canon, many items of which had already become fabulously rare, and almost all of which lingered in esoteric obscurity throughout the 20th century. When Pierre Versins devoted a long article to Restif's Utopian writings in his *Encyclopédie de l'Utopie et de la Science Fiction* (1972), only one of the works he discussed, *La Découverte australe par un homme volant, ou le Dédale français* [Discoveries in the Southern Hemisphere by a Flying Man; or, The French Daedalus] (1781) was reasonably well-known. Of the others, which hardy anyone then alive had ever cast eyes on, by far the most interesting is *Les Posthumes, Lettres reçues après la mort du mari, par sa femme, qui le croit à Florence* [Posthumous Correspondence: Letters Received after the Death of a Husband by his Wife, who Believed him to be in Florence] (1802 but first drafted, according to Versins, in 1787-89 and then rewritten in 1796). The original four-volume text remains extremely rare, never having been reprinted, although a substantial sample was reprinted in 1990 as *Les Voyages de Multipliandre* and shorter excerpts have been published in other samplers of Restif's work. The following translations have been taken from one of these shorter samples (even the 1990 text is now very difficult to obtain).

The text of *Les Posthumes* combines the letter-writer's accounts of his own posthumous activities with a second hand account of the much more elaborate adventures of Jean-Jacob, Duc Multipliandre. That name is intended to be more suggestive of "man multiplied" than "Everyman:" Multipliandre is a kind of superman, who can not only fly but discorporate himself in order to undertake journeys in space and time, enabling him to visit many other worlds and the Earth of the future. Many of his adventures, as related by the letter-writer—occasionally in direct quotation—display his opinions regarding the idiosyncratic limitations of contemporary humankind, especially the problematics of sexual relationships, in a quasi-satirical fashion. His account of his cosmic voyages to other worlds within and beyond the solar system allow him to put those discussions into a wider biological context, examining the nature, languages, folkways and reproductive strategies of many extraterrestrial species, few of which are humanoid and some of which are radically alien. Although Restif follows Mercier's example—in "Nouvelles de la Lune" (1768; tr. as the title-piece of my earlier Black Coat press showcase anthology)—by combining contemporary notions regarding the plurality of worlds with the theory of cosmic palingenesis, he takes the corollaries of the premise much further, just as Multipliandre's glimpse of the future, as summarized by Versins, seems to be considerably more radical than Mercier's classic depiction of Paris in the year 2440.

Restif's imagery of alien life was highly unusual for its time, when the vast majority of depictions of life on other worlds imagined their dominant inhabitants as near-human, or at least closely modeled on familiar animal species. Throughout the 19th century and into the early 20th, in fact, the majority view was that because other planets were made of the same elements as the Earth, and had originated by the same process of nebular condensation, life there would inevitably follow a similar pattern to that on Earth, however it originated and/or evolved—a doctrine dramatized by the other interplanetary stories reprinted in this sampler.

This was not the only respect in which Restif was way ahead of his time as a speculative writer. His utopianism anticipates many aspects of 19th century communism as well as the sexual revolution of the late 20th century. He not only imagined heavier-than-air flying machines in advance of the Montgolfier brothers' first balloon flight, but suspected that such devices would leave a "trail of infamy, fear and horror" in the future when they were used to drop bombs. Although his evolutionary theory was primitive, he deserves recognition as a significant pre-Lamarckian evolutionary philosopher. He was also a significant pre-Pasteurian germ theorist. He was, as even La Harpe admitted, a genius—and he also had far better taste than he was long given credit for. French scientific romance would have been far richer had he had more influence on its early development.

The fragments reproduced here only represent a small fraction of Multipliandre's comic voyage; the full text evidently goes into much more detail about life on Mars, Jupiter and other worlds. The fragments I have translated begin part way through the 207th letter; I have run consecutive letters together, as the breaks between them are arbitrary, but I have separated out the occasional interpolated "responses" by means of an extra line. Where sections of the original text have been omitted, however, I have inserted chapter breaks.

I

When Multipliandre had risen up, by means of his wings, to 32,000 feet above the world's surface, there was no more breathable air. It was impossible to make provision for that; there was only one course of action to take and he took it. That was discorporation. He flew over the highest peak in the entire world and left his body on he inaccessible point of a crag, after having wrapped it up well in furs, having treated it with a health-preserving gel, with which he filled the stomach, the mouth and all the bodily apertures and having placed it so securely that the winds and tempests could not dislodge it. Then, his detached soul could go wherever it wished, because, no longer being in the sphere of corporate life but that of souls, could dispense entirely with entry into a body.

Multipliandre's soul being a finite point, it could not arrive on the world of the Moon instantaneously; the journey would take time, albeit not long—about half an hour. Consequently, he calculated the point in space where the Moon would be in half an hour, and directed his intention thereto, intention being the soul's wings. He arrived there at the right moment, but in entering the tenuous lunar atmosphere he sensed that he needed a body. He displaced the soul of the first large bird he encountered and descended thus to the surface.

As soon as he had arrived, having caught sight of a Rondin (that being the name of the lunar creature that corresponds to an Earthly human), he abandoned the body of the bird—which did not resemble our birds, having one round wing all around the body—and set about displacing the Rondin's soul. He found it to be very weak, and triumphed without difficulty; he placed it in the bird that he had quit.

Multipliandre perceived that the Rondin was the dominant animal on the Moon, not by virtue of its form, which did not resemble that of humans at all—it was entirely round and rolled instead of walking—but because all the other animals drew away from it, or at least would not to allow it to approach. While he was in its body, he allowed its former ideas to follow their habitual course, and immediately sensed how limited they were. The Rondin only thought about four things: seeing, hearing, tasting and touching. It did not have the idea of odor, and lacked a sense of smell.

Multipliandre's soul tried to speak then, and perceived with singular astonishment that the same organ served for eating, speaking, listening and evacuation;[6] it had two different conduits to the interior, one for introduction and the other for excretion. As the Rondins, like all other lunar animals, have no limbs, they have a singular manner of eating. They lick an object and catch hold of it with a multitude of tiny feet, like those of woodlice or the clinging processes of ivy, then they suck it by means of the same tongue; one sees the sucked object diminish in breath or volume, like a fly devoured by a spider, and the sucker increase in size. It is only by that means that one can see which is the eater and which the eaten. In this manner they suck animals, fruits and plants whose species are entirely different from ours.

It was a curious thing to see a Rondin roll after an animal, trap it, attach itself to it and suck it up. Some three or four days later the victim disappeared entirely, and the consumer was as large as the two of them had been—then it diminished by transpiration. If, during the suction, the consumer experienced a contrary need, it stopped, evacuated, rinsed the con-

---

[6] I have had to omit an untranslatable joke here; the term Restif uses for which I have substituted "evacuation" is *démanger*, which is the etymological opposite of *manger* (eating) in French but is not used as such (it is actually used to mean itching); he adds a parenthetical observation to explain that the equivalent term is used literally in the lunar language. I have used "evacuation" rather than "defecation" here because Restif subsequently uses a more direct French equivalent of the latter English word (*déjection*) in circumstances that hint at a similar wordplay; the English transfiguration of dejection is, of course, used quite differently.

duit, then began sucking again. Sometimes, a malodorous excretion of digested matter emerged from the pores of the Rondin or the animals, in parts opposed to that which sucked.

The Rondin language was composed of 24 masculine words and as many feminine ones, the verbs having no tenses and only one participle, which was both substantive and adjective at the same time. Here are the 24 words:

Loving, hating.
Eating, evacuating
Enjoying, depriving.
Beating, vanquishing.
Chasing, evading.
Killing, producing.
Crying out, shutting up.
Flying, walking.
Winning, losing.
Ordering, confusing.
Searching, finding.
Accepting, refusing.
Taking, receiving.
Giving, removing.
Braving, fleeing.
Rejoicing, saddening, frightening.
Honoring, scorning.
Going forward, stopping
Being born, dying.
Warming, chilling.
Illuminating, obscuring.
Existing, ceasing to exist,
Raising, lowering.
Benevolent, malevolent.[7]

---

[7] This last pair—two words (*bienfaisant, malfaisant*) that have the same form as present participles in French, by virtue of ending in –ant, while actually being adjectives—embodies one of several untranslatable linguistic jokes in the list. Number 4 (*battant, vainquant*)—the only item not to feature a blatant

All the passives of these participles—loved, hated, eaten, evacuated, etc.—are the feminines of the pairs. The Sun is called the warming, the Moon the warmed, God the existing, the Rondin the ceasing to exist, or mortal. The word Rondin was invented by Multipliandre because of the rolling motion of the lunar inhabitants, which is particular to them.

Oh, what strange people! At the end of the day, though, it is necessary that everything is varied in Nature, and we all believe that strongly—but men are eternally argumentative. Monsieur de Lagrange [8] has a theory: he says that all the planets must dissolve in their Sun, and all the Suns in God or the central star, and that this amalgamation of all being in God, at the end of a great general revolution, proves that—all the Suns and, in consequence, all the planets having emerged from that homogeneous amalgam—they must all produce the same things. That is well enough reasoned—Monsieur Cazotte was converted on the spot—but others maintain their opinion. They say that it is the difference of locality, not that of sub-

---

opposition—is more complicated than it seems in translation because of the multiple meanings of *battant*.

[8] Joseph-Louis Lagrange (1736-1813) was a noted mathematician, commemorated in a formula that bears his name, who applied his art to astronomical calculations and speculations. The person named as having been convinced of Lagrange's argument as soon as he heard it is the writer Jacques Cazotte (1719-1792), with whom Restif dined twice a week from 1786 onwards, along with other guests. Restif falsely attributed the anonymously-published *Les Posthumes* to Cazotte—who had fallen victim to the Terror ten years before its publication—and the gesture suggests that some of the narrative's details originated in discussions at Cazotte's table, although the basic idea of letters from beyond the grave was allegedly furnished by Restif's sometime patroness, Fanny de Beauharnais, while the world-view of the narrative and its extraordinary range are pure Restif.

stance, which produces and necessitates differences of organization, form and modification. It is truly astonishing that I remember all that.

It is in a language that has only these few words that the two lunar sexes express everything that they have to say, employing neither conjunctions nor adverbs. The Moon is also called the existent, the Earth the illuminating. There are no pronouns; to say "me" the Rondin bounces on the spot; to say "you" he bumps into another; for "him" the same; for "my" he attaches himself.

For erotic enjoyment, the Rondin and Rondine attach themselves together as if they were eating one another; one can see that they are having sex because they increase and diminish in size alternately to a small degree.

Having left the Earth when the Moon was full, I observed at first that it was midday when I arrived. The heat was so excessive that all the living beings retreated into caverns or profound valleys, with which the Moon is strewn, or beneath large trees whose foliage, if they have any, is impenetrable to the Sun's rays. The reason for this is that because the Moon's atmosphere has neither ice nor snow (they hardly have time to form during a half-year or winter of 14 of our nights and days, and have, on the other hand, plenty of time to melt during a hot day) the Moon has no large rivers and very few small ones, only streams; similarly, it has few seas, whether because crystallization is more advanced than on Earth and on Venus, or for other reasons. Thus, there is almost no rain, only abundant dews, during the long night of 14 times 24 hours. The trees and other plants do not have leaves; they are all akin to mushrooms. They grow in the same fashion, after abundant dews, and are all destroyed at about the third hour of the afternoon—which is to say, between the ninth and tenth of our 24-hour days, counting in our fashion. During this interval, they bear their fruit, and the lunar inhabitants harvest them. There are also plants that do not bear fruit; these are bread-mushrooms and they are very tasty. They are eaten fresh, and to conserve them for subsequent days—or, rather, the final hours of the long day—they are fried in an oil furnished by several species of olive-mushrooms, and eaten crisp for supper. Breakfast on the Moon lasts for one of our days, dinner for two and supper for three; thus, there are six days of eating out of 14—which is almost in the same proportion as here.

There is neither rain nor wind during the long day that is a veritable lunar year. Daylight lasts 14 times 24 hours, not counting the morning twilight or the evening dusk. Supper takes up the three times 24 hours before the day's end, dusk included. Bedtime is immediately thereafter, and if anyone takes a nocturnal stroll it is when there is Earthlight on the relevant hemisphere—but it is rare that one has the pleasure of such excursions, as we shall see.

Multipliandre, after what is improperly called sundown, perceived that the air became replete with condensing vapors. Lightning flashed; thunder was audible. In spite of this racket, the man from Earth observed the sky. He saw a gross Moon, 50 times larger than the one we see from here, which sent forth a light strong enough to read, if he had had any books, for 12 hours, and for the next 12 hours left the Moon in a profound darkness, during which the Rondins and all the animals slept.

II

The language spoken on Mars is uniform, as that of Earth once was, very coarse and imperfect but more extensive than that of the Rondins of the Moon. The creatures there have a head and limbs. The terrestrial philosopher sought an individual of the same species, other than the one he was inhabiting, in order to be able to converse. He discovered one, but stouter, more hideous and much more ferocious. This animal, known on Mars as Nususumu—pronouncing the *u* as the French do, which is to say, like the Greek ypsilon, rolling it—threw itself upon him and said to him: "Mumuarumu"—which means, in Martian, "I want to possess you." The poor Duc had just taken over the body of a Nususumu that had earlier pleased the hippopotamus, and he was therefore possessed. He even felt all that a female Martian amphibian would have felt on such an important occasion.

After this operation, which lasted rather a long time, the Nususumu made his mistress, or his spouse, kiss his posterior, effected a few heavy capers and plunged into the marsh, where he disappeared. In order not to be exposed to these rather disagreeable assaults any longer, the terrestrial soul entered the body of a young male, very cheerful and playful, which appeared to be at the end of its adolescence.

He found then that the community of Nususumu, of which he had the honor of being a member, labored on its aquatic habitations much as our beavers do. Their nourishment consisted of a fleshy herb like the thick and leafless plants of our hot countries; the bark of a tender cabbage-like tree; large citrus-like fruits that tasted like cooked apples, which came from soft palm-like trees; and almonds as big as pumpkins, borne by trees resembling walnuts, which made a whole meal for a female although it took three of them to satisfy a male. They also ate dried fish, sometimes living ones, commencing with the head, as we eat a piece of bread. The most delightful meal was serpent, or eel.

What the Earthman found most advantageous about these amphibians, which ruled the animal kingdom, was that no other species was stouter, stronger, more courageous or more voracious than them. They made all others tremble and flee.

Multipliandre saw animals of a thousand species; all of them were smaller than a female Nususumu. As for the males, they were enormous in size; they went into the sea to seize the largest fish and serpents whose length exceeded 600 feet. They broke them up as soon they caught them, and every female that followed them got a 12-foot section for her meal.

III

"Discorporate, I rose upwards, aiming for Jupiter, which I discovered at that height; its light only reaches the Earth weakly. I had quit the latter, and the movement of Jupiter was very slight at first, relative to me. Having approached it for three hours, though, I was obliged to steer a new course in order to catch up with it, for it appeared to be moving away from me with a surprising velocity. The intentions of my soul, however, were even swifter. I had seen the Earth as a large luminous planet; then I saw it diminish as Jupiter grew; eventually, the Earth became a tiny planet and Jupiter a monstrous body. Finally, I arrived in its atmosphere, and then it hid the half of the universe that was behind it.

"I saw then that it was almost completely covered by seas, which were subject to fearful tides; it was an Ocean 2400 times more extensive than ours, immense even to the vision of a discorporate soul. I descended nevertheless, looking for a bird in order to enter its body. Thick and continuous clouds were obscuring my vision, in such a fashion that Jupiter, seen at close range, is very dark. These clouds were composed of vapors of every sort; they passed over three times every day—each of which is only six hours long—leaving clear spaces between them, and also changing places. I could not imagine the sort of beings that might inhabit such a stormy environment, but I could only get to know them by entering into the brain of one of them.

"The winds there are so terrible that nothing can remain very long in place. In my capacity as an unattached being, they had no grip on me, but it seemed to me that there could not be any birds in air so agitated. Nor could I discover any at first. As I approached the surface of the waters, however, I saw massive creatures thee that seemed to me to be round. They watched what was happening above them with a sort of marked anxiety. I was about to decide to enter into one of these bodies when I saw a sort of square tub rising up towards the clouds. I observed that it was a waterspout that was lifting them up and carrying them over peaks that were not merely elevated above the water but the clouds too, covered with vegetable produce on which the square tubs appeared to be grazing. They remained there until another waterspout enveloped them and plunged them back into the Jovian sea."

We can certainly imagine that the inhabitants of Jupiter will not resemble those of the Moon or those of Mars. It is, however, very pleasant to voyage thus among the planets in the wake of a man as enlightened as Multipliandre, for we presume that he places himself within each of the appropriate inhabitants according to the most exact principles of physics. That is what gives us confidence in him and amuses us all.

"I was not sure whether I ought to take the body of one of these flying, swimming and waterspout-borne tubs, whatever they might be. I came to a decision, though, when, having gone to investigate the large masses that were immersed in the water, I perceived that they were anchored to the seabed. I dispossessed the soul of a tub and replaced it. I then attempted to follow the course of its ideas. I had a great deal of trouble. Gentlemen, the tubs of Jupiter only think about two things: grazing and reproduction. Their language has but two words: *pupu*, eating; and *coco*, doing…*that*.

"I could not see that there was anything much from which to profit on Jupiter, where secondary nature was still in its infancy and brutal state. Everything there was very different, then, from things as they stood on Mars, and infinitely far from Earthly existence. By virtue of what I had seen, I calculated that the inhabitants of Jupiter would require a further 200,000 years to reach the same level of development as us.

"I went down then in my fish-tub, wanting to see the large square masses that I had perceived in the watery depths, which I had taken for animals because they had eyes and were watching. I came very close to them. Their gazes turned towards me. 'There is intention here,' I thought. Then, I was bold enough to quit my fish-tub and seek to enter the monstrous animal by way of the eyes. I succeeded in that. Lodge in its brain, my soul was able to act upon its organs freely, as usual. I found them torpid and obtuse; all its ideas were chaotic. I wanted to move, but to my astonishment I realized that I was attached to the crystallized seabed by an umbilical cord! By stirring myself, however, and by force of intention, I gave the heavy machine a few ideas, and I found that it was capable of containing a reasoning soul. I had an intuition that the animal, fixed in that manner to the ground at the bottom of the sea was the embryo of the animal that would one day seize the scepter of the animal kingdom on Jupiter.

"After these reflections I thought about leaving aqueous Jupiter, being eager to see Saturn—but then I thought that it might be appropriate to visit some of the Jovian satellites.

"I let myself down on the first of the four, and found that everything there was much more advanced than on Jupiter. It appeared that the satellites, although planetized later than the principal planets, crystallized much more quickly, doubtless because, their rotation on their axes being much slower, centrifugal force there is much reduced; the centripetal, on the contrary, is very considerable and, in consequence, deposition or crystallization is more prompt."

IV

"I arrived on Mercury in the evening of its day of eight hours—which is to say, a third the length of ours—at a latitude which the daylight only illuminated for two," Multipliandre continued. "I had not wanted to land on the planet beneath the equator, nor in the part that was then in summer. I was in a climate fairly similar to that of Earthly France in the environs of June 25. Before taking a Mercurial body from one of the beings that corresponds to the humans of Earth—which call themselves Oa, incidentally—I wanted to find out what the temperature was on Mercury during its winter.

"To do that, I introduced myself into the body of an animal corresponding to our serpents, called Ii—for the Mercurial language has very few consonants, only including six—b, l, m, g, r and s, and almost all its words have only vowels. Now, the Ii of Mercury are only active in winter. I mastered the reptile's sensations as best I could, and found that the heat of the winter solstice on Mercury could be very similar to that of Earth's Senegal in summer. It might have been much greater if the day had not been so short and the night six hours long.

"I quit the animal's body after this preliminary investigation. Afterwards, I attacked the soul of an Oa that I saw on a river, whose flow was somewhat reminiscent of volcanic lava. It had no boat, and was walking on the surface as if on solid ground or ice. I observed that I had not seen ice or snow on Venus, that the Sors there have six senses, of which the sixth advertised that a Sors remembered something that it had to do—but what I forgot to say is that they had three hands: two like ours and one on the rump, stronger than the other two, which as very useful in defending the against Sorseaters and Sorsrippers, two species of animals that they had finally annihilated, which corresponded to our lions and tigers.

"On Mercury, where the Oa are even smaller than the Sors, being only one and a half feet tall, they have four hands, two like ours and as on Venus, and two on the hindquarters, whose fingers are linked by membranes as if for swimming—but that was not the only difference. The Oa that I examined had two faces, one black like those of our negroes and placed like ours, the other on the buttocks, with the difference that what is in relief on the ordinary face is hollowed out on the posterior one—but both have eyes, ears, nostrils, and especially a mouth. The posterior one does not even lack taste, but it only serves for defecation, and, if it sometimes drinks, it is by order of the superior face, in circumstances where we would wash ourselves. It is not that the posterior face is destitute of judgment; it has a great deal, if, for instance it has a sore throat.

"Until tomorrow, Hortense,"

This is absolutely mad. Why conform these poor Oa thus. But Fillette interrupts me to say, naively: "Do you want him to lie? If that's the way they are, shouldn't he say so?" You see, my dear husband, that there is nothing to say in reply to that. I embraced her.

If the posterior face has a sore throat, it tells the superior face—or, rather, the mouth—to eat the Mercurial equivalent of prunes, cucumber, etc. It looks after itself with a great deal of discretion. The head is in charge of all important affairs, occupying itself with them without thinking of corporeal needs; it is the posterior that has that responsibility, especially the commission of taking tobacco. It sneezes and wipes its nose very properly with the aid of its hindward hands, which are especially devoted to its service. Behind it, in the usual place, are the reproductive parts, which it directs—but it is the superior head that chooses the object, and which appreciates the beauty of the face and the throat, eyes, mouth, lips and hair. The choice is never consummated, however, until the virile posterior has been consulted as to the beauty of the feminine posterior face and its indentations, which are the projections relative to the superior face; often, the repugnance of the posterior for the relevant posterior causes the failure of liaisons that the superior, and the heart itself, have regarded as very well matched. It is the posterior that decides enjoyment and delights. Thus, while the two upper faces caress one another nobly and the mind, in accord with the heart, makes them say charming things, the two posteriors often say very obscene things to one another or snarl at one another, and project very disagreeable things from their noses—but the two superior heads, provided that the pleasure comes, only laugh at them.

"The Oa have only one soul to govern the two brains, and that is sufficient, but with the condition that, when it abandons one head, that one continues to act in a dream, while the other acts consciously. Thus, an Oa always has a double enjoyment: that of reality and that of dreams, which is not a mediocre advantage.

"The Oa have seven senses: our five, that of Venus and counter-taste—which is to say, the taste by which an Oa knows that it is time to surrender the aliments it has taken. By this means, it avoids constipation, colic, etc.

"After this description, let us return to the man that I saw walking on a river, dragging his boat instead of being inside it, as I discovered subsequently. The waves served as wheels."

Ah, that idea is too funny! It's a long time since I've seen honest laughter in our society. As for me, I laughed less and I admired the variety of Nature. We believe that we are very important, very reasonable, with our single brain, but here's someone who has two, and doesn't think that too many! I rather like the distinct functions of the two faces, but I'll leave my reflections at that, and business matters will fill the rest of my piece of paper.

"He had four feet, four arms with their hands, his two faces, etc. He was on all fours, his postface turned towards me when I perceived him. 'There's a singular face, and singularly placed,' I thought. 'How various living beings are!' He turned round, and I saw an entirely different individual, with a face like ours, and very spiritual. 'They're two men, perhaps even a man and a woman,' I thought.

"At that moment, I attacked the soul via the posterior, which I believed to be the man, and introduced myself into the brain. A slight noise made me direct my attention to another creature that was running up. That one was much prettier and more delicate. The first creature embraced it—which is to say that the two faces kissed in the ordinary way. Then I saw them turn round and similarly make their posteriors kiss. I understood then that the two faces, the one in relief and the one hollowed out, belonged to the same individual, which redoubled my surprise.

31

"I seized the opportunity to attack the Oa's soul and chased it out of the superior brain. I usually had a great deal of difficulty dislodging a soul, but in this case I had none. That was because I took the Oa at the moment when it was embracing the female Oa by means of its posterior face. It appeared that all the soul had hastened into the brain of the other head in order to preside over the pleasures of love.

"I wanted then to follow the traces of the Oa's brain, and I succeeded in that with much less difficulty, the fibers not having suffered any violence by virtue of the combat of the two souls—but that which had been set aside was not lost. I followed the memory-traces of the superior head. Ah, my love, what sublime knowledge, and much purer because the superior head was absolutely detached from carnal and coarse ideas! It is, as I told you, the posterior head that is charged with all details of that sort. I found myself endowed with a perfect knowledge of the Divinity; I knew all of Nature, the composition of living beings, the principle and the motive power of life."

The development of the two faces corresponds perfectly to the beginning, and we are very content with this idea. For myself, I have another reason for joy: it is that so much gaiety testifies to a perfect state of health. Courage, my dear husband! Divert yourself by amusing your wife and all her friends—who make my amusement all the more animated, for intellectual amusements have the admirable quality that, the more they are communicated, the more they are augmented. They share a common property with fire, which inflames and grows by communication. I shall do as you do.

Until tomorrow…

Charles Nodier: *Perfectibility*
(1833)

Charles Nodier (1780-1844) was the son of an active Jacobin, and thus, in effect, a child of the Revolution. Although he was living in Besançon during the Revolution rather than Paris, he was deeply affected by it, particularly the nightmare of the Terror—which led to an extreme disenchantment, not merely with the Revolutionaries but other ideologies that he considered partly to blame for it. He was no more charitably inclined towards the Empire that followed in its train, which he considered to be a natural extrapolation of the same ideologies; when a satirical poem he wrote about Napoleon bought down the wrath of the authorities on his head, his animosity was further intensified. The ideology that he considered most culpable of all, however, was not specifically political but more abstractly theoretical: the idea of progress and its utopian corollary, the ideal of social perfectibility.

Nodier made several unsuccessful attempts to find a congenial means of earning a living before turning to professional writing, and struggled to make ends meet during the early part of his literary career. His first novel, *Le Peintre de Salzbourg, journal des emotions d'un Coeur souffrant* (1803) was a chronicle of anguish strongly reminiscent of J. W. Goethe's *Die Leiden des jungen Werther* (1774; tr. as *The Sorrows of Young Werther*). While Goethe initially refused to recognize himself as a member of the German Romantic Movement, however, and had to be persuaded against his will that he was one, Nodier was a wholehearted Romantic from the outset, and became one of the chief propagandists for a French Romantic Movement. He continued to lead by example with *Jean Sbogar* (1818), a novel about a noble Illyrian bandit, and the lachrymose love story *Thérèse Aubert* (1819), but it was his fantastic stories—examples of what the Germans call *kunstmärchen* [art-folktales], most notably *Smarra, ou les*

33

démons de la nuit (1821; tr. as "Smarra; or the Demons of the Night") and *Trilby, ou le lutin d'Argyll* (1822; tr. as *Trilby, the Goblin of Argyll*) that set more memorable and enduring examples.

It was also in a fantastic vein that Nodier worked in collaboration with Jean Toussaint Merle, the director of the Porte-Saint-Martin theater in the early 1820s, working in collaboration with other writers on stage melodramas loosely adapted from John Polidori's "The Vampyre" and Mary Shelley's *Frankenstein*.[9] In a classic anecdote recorded in his autobiography, Alexandre Dumas recalled that he went to the first night of *The Vampyre* when he had not been in Paris very long, and found himself seated next to an irascible gentleman who expressed his continual displeasure with the script loudly enough to be ejected at the intermission; he subsequently discovered that the gentleman in question was Nodier, taking offence at the way in which his contributions to the script had been mangled by Merle.

In 1824, Nodier finally obtained a salaried post that suited him when he was appointed librarian of the Bibliothéque de l'Arsénal. There he initiated a series of what he called *cénacles*—which bore more resemblance to seminars or writers' workshops than Parisian literary *salons* usually did— in which he proselytized Romanticism relentlessly, becoming the effective leader of the French Movement until the younger members of the group, tired of his irascibility and authoritarianism, started their own *cénacle* at Victor Hugo's house. The latter meeting soon took over as the beating heart of the Movement, while Nodier's health deteriorated significantly. His own work became increasingly sparse and eccentric as he grew older.

Félix Bodin named Nodier in one of the appendices to *Le Roman de l'avenir* as the man best suited to write a novel of

---

[9] Available from Black Coat Press in *Frankenstein and the Hunchback of Notre-Dame* (ISBN 978-1-932983-38-8) and *Lord Ruthven the Vampire* (ISBN 978-1-932983-10-4).

the future, but did not mention that Nodier had published a two-part satirical novelette set in the future a year before, in 1833—probably because the supplements had been written some time before the fragment of a *roman* that supplied the book's main text, and Bodin, scribbling furiously during a parliamentary recess, did not have the time or any inclination to update them.

As might be expected, Nodier's satire is an unusually wholehearted assault on the idea of progress—or, at least, the ideal of perfectibility, which Nodier considered both dangerous and absurd. His original intention was presumably to publish the whole story in one go, but it actually appeared in two parts, probably because, as the last few paragraphs of the first part declare, he sat up into the early hours attempting to finish it in one go—and then suffered a writer's block when he tried to pick it up the following day. At any rate, it appeared in two parts, as "Hurlubleu Grand Manifafa d'Hurlubière ou la Perfectibilité" and "Léviathan le long Archikan des Patagons de l'île savante ou la Perfectibilité, pour faire suite à Hurlubleu" in the August and November 1833 issues of the *Revue de Paris*.

The story is significant not merely in its temporal range and acerbic assertions, but also in its depiction of the strange ecology (or non-ecology) of the isle of the Patagons, where all food is synthetic. The notion of synthesizing food directly from the relevant elements rather than using plants and animals as middlemen crops up again in Jules Lermina's "Quiet House," where it is similarly treated as a hideous absurdity, but both stories might ultimately prove more prophetic than their authors intended, as modern food technology continue to advance apace in the 21st century. Nodier used a deliberately esoteric vocabulary in his story, which I have replicated as best I can while preserving my version's readability, and strewed it with contemporary literary and scientific references, some of whose sources I have not been able to identify and have, therefore, been unable to footnote

Part One
Hurlubleu, Grand Manifafa of Hurlubière

"To the Devil with you all!" cried the Manifafa.

"Does that include the Chief Jester of your Holy College of Buffoons?" asked Berniquet

"No," Hurlubleu said. "I'm talking to that rabble of kings and emperors who murder me every evening with their sa-laaming and who insist on caressing the soles of my slippers with vile kisses. I like you, Berniquet; I like you, Chief Jester of the Holy College of Buffoons, because you have no common sense and you don't lack wit, without which everything is humdrum. I must have a high opinion of your worth, to have conferred upon you one of the most eminent dignities of my empire, for I remember that you fell into my house like a bomb."

"Absolutely," replied Berniquet. "I arrived in a cannon-ball at the foot of Your incomparable Majesty's glorious di-van—and the vehicle is still there, encrusted, so to speak, in the marble on which he deigns to set his sublime feet when he is tired of lying down all day."

"That's not the half of it, Berniquet! Your arrival—which was unexpected, and even a trifle brutal—passed for miraculous, because it delivered the land from a frightful schism that had already cost the lives of 100 million of my subjects, the reason for which I no longer recall. Stuff my ca-lumet so that I can refresh my thoughts."

"Eternal and immutable Manifafa," Berniquet continued, while stuffing his master's pipe with all the customary cere-mony associated with that noble office, "the buffoons affi-liated to the cult of the Divine Bat, from which your imperial dynasty is descended, and which has the infallible pleasure of covering the Sun with its wings every night to procure Your Most Perfect and Most Adored Highness a cool darkness fa-vorable to his sleep, were divided into two stubbornly-opposed parties, commanded by two pitiless jesters, with regard to the question of whether the Sacred Bat had hatched out of a white egg, as Bourbouraki proposed, or a red egg, as Barbaroko maintained—Bourbouraki and Barbaroko being, of course, the two greatest philosophers that had ever illuminated the world and other dependencies of the Empire of Hurlubière with the light of science."

"Why remind me?" replied the Manifafa, sighing from the depths of his soul. "It wasn't my fault that I couldn't reconcile Bourbouraki and Barbaroko, or all those damned jesters. I myself, practically on my own initiative, proposed a compromise to the council of my chibicous[10] by which it could have been amicably agreed that the egg of the Divine Bat was white outside and red inside, or vice versa—I couldn't give a hair of my moustache, myself—but the red buffoons and the white buffoons would never accept it, so obstinate and reckless were they in their resolve, with the result that the bitch of a question would still be hanging in suspense if you hadn't descended abruptly from the clouds to settle it."

"I replied ingeniously to Your Serene Highness that the two jesters were lying about it, and proved by demonstrative logic that the Celestial Tetrapod could not have emerged from a white egg, just as it could not have emerged from a red egg, since it was by nature viviparous, mammalian and anthropomorphic, neither more so nor less so than a buffoon; upon which Your Serene Highness hastened in his sovereign bounty to have the heads of the two jesters and all the chibicous cut off, to the great contentment of his people, who were impassioned with joy throughout the world."

"That memorable event was inscribed in letters of gold in the annals of my reign, with the decree by which I named you Chief Jester. I remembered right away, you see—but where the Devil did you get that *viviparous, mammalian and anthropomorphic* nonsense from?"

---

[10] Nodier appears to have invented this world, having run out of readily-available synonyms for "clown."

"I knew it by abstraction, in my capacity as a qualified doctor of all infused doctrines and encyclical propagator of the perfect monopoly in *omni re scibili*[11]—but that story's too long for it to be permissible for me to take up the precious leisure time of the great, the very great, the infinitely great Manifafa."

"Tell me your story, Berniquet. If it's long and boring, so much the better. I only like stories that put me to sleep—but spare me at least half of your formulas of obsequiousness and respect; the fact that I am superior to you, poor dust beneath my feet, is too obvious to both of us for me to forget it. For fear of losing the habit, just call me Divine Manifafa from time to time. That's much better, Berniquet—it's short, it's true, it's clear; and when I'm smoking, with my legs comfortably extended on my divan, I don't pay much attention to etiquette. Speak, Berniquet! Speak, jester!"

"Your Majesty will be aware," Berniquet continued, profoundly moved—as he should have been—by this gesture of benevolent familiarity, "that, 10,000 years ago, I lived in a sort of village, which was dirty, smelly, badly-built and disgraceful in every respect, erected on a part of the site that has since been occupied by the stables of your noble eunuchs, which was known as 'Paris' in the patois of that barbaric era. It did not hesitate to pass itself off as the queen of cities, even though it is scarcely mentioned in the ancient chronicles of the Empire of Hurlubière, whose incomparable capital of Hurlu shines today like a resplendent diamond in the world's crown."

"I've heard talk of your shanty-town," Manifafa put in, excitedly. "Stop there a moment, though. What's this 10,000 years you're talking about, with that clownish face that declares that you're 45 at most? If you know the secret of prolonging for more than ten centuries the existence that the most vigorous of my immortal ancestors accomplished in less than 100 meager years, I'll open my treasure and my harem to you

---

[11] "All things that can be known."

on the spot, and I'll have you set by my sacred side, buffoon as you are, on the throne of Manifafas. Tell me this instant, jester, if you know a means of living forever! I order you, on pain of death!"

"No more than you, Divine Manifafa! We all die in our turn, ever since our miserable universe began rolling in its narrow orbit, and I have some reason to think that it will be thus until a new order emerges. I really am 45 years old, neither more nor less, as Your Highness has granted me with his special grace. And if he takes the trouble to subtract the months of nursing, the age of cutting teeth, whooping cough and spring-strings, time at college and the Sorbonne, the enormous portion of illnesses and sleep, the days of military service, the visits made and received, indigestions, missed meetings, lectures, concerts, literary conversations and the public meetings of 18 academies, he will easily comprehend, in his wisdom, that there remains to me a definitive quotient of one miserable year of life, just like everyone else. On my honor as Great Jester of Buffoons, I wish that lightning would strike me down, if I claim to have existed for one hour more. As for the 10,000 supplementary years that were mentioned just now, I leapt over them in the course of my biography. They lasted no longer, so far as I was concerned, than the time required for the heart to pass from systole to diastole, or a woman to change her mind."

"That's nice," said the Manifafa. "The length of your story is beginning to bore me very nicely, although I'm well accustomed to reading all the nonsense in Hurlubière to put myself to sleep. Go on then, jester!"

In response to the Manifafa's imperious and decisive gesture, the jester squatted on his heels and continued in these terms:

"In Paris, about the year of grace 1933—which, I have the honor of relating to you, wasn't yesterday—there was a universal propaganda of perfectibility to which I was party, by virtue of my polymathic, polytechnic and polyglot erudition, and which received licensed ambassadors on a daily basis from every rhumb of the horizon. The merchandise was somewhat mixed, according to taste, but all savants, in order that no one will understand them, have to be professional imps to some extent. On one foggy winter evening, however, before sharing out the takings, they agreed that it would be rather difficult to create a perfect society if a preliminary means could not be discovered to procure a perfect man, or to produce one, the aggregate always being, according to the apt expression of peripatetics—God bless them—the complex expression of the aggregated elements, as the Divine Manifafa understands a thousand times better than his humble slave, assuming that he is not yet asleep."

"May the Holy Bat shade me with his tenebrous wings in perpetuity," cried Hurlubleu, "if I understood a single treacherous word of it! But take it upon yourself to spare me the peripatetics' aggregate and get on with it!"

"It was thus resolved that they would devote themselves incessantly to the search for the perfect man—which is to say that as soon as they found out where he might be, and having established that he was, they would make him the foundation of the universal propaganda and the regeneration of civilization."

"You were too modest," the Manifafa put in, "for your propaganda and your civilization had no lack of them—foundations that is. You came out with that witticism willingly, although it wasn't in very good taste. But what were you expecting of the perfect man, since you had already reached the supreme end-point of science, which consists of no longer understanding anything?"

"Organic perfection!" Berniquet relied, humbly. "The complement of those innumerable faculties which God has distributed between his creatures so prodigally, but which he has restricted in our species with a malicious parsimony to the exercise of five obtuse and miserable senses, combining them, more maliciously still, with intellectual sensibility, which we only use to manufacture stupidities."

"We also use it," the Manifafa said, "to say them and print them, damn it. These considerations must, indeed, have furnished the propaganda with ample food for thought."

"Softly, softly, milord! Propaganda never thinks that which it has thought before. There was a little Chinese peasant there that you could have passed through the eye of a needle, but who knew that it was as long as it was broad, and who swore to us that the perfect man had been manufactured by Zeretochthro-Schah [12] nearly 4000 years previously, but no one had any idea of what had become of Zeretochthro-Schah or his automaton."

"I can't give you any news of that. Who ever heard mention of an animal of that name?"

"Zeretochthro-Schah, Divine Manifafa, was, as they say, *si res parvas licet componere magnis*, [13] a sort of incongruous cross between a manifafa and a buffoon, who lived in the time of Gustaps and came from Media to indoctrinate Bactria. In addition to the Zend-Avestra and a few other books, it is generally believed that that he left behind a formula well-accommodated to the most vulgar intelligence for the confection of the great work of perfectibility, which is the perfect man; but, as his luggage was being transported, it was unfortunately flooded by a bottle of ink, and has never been seen since. No other means of obtaining cognizance of it, therefore, remained to the universal propaganda but to consult tradition, making a journey to the relevant places at the State's expense. According to every indication, we would have obtained good results from that great enterprise if another manifest obstacle had not cropped up at the time—which was that Bactria was swallowed up by an earthquake between two of our meetings, taking Zeretochthro-Schah, his traditions and his formulae with it."

---

[12] Zoroaster.

[13] "If, in this instance, it is permissible to compare small things with large ones."

"Goodbye perfect man and perfectibility. I imagine that the nose of universal propaganda was put out of joint."

"I have already had the honor of telling Your Divine Highness that the impeccable propaganda never went back on its decisions. A dozen of us set forth, firmly resolved to search for the Bactrian all the way to the center of the Earth, into which frightful confusion, according to every indication, he must have descended by virtue of the law of gravity."

"You're putting me on the track, wise jester. Did the reputation get there by artesian well?"

"Your ever-august Majesty's immense penetration is as sudden as genius, but we were not so ingeniously advised. It seemed appropriate to complete an exploration of the entire surface of the globe before visiting its entrails."

"Marvelous! I can see you now in a speedy conveyance, like the scientists of the common people. Propaganda on the high road!"

"There was no means, sire. One could no longer travel without mortal peril, since the invention of railways."

"I had forgotten that. Continue then—for I've been making mental efforts for a whole quarter of an hour, which are waking me up."

"We embarked on the steamboat *Progress*—a fine vessel, I assure you—with three funnels and a powerful engine, which sailed so boldly, triple port, that my friend Jal[14] would not have had time to count the knots on the log line. We traveled nearly 1800 leagues, at the stoker's estimate, until we were reduced, for want of combustibles, to throwing our furniture, our tools, our petty possessions, and even our hydrographic charts, our scientific textbooks and our patents, into the boilers."

"You would have been wise to begin with those, jester," said the Manifafa.

---

[14] Augustin Jal (1795-1873) published a glossary of nautical terms.

"At first, that made a bright and brilliant fire, which filled our hearts with joy, all the more so because the guardian of the valves already thought he could see land through his achromatic telescope. The fanatic would have done better to attend to his valves however; the three steam-engines, which I had the advantage of mentioning before, profited from the occasion by exploding all at once, with such perfect harmony that one would have thought that they had given one another a password."

"The explosion of a steamboat—the capricious and jerky speed of which has discomfited me many times—necessitates the observation, Berniquet," said the Manifafa, "that this mode of navigation is a furious demonstration of its inventor's intelligence, and has a great deal of pleasure in it."

"When one has come back, milord. We were thrown so rapidly to an enormous height that I had not time to measure it with exactitude, because there is an essential lack of objects of comparison at sea. We soon perceived, however, in accomplishing our parabolic trajectory, in the manner of projectiles, that we had had the good fortune to be steered close to shore—without which death would have been inevitable. Undoubtedly, no country so delightful had ever presented itself to the gaze of an astonished traveler. Calypso's isle, of which you have perhaps heard mention, was only a miserable sandbank by comparison, unworthy of the imagination of poets.

As we drew closer, we were able to see developing before our eyes—and that figurative expression is quite exact in this instance, for we were falling head-first—all the marvels of an Elysian vegetation, crowned with flowers and fruits. There were none but orange-trees with golden apples, banana-trees with floating clusters, and vines with purple grapes, which linked their opulent arms with the branches of mulberry-bushes and elms; there were none but cherry-trees weighed down by the weight of a multitude of rubies, their flexible boughs swaying gently in the breeze; there were none but laurels with berries black as jet, or acacias with perfumed sprays, which mingled their intoxicating odors with those of violets, carnations, heliotropes and tuberoses, the fresh verdure of whose meadows was punctuated everywhere by streams of crystal and silver, like threads of elegant embroidery. Roses being relatively rare in the region, however, we did not notice any at first glance."

"I'm only astonished that you were able to notice so many things," the Manifafa commented, "but I presume that you decided to make landfall after having tacked for as long as you say—let's leave it at that."

"By hurtling from branch to branch, in the manner of Christopher Morin when he took the *piau* from the nest, Divine Manifafa. Our first concern was to count ourselves. Of the 800 individuals who had composed the crew only six of us remained, but thanks to the special effect of the providential wisdom that watches over the progress of humanity, all six of us were delegates of the élite of the universal propaganda."

"I have often heard it said, my friend, that people of that sort always land on their feet. But do me the honor of informing me whether the providential wisdom you mention had conserved the little Chinaman for you?"

"The little Chinaman had done his bit, Sublime Highness; by virtue of his natural extreme slenderness, one may presume with considerable assurance that he had returned, in impalpable atoms, to the perpetual fire of creation."

"So much the better!" cried the Manifafa. "He was the one who got you involved, in this interminable story, with the pursuit of Zeretochthro-Schah, and I do not feel capable of forgiving him that in this lifetime."

"We were a little bruised; that's the least one can expect when one falls from on high without preparation, but that only increased our pleasure in the midst of the happy people who were dancing in the shade. We hastened to join in their innocent games, as naively ass if we had been simple shepherds, and our cheerfulness increased considerably, as you can believe, when we learned that this pastoral festival was being held to celebrate the departure of a freight-balloon for a very distant region, to which it would take us in a little while."

"Did you know, savants as you were—and you being a particularly savant jester—where this balloon would take you?"

"What does it matter where a balloon might take one when one does not know where one is going? That is the road taken by savants, empires and the world."

"Take ship for the skies, Berniquet! Go, my son, my jester, wherever the demon drives you! But an aerostat that one cannot steer is no more than a child's toy, only good for amusing kings. Old women and academies."

"A mere bagatelle! The subtle perspicacity of your mind is still transporting you, increasingly extraordinary Manifafa, in advance of the discoveries of ancient civilization, as if you had divined them! The direction of balloons had become the simplest of all problems to solve, since steam-engines had been applied to navigation; the resistance of air-currents is less difficult to vanquish than that of the waters. We therefore climbed resolutely into the steam-balloon *Well-Insured*, which was an imposing vessel, perfectly equipped and armed for that great expedition because of the large number of aerial corsairs that had been ravaging the regions we were going to visit for some years, thus causing an immense prejudice against atmospheric travel, in spite of all the precautions of customs officers and the police. We were furnished with 24 good Siamese cannons, 52 feet long, and a 182 pounds of cannonballs, which could hit their targets at a range of seven leagues, and we had no less than 6000 fighting men, organized into troops armed with every possible weapon, save for cavalry and sappers, not counting the chiurm[15] and the boarding parties, who were stationed at the grappling-irons—with the result that we took to

---

[15] The English word *chiurm* is as esoteric as Nodier's direct French equivalent, *chiourme*, but there is no ready alternative; it refers to any means of calibrating the rhythm of a crew of galley slaves. It is, alas, not obvious what contribution a crew of galley slaves could make to the propulsion of a dirigible balloon.

the air, without anxiety and without difficulty, followed by the acclamations of the multitude."

"I recommend, jester, that you keep an eye on the valves! But how did you and your fellow savants pay for your passage? Were the propagandists of perfectibility stationed at the grappling-irons or at the chiurm?"

"Eh?" Berniquet replied. "Set aside that needless concern, Divine Manifafa! In all the terrestrial, maritime and celestial conflagrations that you can possibly imagine, the first thing the savants of my time made sure of was to carry their purses with them everywhere, and the perfect consideration they enjoyed in that distant era procured them much credit everywhere the name of man was known. Their diplomacy was worth bars of gold."

"Might I permit myself to observe, Berinquet, that that is not the case today?"

"I agree, milord. Whatever the circumstances, we were able to go nearly 4000 leagues[16] without knowing exactly where we were, because Your Majesty is not unaware that the compass has drifted a few degrees since then, and at that height it can move randomly, turning entire circles at times, with no other motor than its own capricious oscillation, the attractive action of the pole being considerably altered in those elevated regions."

"That was a good opportunity to graduate the scale of the blueness of the sky, which gave so much trouble to Monsieur de Saussure!"[17]

---

[16] A metric league is four kilometers; the Earth's circumference is approximately 40,000 kilometers. Given that the steamboat had already carried the travelers 1800 leagues, therefore, a balloon journey in a similar direction would have taken the travelers more than halfway around the world, probably ending up somewhere in the Pacific.

[17] Horace de Saussure (1749-1799) was a physicist and geologist who invented or improved numerous measuring devices,

"The sky was as black as ink. However, we consoled ourselves in our isolation by giving names to the occasional clouds. It was a very ingenious pleasure, a human joy, gone with the wind like those of Earth. Besides, we would have run the risk of a serious accident if we had not escaped, by means of a skilful maneuver, the eruption of an accursed volcano, which almost put the *Well-Insured* up the spout."

"I can't let that pass," Hurlubleu interrupted, "and God knows that you've made me swallow a lot over the last hour. Never, and I mean never, has a volcanic eruption climbed so high!"

"It often happens, superhuman Manifafa, that the eruptions of aerial volcanoes descend much lower, at least when the ambient rotation of the atmosphere does not transform them into pretty little pocket satellites, as I have often seen in my travels. The explosion that threatened us at such close range could have been the one that destroyed Paris. It was, to tell you the truth, that of one of those wretched provincial planets that the Earth carries away, like a scatterbrain, in its stupid revolutions, like one of those baskets of plums that children whirl around in a sling without letting a single one fall, and which, being composed of inflammable elements tormented by an igneous principle, end up brutally dissolving into a rain of aeroliths when poor passers-by least expect it. Considering its apparent diameter, we judged that it was scarcely any larger than a third-class prefecture, which the least of your civil servants would not have wanted."

"He would have been quite right!" replied the Manifafa. "A prefecture composed of inflammable elements tormented by an igneous principle would be no favor. The description that you have given me of these aeroliths appears, moreover, to be very instructive and very amusing, and I excuse you, because of that, for having taken this route to the center of the

---

and was one of the first people to reach the summit of Mont Blanc.

Earth, even though, looking at the thing rationally, it was not the shortest."

"That was not the only inconvenience of our journey. We had just dropped the pneumatic sounding-line into a rather beautiful depth of atmosphere—from which it brought back, entirely to our satisfaction, a mixture of oxygen and nitrogen, formed according to the proportions that the chemists consider most suitable for everything that breathes—when we were distressed to perceive that the hull was leaking air in two places."

"And there's another, damn it, Berniquet! I've heard mention of water leaking, but I never heard of leaking air."

"There's nothing easier to understand. It means that gas was escaping in abundance through fissures in the capsule, for want of repair. Your Majesty can imagine that we lost no time sending out caulkers, but Castor and Pollux, the protectors of mariners, permitted one lad of tender age and little experience to bring the flaming tar so close to the breach that the hydrogen suddenly caught fire, decorating the balloon superbly with a marvelous girdle, which radiated a dazzling spray, and must have given it the appearance to those below—for the Sun had been hidden for a long time throughout that hemisphere—of a shining meteor. On my jester's honor, I might live through my 10,000 years, so quickly passed, and 10,000 more, but time could not efface from my memory the sentiments of admiration with which I was filled by that sight of that fiery globe…"

"Which burned on an equal footing with planets," Hurlubleu interrupted. "I willingly put myself in your shoes at the present moment—but not otherwise, parenthetically. Admiration presumably did not absorb you, though, to the extent that you did not pay attention to anything else?"

"We made haste to disencumber the vessel of its useless cargo, for it had no excess ballast in reserve: the steam engine first, then the Siamese cannon! Their like had never been seen for the excellence of the work and he richness of the carving. After that, a whole encyclopedia, in order of topic. I did not regret them much. After that, the entire record of laws, decrees and ordinances, with all the speeches from the two chambers. That was a terrible loss! After that, someone had the impertinence to say that it would have been better to commence with the savants. I took the plunge along with the others, but I was so fortunately favored by my particular weight—heaven be eternally praised!—that in the course of my perpendicular flight I overtook one of those aerial barges, which was foundering. As it was made in the form of a seahorse, according to the fashion of the period, current since the famous cetacean of Monsieur Lennox,[18] I bestrode it as gently as could be in such circumstances, in such a manner that I found myself firmly saddled, with my right hand in the mane, maintaining a good seat, planted like a Saint George."[19]

"And then Berniquet, you dug your spurs in, as your position demanded, and I see you with pleasure on the road to the land of Zeretochthro-Schah, if the aggregate weight is reciprocally multiplied by the square of the velocity."

"I came down, as chance would have it, in a large rut set in the exact middle of the highway, where I was only embedded up to the neck, because I had soon recovered my courage as I recognized, from the nature of the soil and the geological configuration of the locality, that my lucky star had set me on my feet in one of the most civilized countries on Earth."

"Setting on the feet is a hyperbatic manner of speaking, to which I will gladly subscribe if it pleases you, but I warn you that I shall have more difficulty in agreeing to the indefi-

---

[18] Lennox was the family name of the Dukes of Richmond, but this reference is otherwise obscure.

[19] Although this comparison can be read innocuously, it might be worth observing that the term "un saint Georges" is used in French to refer to a particular position in sexual intercourse, in which the penetratee sits astride the lap of the penetrator; the phrase is probably intended to imply that Berniquet's sitting position was not quite as comfortable as he suggests.

nite perfection of a country in which there are such large and profound ruts is the exact middle of the highway."[20]

"Oh, that was because the philosophers of that country, Divine Manifafa, had something much better to do than fill in ruts."

"What were they doing, then?"

"Cookery," Berinquet replied.

"Well," replied the Manifafa, "I can't blame them—but begin at the beginning, jester, for we just left you, to my great regret, in a situation that was scarcely convenient for exploring the terrain."

"It was, however, favorable to meditation—and, as for the terrain, I knew it thoroughly, independently of my personal experience, by virtue of what I had read in cosmographies and traveler's tales, which never lie. The isle of the Patagons,[21] so

---

[20] Hyperbation is a rhetorical term referring to a deliberate inversion of meaning. The French term that I have translated here with excessive literality is *prendre pied*, to which Hurlubleu is presumably objecting because Berniquet has ended up neck-deep in the mire. The other key phrase in this passage is *juste milieu* [exact middle], which had a very specific reference in the context of French politics before and after the July Revolution of 1830, when it was proposed—and, to some extent, implemented—as a means of arbitration to balance the opposed demands of the Royalist right and Republican left, involving the calculation and subsequent steering of an exactly-balanced middle course between the two. This extends a sketchy series of analogies in which the progressive savants' steamboat journey and trip in the dirigible airship, both ending in disasters, represent the Revolutionary and Imperial phases in recent French history.

[21] Patagon is used in French to refer to the inhabitants of Patagonie [Patagonia], and thus invites translation as "Patagonian," but as Nodier's island bears no resemblance to the actual South American region of Patagonia, I have transcribed it directly.

50

far as I had been able to judge by sight while plunging into that mid-Atlantic empire, forms a circle about 1130 leagues in diameter, which gives a circumference of 3550 leagues—or should, if Adrien Métius of Alkmaar is no fool.[22] It is the fact that it has never produced any living thing that renders it particularly appropriate to civilization."

"Which remains to be explained," cried Hurlubleu, shaking his head defiantly. "An island that produces no living things, but where there are philosophers! It's true that they crop up everywhere—according to you, though, their cuisine must be rather meager."

"The most perfect that could ever be savored at a royal table. It would only be necessary to *presuppose*, if 'presuppose' were admitted to the Hurlubièrean language—which depends on the Academy—that the island of the Patagons is the center of an archipelago entirely populated by philosophers, who are methodically arranged in their islets, according to the encyclopedic system of Bacon, with such technical precision that the languages of Earth merely require labels to figure in the topography of perfectibility the *universal compendium* of human knowledge.[23] This species being very populous, because it is extremely idle, it decided one day to take advantage of the proximity of he metropolitan island, where I was presently in the situation of which you are aware, and

---

[22] Adrien Métius (1571-1635) was the Dutch mathematician credited with the discovery (or rediscovery) of the constant *pi*, which expresses the relationship between the circumference of a circle and its diameter.

[23] This passage links Nodier's imaginary island with Francis Bacon's New Atlantis, as described in the first utopia (written c1609; published posthumously in 1627) to argue flamboyantly that technological progress was the key to a better life. Bacon never finished it, any more than he finished the great encyclopedia of human knowledge that he intended to produce.

where I beg you to permit me to remain for a little while longer..."

"As long as you care to, jester," said the Manifafa. "Take your time."

"It decided, as I said, to send a creative colony there, and that only required laboratories, since it knew how to produce by chemical combination all that Creation produces. It was by this means that the philosophical consistory of the Isle of the Patagons devoted itself to culinary manufacture, to satisfy the communal necessities of healthy individuals who took pleasure in eating two meals a day, when they were able to afford them—I'm not taking about poor authors, those innocent proletarians of speech, disgraced tributaries of the press, honest people who scrape a living when they live at all, and who have lost their pensions through the malice or ineptitude of a chibicou; they are hardly to be seen there. But suppose, for example, that Your Highness had a sudden desire tomorrow to dine on an excellent *tête de veau en tortue*,[24] as could happen to anyone; you send your menu to the mammalogical section, which makes a calf and puts the head aside for you. The section's Architriclin—that's a highly-placed official—immediately sends your menu to his colleague in the ornithological section, who makes you a cock, and dispatches the comb and the kidneys to the first laboratory; the same with the crustaceological section, which concocts superior crayfish. After that, everything proceeds as normal, and it is served hot. It's a delicious meal."

---

[24] *Tête de veau en tortue* is an elaborate recipe found in the pretentious gastronomic guides popular in Nodier's day. Its basic constituents are a calf's head and rice, but it also requires numerous truffles and quenelles (meatballs), twenty prepared cockscombs and a crayfish. There is a certain irony in the fact that the Patagonian food scientists produce the cockscombs, crayfish and raw material for the quenelles artificially while apparently taking the truffles (by far the most expensive ingredient) for granted.

"Who are you talking to?" said the Manifafa. "All that appears perfectly in order to me, and I would take great pleasure in interrogating you on a few details, if I weren't too scrupulous to retain you in that rut any longer than is appropriate to a man of your age and quality."

"I was there for 100 hours and I don't know how many minutes, Divine Manifafa."

"Then we have time—so amuse yourself by answering me; it will give you a rest. How is it that these philosophers, who were making so many things, had not succeeded in making the man for whom you were searching with such rare intrepidity?"

"Eh! Be assured, Lord, that they were making such men very well. A man is no more difficult to fabricate than a wild rabbit when one knows his composition. The anthropological section had no other occupation from dawn to dusk, in contrast to backward and mechanized countries where people voluntarily occupy themselves with it, in a more specialized fashion, from dusk to dawn—and it must be admitted that it has not spare its efforts, since it has made the Patagons, in the least of which there is material for the dozen drum-majors of the dozen legions of your capital, including those of the suburbs. But beyond the five natural senses, it had found itself considerably embarrassed, the ideological section never having been able to furnish the intellectual sense in good condition. The intellectual sense! Divine Manifafa, you would have reduced the ideological section to rubble, because you would not have been able to obtain enough of it therefrom to make a vaudeville—and when that is distributed in equal parts between 50 million giants, it's almost as if they had none of it at all. That's why the unhappy race of Patagons is so stupid that the nations of the world have since adopted into their speech the proverbial usage *as stupid as a Patagon*."

"Heaven help us—and the Holy Bat too!" said the Manifafa. "With what did these poor people make kings?"

"That's a great pity," Berniquet replied humbly lowering his eyes. "They made them with Patagons."

"That proves, jester, that there was no great profit in this method, since the philosophers did not preserve it for themselves."

"One is careful with kings and peoples, sire, when one calculates their living expenses! The philosophers, who had continued to reproduce in the vulgar manner, because it is slightly more amusing, remained very small—which forbade them the chance of acquiring positions of public authority in the country of the Patagons, where all such positions are determined by height, including the crown. When the king dies, the population is passed beneath a hectometer, and his successor is selected by the ruler."

"With the result that the reigning sovereign," the Manifafa put in, "has a perfect right to judge himself *the Great* and receive that title from his court without anyone having grounds for criticism—which seems quite agreeable to me. But what happened, Berniquet, if some petty Patagon peasant took it into his head to grow immeasurably all of a sudden, surpassing his legitimate prince by a cubit or two, while the latter was peacefully enthroned on the word of the ruler, geometry and the philosophers?"

"He would be recognized as the heir presumptive, lord, and proclaimed Caesar, until another came along to contest his rank. I've heard it said that this had spared them many revolutions and civil wars, and they were no worse-governed for it."

"I can easily believe that, jester. It's the most reasonable electoral system that anyone has ever invented, to my knowledge, and I'll try it out on my chibicous before long. Whatever happens, I'll be almost certain not to lose by the change. If your report is accurate, though, there are still two things that bother me. My first concern, Berniquet is to know what becomes of Patagon women in a country where the anthropological section takes the trouble to make the children?"

"Oh, the women are very busy, sire; they discuss, they manage, they administer, the judge, they govern, they formulate plans of campaign, statistics, laws, constitutions—and, from time to time in their spare moments, write little eclectic pamphlets: treatises on ontology, epic poems in 36 songs. They do a great deal of harm! But what is Your Highness's second concern, Divine Manifafa?"

"My second concern, Berniquet, is to know what you did to extricate yourself from that diabolical rut?"

"I did not spend all my time reflecting on the notions recalled confusedly from my reading. I made every effort to shout at the top of my voice, and with all the force of my lungs, that I was the sole survivor of a dozen members of the universal propaganda, who had come to pay homage to the civilization of the Isle of the Patagons. I added, with a compassion easier to imagine than to express, that that I would probably be the last propagandist who tried to land in that philosophical rut, especially by the route by which I had come— unless, that is, one of my comrades had succeeded in remaining in the air longer than me, and I saw no possibility of that."

"My Grand Orator could not have put it better, dear Berniquet, even though that is his profession, for which I pay him a fat salary, and he has raised his voice several times in opposition—but to whom did you address this eloquent and naïve discourse?"

"To a handful of wretched children, 25 or 30 feet tall at the most, who were playing follow-my-leader and other similarly puerile games on the roadside."

"On the side of the rut, you mean. And what happened after that, jester?"

"Alas, milord, you know what happened: a legion of philosophers in fancy coats and silk stockings, with gloved hands and umbrellas under their arms,[25] came to sit down around me on folding chairs to arrange the means of getting me out of it. On the first day they were not excessively embarrassed. The judged almost unanimously that I appeared to have fallen into the rut accidentally. On the second day, they decided that it

---

[25] Louis-Philippe, who acceded to the French throne after the July Revolution, was routinely caricatured by reference to his habit of carrying an umbrella with him when he went out.

would be best to extract me by means of some machine. On the third day, they contrived a marvel…."

"They finally got you out!"

"No, Divine Manifafa. They appointed a commission composed of scientists highly-skilled in mechanics. I thought I was lost, that time. Holding out my shaking hands, which I had succeeded in detaching from the rut, at the level of my head—where they had made themselves very useful by chasing away the flies—I renewed my futile supplications with a great abundance of tears. The philosophers were already some distance away. What saved me was that among the numerous brats that I had the honor of mentioning a little while ago, there were two who had made a monstrous seesaw out of the mainmast of a three-decker sailing-vessel and were indulging themselves wholeheartedly in that ridiculous exercise—which is, as I had made sure to tell them, unworthy of occupying human thought.

"One of these little brutes, whom I had observed paying a stupid but nevertheless rather crafty attention to the philosophers' discussion, brought his mast closer when they had disappeared, and, having carefully established the equilibrium of the large moving part on its fulcrum, set about turning the extremity towards the place where my convulsive hands were still agitating vainly. I took hold of it mechanically, but firmly, to avoid a collision between my head and the gigantic joist that would probably not have been to my advantage. At the same instant, the miserable Patagon ruffian jumped up to a considerable height to reach the other end, and pulled it towards him with al his weight, with the result that I sprang forth from the rut like a dart; by letting myself slide along the beam, of which I had not let go, I landed quite comfortably on solid ground of rocks and pebbles that would not have given way beneath and army of Patagons.

"The fortunate meeting with that instinctive expedient caused me to reflect bitterly upon the misery of those unfortunate Patagons, who were reduced by the deprivation of the intellectual sense to be stupidly confined to the exercise of their animal faculties, without any hope of becoming savants, and whom civilization—ordered and gentle, to be sure, but set up like an instrument—turned perpetually like cogwheels. That is harmful."

"I recognize your good heart there," said the Manifafa, "but that's the fault of the ideological section, which is not in the land of the Patagons for nothing, and who, if I understand you correctly, diminished the intelligent and perfectible minds of these islanders. Since their civilization is ordered and gentle, however, Berniquet, and they do not lack instinctive expedients for getting themselves—and others—out of difficulties, what more, and what better could they desire?"

"Better, I don't know; but more, progress—or, to explain myself with all the precision and eloquence required in these elevated matters, I wanted them to be making progress. Good God, what good is a nation that isn't making progress? The essential destiny of man is not to furnish with simplicity his brief career in the midst of his family, faithfully fulfilling his duties to God, the state and humankind, as those miserable driveling moralists preached in ignorant antiquity. The essential destiny of man is to make progress; and, whether he likes it or not, he *will* make progress, mark my words, or he'll explain why he isn't...

"These Patagon children were, however, naturally benevolent. The poor little fellows hastened to plunge me into a pool of pure water, at a rather bitter temperature, which washed away the mud of the rut and restored a little suppleness and elasticity to my painful limbs. They dried me off afterwards, in the rays of an ardent and reparative Sun, while fanning my forehead with a few balsamic leaves with which they had equipped themselves for that purpose; and, without further delay, they delicately peeled the remaining detritus of their breakfast, in order to prepare me a good meal—which proved very copious, for one could easily live on a Patagon's crumbs. I had scarcely expressed my gratitude, by means of gestures of which they took little or no notice, when they returned to their seesaw, after having pointed me in the direction of the city of philosophers, where I expected to find someone with whom to talk.

"As I was on the point of arrival, I saw a vast procession emerging from the walls with great ceremony, which headed towards me. I immediately recognized the objective of that scientific excursion equipped for travel. There were planks, poles, ladders, ropes, pulleys, rails, levers, weights, counter-weights, wheels, capstans, tackle-blocks, cranes, dredgers, clamps, measuring implements, pick-axes, hooks, jacks and all the movable equipment of the Conservatory of Arts and Crafts, with the exception of a seesaw. I was very flattered by the foresight of these great men, and tried to make my senti-ments manifest to them in some 20 languages—of which they appeared to have no knowledge. For my part, I understood nothing at all of theirs, which made me think with admiration that they might well have invented the universal language, or at least discovered the primitive one.

"This little difficulty, which naturally injected a certain obscurity into our conversation, prevented me from making them understand clearly how I had succeeded in getting out of the tight spot in which they had found me, but they seemed so enthusiastic to honor that difficult operation, in which I saw no great inconvenience, that I gladly abandoned the attempt to compose an autoptic description for them. I consented, there-fore, to the frenetic acclamations of a great crowd of Patagons, who had lined all the streets along their route—to which wel-come they deigned to respond with proudly modest benevo-lence, smiling graciously to the left and the right, to the extent that I came very close myself to believing in the efficacy of the help that they had been taking me. In any case, I was too well-accustomed, and had been for a long time, to the tradi-tions and customs of academies, not to do likewise.

"I was conducted in this fashion—triumphantly, so to speak—to the palace of the Supreme Consistory, where I was deposited, like an object of curiosity put on display, on the Architrichlin's green baize: a solemnity much more flattering for its object than for one who is always sure of the approbation of a Patagon audience—for these people are essentially admiring, by virtue of their great innocence."

"The innocence of the Patagons is all very well, but I'm not without anxiety regarding the anthropological section. They must have wanted to have you stuffed."

"There was no question of that for the moment, Divine Manifafa! The Great Architrichlin made a speech tailored to the Patagon audience, whose galleries were overflowing, which did not at first enlighten me as to the difficulties of that philosophical language. I had a great deal of difficulty distinguishing between the apheresis, the dieresis and the synthesis, getting past the apocope and the syncope, struggling with the contraction, making sense of the syllables and the euphony, invoking the conciliatory paragogy in which to take refuge from the tenebrous anagogy, and I could not, no matter how hard I tried, catch up with my radicals. Wise and savant Edwards,[26] if only you had been there!

"Eventually, the frequent repetition of a locution in which I had captured in passing the mystical metathesis suddenly revealed to me that this beautiful and erudite idiom was quite simply the native patois of Villeneuve-le-Guyard, where I was born, but elegantly inverted in the order of the disposition of the letters, in the manner of a boustrophedon,[27] to which I had had the good fortune to have initiated myself in my early youth, by reading signs backwards—which meant that, within a moment, I had as much mastery as the most experienced linguist of all the delicacies of the hieratic language in use in the isle of the Patagons. I therefore began speaking after the Architrichin, with an easy confidence that astonished

---

[26] Possibly the American theologian Jonathan Edwards (1703-1758), who commented in learned fashion on the rhetorical style of religious revivalism.

[27] A boustrophedon is a document in which alternate lines are written in opposite directions, those reading from right to left being constructed in mirror-writing, but Nodier appears to be using the term here simply to refer to inverted speech.

everyone—and the due reserve that modesty imposes upon historians who are speaking about themselves cannot make me keep my mouth shut regarding the prodigious effect of my speech, since the results of that inaugural session still made themselves felt after 10,000 years of my short life.

"The thunderous applause that followed my harangue disconcerted me to such a degree that I remained as if enraptured between the four candles on the demonstration table—to the extent that that an idiotic savant, who was fulfilling the functions of a majordomo, was dispatched to the chemistry section to fetch a soothing spirituous beverage, of which they make use themselves on similar occasions instead of sugared water, to calm the senses of an orator during the heat of enthusiasm and the hullabaloo of applause.

"I only took a drop of it, but I had scarcely finished downing the potion when, instead of impressing on my physiognomy the tonic and hilarifying influence of a salutary liquor, I was seized by a frightful spasmodic yawning, which immediately caused all the spectators to judge—as was only too true—that I had just fallen victim to a philosopher's mistake. It is necessary to tell you, moreover, that philosophers' mistakes are even more dangerous than an apothecary's mistake. The Architrichlin made haste to check the suspect phial, and he had no need to go any further than the label to say, expansively: 'A fatal and irreparable mistake has been made. It isn't the water of health and rejoicing that has just been administered to our beloved colleague—it's the water of eternal sleep!'

" 'Eternal sleep!' I cried—to the extent that one can cry out when one is yawning, while the hiatus assiduously punctuates one's every word! 'Eternal sleep, accursed Arichtrichlin! May the lightning strike you down, along with the entire Isle of the Patagons!'

" 'Eternal isn't strictly accurate,' the Architrichlin put in, benignly. 'The dose wasn't strong enough for that. You haven't had enough for more than 10,000 years, according to the prescription, which is calculated to perfection, and you'll obtain a great advantage from this slight interruption to your academic work, since you've dedicated your life to the search for the perfect man. Who knows? Perhaps you'll find him when you wake up.'

"Meanwhile, I yawned with all my strength. 'A slight interruption!' I replied, in the most violent fit of temper that can grip a man who is falling asleep. '10,000 years, a slight interruption! You don't imagine, then, pitiless Architrichlin, that I have business to take care of at home! My civil list pension is in jeopardy, for want of a certificate of life, and I was in a position to formulate a nice establishment with a rich and pretty young woman who will probably not wait for me!'

" 'I dare not make you any promises with regard to her,' the Architrichlin replied. 'If she were here, and if she agreed to it, I could offer to put her to sleep with you; it wouldn't cost me anything more—but that's the only condition in which young women can await a future that has 10,000 years to sleep. It's a petty inconvenience anyway. Good-looking as you are, you'll easily find other mistresses, and 10,000 years pass so quickly when one's asleep!' "

"They aren't squeamish," said the Manifafa.

"And having said that, the gentleman bore me away, without my being able to put up much resistance, in view of the soporific state into which their infernal specific had put me. By one corridor after another, I arrived, still yawning, in the Hall of the Oneirobes.[28] That's a local sect of sages who spend almost all their lives asleep.

"I perceived in the blink of an eye, beneath glass bell-jars numbered in indelible ink, a number of worthy individuals who had spontaneously embraced that vocation of centuries-long sleep, whether out of disgust for the world in which they lived, or by virtue of a quite natural impatience to see another. It was, I swear to you, a perfectly select society. There were

---

[28] I have transcribed this improvised term directly; oneiro- is a Greek preface signifying "dream."

some there who were stirring already, so near were they to resuscitation. As I no longer had any need but sleep...."

"Me neither," said the Manifafa.

"As I was half asleep..." Berinquet continued.

"Me too," said the Manifafa.

"I wished them much pleasure, internally," the jester went on. "I went unceremoniously into my bell jar—which covered a bed that was very comfortable, at least for a man who is asleep—and I went to sleep in a flash."

"Good night, Berniquet," said the Manifafa, letting his pipe fall. "Sleep well and don't have bad dreams."

"The first thing I did, when I woke up, was to look at my watch; it had stopped. When I was woken up..."

"What? Damn it!" the Manifafa put in, arranging himself on his divan. "When you woke up, I was probably asleep! At least, if the Devil doesn't take a hand, I can surely sleep for an hour or two during the 10,000 years that I've had the pleasure of granting you between the beginning and end of your long story. Not that I didn't take a certain pleasure in it, Berniquet—I was particularly amused by the naval combat between the seahorses and the genteel saraband of the four little blue guenons. It's really very amusing."

Berniquet, who had an extremely penetrating mind—as was noticeable at various points in his narration—saw clearly that the Manifafa had not been listening thus far without taking the time to have an occasional nap. "It is necessary that kings be very stupid," he murmured, in a very low voice, "else they are every ill-intentioned. Here's one with whom I've been discussing the most transcendent and abstruse questions of morality, philosophy and politics for an hour, and who takes advantage of such precious moments to dream about seahorses and sarabands of little monkeys!"

"What are you muttering between your teeth, Berniquet?" cried the Manifafa. "You look as if you're making faces at me!"

"I thought, Divine Hurlubleu, that my expedition was worth the trouble of being recounted to its conclusion—and I intend, moreover, to make it an element of a trilogy whose title will be of some consequence to my editor. That's what will make it a success."

"How scrupulous can the soul of a jester be, Berniquet? The people for whom you write are so well-accustomed to three-letter monograms that you'll risk nothing, on my word as a Manifafa, by throwing them a four-part trilogy. They'll see many others! For God's sake though, Berniquet, go to sleep and let me sleep!"

"A trilogy in four parts for a time that goes quickly! Why not?" said Berniquet, in an aside. While he reflected, biting his fists, on this new mode of composition, the sublime sovereign of Hurlubière had already snored three times. He was asleep.

The jester lay down at full length beneath his master's feet, to meditate more at his ease on the dignity of the species and its progressive improvement. He went to sleep.

I, who am transcribing this with difficulty from Berniquet's manuscripts, as 3 a.m. chimes on one clock after another, by the dying light of an oil-lamp whose price my grocer is clawing back with dishonest lawsuits, feel the quill slipping from my fingers. I'm going to sleep too.

What about you, Madame?

Part Two
Leviathan the Long,
Archikan of the Patagons of the Savant Isle

At 6:45 a.m., Hurlubleu sneezed three times in succession. It was the signal in response to which his attentive eunuchs were accustomed to bring him his chocolate.

Berniquet, who was lying on his back, as is usual when one is asleep—at least when one is not lying on one's right side, or even the left—perceived that the Manifafa was no longer deigning to sleep, so he turned over on to his belly. That done, he sprang abruptly into a sitting position and resumed speaking thus: "When I woke up, Divine Manifafa—and I admit that I had a bit of a headache..."

"Is that you, jester? 10,000 years have gone by since you were last seen! Finish, then, if you must. Tell me the rest of your adventures in detail; perhaps they'll send me back to sleep."

"At first, I was as red-faced as a bell-founder to find myself alone under my bell-jar. All the other Oneirobes had departed without the accompaniment of drums and trumpets—which was a matter of indifference to me because, sleeping as I was sleeping, I wouldn't have been able to hear them. It occurred to me that I might have been forgotten during my siesta, and I hurled myself so impatiently against the walls of my transparent prison that we both rolled along the floor. It was as well for me that it was made of a malleable, elastic and unbreakable glass invented by the Patagons, since I did myself no more harm than a man who falls out of bed wearing an excellent padded dressing-gown.

"The savant on duty came running in response to the noise, followed by his assistants, and—after having observed from my notes that I had conscientiously completed my 10,000 years, with a small surplus—he obligingly provided me with a passport to go wherever I wished. He didn't even demand the requisite declaration of witnesses to my identity, which I would have had difficulty procuring. In exchange, to keeps his accounts in order, I gave him a proper receipt for my person, establishing that he had delivered me to myself duly and integrally, *in ossibus et cute*,[29] at the expiry of an interval fixed in advance at 10,000 years, healthy, safe and well-conserved—which is to say, without any apparent breakage, damage or wastage—and in working order, thanks to the expertise of the authorized conveyors, all to the general satisfaction and my own. Then I got ready to leave.

" 'Wait a minute, my good man,' he said, grabbing my by the sleeve. 'You European doctors must know almost everything, or not far short of it.'

" 'I know more than everything,' I told him, 'since I'm a delegate of the intellectual propaganda of perfectibility.'

" 'That's good,' he continued. 'We won't ask you for that much—just whether you know medicine. It's not a matter of drinking the sea.'

" 'As much as is necessary,' I replied, 'to cure completely a man who is not sufficiently churlish to insist on dying. I swear to you that the physicians of my time knew no more than that.'

" 'Then you're my man. Imagine that Leviathan the Long, who is a very imposing prince—he's more than 40 cubits tall—has promised *in petto*[30] to have us all quartered before sunset if we haven't brought him a physician capable of curing him. Of what, I can't tell you: of some trifle, the tedium of some ostentatious speech, the resentment of some ill-received ordinance, a malady of the court—but we take such things very much to heart, for kings are capable of anything.' "

"Take care, Berniquet. There were no physicians in that Academy of philosophers! What the Devil were they playing at that day?"

---

[29] "Skin and bones."

[30] Secretly.

"Perhaps they were distributing St. Michael ribbons, Divine Manifafa. I have had the honor of informing you, if I am not mistaken, that the Isle of the Patagons was extremely civilized."

"That's true damn it, but I don't think so any longer. Unfortunate Leviathan the Long: a king of 40 cubits, and not a single petty physician comes to soothe the anguish of his death, to administer the last rites!"

"I had no sooner examined the colossal Archhikan of the Patagons than it appeared to me, pending a better opinion, that he had suffered a cut on the index-finger of his right hand."

"Don't deceive yourself, Berniquet—a cut on the index-finger of the right hand causes a sharp pain that would damn a buffoon. I was often subject to them in my childhood; that's what prevented me from learning to write."

"The diagnosis being sufficiently confirmed, in my opinion, by a strict autopsy…"

"Curses!" cried Hurlubleu. "Did you really have the ferocious courage to eviscerate this Leviathan for the sake of a cut?"

"Oh, no, milord, I'm only taking about the kind of clinical autopsy carried out on living invalids, whose investigations stop at the epidermis, while awaiting something better. I hastened, therefore, to order 80,000 hungry leeches from the helminthological section, and applied them to my patient."

"To your patient—I like that. He was neither more nor less than the Archikan of the Patagons—but I'll wager that you'd forgotten one thing."

"I say nothing to the contrary. One often forgets something in practical medicine. But what, Divine Manifafa?"

"A mere bagatelle—to give notice to the hereditary prince to hold himself in readiness for his enthronement. 2000 leeches a cubit! My God, what a bleeding! I shall be quite astonished, jester, if the Archikan of the Patagons lasted much longer."

"Bah! An Archikan is as strong as a buffalo. I assure you that his cut felt better after six months. He wasn't able to move a hand or a foot."

"There's an invalid who must have owed you a great deal, Berniquet. I like to think that he died cured."

"You have arrived, Divine Hurlubleu, at the most extraordinary part of my story. My invalid did not die at all. After a further 18 months of convalescence, and as many tons of analeptics, the least of which exceeded in capacity the giant cask of Heidelberg, I had the satisfaction of rendering him hale and hearty, save for a sort of hemiplegia, which badly inhibited the movements of half his body, and a rather disagreeable species of claudication, which completely prevented him from walking."[31]

"Which is to say that you had extracted him from the predicament in good order to the tune of 75%. Poor Archikan!"

"The most honest man in the world. He sent for me in order to give me his thanks in person."

"Had he lost his mind, then, this Archikan of the Patagons?"

"Impossible, milord. No Archikan of the Patagons has ever lost his mind, or anything resembling it. 'European doctor,' he said to me, 'it's a pleasure to see you with the one eye of which we can still make use. With the intention in mind of awarding you a prize proportional to your services, and having taken advice, we have resolved in our wisdom, and for your own good, to put you discreetly back to sleep. What do you think, amiable and savant foreigner?'

"At these formidable words, I shivered from top to toe, and my hair stood on end in terror."

"I imagine, Berniquet," observed the Manifafa, "that you prostrated yourself before him and embraced his knees."

---

[31] An analeptic is a tonic; a hemiplegia is a partial paralysis (nowadays attributed to a haemorrhage in one hemisphere of the brain); a claudication is a limp.

"I would have liked to, but there was no way to do it. I simply embraced his ankles. 'Bright light of the world,' I cried, 'my emotion tells you how sensible I am of the gratitude that it pleases you to heap upon the least of your slaves, but that would not be in accord with the duties of my mission, which have been languishing far too long, and injurious to the propagation of a multitude of discoveries that ought to be turned to the glory and the profit of the human race. It is indispensable that I wake up from time to time to correct my proofs.'

" 'That is a laudable and worthy occupation, to which I have an infinite inclination myself,' replied Leviathan the Long, 'but what can I do for you, then, and by what benefits can I display my gratitude and your merits. Speak! Would you like to be Quasikan?'

" 'The title of that office is beautiful,' I replied, 'but I do not know what it entails.'

" 'It is almost self-explanatory,' he continued. 'The Quasikan is the second person in my empire, and in that capacity he has the right to adore me perpetually, to amuse me when I am bored, and to do everything I wish.'

" 'I understand perfectly, light of the world—in return for which he is lodged, fed and clothed…'

" 'Shaved, sheared and buried—with all the benefits of life, of course—and enjoying in addition the disposition of all my treasures.'

"I bit my tongue just in time. 'What astonishes me,' I said, cleverly, 'is that such a beautiful situation is vacant.'

" 'By accident,' he said, shrugging a shoulder—I would have challenged him to budge the other. 'Can you imagine that that there have been 14 on the trot that I have had impaled, in vain, to correct their distractions? Not one of them was able to remember that my left slipper must be presented to me in the right hand, and my right slipper in the left hand. It's the most express condition of the ceremony, and it is recorded as such in the fundamental laws of the Savant Isle. I too am rather distracted, and I admit that the fundamental law scares me.'

68

" 'Mighty Sun of the Patagons,' I murmured, in a tremulous voice, 'the sublime rank of Quasikan is far above my unworthiness. You would reward my feeble offices too nobly by sending me home as soon as possible, by the shortest route, provided that it is not in a boat with a triple compressor, nor a balloon armed for war, because I hold hose two vehicles in execration, for reasons that are particularly personal.'

" 'What!' retorted the Archikan. 'I gladly give you permission to return there on foot, if you know the secret. It's a means that my islanders have very rarely used, so far as I know, for transporting themselves to the continents. Since you are proposing to return whence you came, though, do me the favor of letting me know where that is. You will find that I have an astounding erudition in that regard. After hunting and heraldry, the subject in which we Patagon kings are especially well-informed is geography, because it opens the minds of young people wonderfully, and stimulates the appetites of sovereigns for conquest. It is no less necessary for government, at least as we govern.'

" 'My intention,' I replied, 'is to go to that capital of science, that metropolis of art, that headquarters of civilization, that inexhaustible arsenal of perfectibility, Paris. It's near Villeneuve-la-Guyard, only half a day away by diligence.'

" 'To Paris!' he cried, with a deafening laugh. 'It's 10,000 years and more since Paris was destroyed by a rain of aeroliths.'

" 'I always suspected as much,' I riposted, striking my forehead with my hand. 'I was there.'

" 'That astonishes me greatly, doctor. If you had been in Paris on that day, you would not have been sleeping for 10,000 years on the Isle of the Patagons.'

" 'What! Sire, I was not in Paris; I was in the rain of aeroliths, which I did not deem it appropriate to follow as far as the ground.'

" 'That was wise on your part, for at the contingent point, I would not have given straw for the difference. You should know, then, that the place where Paris was is occupied today by the superb city of Hurlu, which was founded by Hurluber-lu, and which has the inestimable good fortune of now living under the most gracious, the wittiest and the most illustrious of all his descendants, the magnanimous Hurlubleu, grand Manifafa of Hurlubière. You can verify that immediately in the *Royal Almanack.*' "

"Stop there, Berniquet," the Manifafa interrupted. "Is it really true that Leviathan made that speech?"

"May I never go back to the land of the Patagons," replied Berniquet, "if I have altered a single word of it."

"I have difficulty understanding, then, why you give so little credit to the mind of the Archikan, for those phrases seem to me to be exceptionally well-turned."

"Everything is relative, divine Manifafa; a fool may utter such phrases as would do honor to a man of genius, and the expression of so natural and so facile a sentiment is only feeble and vulgar in proportion to an eloquence and style of 40 cubits."

"That's fair, jester; I'm not unduly flattered to be placed at that height in the estimation of that great personable. Continue."

"Leviathan continued speaking: 'I cannot see the slightest inconvenience,' he said, 'in sending you back to Hurlu, but I'm afraid that you'll find it a long journey if you obstinately refuse to use speedy means. It's a terrible problem to untangle.'

" 'It seems to me,' I replied, 'that on a globe whose circumference is calculated at 9000 leagues, it requires scarcely 3000 leagues by the axis and 4500 leagues by the semicircle to reach the antipodes. Now, we both understand by antipodes the two opposite points of the sphere through which the greatest possible perpendicular could be passed.'

" 'I could not prove the contrary in a quarter of an hour,' the Archikan replied, 'but I have a suspicion that you are mistaken regarding the actual dimensions of the Earth—and that would be an entirely understandable illusion after 10,000 years of sleep. Observe first, savant, that you are not taking account of the gradual increase of the geological and mineral world by juxtaposition. A tree elevates a bird's nest imperceptibly while it sleeps momentarily, with its head hidden beneath its wing, but you're supposing, doctor, that you have spent 10,000 years under your bell-jar without changing your relative position in space!'

" 'No, truly,' I replied to the Archikan. 'There must be something in it, or I don't understand anything.'

" 'Reflect a little further,' Leviathan the Long went on. 'You have seen satellites dissolve and rain aeroliths upon the Earth. You have seen them bury cities and cover vast regions without anything of indestructible matter being destroyed but a transient form. What do you say about the geoliths that volcanoes vomit forth as they deepen their craters, a common phenomenon that will perhaps be repeated until the empty globe is reduced to an immense shell, which must necessarily gain in surface what it loses in solidity?'

"I thought privately that this accident would be very favorable to the exhumation of Zeretocthro-Shah and his man, and that it would be rather prudent to postpone to that epoch the definitive advent of perfectibility.

" 'What do you say about all the organic creatures, living and sensitive, which accumulate in humus, which stand out from cliffs, which lie in ossuaries? About mountains that collapse, and which, in flattening out their abnormal unevenness, increasingly raise up the soil that serves as their base. What do you say?' "

"What do you say, Berniquet?" cried the Manifafa. "I don't understand the Patagon any better than the propagandist, or the propagandist than the Patagon, but it seems to me that there can't be much in it. When you put your story into print, don't make this huge Leviathan so stupid; he talks at least as well as the books of buffoons."

"Instinctively, milord; there is nothing as crushing as the simple reasoning of an ignoramus, but Your Majesty probably no longer remembers that these poor people have no intellectual sense?"

"I remember quite clearly, jester, that the ideological section appeared not to have found it—but if it ever does find it, against all expectations, and you still have credit in those lands, I suggest that you ask them to keep it to themselves. That can't do the ideological section any harm, and I think it would be as well for them if our Patagons did without it."

" 'Finally,' said the Archikan, still talking, 'you are not taking into account certain fortuitous aggregations like the one that resulted from the fall of the Moon while you were sleeping so soundly. There's a protuberance that extends your diameter a little!'

" 'What!' I riposted immediately. 'The Moon, gone astray by virtue of one of those perturbations to which it was so liable, has become united with its metropolis? That meeting must, indeed, have produced a rather remarkable bulge on the sphere.'

" 'Don't speak any longer of a sphere, my dear doctor; the world that your century labeled thus now resembles one of those spinning-tops with irregular and unequal rhombs, which children cause to leap about on rope—or, if you prefer, it is exactly the same shape as one of those pumpkins from which pilgrims fashion gourds. The most unfortunate thing about that collision was that it struck in a horrible fashion that beautiful kingdom of diamonds in which the Regent would only have passed for a miserable paring, because they had succeeded in fabricating the richest of nature's works in enormous dimensions. We have carefully retained the recipe for them, but we have searched in vain ever since for the proportions and the procedure.'

" 'That's what we lack too,' I told Leviathan the Long, 'but I ought to add that we don't have the recipe.'

" 'It comes down,' he said, 'to two rather common principles: charcoal dust passed through a sieve, which can be extracted from bladder-nut trees, and a vegetable element called *fagotine*, which the botanical physiology section has discovered in bundles of firewood.' "

At this point, the impatient Manifafa once again abruptly broke into the jester's interesting narrative. "I'd like to know, Berniquet, why the botanical physiology section got mixed up in it. Diamonds are losing all their value."

"Right, milord! The street urchins no longer want them for playing marbles—but bundles of firewood are priceless."

"I can't see, then," he continued, joining his hands together piteously, "what advantage one can derive, in terms of political economy, by debasing a stupid jewel whose rarity alone made all utility unnecessary, and making it impossible for good folk to acquire the joyful firewood that adds charm to winter evenings?"

"It's necessary to make a distinction, Divine Manifafa; I didn't say that it was advantageous, merely that it was progress."

"My word, you're right, Berniquet. That distinction had escaped me. Resume your story immediately, jester, for I'm finding it very instructive."

"The Archikan continued the discourse from the point at which we left him in this manner: 'You see, doctor,' he said, 'that, the world has grown unexpectedly in your absence. It will be difficult to reach the fine city of Hurlu, by the most direct route, in less than ten years, to which you must add ten years more that you will inevitably spend at custom-barriers, hospitals and police stations, and another ten years spent in waiting for passports and visas. Factoring in fatigue, accidents and, most of all, the infirmities that increase every day at your age, and you'll be doing well if you only have to give yourself another 30 years. With the virile maturity that you display, strong resolution, an intrepidity proof against anything, good feet, a good eye and a little luck, you might well make your entrance into the splendid capital of Hurlubière in 60 years or thereabouts, save for submitting to preliminary inspection of the gendarmerie, the *sergents de ville* and the officials at the toll-booth.'

" 'You don't say,' I replied to Leviathan the Long, in a humorous tone. 'That will make at least a century since my emergence from the baptismal font.'

" 'You'll be all the more respectable. On the other hand, if you decided to take the indirect route—which is infinitely more comfortable—we would be able to offer you, in truth, suspension bridges ending in 800 planets.'

" 'Great God—800 planets! And planets with suspension-bridges! All those ruined entrepreneurs!'

" 'That's where you're mistaken. All the men who grow bored on one planet spend their poor lives going in search of another. It's a perpetual shuttle; but that mode of traveling presents quite a few inconveniences, according to the celestial mechanics section. The first, savant friend, is spending your valuable spare time in journeys that are instructive but fruitless, for 200,000 or 300,000 solar cycles—I'm giving you approximate figures, because I don't remember them.'

" 'Oh, milord,' I cried, lamentably, 'I gladly give you dispensation for the approximate figures and the other inconveniences. After a figure and an inconvenience like that, I'm quite certain of never seeing Hurlu again.'

" 'You'll be there in ten minutes, if that's agreeable to you,' the Archikan relied, laughing.

" '2000 or 3000 solar cycles, and the space that their revolutions embrace, in ten minutes! I must be dreaming.'

" 'That wouldn't make things worse,' he went on. 'All the time one isn't dreaming is time lost.'

" 'I can't deny,' I ruminated, understandably, 'that fulminating gold promised to make a very pretty projective in my youth, but these thousands of solar cycles reduced to minutes must surpass the range of the propaganda.'

" 'Gold! Truly a beautiful poverty. Get it into your head that we have discovered ten metals superior to gold on one planet alone, and 10,000 projectives for fulminating gold. The common people don't make matches from it.'

" 'That's strange!' I replied. 'Gold was quite valuable in my time, if one can judge by hearsay.'

" 'With rhinoceros-loads, hippopotamus-loads and camel-loads, dear doctor—so many years have you slept—with mammoth-loads, you would not be rich enough to but a handful of rice, barley or sesame.' "

"Oh, how I would like," said the Manifafa, "to see that double-dyed fool Croesus resuscitated in the midst of his treasures in the Isle of the Patagons, to laugh at his idiocy! That bewilderment would do great honor to the gaiety of Providence."

" 'Come on,' Leviathan continued, in an imperious voice, 'decorate this famous doctor with a ceremonial gown that will not be useless to him in the cold regions through which he will pass, and send a forced projection to Hurlu, even if it bursts the mortars. You'll answer to me with your head!' As I was carried away, he added: 'By the way, European philosopher, don't forget to present assurances of my esteem and fraternal amity to your master.' "

"I kiss his hands," said the Manifafa, "and I approve of the way he treated you, because it was quite gallant. There you are in a carriage, then."

"It was a comfortable chair, elegant, light and well suspended, but devoid of wheels or shafts—those vulgar means of vehiculation being quite useless to it. It was simply fixed in front of a horizontal metal bar—have the generosity to imagine it, for I did not have time on the way to make a drawing—the extremities of which ended in two large-caliber cannonballs at the orifices of two artillery pieces, which were placed at exactly equal distances, similar to my tilbury, with the result that I was enclosed in a sort of iron horse."

"That's rather ingenious," Hurlubleu interrupted. "I'm waiting for you at the projective."

"Behind me the openings of the two cannons were furnished with two convergent conductors, which inevitable slanted towards a common summit, geometry not having changed between here and that disposition. I was not made to wait. Scarcely was I arranged on my cushions to sleep when a lanky postillion arrived…"

"Match alight!"

"No, Divine Manifafa, Leyden jar in hand. The electric spark was preferable because of its synchronicity. He presented the switch to the conductors' point of contact, and I departed with a rapidity that is difficult to imagine, especially if one has only ever come from Villeneuve-la-Guyard by way of a mail-coach."

"Did the mortars explode?"

"I have never been able to find out, milord. Sound travels at little more than 200 fathoms a minute; I would have been hard pressed to catch it."

"This means of travel, Berniquet, must be rather inconvenient for people who are short of breath."

"Not as much as you might think, Divine Highness, because the rarefaction of the air, which is incalculable at those heights, makes more than adequate compensation, and because the rapidity of the flight almost makes up for the lack of atmospheric density. The greatest danger that a traveler might run is that of encountering a body more solid than the medium it is penetrating."

"An aerolith, for example, worthy jester—that would be a dire occurrence."

"Very dire, Divine Manifafa. I almost cracked my skull on a thin grey mist of flax which was no larger than a fist, and which arrived, bobbing around insouciantly, exactly in the middle of my two cannonballs. God, what a crash!"

"You blew it away."

"I couldn't—but it was obliging enough to take its right of way, like a taxi-cab."

"What I find most irritating about this method, jester, is the monotony of the eye-blink, for nothing can be as disagreeably uniform as a route where little grey mists of flax count as events, when one is accustomed to observing as one travels, ending up reading the signs."

"The monotony! Don't believe it, milord. I took an inexpressible pleasure in contemplating the 800 planet-to-planet suspension-bridges that were hurtling from horizon to horizon in marvelous arcs, all charged with trophies, obelisks and statues in rather good taste, and exactly the right proportions, at least by comparison with those on the Pont de la Concorde. I can't describe it."

"No one else would be able to describe it any better than you, Berniquet. You're talking about an admirable view."

"I was enjoying it with all my heart when the shaft of my cannonballs, probably overheated by friction, and heat-sensitive by nature, suddenly dilated with a screech—and broke into two exactly equal parts, because of the homogeneity of the material and the perfect equipollence of the two projective impulses."

"By virtue of the homogeneity and the equipollence," said the Manifafa, yawning and climbing his jaw, "it could not have happened otherwise. You're now well on track to describe the world upside-down again, for I can't believe that you're the kind of man to give up the habit of falling head-first, as the variety of your tale would require."

"I beg Your Majesty to recall," Berniquet riposted, "that I fell feet first into the rut."

"My word, that's true, jester," Hurlubleu replied, "and I've sometimes regretted it slightly, for if you had struck the bedrock with your head, I fancy that the story of your travels would already be over and done with."

"It's only a matter of patience, Divine Manifafa, and we're nearing the end, if you wouldn't prefer that I start again. As I was leaning on the bar at the instant when it shattered, which is an entirely natural posture when one goes out to see the world, I had the good fortune to retain the side I was holding and to follow my flying cannonball, while Leviathan's royal chair went to the Devil. Your Sublime Highness already knows the rest. I passed over the high wall of the palace and the tenfold circle of your guards, in which I made a nasty hole, as far as the small apartments, where I was carried quite naturally to your sacred knees—which seemed to cause you some slight surprise, in view of the rarity of the event."

The Manifafa was snoring like an organ. Berniquet concluded, logically, that he had gone to sleep.

It is at this point that the jester's adventures appear to come to a stop, but it was not the end of his troubles. This great man remained human, by virtue of a few weaknessness of organization for which no one had found the remedy in his time. Several times, while he was telling his tale, he had noticed a certain trembling of the silk screens whose light hangings closed the communicating door between the harem and the bedroom, and he had rightly attributed this to a moving body more intelligent than the external air, for it surely must have heard him talking. Astonished by the unaccustomed absence of their royal spouse, and perhaps also curious to make a more leisurely examination of the unknown philosopher who had passed so suddenly through their midst in the wake of the shafted cannonball, without having time to let them see him, the Manifafa's wives had slipped furtively, one by one, to all the exits—and Berinquet even thought he had caught two or three glimpses of the crafty brown face of an odalisque, so barely mature that it impressed a singular preoccupation on his mind. This was the fortunate male's favorite sultana.

The hands of the clock had not marked out an entire quarter-hour when the Manifafa awoke with a start from some preposterous dream or other. One might perhaps have guessed that he did not find the jester nearby; on the other hand, he had scarcely passed the nearest screen when he found him extremely close to the favorite sultana, where the savant chief buffoon, surprised by a gentle and deceptive drowsiness, had yielded to the charms of a sleep similar to that of innocence.

The unfortunate Berniquet reopened his eyes to the gleam of the yataghan.

"Do you recognize the master of your body and your soul, detestable hypocrite?" cried Hurlubleu.

"Mercy, have mercy on the body of your humble and devoted jester!" sobbed Berniquet, in a stifled voice. As for his soul, the philosopher had arranged that it would require no more preparation than the fleshy, sweet and edible tap-root of

Brassica napus, which is the third variety of the Linnaean *Asperifolia*.[32]

"This is a fine way for a spineless wretch to carry on, on the pretext of being a savant," the Manifafa said. Sheathing his blade again, he continued: "That's all right. Never let it be said that I deprived perfectibility of such a great hope merely to satisfy the vengeance of my mad jealousy. I can exploit you in a fashion more advantageous to my glory. I would gladly sent you on a shafted cannonball, on my behalf, to visit that honest Leviathan who said so many nice things about me, if I had the means—but you will give me great pleasure by returning, as soon as possible, to the quest for Zeretochthro-Schah by way of the bottomless well that has been newly opened up in the middle of Hurlu's main square. I often thought about it during your story, and I am happy and proud to be able to offer you, within my own State, a favorable means of accomplishing your great destiny. Make an amicable will, therefore, in which you will take care to give me all that you possess, as our mutual friendship requires, and make ready, seductive jester, to depart for Bactria this evening. I am curious to know whether you will come back as easily from the nucleus of the Earth as from the most eccentric points of its rotation."

Berniquet, who was discreet, respectful and courteous, had not uttered a single word in reply to this paternal allocution. He was interred that evening.

The jester of the buffoons was as fundamentally wise as one can be when one is a philosopher, and as good-natured as

---

[32] *Brassica napus* is rape, which does not have an edible root, although its seeds are a rich source of oil; the use of botanical analogies in the euphemistic representation of human genitalia and sexual activity was, however, commonplace in the 18th century—a circumstance not unconnected to Linnaeus' decision to classify plants according to their sexual organs—so Nodier's reference to rape's "tap-root" is presumably not intended literally. *Asperifolia* means "plants with rough leaves"—another reference that is presumably metaphorical.

one can be when one is a philanthropist. Although he was quite obstinate in his systematic whims, his adventurous voyages and his negative longevity had disillusioned him somewhat with regard to indefinite improvement, and it was noticeable that he had often spoken of it lately with a muffled laugh. It is probable that he did not arrive at the grand *vade in pace* of Hurlu's main square without inwardly desiring that he had never got involved with propaganda, Zeretochthro-Shah, Hurlubleu and the favorite sultana, but he put on a brave face—and the sensitive populace, who sometimes take account of powerful people who have come to harm when none has been done to them, accompanied him with the most energetic evidence of sympathy and regret of which common people are capable in cases of noble distress; they said nothing at all.

The ceremony was pompous and magnificent. All the Hurlubierians were there—ten million individuals, not counting the women and little children. The jester, with a lantern attached to his doublet, a basket of provisions in his hand and a voluminous album under his arm—for his notes and drawings—took his place in the miner's basket with all the dignity of an ambassador thoroughly convinced of the importance of his mission.

"Irreparable man," said the chibicou who was accompanying him at the moment of his leave-taking, "if our prayers for your return go unanswered for a long time, as seems only too likely, what information will you deign to leave us, in your infinite prudence, as to what we ought to think of the utility of science and the goal of wisdom?"

"I should like to communicate to you all that I have learned in more than 10,000 yeas of existence," replied the Curtius of perfectibility,[33] "saving the rectification of my

---

[33] Curtius was a legendary hero of ancient Rome; when an earthquake opened a deep fissure in the Forum he declared that the strength of Rome was embodied in the arms and courage of its citizens, and leapt into the gulf on horseback. The

judgment by new discoveries. Science consists of forgetting what one thinks one knows, and wisdom is not worrying about it."

On that sentence, in which all human philosophy is summarized—and which is sufficient for me to conclude, insouciantly, my laborious pilgrimage through this vale of tears, the inexplicable Jehosaphat[34] of the living—the activation of the cables sent Berniquet speeding into the bowels of the Earth.

A week later, the watch-officer's rope brought back a nice packet of geological rarities, the most curious of which was a fossil cockchafer which had eight legs and an inverted prothorax. The former jester informed his colleagues, by means of a missive attached to this subterranean gift, that the shaft widened out into an immense cone as it approached its utmost depths, which considerably increased the difficulties of a return journey, at least by means of ordinary ambulation, but that he was happy to write them a polite note informing tem of his determination to proceed to the central point of his excursion.

After that, all the cables were withdrawn, and the philosophical shaft was covered over by an enormous monolith in the form of a millstone, in the style of those fabricated at Ferté-sous-Jouarre, between Meaux and Château-Thierry. A regiment of Patagons could not have lifted it.

I regret now not having the pen of Tacitus—or a better one if you can imagine that—to describe the terrible events that followed Berniquet's departure. His partisans, who naturally saw his unexpected and sudden message as a sort of covert exile, gradually roused the cruel civil emotions that subsequently gave way to the bloody war of the buffoons: THE

---

fissure than closed up again, as if to signify the Earth's agreement.

[34] The Valley of Jehosaphat extends between Jerusalem and the Mount of Olives. In apocalyptic mythology it is where the dead will assemble for the Final Judgment.

WAR OF THE BUFFOONS which, you will remember as vividly as I do, furnished history with such beautiful pages, and over which the tragic muse has shed so many tears!

The advantage lay at first with the august dynasty of Hurluberlu, but it soon turned in a calamitous fashion; that was the effect of a particularity too memorable for me to pass over it here in silence, although the solemn dotard Attus Navius has not said a word about it in his chronicles. It appears that, as the etymology—which is the true luminary of facts—suggests,[35] official congratulations in the court of Hurlubière really did consist of tickling carried to the extreme of reducing the conqueror to helpless spasms; it is generally believed that the magnanimous Hurlubleu quite this life during one of these glorious epilepsies. It must at least be admitted that critics will be hard pressed to prove the contrary, and I am all the more enthusiastic to accept this lesson because it furnishes me with a precious example of a king who dies laughing—which has probably never happened before, and will certainly never happen again, the way that monarchies are going.

Hurlubleu having died childless, the kingdom's Great Charter necessarily rendered power to the buffoons, who would have been quite content without it, in accordance with their immemorial habit—for one never saw anything emerge from any of that deplorable empire's revolutions but buffoons: buffoons against buffoons; buffoons on top of buffoons; a whole host of buffoons. The people had plumped for white buffoons, red buffoons, buffoons of every color, buffoons with long robes and buffoons with short robes, buffoons in buskins and buffoons in boots, buffoons in togas and buffoons in armor, buffoons with pens and buffoons with swords, buffoons

---

[35] The etymology of the terms Hurlubleu and Hurlubière relate them to the verb *hurler*, to howl. The former suggests a condition akin to that expressed by the English phrase "howl [with laughter] until [one is] blue in the face." Bière has two meanings, equivalent to the English "beer" and "bier," the latter presumably being the intended one.

by birth, buffoons by chance, buffoons with money, buffoons with doctrines, buffoons of industry—but they were always buffoons. The wretched Hurlubierians, having something of the buffoon innate within them, always opted for buffoons and perennially devolved into buffoons. In the final analysis, who would vote for buffoons if he were not a buffoon?

The sovereign buffoons, as is reasonable, erected a pedestal on the stone that closed the shaft into which Berniquet had descended: an unequal dodecahedron depicting the dozen continents of the known world. If ever a 13th were discovered, I sincerely declare that I don't now where one could put it, but Heaven preserve me from such a great problem!

Berniquet had left a popular legacy equivalent to the almost 300 sesterces that Caesar had left to each Roman citizen—which amounted, according to Monsieur Letronne,[36] to 59 francs 61 centimes. That's what I call a good prince! The poor jester, however, had not a single brass *uncia sextula* to dispose—and that, more than anything else in his life, inspired the profoundest pity in his biographers. On the largest face of the base, therefore, in a lapidary style not seen again in the Academy of Inscriptions, the last lines of his will were inscribed:

May God Deign To Give To All My Good Friends,
All The Patience Required To Tolerate Life With Love
And Benevolence, To Render It Sweet And Useful,
And The Gaiety Required To Laugh At It.

A statue of the jester erected on the monument was inaugurated the following day, and, as the sculpture of that improved era was naïve and bourgeois, the skillful artist represented him in a nightcap and slippers, breaking wind.

It is a beautiful piece.

---

[36] Jean-Antoine Letronne (1787-1848), a contemporary polymath particularly distinguished in the fields of geography and archaeology.

Louis Ulbach: *The Story of a Naiad*
(1864)

Louis Ulbach (1822-1889) was a protégé of Victor Hugo, who published a volume of verse, *Gloriana* (1944), before undertaking a career in journalism, as an enthusiastic supporter of Republicanism. Following the revolution of 1848, he founded the *Propagateur de l'Aube* [Propagator of the Dawn], in which he published a dialogue in the form of two series of letters, one signed "Jacques Souffrant, ouvrier" [Suffering Jack, workman] and the other with his own name. These letters caused something of a sensation, renewed when they were subsequently reprinted in book form, but they identified Ulbach as a potential trouble-maker when Louis-Napoléon staged his *coup d'état* in 1851; the *Propagateur de l'Aube* was suppressed and Ulbach went to work for the *Revue de Paris*, becoming its editor in 1853.

In 1858, the *Revue de Paris* was suppressed in its turn by the Emperor's censors, and Ulbach embarked upon a career as a *feuilletonist*, producing novels and short stories in considerable quantity, almost all of which are now completely forgotten. He also became the drama critic of *Le Temps* in 1861. In 1867, he started working for *Le Figaro*, in which he published a series of satirical letters above the signature Ferragus, which he used as a pseudonym on some of his fiction. He also became a significant contributor to the evolution of French Freemasonry. In 1868, Ulbach founded another periodical of his own, *La Cloche*, but it was quickly suppressed and Ulbach was jailed for six months. When he was released, he was unable to revive *La Cloche*, but he continued to express his opinions stridently.

The fall of the Second Empire did not put an end to Ulbach's troubles; indeed, he contrived to annoy both the Commune and the new Republic that succeeded it, and was imprisoned again in 1871-72. His argumentative tendencies had by now become legendary, although the controversy for which he is nowadays best remembered is a purely literary one; following the publication of Emile Zola's *Thérèse Raquin* (1867), Ulbach published a fierce denunciation of that novel under the title "La Littérature putride" [Putrid Literature], to which its equally combative target responded with a fervent diatribe that became the "manifesto" of Naturalism. From 1878 until he was forced by ill-health to retire, Ulbach completed his career, as Charles Nodier had done before him, as the librarian at the Bibliothèque de l'Arsenal.

"Histoïre d'une Naiad" was reprinted in book form in *Voyage autour mon clocher: histoire et histories* (1864), but was presumably published in a periodical some time before that date. It might seem a peculiar inclusion in a collection of this sort, given that, with the exception of a couple of under-developed asides, it is not speculative, and is not even fiction. It is, however, an early technological romance of a sort that was subsequently to become commonplace in the context of the popularization of science. Ardent champions of progress never found it easy to express their enthusiasm in the form of futuristic fiction, but they found it much easier in essays celebrating the past achievements of technological innovators. By the mid-20th century, popularizers like Isaac Asimov and Martin Gardner—both of whom also dabbled in science fiction—had perfected a kind of "science non-fiction story" used to turn accounts of scientific, mathematical and technological discoveries into heroic fantasies, gradually building a new "factual mythology" that has become the main narrative component of the history of science.

Most "human interest stories" of this kind foreground ingenious inventors rather than their inventions, but some fetishize and mythologize the machines themselves, and Ulbach's essay in tragic drama is one of the earliest accounts of this sort. It makes an interesting contrast with more orthodox literary accounts of potential technologies, which far more readily fall prey to the effects of the Frankenstein complex, and its careful reflective reference to another (even more obscure)

85

literary work featuring its doomed heroine provides a deft reminder of the fact that technology, like art, is a form of "secondary creation."

It is a beautiful spectacle to see Louis XIV, young, magnetically attractive and replete with all the prestige of nature and power, progressing with smiling majesty towards the realization of one of his Olympian fantasies. I do not seek to hide the fact that the pompous scaffolding in question was founded in sweat and tears; I know perfectly well that all that wealth had a heavy counterweight in the misery of the common people; I know perfectly well that the construction of the palace of Versailles might have cost the lives of an army; but why reproach the sacrifices made to ambition more bitterly than those made to art and science? Hecatomb for hecatomb, I prefer those that are immolated to genius to stupid massacres for reasons of State. Is it less honorable to die for a masterpiece than to avenge the human vanity of a statesman or repair the ineptitude of an imprudent ambassador?

We shall not review all the titanic playthings with which Louis XIV capriciously amused himself; we shall not read through that epic poem hewn in stone—the only true epic of which France can be proud; we shall proceed bucolically through the laughing woods and hillocks to talk about the naiad whose powerful conch exhaled water into the fountains of Versailles, and previously exhaled it from the stone noses of horses at Marly—which means, shorn of hyperbole, that we shall visit the hydraulic machine whose aqueduct, with its enormous arches, mingles so picturesquely with the landscape of Bougival, and recalls, in setting aside the verdure, one of those horizons set in the depths of the Italian landscape around Tivoli.

If we were still in that eminently artistic epoch in which art replaced natural ornaments in the mind, in which artificial hairpieces maintained the inspiration of poets in mild warmth, and in which illusion—of which frequent use was made—created belief in the operatic mythology enthroned everywhere, this would be a mater of intoning a ode or epistle in the manner of a description of the Rhine. Under what periphrases the workings of the machine could be dissimulated! How reeds might be dressed and weeds crowned! How little tritons and dolphins might be made to swim and leap in the silvery moss scattered in that river region!

Unfortunately—or, rather, fortunately—the abuse of hydraulics has engendered skepticism with regard to naiads, and steam, applied to the Marly machine, moves so brutally that it only seems to us that the poor nymph must be suffering a horrible dismemberment. There would be little chance of waking her up or invoking her. Nor do we wish to issue a technical description, and we have excellent reasons for that, which require the dispossession of one alderman in order to give to the others. We are in perfect ignorance with regard to hydrostatics; we shall simply relate what we know; we shall forge the legend of the machine; we shall visit her in this story as we have visited her in reality, by way of fantasy, without industrial preoccupation or pedantic afterthought, restricting the point of view…to the point of view.

I have often wondered what might have happened if Louis XIV had had steam-engines, railways and gas at his disposal. I do not doubt that these inventions would have been exploited marvelously, and that the hydraulic enchantments glimpsed periodically would have been unable to perpetuate themselves and last the night. Imagine the grounds of Versailles illuminated in the regal fashion in which everything was done then; imagine that the light employed had the same range as a lighthouse: what a dream! Unhappily, they had nothing but water at their disposal—but they did not hesitate to use it and get as much out of it as possible.

In 1676, Mansard, with the plans on which Marly had been built, demonstrated to Louis XIV the need for a machine of some sort to bring water up to the gardens of the château. It was simple to imagine, difficult to execute. Louis XIV did not get any more excited than was necessary; he simply notified the scientists of Europe that they were to provide it, and not to take too long about it. Projects immediately began to flourish.

Heads heavy with calculations bowed down stubbornly in search of a glorious solution.

The Baron de Ville, a native of Liége, already well-known in France for several hydraulic systems, offered his services to build the machine in question. His project approved, he set to work, stoutly aided by one of his compatriots, a highly-skilled technician named Rennequin Swalem.[37] Some people even claimed that Rennequin was the inventor, and that the Baron de Ville was only one of those dangerous collaborators who lend their name but take the glory—one of those usurpers for which the verses were written that begin *Sic vos non vobis*....[38] There is, however, no justification for the Rennequists' claims. All the evidence suggests, on the contrary, that the Baron de Ville was a serious inventor. There is much argument regarding a certain epitaph that describes Rennequin as an inventor. On the other hand, however, it is said that the Baron de Ville had come to France to construct a machine to raise water to the château and gardens of Sant-Germain, then occupied by Queen Anne of England; that the machine was completed, and later proposed, copied and re-constructed at Marly. This repetition would be an important argument. Rennequin supervised the work and the workmen and, when the machine was finished, the Baron de Ville was appointed its governor, with a proportionate salary. He lived in the Pavillon de Luciennes (or Louveciennes); as for Rennequin, he remained a supervisor with a salary of 1880 francs. He died at the machine, in 1708, at the age of 64, without ever having protested against the Baron de Ville's alleged usurpa-

---

[37] Modern textbooks give this surname as Sualem, but I have retained Ulbach's spelling.

[38] According to legend, this was the common first line of four verses deliberately left incomplete by Virgil by way of a challenge Bathyllus, who had claimed authorship of some of the great poet's verses; Bathyllus was, of course, unable to complete the verses. The phrase is approximately translatable as "Thus ye do, but not for yourselves."

tion. Moreover, this is what can be read on an old diagram representing the former Marly machine, designed in 1688:

This machine served to embellish the royal houses at Versailles, Trianon and Marly, and might have served at Saint-Germain-en-Laye. It was constructed by order of the king, according to the plans and under the direction of Monsieur le Baron de Ville.

Work was begun in June 1681, and the water rose up in 1685. That was a fine day, but rudely bought with innumerable efforts, researches and tentative experiments. As for the expense, no one was astonished. It was six or seven millions then, which would be a good 14 today; it is also said that it was not all written down. The naiad's running costs rose to 71,016 livres, but that is said not to include wages. Nothing seems to have been exaggerated. Beside, who would have complained? The people? It did not concern them. If that money did not buy bread, at least it bought spectacles; that was enough. As for Louis XIV, such trivial considerations did not bother him. He had needed water for the reservoirs, for the swans, for the stone and bronze tritons, and he had said: "Go, I give you the mountain, take the valley, and, if necessary, confiscate the river." He had been obeyed; the sunlight played upon the water of his pools; it cost a good few millions—a mere bagatelle! It was paid, everyone was content. There was no Chamber to dispute his expenses, no newspapers to scatter their writings in the crystal waters of his fountains! He was the king, he was a god, he was everything!

Marly alone profited from the machine at first. It was only 20 years after her completion, when the population increased considerably at Versailles and the wells dried up in periods of drought, that the reservoirs of Marly were transferred there. We would certainly like to give an accurate description of the ancient machine, and we declare that to that end we have riffled through the pages of books with which we were strangely unacquainted, but how can she be recognized in these wheels, chains, pumps, pistons and sumps? On the basis of our studies, we can say to our readers that what remains clear to us is that all the water stirred, captured and swallowed by the machine was raised with the aid of 221 pumps, arranged in three rows, and two sumps, mounted on a platform that was 500 feet or 162 meters above the river.

From that tower the water falls into a basin that serves as a gauge; from there it runs into an aqueduct 310 fathoms long, sustained on 36 arches, constructed in millstone grit, all of whose angles and all of whose pillars are made of cut stone. At the end of this aqueduct is a tower about 44 feet high, constructed of the same materials as the large tower and the aqueduct. The water is received in a cistern, at the bottom of which are the valves that distribute the water to Marly and Versailles. That is a summary of the digestive apparatus with which the monster drank from the Seine that which she subsequently blew out over the gardens.

If all men—or, at least, nearly all men, as one of Louis XIV's court preachers rephrased it—are mortal, the works constructed by men are subject to the same destiny. After a century, by dint of twisting the waves in her throat the old machine felt profound internal lesions; her stomach was ruined, her teeth were broken, visible cracks appeared in her skull, and she began to cough and shake her head. She had become terminally asthmatic, without taking into account the fact that, incurable as she was, the centenarian's malady was costing the State dear. A conference of mechanical engineers was therefore assembled. The hope was ignited in their eyes of a glorious recompense if they found a means of galvanizing the decrepit body and simplifying the expenses of her upkeep. However, in the middle of the consultation—which was prolonged—a knock on the door was heard; the French Revolution was passing that way, and wanted to stamp the scientists' certificates of citizenship. One of them, the author of the restoration project, was arrested as a suspect, and the whole thing was abandoned.

The vestige of absolutism was left breathless in her corner, for there was then a machine in Paris, perennially active in one of its great squares, which engaged in rivalry with others. The poor invalid was then overtaken by a series of misfortunes and dolorous alternatives. Here the demolition hammer was set to work, there scaffolding was erected. She was sold at auction, abandoned, betrayed and crucified. One of her worshipers, in despair, then began, in slightly irreverent language, a history of its martyrdom entitled: *The passion of a very respectable lady, aged 123 years, god-daughter of a very magnificent prince and daughter of a man of genius, delivered into the world in the year 5804, among the apostles of truth.* It was an imitation of the Gospel, by which no one then dreamed of being shocked, but which nevertheless had a sacrilegious frivolity about it.

This opuscule begins thus: "At that time, the god-daughter of one of the greatest and most magnificent princes who had ever existed said to her friends and admirers: 'You know that judgment will be passed in two days and that the daughter of Swal [Rennequin Swalem] will be given over to be dismantled.' Then the princes of theory and the speculators assembled in the hall of their leaders and they deliberated on the means of skillfully taking her apart and killing her."[39]

The imitation is faithful; it continues thus word for word. We shall cite another two fragments:

"The morning having come, the leaders of the princes of theory and the speculators held council against the god-daughter to put her to death; and having already sold her they delivered her to the demolisher, in consideration of 180 kyliades, which were divided between them. Then the one who had betrayed her, seeing that she was condemned, said: 'I have earned my money.' He rejoiced in it, and he bought a house of ease and a field, putting all thought of doing away with himself out of his mind."[40]

---

[39] The parody is not exactly word-for-word, as Ulbach suggests, but is obviously derived from Matthew 26:1-4.
[40] Derived from Matthew 27:1-5—except, of course, that in the gospel Judas hangs himself.

The judge, who wants to save the unfortunate machine, but is unable to do so, washes his hands in vinegar and all the speculators respond: "May her blood fall back into our pockets and those of our children!"

She is mutilated, and a placard is put on her forehead bearing a bizarre inscription, which is incomprehensible if one does not bother to read the large letters together, independently of the small ones, and then the small ones, independently of the large:

CEN'EcondSTQUEamnPARéeCEàêt
QUENrevenOUSdueVOetdéULONchir
SDEVéccaORErlarRLAemplacMACera
HINquiEDEpourMARraLIpeun
QUENousimOUSLporteAVOànoNSus.[41]

The minor wit responsible for this *complainte* is unidentified. The machine was resuscitated before being entirely defeated. In 1807, work on the project began, but enormous sums were expended in vain. In 1811, Monsieur Cécile took over the direction and overcame the difficulty. He it was, jointly with Monsieur Martin, who put air back into the broken-down lungs, or rather fitted new lungs. He it was who applied steam-power and equipped the edifice with a Greek fronton, in which the poor nymph was blackened and bruised by the gears while releasing frightful sighs. One would have thought it a temple without the black plume that was almost always suspended above her head, which attests the alimentation of a more ardent fire that a tripod or incense-burner of our own day.

This machine is 64 horse-power. She consumes between 96 and 100 hectoliters of coal every 24 hours, and raises up 90

---

[41] Deciphering the inscription as instructed, it reads in translation: "It is only because we want to destroy the Marly machine that we have condemned it to be sold and taken apart, for to replace it would be of little consequence to us."

inches of water in a single jet to the summit of the large tower, which is equivalent to 1.8 million liters of water. She was put into operation in 1826. In 1818, the entire mechanism of the old machine was demolished and sold, replaced by another that raised up the water in a single stream. The latter was supposed to be provisional, pending the installation of the steam-engine. That provisional apparatus still exists. It comprises only two hydraulic wheels, each connected to a complement of four pumps. The maximum product of this machine is 60 inches or 1.2 million liters of water every 24 hours.

Such was the origin and the story of this glorious establishment, for whom new destinies are perhaps reserved in the future, but which, for the moment, no longer enjoys any but the obscure esteem of competent men. She is no longer the beloved *god-daughter* of kings, as the *complainte* quoted above makes out. The latter only take note of her occasionally. Louis XVIII was asked to visit her one day, but the constitutional obesity of the monarch, who did not have the full use of his legs, had to be taken into account. A miniature model of the machine was therefore constructed, which was mounted on little wheels on the day of his visit and pushed into the middle of the road, where the prince from the height of his carriage, set the hydraulic toy in motion. The courtiers then praised the condescension of the prince, who could have ordered that the machine be rolled all the way to Paris and installed his study. Charles X and Louis-Philippe each consecrated a single journey to her. The Comte de Paris came occasionally, and took extreme pleasure in having the workings of the steel limbs explained to him.[42]

Fountains of warm water have been organized on either side of the peristyle, thus serving the culinary needs of inhabitants of Bougival and Marly. It is the first concession made to humanitarianism. In the great century, that positive application would have been strictly avoided; it would have been consi-

---

[42] The Comte de Paris was Louis-Philippe's similarly-named grandson, born in 1838.

dered a sacrilege had an object designed for luxury not been completely useless. What would Louis XIV have said if, like us, he had heard a scientist and engineer, whose strange social preoccupations have somewhat encumbered his scientific ideas, make the bold and frank proposition that great steam-engines might be employed in the quasi-realization of Henri IV's prayer!

What this enthusiastic dreamer proposes (we leave the entire responsibility for his utopia to him) is that, by means of slight modifications familiar to him, residual water in steam boilers might serve admirably to cook the humble beef of poor people who are frightened by the idea of keeping a fire lit at home for a long time. In every region where the benefit of the smallest steam-powered factory or the most negligible steam locomotive were admitted, every inhabitant would bring his supper, carefully bound up and labeled, and the communal boiler would then return his beef, cooked sided-by-side with his neighbor's beef, or perhaps his enemy's. Who knows, even—this is the transcendental gastronomy of culinary philosophy—whether the idea of a communal boiling of nourishment prepared in the same receptacle might not extinguish rebellious hatreds and give birth in the minds of men to the idea of a reconciliation commenced by the vital element? Such a short distance separates beef and man—perhaps only the distance between food that is edible and that which is not.

Louis XIV, we may be certain, would be quite astonished by these projects, which will come to pass on the day when the Sun, on rising, plays in the arms of the humanitarian telegraph. In that happy time, people will set forth without anxiety, and everyone getting into a railway-carriage might enjoy the delightful assurance of being preceded by his dinner and traveling by courtesy of his cooking-pot.

X. B. Saintine: *Astronomical Journeys*
(1864)

X. B. Saintine was the by-line used by a prolific dramatist and novelist who was born Joseph Xavier Boniface (1798-
1865). Although he is largely forgotten today, two of his
works, both fact-based novels, remain fairly well-known: *Pic-
ciola*, about a political prisoner who conserves his sanity by
investment in the fate of a flower growing in a crack between
the stones of his prison; and *Seul!* [Alone!], which purports to
tell the true story of the castaway on whose experiences Daniel Defoe based the story of Robinson Crusoe.

The fascination with strategies of psychological survival
exhibited by these two novels resonates in many of Saintine's
other works, including a curious book of visionary fantasies,
ostensibly (and perhaps genuinely) drawn from a notebook in
which the author had long compiled a record of his dreams, *La
Seconde vie* [The Second Life] (1864). The following two-part
episode is taken from that book, where it forms chapters IV
and V; the second is there separately titled "Une Autre visite!
Une Autre planète!" [Another visit! Another Planet!]. It is not
the only dream recorded therein that is of interest in the context of scientific romance; others deal with hypothetical microscopic life-forms named "animules."

Most of the dreams related in *La Seconde vie* are earth-
bound fantasies mingling broad comedy with sly philosophical
and psychological speculations, but this brief cosmic odyssey,
while remaining as cheerfully nonsensical as any of the other
dreams narrated in the book, boldly involves itself with contemporary debates regarding the evolution of the Earth and its
living species. Camille Flammarion employed similar visionary artifice in some of contemporary popularizations of astronomy and discussions of the possible habitation of other
worlds, especially *Lumen* (1866-69; 1872 in *Récits de l'infini*;

revised for separate publication 1887), but Flammarion's evolutionism was responsible for a sharp ideological contrast between the imaginary excursions described in *Lumen* and those detailed by Saintine.

Saintine's fantasy, which takes some inspiration from the endeavors of followers of the anti-evolutionist anatomist Georges Cuvier, makes an interesting comparison with Eugène Mouton's "The Origin of Life," whose inspiration was similar. Its graphic depiction of animate matter anticipates the imminently-impending public clash between Félix-Archimède Pouchet and Louis Pasteur regarding the viability of the theory of spontaneous generation—an issue not yet regarded as conclusively settled at the turn of the century, when Gustave Le Bon wrote *L'Evolution de la matière* (1905; tr. as *The Evolution of Matter*) and Gaston de Pawlowski dramatized its substance in *Voyage au pays de la quatrième dimension* (1912; revised 1923; tr. in a Black Coat Press edition as *Journey to the Land of the Fourth Dimension*).[43] Saintine does not, of course, attempt to address these issues seriously, but his flamboyant celebration of their potential as aliments of nightmare testifies to the extent to which thinking men of the time were haunted by the possibilities that contemporary scientific research and speculation were releasing into the public domain

---

[43] ISBN 978-1-934543-37-5.

1.

Where am I? What eager whirlwind is carrying me into the depths of the Heavens? I am floating, rising up with a speed that only the rapidity of the electric current can approach. The Earth vanished from my sight some time ago: poor wretched little Earth, I watched it shrink, gradually diminishing until it seemed no more than a schoolboy's ball, rotating after having touched the ground—and my heart was touched, my eyes moistened. Poor, poor little Earth, where so many grand passions seethe—and vanities no less grand!—little grain of sand from which I saw the Sun for the first time, on which I have loved and suffered, shall I ever be allowed to return to you?

My emotion was not long delayed in changing its object. Still rising up, I was swallowed up by profound darkness, and the dread took hold of me that I might crack my skull on some unperceived celestial body. A feeble radiation dissipated the obscurity around me somewhat; I glimpsed a sort of reddish globe that was heading towards me. Was it a comet ready to crush me in its passage? What could I do to avoid it? I had no wings to regulate and direct my course.

With a vivid sentiment of joy, I then perceived that my own will was adequate in itself to move me the direction I desired. At first I had difficulty believing myself to be endowed with such power, but what could be more logical and natural, in accordance with the universally established order? When I was an inhabitant of the Earth, could I not cause my limbs to move solely by means of a mental instruction? Now my thought—my will, in the final analysis—was similarly steering my body: a body freed from the bonds of gravitational attraction, and consequently almost weightless.

Assured of this precious faculty, after having tacked back and forth for a while, gently cradled by the waves of the ether, intoxicated by that pure essence of life, I was emboldened to resume my ascent, continuing my course through the higher regions of space.

I saw that same reddish globe again, my first discovery in my voyage through the Heavens. It seemed paler to me. Whatever it was, it was definitely not a comet; it had neither the dazzling head nor the long atmospheric tail that is the obligatory accompaniment of all comets; no more was it a star, properly speaking, no scintillation within it indicated an active flame. What was it, then? Suddenly, a sort of grotesque face turned towards me; I recognized it. My reddish globe, my tailless comet, my ray-less star was the Moon!

On that subject, I had read all that dreamers had thought and all that thinkers had dreamed, from Pythagoras to Seneca, and from Cyrano de Bergerac and Fontenelle to Humboldt and Arago.

Among the scientists, one alone had not been content to think and dream; he had wanted to see with his own eyes.

From Easter to St Michael's Day,
He built a telescope
So large, so large, that Herschel's
Was myopic by comparison.[44]

Then, he saw...what did he see? Huge bats in human form, *Homo vespertilio*—and I was consumed by desire to know that which all these scientists had thought, dreamed or

---

[44] The first line of this verse, "De Paques à la Saint Michel" is a popular way of indicating the summer months in France. Subsequent references to "Monsieur Nicolet" are presumably to the author of the poem, but I can find no reference to any lunar fantasy written by a man of that name or to any contemporary work that populates the moon with giant bats; it might have been a fashionable *complainte* whose popularity proved brief. The term *Homo verspertilio* was once used in a German work by Heinrich Hoffmann, but I cannot find any French reference to it.

seen, in the direct line of incontestable truth, Could I ever hope to have a better opportunity to clear up my doubts? The Moon was there, right there in front of me, accessible to me!

Exerting all my will-power to one unique purpose, combining all its force into a single impulse, I precipitated myself in headlong flight, and a few minutes later I touched down on a high mountain that presented hardly any other view than that of immense glaciers. The natural location of glaciers is on high mountains; I was not surprised.

I left these lunar Alps, or Cordilleras, to descend to the plain. There, the soil was covered with snow of dazzling whiteness, doubtless fallen the previous day; I had presumably arrived on our satellite in the winter season.

Winter could not be manifest everywhere, though. I visited the Moon's four cardinal points; I descended into its valleys, and also into the craters of its volcanoes. I traveled over its seas, its gulfs. Everything there was rigid, motionless; it was all frozen. The place was fully illuminated by the Sun, but the Sun's light did not brighten or heat up anything there; its rays arrived there chilled, without the power to melt a snow-flake, without awakening an atom of life. On the plains, there was not a tree; on the receding flanks of the rocks, there was not a blade of green grass or patch of moss; in the air, which was so clear that I could see every planet gravitating around its orbit, there was not a cloud, nor a bird in flight; no cry or insect hum could be heard there!

I could only perceive a single breath—that which emerged from my own breast.

The Moon is dead, dead, dead!

"Has it, at least, lived its planetary life? Was it once inhabited?"

To that double question, I can give a bold affirmative response.

The cadavers of cities lie upon its plains; though covered by their shrouds of snow, the remaining indications of rounded shapes and rectangular lines are sufficient testimony to the hand of a constructor. Now, was this constructor Fontenelle's human being or Monsieur Nicolet's bat?

To decide the matter, it seemed at first that I would only have to dig down into the layers of snow, to go into one of the houses, which must surely have retained traces of heir inhabitants, even better than those of Pompeii. Any tool that came to hand, of iron or wood, would be sufficient to the task. But one does not travel through the impalpable ether with arms and luggage—except in extraordinary cases, as we shall soon see.

I had brought with me neither a spade nor a pickaxe, and I could not excavate a path through those towns and ice-sealed tombs with my fingernails. Besides which, the land's more-than-Siberian cold rendered me incapable of action. I was already thinking of leaving, and in thinking that, became depressed. Had I, then, undertake this long journey only to register the Moon's death-certificate? Would nothing help to enlighten me as to the nature of its former inhabitants?

Providence came to my aid!

Numbed by cold, with frostbitten fingers and chattering teeth, I was on the point losing all hope and was about to resume my flight, when a large corridor formed by high white rocks, decorated externally by a layer of ice that gave them the appearance of immense blocks of porcelain, opened before me. On the hardened ground and along the walls, a series of objects were scattered, the nature of which it was impossible for me to make out. I drew nearer, only expecting to find a few outcrops of rock or a few tree-trunks not covered by the snow—which would have been a victory in itself—but a much greater surprise and an unexpected triumph awaited me! I had before my eyes a complete specimen of the ancient population of the Moon. These sad specimens of an entire vanished race must have taken refuge there at the very moment of the great cataclysm. There were there still, conserved intact by the cold, with their last anguished expressions and in their final stances, perhaps hundreds of centuries old.

I therefore found myself in a position to answer, with complete authority, the great question of the inhabitants of the

Moon—a question that had so keenly preoccupied the scientific world and myself!

The Moon had once been populated, not by giant bats, as Monsieur Nicolet had believed, or pretended to believe, but by beings much closer to the form and nature of humans, although they were quite different in certain essential respects.

The double man, Plato's *homo duplex*, brought back into favor in our time as an anatomical reality by the savant Dr Serres of the Institut, was displayed there in the full expansion of his duplicate individuality.[45] Male in the right half of the body, female in the left side, the lunar human possessed two arms and two legs, exactly like the humans of Earth, but had in addition two distinct and separate heads, elegantly rising from articulated clavicles, capable of certain movements that are forbidden to us. Each of these heads had an elongated neck for a stem, which drew apart progressively from their bases. Evidently, this neck, instead of supporting only seven vertebrae, as ours do, must have accommodated at least 22, like those of birds.

The broad chests of these strange beings presented, not quite in the middle but slightly to the left, two breasts, to which the double mouth of a bicephalous infant could be simultaneously applied. To the right, there was no trace of the vestigial nipple with which nature has decorated us, more in accordance with harmonic law than the law of necessity.

A double spinal column, branching from a junction, permitted the conjoined individuals to look one another in the

---

[45] Plato's *Homo duplex* conceives humans as duplicate beings in terms of body and soul, although Plato did also speculate about sexuality in terms of the figurative division of a hypothetical hermaphrodite form. The anatomical observations of Étienne Serres (1786-1868)—in accordance with the remainder of the passage—had more to do with bodily symmetry. A similar calculated ambiguity forms the ideative basis of one of the chapters in Pawlowski's *Voyage au pays de la quatrième dimension*, which might owe something to Saintine.

102

face in order to smile, to talk—for I cannot doubt that they were possessed of the gift of speech—and to put their hand on one another's shoulder in a sign of friendship. That affectionate pose must have been habitual to them in moments of great stress. Almost all the poor coupled creatures that I had before my eyes gave me evidence of that.

The inhabitants of the Moon were certainly the most complete hermaphrodites among the superior races, and love, among them, must have been practiced according to the strictest rules of moral hygiene. Brother and sister at first, later husband and wife, linked by custom and by blood, exempt from suspicion and jealousy, since they were never apart, unable to take a single step without one another, since they were born together and would die together, can they not offer perfect models of conjugality? If there were ever a Golden Age of happy households, it must surely have been on the Moon.

At this point, before having reached my conclusion, I felt my thoughts clouding over because of the intensity of the cold, and I suddenly lost consciousness. I only recovered when I heard two voices: two quarrelsome voices, which increased in volume as they argued, replying to one another in the angriest possible tones. To the extent that I could understand, at first, the argument concerned furniture (how strange dreams are!). One of the voices was that of my upholsterer; my upholsterer as arguing with someone, and that someone, who was shouting the louder, was me!

And yet, my astronomical voyage continued.

This is what happened.

2.

Chilled to the bone, half-frozen, almost as dead as the Moon itself, I took advantage of the feeble residue of my will to head for the first available planet. Desirous above all of warmth, rest and comfort, I had told my upholsterer—don't ask me how!—to send me all the furniture in my bedroom.

My upholsterer is punctiliousness personified. When I arrived at my planet, I found him waiting at the landing-stage with his baggage. It was the dead of night; without listening to his observations, of which I heard not a single word, and without even bothering to find out whether there was a hotel in the vicinity, I instructed him to set it all up in a beautiful grotto of slate-colored basalt, whose entrance, in the form of a portico, opened on to a lake.

Nothing was lacking in my improvised apartment, not even central heating; I perceived a gentle warmth there, which did not take long to bring me out of my glacial torpor. I could have believed that I was in Paris, surrounded by my furniture in the Renaissance style—I had a penchant for the Renaissance at that time.

Monsieur Durand, my upholsterer, had brought my old Gobelins tapestry, decorated with great characters of mythology, my Palissy faiences ornamented in relief with lizards, snakes and frogs, and even my famous Giotto canvas, *The Massacre of the Innocents*. I could certainly have been satisfied with less, but, I repeat, Monsieur Durand is punctiliousness made man; I had asked him for all my furniture, and he had brought it to me complete—and if he had not delivered the doors and windows along with the furniture, it was doubtless because the landlord had opposed it.

I threw myself on my bed, where I went to sleep immediately.

In the middle of the night, dull cracking sounds became audible above my head. The walls of rock seemed to be splitting noisily—and, from time to time, small flakes of basalt were falling on to my bed. Twenty other noises were not long delayed in mingling with these sounds; I heard sighs and all sorts of murmurs—even the murmur of water, which seemed to be lapping spasmodically against the entrance to my grotto.

"A fire has broken out, caused by my central heating, and the firemen are in the process of putting it out." That was my first thought.

Frightened, I hurled myself out of bed in order to get out of that inferno as quickly as possible. The exit was closed! The tall portico of rock had subsided, now leaving only a narrow aperture at its base, through which the hissing waves were coming.

"If it's not a fire," I said to myself, "then a storm has broken out over the lake—a tempest, most certainly, complicated by an earthquake!"

My situation, already terrible, was about to get even worse.

On going back into my room, I stood petrified by the spectacle that offered itself to me, which a phosphoric leakage from the frock permitted me to contemplate in all its marvelous horror.

All my furniture had come to life. Just as the high basaltic mountain into which I had come in search of shelter was cracking and moaning, and just as the little lake, my neighbor, had come swirling to besiege me in my refuge, every item of my household goods was playing an active role in its turn.

My four-poster bed, made of old oak-wood, entirely disarticulated in its limbs and joints, was attempting to return to its primitive and natural state. Its twisted feet and pillars were unrolling their spirals, standing upright, digging into the ground in order to implant themselves there; they were also implanting lively cuttings, by means of roots abruptly emitted by their nether parts, while a thin layer of bark began to cover each new stems as soon as it set itself upright.

Inlays in mother-of-pearl or tortoiseshell were detaching themselves from other items of furniture and becoming curved, rounding themselves off, acquiring the forms of shells and carapaces. The leather and morocco upholstery of chairs was distending and taking on the appearance of the animals that had furnished it. The horsehair with which the armchairs were stuffed was escaping in order to attach itself to strange animals, comprising their manes or fleeces.

All around me, everything that was conscious of a previous organic life, animal or vegetable, seemed to be trying to return to it. Nor did the miracle stop there. My night-stand started to dance; one by one, with a menacing air, it lifted each of its feet, which terminated in powerful eagle's claws—and these claws were opening and closing again as I approached, as if to seize their prey.

Further amazement! The mythological characters depicted in my Gobelins tapestry—Mars, Pallas and other gods of the first rank—were suddenly taking on a frightful three-dimensionality; their eyes were lighting up, their muscles stirring, their mouths murmuring confused threats. The lightning-bolt that old Jupiter was holding flashed momentarily, and three times the mountain trembled on its base. Then, all those fallen gods began to flex their backs and stretch their arms in order to rid themselves of the weave that retained them—but they could not complete the task.

Less encumbered than the gods, the Roman soldiers in Giotto's painting launched themselves out of the canvas with wild-eyed gazes in pursuit of poor little innocents; I saw the blood running, and heard the screams of the victims and the imprecations of their executioners....

By means of a bizarre phenomenon, already observed by Pascal, I was momentarily conscious of my sleeping state. "I'm dreaming; it's a dream: a frightful nightmare, which my dear doctor would not hesitate to class among his *symplegadics!*"[46] I told myself—but after due consideration, I replied in the negative; "No, I'm awake, I'm fully conscious; it's all true, all real!"

---

[46] The Symplegades are two rocks featured in the story of Jason and the Argonauts, which periodically smash together; that term is thus used metaphorically to refer to any course steered between two parties in imminent danger of clashing violently. I cannot find any evidence of the term being incorporated into 19th century psychology to describe a category of nightmare, but it could have been, although it is also possible that Saintine, who was obviously very interested in oneirology, might have improvised the term himself.

And I continued to be subject to my dreamer's torment.

A formidable cracking sound warned me of the imminent collapse of that fatal rock, under which I had voluntarily imprisoned myself. From the obscure corner in which I curled myself up, with sweat on my brow, a violent shaking threw me back to the middle of the grotto; the cave, doubtless in consequence of an upset effected within the mountain, became narrower, gradually closing in until I was only left with just enough space to avoid contact with all the monsters by which I was surrounded.

Soon, enormous blocks of basalt detached from the ceiling fell upon the gods of old Olympus, who were more entangled than ever in the threads of their tapestry, and the infamous Roman soldiers, who had not relented in their massacre of innocents. The trees and animals of my furniture, crushed and broken, were no longer anything but shapeless debris. Only my distraught night-stand, as if overcome by madness, ran away from that rain of rocks, using its powerful eagle's claws to clamber up the wall, scaling it all the way to the top.

To cap it all, the frightful reptiles—Palissy's lizards, snakes and frogs—which had retained for some time in the torpor habitual to them, were now sliding, running and hopping through the bloody debris; impregnated with that blood, they were swarming around and crawling up my legs, mingling their sinister hissing and frightful croaking with my cries of distress.

It was horrible!

However, the greatest suffering I endured did not arise from the perils I was running, nor from the spectacle before my eyes, nor from the venomous touch of the serpents; it came from the intolerable heat that reigned within the grotto. I was suffocating, choking; I thought I was dying.

In that supreme moment, a resounding voice burst out, overwhelming all those noises, all those rumblings and all those sobs.

The voice was my upholsterer's. "Quickly! Quickly!" he cried, seizing me by the hand. "The way out has been opened

up for us again by a landslide. We haven't a moment to lose—
hurry up!"

Would you believe it? At the very moment when I owed
my salvation to the honest Monsieur Durand, I elected to in-
flict upon him the most unjust outbursts of temper. All my
fears and all my suffering had just degenerated into furious
anger. I reproached him for his disloyalty; I accused him of
knavery. The furniture he had brought me could not be mine;
it was bewitched! He swore to me by his greatest gods that he
had never played a practical joke in his life. I replied that he
was a miserable liar! It was with malevolent, criminal intention that he had fired up the central heating to the point of asphyxiating me. I finished up threatening him to take him to
court.

O triple Hecate! O Bombo, Mormo, Gorgo![47]

Fortunately, my brave upholsterer continued to drag me
along with him, without paying overmuch attention to my re-
criminations.

Once outside the grotto, I looked for the lake that bathed
its edge and could no longer see it. The lake had evaporated
into steam, and now formed a large dark red cloud, in which
the glow of a fire seemed to be reflected.

I scanned the high mountain of which my grotto was the
base; it had been turned upside-down and 20 craters now open

---

[47] Hecate is called "triple" here because she was thought by
some writers to have three different aspects, being Selene or
Luna in the Heavens, Atrtemis or Diana on Earth and Per-
sephone or Proserpine in the Underworld; she was thus represented, on occasion, with three bodies or three heads, one of a
horse, one of a dog and one of a lion's and afforded such epi-
thets as Tergeminus, Triformis and Triceps. A supposed hymn
to Hecate exists in which the three aspects of her personality
are addressed as Bombo, Mormo and Gorgo, although the last
of the three terms is more commonly associated with the gor-
gon better known as Medusa—who was also part of a set of
three, according to Hesiod.

simultaneously along its torn flanks. The horizon traced in front of us was nothing but a circle of volcanoes.

"Where are we?" I asked, gripped by terror.

"On Monsieur Le Verrier's planet, incorrectly called Neptune," Durand replied, with the utmost calm. "You've come from the Moon, haven't you?"

"What! You know that?" I cried, interrupting him. "My dear Monsieur Durand, do you also know how the Moon died?"

"That's an old story," he answered. "After having created the terrestrial globe. God put the Moon at the service of the Earth, in the capacity of its satellite. It was charged with restraining and moderating the seas by means of its gravity, and for a few centuries things went according to plan—but the day came when, weary of turning on it axis, the Moon broke its chain and tried to wander away from its regular orbit. Then there was the Deluge; in addition, to punish it for its disobedience, God struck it dead; since that time, it accomplishes its duties as a star entirely automatically, no longer doing anything but obeying the general laws of gravitation. Now, my dear client, let me resume what I was saying. Yes, as you have been able to verify for yourself, the Moon is dead, and quite dead; here, entirely to the contrary, you have before your eyes a world in formation, where the forces of organic life are presently constituted with a frightful intensity. Here, due to the excess of heat, solid bodies liquefy and liquids evaporate into gaseous form, thus forming the atmosphere indispensable to every planet that wishes to live."

I stood in front of my upholsterer, rapt. Never had I suspected him of being well-informed on these sorts of things.

"The brute matter has now been sufficiently warmed up and ground down," he went on. "Some of these volcanoes are beginning to die down; their fire is becoming central. The moment has arrived when the germs of animate beings can develop here, and they will develop, at first to excess and with prodigious rapidity. Examine the terrain on which we're treading at this moment; every atom of matter here is restless, avid

109

for friction. Throw down an acorn here and it will germinate instantly, immediately growing and pushing up towards the heavens; tomorrow there will be an oak-tree, which will have taken on immense proportions in no time at all—but that gigantic tree will soon perish, empty and flaccid, exhausted by its effort.

"Instead of an acorn, set down the egg of a lizard here, or that of a hummingbird; out of it will come an eagle or a crocodile. This is the phenomenal epoch of monsters, of which Monsieur Cuvier had spoken to you, and the Marquis de Laplace before him. Here the globe is so avid to produce that everything that has form is alive. Here, a wooden horse will become a horse of flesh and bone, a doll will become a woman—and we ourselves, if we prolong our sojourn here imprudently, might well be transformed into giants."

I took three steps backwards. Monsieur Durand took hold of my arm again, with a smile full of irony. "Now, my dear client," he continued, "do you understand why, without any witchcraft on my part, the mother-of-pearl and tortoiseshell of your bed, the leather and horsehair of your chairs, the feet of your night-stand and Bernard de Palissy's frogs and serpents, as well as the people in your tapestry and Giotto's painting, tried to recreate their life, their form, their activity? And also why, without any other central heating but the volcano that warmed the ground beneath your feet, you almost died of asphyxia? Whose fault is that? Is it mine, who was only carrying out your instructions, eh? Answer me."

I gave him no answer; I had none to give. Besides, I was quite out of breath, with my tongue stuck to the roof of my mouth. The open air had become as hot as that of the grotto. Having almost died of cold on the Moon, I didn't want to meet my end by virtue of an excess of heat; in any case, the prospect of turning into a giant was not at all tempting to my vanity.

I looked down at myself...my feet had already begun to develop considerably; my knees seemed to me to be more highly placed than before...

I hastened to quit Monsieur Le Verrier's planet, my mind anxiously full of the idea that creation is not yet terminated, and that God, instead of being at rest, as tradition affirms, is actively continuing his work.

Adrien Robert: *War in 1894*
(1867)

Adrien Robert was the principal pseudonym employed by Adrien-Charles-Alexandre Basset (1822-1869), who could not use his familiar name—he was called Charles within the family—because his father, André-Alexandre Basset had already used the by-line Charles Basset in building a successful career as a dramatist. Adrien Robert was the by-line attached to a number of *feuilleton* serials of a more-or-less melodramatic nature, mostly in the *Journal pour tous*, beginning with *Les Amours mortels* [Fatal Love Affairs], reprinted in book form in 1857, and concluding with *Le Bouquet de Satan* [Satan's Bouquet], posthumously reprinted in book form in 1872. The author's early work, however had mostly consisted of humorous short stories, many of which were collected in *Contes excentriques* [Eccentric Tales] (1855) and *Nouveaux contes excentriques* [More Eccentric Tales] (1859), the first of which was initially signed Charles Newil and the latter Charles Newill; those collections were, however, reissued under the Adrien Robert by-line when it became more famous, and the best of all the author's collections, *Contes fantasques et fantastiques* [Offbeat and Fantastic Tales] (1867), was only issued under that name, in an edition handsomely illustrated by Horace Castelli.

The only one of Robert's works that retained much of a reputation after his premature death was the folkltale-based *Jean qui pleure et Jean qui rit* [John Who Weeps and John Who Laughs] (1859), which was not only lighter in tone but more consciously sophisticated than his other novels; he wrote a stage version of it in collaboration with his fellow *feuilletoniste* Paul Féval, to whom *Contes fantasques et fantastiques* is fulsomely dedicated. Robert's short stories are, however, considerably more adventurous thematically and often quite original. "La guerre en 1840" is one of three items in his last collection of some interest with respect to the history of scientific romance, the others being "La main embaumée" (tr. as "The Embalmed Hand" in *News from the Moon and Other French Scientific Romances*) and "Berthold Schwartz," an account of the mythical inventor of gunpowder.

"La guerre en 1894" was probably written only a few months before the publication of the collection; internal evidence strongly suggests that it was inspired by the extensive sequence of invasions carried out by Prussia in the latter months of 1866, beginning with the annexation of the Duchy of Holstein in June of that year: invasions that laid the foundations of the unification of Germany, and its establishment as an ambitiously bellicose nation-state. The story thus anticipated the boom in future war fiction that began in England in 1871, under the immediate provocation of Prussia's successful invasion of France. Anxiety regarding the probable effects of future technological developments on warfare was communicated to France on a much more generous scale in the 1880s, where it was extravagantly dramatized by Albert Robida—thus providing the fledgling international genre of scientific romance with one of its key subgenres—but Robert's brief anticipation of chemical warfare is entitled to be regarded as a significant and prophetic precursor.

CADET SCHOOL FOR THE DESTRUCTION OF ARMIES

To Monsieur Edmond R   , captain of the first battery of steam bombardiers, at Strasbourg.

Grand Duchy of *** , June 5, 1894.

I have finally succeeded in discovering the great state secret that has intrigued me so powerfully during the month I have spent in the territory of the Grand-Duke *** (a tract of about 15 square leagues). As this discovery cannot fail to interest you from the double viewpoint of politics and the art of war, I am sending you a few pages from my travel-notepad.

At the Queen of Hungary hotel, where I established myself, in the salons of the Kursaal, at the Great Elector Bierhaus, to which I went from time to time to empty a few seidels with a dozen students from the university, at the public bathhouse where I performed my morning ablutions—in the company of an old Austrian general, ankylotic from top to toe thanks to five wounds received in the war against Prussia in 1866—from dawn to dusk, sitting down, standing up or lying down, in sunshine or rain, in good humor or black depression, I heard these three words perpetually whistling in my ears: *Cadettenschulefur die Ganzlichearmeenzerstorung!* Which means "Cadet-School for the Complete Destruction of Armies": a pretty formula, which outdoes the most ferocious advertisements for insecticide powders by as much distance as separates the human race from the tribe of Reduvians.[48]

---

[48] Reduvidae are a family of predatory hemipteran insects more familiarly known as "assassin bugs," which live vampirically on the ichor of other insects, and occasionally (but rarely) feed on the blood of higher animals.

However, the Cadettenschulefur, which only got on my nerves at first, began to worry me. The Grand Duke had sent all his rifled cannon, howitzers and mortars to the foundry, and the Ministry of War had made a deal to sell all the Grand-Ducal army's Dreyse rifles—weapons employing the Papferstrof system, firing 35 rounds per minute—to a small South American republic.[49] The entire cavalry, save for the 20 men-at-arms allotted to the service of the community of thieves, has returned to pedestrian status, but the 200 men comprising the main body of His Excellency's army have received new armaments and a special uniform.

Officers and soldiers carry a long bronze-plated iron blowpipe, and a cartridge-case containing wooden darts fletched with swansdown and terminating in a little glass capsule. In addition, each one has in his belt a wickerwork-clad bottle, the metal stopper of which is flared, like the openings of apparatus that is used to anaesthetize patients with chloroform.

The uniform is made of very light black leather, with red braid; a number embroidered on the collar is the only thing serving to distinguishing the officers. Corporals open the series with the number 1, and the field-marshal closes it with the number 13. These numbers are so small that one can hardly make them out from five or six paces away, but the numbering system—borrowed from the Watchmen of London—seems to me to be very advantageous in the field, especially since the creation of units of sharpshooters, specially charged with creating vacancies in the ranks of enemy officers.

This paltry little army maneuvers 20 so-called compressed-air catapults mounted on wheels and considerably complicated by gears—which, I am assured, launch volleys of

---

[49] I have substituted "Dreyse rifles" for Robert's "*fusils à aiguilles*" [needle-guns] because a literal translation would now be confusing, although the term was used in English at the time. The Dreyse rifle was so-nicknamed because of its exceptionally long firing-pin.

a special sort nearly 300 meters. But what is the special nature of these volleys, and what do the glass capsules fired by the *blowpipers* contain? Only General Moufette, director of the Cadet-School (I shall omit the rest of the formula henceforth) and the Grand Duke knew that terrible state secret.

My old Austrian general, who is very much in the know with respect to these matters, gave me some very curious information yesterday while we were plunged chin-deep in the redemptive well known as the Fiery Achilles,[50] in which one would be able to cook crayfish in two hours.

"General Moufette," he said to me, "has only been under the flag for 18 months. He's an ex-apothecary from Louvain, who has led a very eventful life. A very skilful chemist, Moufette—some names are predestined[51]—was searching for a new gaseous compound to destroy a legion of rats installed in a large Beguinage.[52] He asphyxiated his assistant in a quarter of a second, killing him stone dead—accidentally, of course—by virtue of having forgotten to put a stopper in a certain glass tube connected to a boiling retort.

"The sacrifice of an apothecary's assistant is always a painful matter, I admit, and to begin with, Moufette, as a Christian, was afflicted by bitter regrets, but the second quarter of an hour was an apotheosis, a demigod-like triumph for the chemist.

"To confess the truth to the law, which loves circumstantial details and scientific explanations, would have been to

---

[50] I have translated this pun as best I can; the French *bouillant*, literally "boiling," also means "hot-headed" in a metaphorical sense.

[51] The reason that Moufette's name is "predestined" is that *mouffette* is the French name for the animal known in English as a skunk.

[52] A Beguinage is a community affiliated to an order of laywomen (Beguines) founded in the 13th century and devoted to charitable works, resembling a nunnery in all its essential respects, although its members do not take vows.

deliver the secret of the prodigious chance discovery, to annihilate at a single stroke an entire future of glory and wealth.
The apothecary made a heroic resolution; he buried his victim
in his cellar and, under the pretext of going to Antwerp to by a
cheap consignment of quinine bark—*Cinchona scorbiculata*—
he fled to Brussels, where he took the train for Cologne that
same evening. He preferred to be taken for a murderer and
save the strongbox—which is to say, the discovery.

"Two months later, he performed a decisive experiment
in front of the Grand Duke of   and a commission appointed
by the Ministry of War, asphyxiating at a distance of 150 meters three men condemned to death by the high court, lent for
the demonstration of the system. Immediately created a baron
and battlefield general, Moufette was also charged with organizing without delay the *Cadettenschulefur die Ganzlichearmeenzerstorung*, at a salary of 20,000 florins a year. Since
then, with the authorization of the Grand Duke, he has added
the name of Bellone to the name of Moufette, to give it little
more shine.

"He has converted a former powder-magazine, sited
three leagues from the capital, into a vast chemistry laboratory
and arsenal of war. It's there that the cadets prepare, under his
direction, the capsules and shell-casings of blown glass for the
blowpipers and war-catapults, which he immediately fills with
a yellow liquid, which evaporates into smoke on contact with
the air.

"These asphyxiating capsules, which are no larger than a
hazelnut, break on impact with the soil and kill everything
within 100 square feet, even more if there is a wind. The shell-
casings, which contain two liters of liquid, can wipe out a bat-
talion at a single stroke. The skill of the shooters consist of
aiming four paces in advance of the enemy.

"A few days before your arrival, there was a blowpipe
duel between two captains on the drill-field. The younger, who
was from the Cadet-School and was reputed to be the finest
shot in the Grand Duchy, broke his capsule on one of the but-

tons of his adversary's uniform. The latter fell down dead without having had time to blow out his own projectile."

Drawing closer to me on the steps of the bath, the old general whispered: "I've heard rumor in the offices of the Minister of War that a top secret field-laboratory is being constructed for an imminent expedition; I have every reason to suppose that the Grand Duke has the firm intention of annexing France to his Duchy, having long desired to possess a coast. You understand very well, my dear sir, that with the means of destruction at his disposal, his army will be under the walls of Paris within a month, and that the steam-artillery of which you are so proud will be no use at all. Ten Moufette-bombs on Paris, and that's your nationality done for.

"General Moufette's secretary, who was formerly my administrative officer, has told me confidentially that there are 15 tropical hardwood barrels in reserve in the arsenal, labeled thus:

For an army of 1200,000 men.
  Half for 60,000.
For a cavalry division.
    (Ultra-concentrated).
  Half 30-inch shells.

"In sum, there's enough there to kill a million men.

"It's forbidden, on pain of death, for foreign members of the establishment to go into the arsenal building, but the Ministry of War issues permits to visit the laboratory and the glassworks on Mondays from noon to four p.m. If you are would like to undertake such an excursion, I shall have two entrance tickets, and I am happy to offer you a place in my caleche."

I accepted enthusiastically.

Eugène Mouton: *The Origin of Life*
(1877)

Eugène Mouton (1823-1905) was the son of a military officer who spent his childhood in Guadaloupe. He embarked upon a career as a lawyer which culminated in an appointment as a prosecutor in Rodez. He began writing humorous short stories on the side, using the pseudonym Mérinos [Merino sheep or wool], making his debut in *Le Figaro* in 1857, and gave up his legal career ten years later to become a full-time writer. He remained best known for his humorous short fiction, much of which was fantastic in a vein somewhat akin to the "nonsense literature" produced in England by Edward Lear, Lewis Carroll and W. S. Gilbert, but he also wrote various non-fiction books, including one on French penal law and of the first ever guide-books for would-be authors. Partly inspired by the example of Mouton's professionalism, his nephew by marriage, Paul Duval, went on to become one of the leading lights of the *fin-de-siècle* Decadent Movement as Jean Lorrain.

Mouton produced a number of items directly inspired by reading contemporary popularizations of science, of which "L'Origine de la vie" is one; the internal evidence suggests that it first appeared in 1877 before being reprinted in his collection *Fantaisies* (1883). Two other scientific romances, "L'Historioscope" (translated as "The Historioscope" in the Black Coat Press anthology *News from the Moon and Other French Scientific Romances*) and "La fin du monde" [The End of the World] had earlier been reprinted in *Nouvelles et fantasies humoristiques* (1872, by-lines Mérinos). The latter item offers an account of the end of the world quite different from the one briefly sketched out here.

Like Mouton's other exploits in this vein, "L'Origine de la vie" exemplifies the perennial problem that early writers of scientific romance had in finding appropriate narrative forms for their speculative excursions, being more essay than story. It also provides a particularly clear illustration of the license that the adoption a humorous tone gave to a laconically casual imaginative extravagance that would have seemed inapt in more earnest work; in this sense, Mouton's jesting exercises in scientific romance, uneasily but fruitfully suspended between fiction and non-fiction, laid groundwork for the more elaborate and sophisticated speculative adventures of Alphonse Allais, Alfred Jarry and Gaston de Pawlowski.

Given that the Earth was, in the beginning, a mass so in-candescent that the most durable substances were then in a vaporous state heated to 2000 or 3000 degrees above zero, we cannot imagine, even in our dreams, that there was any organic matter therein.

Above 40 or 45 degrees, all organic compounds are destroyed; the roast meat that we eat, even when it is cooked, is no more than 50 or 60 degrees above zero. Thus, the temperature of the Earth being immeasurably higher than our most thoroughly-cooked roasts, no organic life could ever have begun in such an environment, and if there had been any seed of life within it, it would have been annihilated. The igneous origin of our planet—take note of this point—is not, moreover, in any doubt; it is proven geologically and demonstrated astronomically by Laplace in his celebrated *Précis de l'histoire de l'astronomie.*

If one cannot contrive an alternative hypothesis to explain the origin of living creatures, it is necessary to conclude that they have not begun, and to conclude in consequence that, having not begun, they do not exist—which is absurd, to be sure, but much less absurd than the Darwinian hypothesis.

If, on the contrary, one wishes to claim that the first living beings appeared when the Earth had cooled sufficiently, one is no further forward, given that animals mostly eat one another and one is bound to wonder what the first ones lived on while awaiting the appearance of those which would serve as their prey.

One of two things must therefore be the case: either living things cannot, and therefore do not, exist; or, if they have been created and exist, Darwin's theory is false.

With this starting-point clearly established in my mind, I was led to recognize that, in view of the indispensable relationships that make the existence of every organized creature a necessary condition of that of all the others, the appearance of living creatures upon the Earth *could not have been other than simultaneous*—not only for animals but for vegetables, because the chemical operations that render the air breathable are equally shared between vegetables and animals; if the animals ceased to respire, the vegetables would perish, and the other way around.

Having arrived by this route at the hypothesis of simultaneous and instantaneous creation, I must admit that I felt my embarrassment increase. I confess that I could not get my head around the idea of a hippopotamus emerging from the ground like a mushroom, any more than the idea that a cheese-mite might become a hippopotamus by force of ambition; they were two absolutely equal absurdities.

On the other hand, the study of nature shows us that, without a single exception, no living creature exists, or ever has existed, that did not emerge from a pre-existent father and a mother similar to it. Now, if all life originates from a mother fertilized by a father, how could a violation of the essential law of life ever have served as the origin and point of departure of the appearance of living creatures on the planet?

Naturally, I was brought back to *Genesis*.

Here I must make a declaration. I declare, therefore, that I hold all ancient traditions as true on principle. I firmly believe that none of them, fundamentally, can be a lie—firstly, because every time it has been possible to verify them, they have been recognized as exact; and secondly, because, in view of the mental poverty of men in general, and the first men in particular, I cannot imagine how they could have invented false facts, nor what interest they could have had in deceiving themselves with regard to their own memories.

What requires interpretation in ancient traditions is their form; in that respect, yes, it is necessary to take account of the time when the traditions were laid down and the much later time when they were collected in writing. The manner of conceiving ideas and the fashion of expressing them differed considerably from our present conceptions and language, and it is for want of taking this into account that people are so hasty, where matters of traditions are concerned, to declare them all false.

I, however, who never throw in the sponge, have meditated and reasoned, and by dint of thinking hard, like Newton, I believe that I have finally found a plausible hypothesis to explain the origin of life.

The origin of life is Noah's Ark.

As is usually the case with all great discoveries, it was by way of long detours and paths unfamiliar to myself and other men that I found myself one day, quite unexpectedly, confronting the unanticipated solution to this great problem.

So long as, in my researches and my reflections, I had not got past the fifth chapter of *Genesis*—holding as true, in conformity with my principle, everything I saw written there—I could see nothing but the hippopotamus sprouting like a mushroom, and that mushroom-hippopotamus appeared to me to be increasingly hard for my intellect to swallow. When I arrived at chapters six, seven and eight, however, after having ploughed through the most inextricable thickets of the most colossal difficulties that my reason had ever been able to surmount, I arrived at an unexpected result—and I cling to my hypothesis, which nothing will make me release, because it is new, original, seductive and entirely adequate to put a stop to the headache of the origin of life. For this hypothesis has the decisive advantage of projecting the givens of the problem back beyond the present limits of the world and, in consequence, of relieving us of the problem forever.

You know how God, irritated by the increasing corruption of human beings repented of having made them and, full of anguish, said from the bottom of his heart: "I shall exterminate them all, men and animals alike, from everything that crawls on the Earth to the birds in the sky, for I regret that I ever made them." But Noah, descendant of Seth, found grace before him, and God ordered him to make an ark from pieces of planed wood, divided into little compartments, coated within and without with bitumen, 300 cubits long, 50 broad and 30 high, with a one-cubit roof, three decks, a window at one end and a door at the other.

The Lord then instructed Noah to take two individuals of every species of animal, male and female, in order that they might live with him, along with everything that could be eaten, to serve as nourishment for him and all the animals.

When Noah had carried out these orders, God told him to go into the ark with his family and to take seven males and seven females of all the pure animals, and two couples of all the impure animals, and likewise with the birds of the sky.

For 40 days the deluge spread over the Earth, and the waters covered it for 150 days, after which God, having remembered Noah and all the animals that were with him in the ark, caused a wind to blow over the Earth, and the waters began to diminish.

After ten months, the summits of mountains began to emerge. Forty days later, Noah opened the window and released a raven, which did not return until the waters had dried up. Seven days after the raven, Noah released a dove, which came back without having found anywhere to perch. Seven days after that, he released the dove again, which came back bearing in its beak an olive branch, the leaves of which were entirely green. Finally, released a third time, it did not come back again.

A year had gone by. The Earth was nearly dry. Noah waited another 27 days, and then God spoke to him, telling him to come out of the ark with his entire family and all the animals, to go forth upon the Earth, to increase and multiply.

I do not know whether everyone else has done as I did, but I must say that, until that moment, it had never occurred to me to look at this sort from a scientific viewpoint. For me, Noah's ark had always remained one of those little chocolate-brown boats surmounted by a pink house with a red roof, filled with little wooden people and animals. But when I had re-read those chapters, with a view to searching for the solution to the problem that I was seeking to resolve, I saw looming up before my reason the most gigantic objections that had ever been equipped to confound a poor human brain.

Unable to resolve these problems, I had, so to speak, to *turn them around* by supposing, that the story of the ark was merely symbolic. Beneath this symbol, however, there is a genuine fact: that of the initial population of the globe. The population was achieved at a single stroke, and the living creatures, collected on a ship that had floated on an agitated fluid, had sailed for a certain period of time and had finished up landing on the Earth, where Noah disembarked his assembly.

Well, personally, I found in that a complete explanation of the origin of life. This is why:

Life cannot have begun at the time of the Earth's cooling, because any formation of organic matter would have been impossible during the igneous period.

Species cannot have formed by sequential transformation and improvement, because no living being can be produced except by two parents anterior to and similar to itself. For the same reason, they could not have emerged fully-formed on the surface of the globe. They must, therefore, have come from elsewhere, and arrived fully-formed.

Noah's ark is the symbolic account of a great event. It informs us that in a particular era—I shall not attempt to calculate it—in that immense ocean of space in which the planets and stars float, two worlds collided.

One of these worlds was the Earth; the other was one of those aeroliths like those we see from time to time falling to the surface, the substance of which contains minerals and organic carbon compounds similar to those found on Earth.

How that collision happened, and how the passengers from the aerial world were able to resist the shock of arrival, I shall have to reserve for future research; but sufficient unto the day the evil thereof, and it seems to me that I have earned the right to take a short breather and wipe the sweat from my brow.[53]

The corollary consequences of this discovery will certainly not escape the sagacity of our readers; they are that it is necessary to relocate everything in *Genesis* that precedes the Deluge to another world: the terrestrial paradise is transferred to another planet.

And when one sees the sad state in which our satellite presently exists, it is very difficult to avoid the certainty that the Moon, a world so cracked and eroded that it is reduced to the condition of pumice-stone, is the accursed world on which God, in his justified wrath, caused the destruction of the degenerate race of the sons of Cain—an impious race which, after all, was not embarrassed to associate with giants.

And have you seen any giants on Earth?

If there is one thing that holds true down here, it is that NOTHING IS LOST, NOTHING IS CREATED. The truth is that life, neither more nor less than the world, never began and will never end; it can only be displaced—or, to put it better, moved, since movement is the same thing.

We are too trivial a thing in the midst of infinity ever to understand how the parts of the universe might be connected to one another; but the sole fact of the existence of this world in which everything is linked suffices to demonstrate that they are connected, since they are all absorbed and confounded in the absolute unity and infinity of universal life.

Between two equally inadmissible hypotheses regarding the origin of living creatures, I cannot choose, and beyond those two hypotheses, I take the only third term that is conceivable—and if, in order to propose a solution to you, I have

---

[53] Pierre Versins suggests, in his *Encyclopédie*, that Mouton might have borrowed this thesis from the Baron d'Espiard de Colonge, who had proposed it "in all seriousness" in *La chute du ciel* (1865). Unless the subsequent postscript really is a belated afterword, however, Mouton acknowledges his actual source therein.

chosen a slightly playful form, I have done so by design, wishing to honey-coat the rim of the cup that I have offered you, from which, *perhaps*, to drink the truth....

P.S. A propos of this mediation on the origin of life, I have received the following letter, which confirms my theory of the origin of living creatures in a manner as striking as it is unexpected:

Paris, 3 February 1877
Monsieur,
Noah's ark is obviously a symbol. The arguments you put forward to demonstrate that are sound, especially from the picturesque viewpoint that you have adopted. But there are others more persuasive from the technical point of view.

The impact of two celestial bodies, to which you allude, is not a hypothesis, it is a matter that one may regard as proven by science and transferred into the domain of accomplished facts. But the Moon is entirely out of the question. If a collision had taken place between the Earth and the Moon, the conditions of our globe's movement would have been so altered that we would be far from our present state. I shall take up this question again shortly.

Twenty-five years ago, a mining engineer resident in Toulouse[54] published a brochure in which he gave very plaus-

---

[54] Mouton adds a footnote of his own to identify this individual as "M. de Boucheporn." The reference is to Baron Bertrand de Boucheporn (1811-1857), who was, indeed, a mining engineer, but was better known as a grand theorist of natural science passionately interested in the implications of geological discoveries. He was a member of the last generation of fervent anti-evolutionists. His *Etudes sur l'histoire de la terre et sur le causes des revolutions de sa surface*, published posthumously in 1861—undoubtedly the book that Mouton has in mind—belonged to the catastrophist school of geology, but was unusual in attributing the transformative catastrophes that had allegedly shaped the Earth to impacts with extraterrestrial

ible reasons for the existence of a former satellite of the Earth, annular in form, analogous to Saturn's ring. For reasons that it is necessary to seek in the increasing density of the terrestrial globe following its cooling, and in consequence of the augmentation of its mass and its attractive force, the equilibrium of the ring was upset, and the satellite fell upon the Earth. It can still be seen on the surface of the globe, for it has formed the highest terrestrial mountain chains, all disposed on the same meridian.

The collision of these two celestial bodies caused the globe to experience a frightful commotion and must have engendered a cataclysm at its surface and within a considerable depth of its crust, of which it is difficult form an idea: from that came the universal Deluge; Mount Ararat is merely a fragment of our former satellite.

Let us return to the Moon.

The Moon, a once-fluid body, has seen the disappearance, in consequence of its progressive cooling, first of the water that covered parts of its surface, then of its atmosphere. In future (when? relative to infinity, no one can say) the moon will disintegrate and fragment. Some of its fragments will fall on the terrestrial globe, augmenting its mass; the conditions of this globe's equilibrium in space will be significantly changed; its orbit, already almost circular, will become entirely so and will draw nearer to the Sun. In addition to the cataclysm produced on Earth by the impact of the lunar fragments, the terrestrial globe will become suddenly and utterly uninhabitable due to the excess of solar heat. It will be the end of the world.

Reserve the Moon, therefore, for that final eventuality.

Accept, I beg you Monsieur, the expression of my respectful sentiments.

IGNOTUS.[55]

---

objects rather than internal events; deluges and multiple volcanic eruptions thus became secondary effects rather than primary causes.

[55] Ignotus means "unknown" in Latin.

Jules Lermina: *Quiet House*
(1885)

Jules Lermina (1839-1915) embarked upon a career in journalism in 1859, having previously tried out various clerical positions following an early marriage at the age of 18. He became a radical socialist, founding the political periodical *Le Corsaire* in 1867, which led to his being imprisoned. He was released in response to protest—from Victor Hugo, among others—but promptly repeated his crime, founding a new journal called *Satan*, and was imprisoned again, thus initiating a template subsequently followed by Louis Ulbach.

When the Second Empire gave way to the Republic in 1871, Lermina was released again, and then—having presumably learned his lesson, and perhaps taking some inspiration from Ulbach—launched a successful career as a prolific writer of popular fiction. Although his political beliefs are explicitly manifest in some of his novels—especially *To-Ho le tueur d'or* (1905; tr. as *To-Ho the Goldslayer*), in which a noble savage who is one of Tarzan's more significant literary precursors declares war on the symbolic foundation of capitalism—and are always lurking in the background, most of his fiction consists of crowd-pleasing entertainment in the great tradition of French *feuilleton* fiction. He clearly considered himself a direct descendant of Eugène Sue and Alexandre Dumas and did his best to extrapolate their heritage; he wrote a Suesque *Mystères de New York* under the pseudonym William Cobb and produced two sequels to *Le Comte de Monte Cristo*.

Jules Clarétie, who wrote an introduction to Lermina's first collection of fantastic tales, *Histoires incroyables* [Incredible Stories] (1885), records that he and his friend had both been strongly influenced by E. T. A. Hoffmann and Edgar Allan Poe, the presiding geniuses of the 19th century French *fantastique*, and that they had both become increasingly interested in the sinister mysteries and marvels of human psychology. Lermina's work tends, however, to exploit the humorous aspects of the grotesque and arabesque to a greater extent than the horrific, and he was certainly strongly infected by what Poe called "the imp of the perverse." "Maison tranquille," here translated as "Quiet House"—which ought to be its title even in the French version—is the only scientific romance in *Histoires incroyables*, but two more appeared in a second volume entitled *Nouvelles histories incroyables* (1888) and Lermina had already produced a lurid pseudoscientic romance about "magnetism" in *La Comtesse Mercadet* (1884).

Although his increasing interest in occult science drew most of his later fantastic fiction back towards the supernatural, Lermina went on to write several more scientific romances, of which his contributions to the Vernian *Journal des Voyages* are perhaps the most significant; in addition to *To-Ho le tueur d'or*, these included the *nouvelles* "L'Arbre anthrophage" [The Man-Eating Tree] (1878; reprinted in *Nouvelles histoires incroyables*), about a man-eating tree, and "Mystère-Ville" [Mysteryville] (1904 as by William Cobb), which describes a technologically-advanced breakaway civilization founded in the Far East by French protestant refugees. His last novel of this sort, *L'Effrayante Aventure* [The Frightful Adventure] (1910), describes, in a typically flamboyant fashion, an extraordinary catastrophe provoked in Paris by the crash of an advanced flying machine. The two last-named items will hopefully be featured in future volumes from Black Coat Press.

Clarétie says that Lermina began writing fantastic fiction for *Diogène* in 1859, so the present story might have been written long before it was reprinted in *Histoires incroyables*, but it seems more likely that its inspiration owes something to Villiers de l'Isle-Adam's *L'Eve future* [The Future Eve], which had begun serialization in *Le Gaulois* in 1880 before a different version (similarly abandoned while still incomplete) was launched in a rival newspaper, *L'Etoile Française*. The complete version of Villiers' novel did not appear until 1886, a year after *Histoires incroyables*, but the newspaper versions

130

had made its theme perfectly clear. Lermina's story also has also echoes, further emphasized by its American setting, of Nathaniel Hawthorne's "Rappaccini's Daughter," which similarly belongs to a rich tradition of overblown and allegorically-weighted *femme fatale* stories descended from Hoffmann's classic "Der Sandmann" [The Sandman]. Lermina's farcical parody is pure and simple mockery, but he who mocks allegories cannot escape allegorical implication, and there is a sense in which *Quiet House* cannot help but stand for a world in the process of disturbance by scientific enterprise, which thus becomes inhospitable to noble dreamers and transcendental moralists of the sort that Villiers and Hawthorne—and their protagonists—believed themselves to be.[56]

---

[56] Villiers de l'Isle-Adam's *The Scaffold* (ISBN 978-1-932983-01-2) and *The Vampire Soul* (ISBN 978-1-932983-02-9) are available in Black Coat press editions.

I

In truth, was it really a house? Four walls, almost black in color, pierced by four decorated rectangular holes that passed for windows, a brown door with sturdy powerful hinges and large nails, dark and dismal throughout, reminiscent of the face of a slave who has just been whipped.

Stones have a resignation of their own; these had the appearance of hardly being able to tolerate their fate. No shouting voices had ever enlivened them, no song had ever made them laugh. They had atrophied in their immobility, and were leaning against one another heavily, as if to help one another to bear the weight of the silence. The mass was world-weary. It did not even have the resources to frighten passers-by.

Quiet House[57] did not frighten anyone: a banal mausoleum, square in design and benign in appearance; a yawn in stone—that was all. People passed back and forth in front of that curiosity, as inanimate as a sphinx, without even turning their heads.

It was situated on the very edge of the city, beyond Hoboken, near the Elysian Fields, whose trees had the dull color of cemetery plantations. Why had the house been placed there, like a lost outpost? No one came to it and no one came from it—which implied that it was uninhabited.

The house had grounds of a sort attached, surrounded by walls that were too high for curious eyes to attempt any indiscretion. In reality, no one dreamed of committing such a sin. The habitation was isolated, so there were no neighbors interested in investigating its mystery, even if it had been worth the

---

[57] Lermina gives this name in English, and subsequently adds a footnote to inform readers that Hoboken is in New York, although he refrains from explaining that his supplementary reference to the "*Champs-Elysées*," which might have puzzled some Parisians, is to the location where the world's first baseball game was allegedly played.

bother. The road to which it displayed its grey façade had little traffic, and it would have been rather surprising to see anyone walking there after sunset.

The most curious thing, however, was not what was unknown but what was known. It was a matter of public notoriety that Quiet House was not abandoned. It actually served as a residence for three people—or, to be strictly accurate, four. They were two physicians, Doctors Aloysius and Truphemus, the former's wife, Tibby, and their daughter, little Netty.

How they obtained the aliments necessary to life, no one could say—and on my honor, well as the house was guarded, that secret had to be well kept, for no one had been able to discover it. Indeed, John Clairfax, the Hoboken butcher, Smithson, the grocer whose shop was next door, and Parden the baker, had not been able to accept, at first, that the clientele of Quiet House was beyond their reach. They had presented themselves, at one time, to offer their services; they had stopped their carriages loaded with provisions outside the door, the first with its hanging legs of mutton and quarters of beef jiggling as the wheels jolted, the second with its sausages and candles disposed in garlands under its leather awning, and the third with its shiny gilded loaves. They had knocked for a long time before anyone opened the door, which was shuttered without and worm-eaten within—but suppliers have patient souls, to the extent that the batten finally swung back on its creaking hinges and a soft and sickly face, framed by graying hair, appeared, gazing in wide-eyed astonishment at the tenacious individuals who had not been put off by the long silence.

"What do you want, gentlemen?" asked Dame Tibby, the wife of Aloysius, in a soft voice. Realizing very quickly who she was dealing with, though, she added: "Oh! We don't need anything, thank you!"

"Today," insinuated John, the butcher with the cheerful face. "But tomorrow?"

"Not tomorrow either," replied Dame Tibby.

"It'll be next week, then," Smithson and Parden put in, simultaneously.

133

"No need to trouble yourselves, gentlemen," the woman insisted. "We don't need anything and never will."

"Never!" groaned John.

"How so?" cried Smithson.

"Does no one ever eat here?" exclaimed Parden.

At that moment, a blonde head appeared, neck high to Dame Tibby: the head of a child whose complexion was singular, so clear and uniform was it, though devoid of color.

Netty—for this was Aloysius' daughter—let out a cry of joy and admiration on perceiving al the victuals proudly displayed by the tempters. "Oh, Mama!" she cried. "What's that?"

"Nothing, nothing, my child," said Dame Tibby, shuddering and looking behind her as if she dreaded being taken by surprise. Then, pushing little Netty back, she said: "Go away, my love! And goodbye to you gentlemen. I tell you…I'm sorry to tell you that there's no point in coming back…"

And the door closed again.

The three tradesmen looked at one another, but it was evident that none of them could find a solution to the strange problem that had just been posed to them; they took hold of their horses and sent them back towards town with vigorous cracks of their whips.

I tell you…I'm sorry to tell you… Dame Tibby had said. In fact, she had accentuated the two key words—*I'm sorry*—in a bizarre fashion, and if one were not afraid of being mistaken, one might have affirmed that while pronouncing them she had looked at the legs of mutton, sausages and loaves of bread with an almost ardent gaze.

She had, however, added that they would never need any!

Back in Hoboken, the tradesmen declared that they had encountered a family of people who did not eat. One practical man relied that the people in question were very fortunate; several others added that it must be a significant financial economy—and, as no American ever wastes time in useless reflections, no one gave another thought to the inhabitants of Quiet House, who remained free to live as they liked.

II

A third person: Doctor Aloysius, master of the house. To summarize what was known about him is easy, for he alone was seen to leave the sealed house four or five times a year. On each such occasion the door would let out a sort of animate emaciation, which had a head, arms and legs and evidently had the pretension of belonging to the human race. The head was elongated and angular; on the front of it there was a yellow face, which, if the skin had been scraped, might perhaps have revealed the most curious of all palimpsests. That face had a pre-eminence that one could just about recognize as a nose, the tight nostrils of which made it reminiscent of part of the blade of a knife embedded between two flat and hollow cheeks. The mouth was a pale slit, in the depths of which one sought in vain for teeth. The gums had the color of lips—which is to say, no color. The eyes were black as anthracite, the cranium bald, and the beard absent. There was nothing of the bird of prey about it, though; there was a bleak wishy-washiness about the entire physiognomy, an inertia that was perhaps inoffensive, but might be hiding the most absolute indifference—to good as well as evil.

The legs, veritable spindles, emerged from a formless sack that should have been matt black but was lustrous with wear and antiquity. The bony hands projected from worn and completely frayed sleeves.

Thus Doctor Aloysius appeared on the threshold of his house. Another person accompanied him as far as the doorstep: the fourth inhabitant of the house, Master Truphemus, a living antithesis in flesh and bone—especially of flesh. Truphemus was round; he represented the circle as Aloysius did the straight line—and, in truth, less the circle than the sphere. Everything about Truphemus was round, the whole and the details: an agglomeration of balls forming a ball.

135

The head first: round, with round, bulbous eyes; a round mouth, round cheeks, a round chin, and a round nose. The shoulders drooped with a gentle slope to frame a thorax that fused with the pre-eminent abdomen, which melted into the hips, the thighs and the rest. The arched back did not spoil that sphericity; nothing straight interrupted its curve. The legs completed it, supplying a south pole as the head supplied the north. One might have thought him a bottle that a glass-blower had just filled with vigorous breath.

The two doctors chatted briefly on the doorstep. Master Aloysius took a piece of paper from his pocket, which he unfolded, and from which he then read something to which Master Truphemus listened with the most profound attention. It was a list. Truphemus either nodded his head approvingly or stuck out his lips as if to say: "Hmmm! Not really necessary." Then Aloysius scratched the item out. When this work of verification was complete, Aloysius put the piece of paper back in his pocket, held out his elongated hand to Truphemus, and squeezed his companion's chubby fingers.

The door closed again. Aloysius set off.

His absence extended until the evening. At about 6 p.m., something unusual became visible on the road. It was a hand-cart, drawn by a man. Master Aloysius was walking behind it, directing his black gaze at the vehicle's cargo.

It was a very strange cargo: a pile of scrap iron, metallic debris of every sort; then bottles, heaped up pell-mell, full of materials of every color—blue, yellow, green, red, and even white. The cart was heavy, for the man was sweating, and his shoulders, hunched forward, were arching under the pressure of leather straps. Fortunately, the road was flat.

The procession arrived at Quiet House. Master Aloysius told the porter to stop a few yards in front of the house. Then he went to knock on the door personally, in a particular fashion, and it was opened from inside without delay.

Master Truphemus appeared again, like one of those clock-figures that appear from their niches at certain times of day. He came to help his colleague remove the objects from the cart; it was rather a long job, for they were piled up above the side-walls—and Master Truphemus paused occasionally to study the precious burden he was carrying in his arms—which might, for example, be an old piece of guttering or a few rusty stair-rods. He gazed at them amorously, and it was evident that, were it not for human respect, he might have kissed them.

But Aloysius was in a hurry and, perceiving his companion's disturbance, said: "Get on with it, you old gourmand—quicker than that! You know full well that dinner's waiting."

Dame Tibby joined the parry, and the three individuals passed the objects from hand to hand like the bricks that masons send up from one floor to the next. Even Netty had her role to play; Aloysius gave her the smallest pieces, with a friendly pat on the head.

The workman was paid, and left with a visible air of satisfaction, proof that the work had been well-recompensed.

III

Let us go into Quiet House.

It is 7 p.m. It is almost dark. Bizarre as it is from the outside, the house is even stranger inside. There is not a single regular room that is really entitled to that title. We shall, however, try to describe it.

First of all, the cellars are one with the ground floor and the first floor. Only the second floor seems to be sustained by fixed floorboards. The entire space that extends from those floorboards to the ground in which the foundations are set is filled by boxes of various sizes, sustained in the void by chains and ropes movable by means of pulleys fixed to iron poles.

These boxes are of considerable depth, taller than an average man, and their form is cubic. They are furnished with doors. The iron poles have mobile arms that rotate, with the effect that the boxes can change position throughout the breadth of the house. By means of chains and pulleys set in motion by a mechanism whose gears are visible on every side, one can lower them to any desired height. When all the boxes are elevated in mid-air, they leave the depths of the cellar absolutely free.

Here, it is easy to take account of the nature of the place. There is nothing here but bizarrely-shaped stoves, laboratory equipment of every sort—retorts, alembics, long-necked flasks—and mechanical instruments, and an enormous electrical machine whose glass disk measures more than two meters in diameter. There is no doubt that they are the materials of a chemist and physicist.

The entire breadth of the façade that overlooks the garden, of which we shall say more in due course, is pierced by high openings, which can be closed at will by means of shutters sliding in improvised grooves.

In the corners, there are heaps of dark-colored materials and rusty metallic debris. Along the walls, almost at ground level, shelves support bottles half- or completely filled with crystal salts, powders and extracts, all carefully labeled.

At one particular point, a small board is nailed to the wall, perforated with holes, in the midst of which white buttons can be seen, surmounted with little placards bearing the words: *Dr. Aloysius; Dr. Truphemus; Dining Room; Library.*

These same indications are repeated on the wooden boxes. The buttons activate electrical apparatus. Depending on whether one presses the one to the right, the left or one of the middle ones, the chain that unrolls lets down Aloysius' study, the library, and so on. A ladder is positioned so as to extend from the ground to the box, the door is opened, and one is introduced into the box.

When we dart our indiscreet glance into Quiet House, Truphemus is in the depths of the cellar; by the light of a bizarrely-shaped lamp radiating white electric light he is tracking the progress of a transformation taking place in a crucible. Truphemus is visibly preoccupied, though; his round eyes are not focused, and his thoughts are not proceeding in a straight line. At one particular moment, he makes a gesture of discouragement, followed by another gesture of decision; he has just

138

formed a resolution. Then he heads for the control-panel and presses Aloysius' button violently—a little too forcefully, in fact, for the chain turns on its pulley with a rapid screech and the box in question comes down as if falling—but the springs are solid. The box stops with a shudder.

Truphemus climbs the ladder, his arms at full stretch to permit the ascent of his protruding belly. He opens the door.

Aloysius has been half-knocked-over by the shock, and his bony limbs have suffered somewhat from the abrupt descent. "What the Devil are you doing, my friend?" he cries, as Truphemus appears. "Your visit is reminiscent of a landslide."

Truphemus does not reply. He closes the door firmly behind him, and instinctively looks round to make sure that no indiscreet ear can hear what he might have to say to his colleague—and in fact, given the disposition of things, that would certainly not have been easy.

"The simile is inappropriate," Trumphemus says, belatedly responding to his friend's remark. "Landslides go downwards; I've come up."

"True. Anyway, it hardly matters, and your purism can excuse me this once. What is it, then? Has there been an accident down below?"

"None."

"Is the bromide all right?"

"Admirable."

"The potassium cyanide's behaving itself?"

"As well as can be expected."

"I'm glad to hear it—you gave me quite a fright!"

"Fear is merely a muscular contraction."

"And involuntary. But that's not the issue. Explain, I beg you, for I'm in a hurry to get back to work."

Master Truphemus, thus summoned to get to the point, placed his rotund person on a pile of books stacked on the floor and, put his elbows on his knees and his face in his hands, and looked at Aloysius with dull blue eyes. "My dear friend, I think that, since our relationship—or, rather, our scientific collaboration—began, we have to congratulate ourselves on the progress made…"

"I agree with you gladly as to that—and, since the opportunity presents itself, permit me to recognize the astonishing faculty of intuition with which you are endowed, and which has permitted us to resolve problems before which the greatest minds have recoiled…."

"As I also ask of you the authorization to render justice to the surprising qualities of tenacity and perseverance of which you have given extraordinary evidence."

The two scientists bowed to one another. One might have thought they were in an Academy.

"Let's pass on!" said Truphemus.

"Let's!" said Aloysius.

"And among those problems," continued Trumphemus, "I shall take the liberty of calling particular attention to that of alimentation. You know the question very well—better than me, I ought to add—but allow me to summarize the discoveries that we have made."

Aloysius closed his eyes and cracked his knuckles. He listened.

"With what does the human body nourish itself? Let us resume, for a few moments, the language of ignorant stick-in-the-muds. To that question they answer…what? That the body is nourished by animal and vegetable substances; that nutrients must be drawn from those two natural species, excluding purely mineral substances."

"As if the Otomaques and the Guamos of the banks of the Orinoco did not content themselves with earth alone!"[58]

"Indeed!" Truphemus resumed, his tone indicating his annoyance at being interrupted. "I'll continue. But what are animal and vegetable substances, if not various compounds of primordial elements necessary to nutrition: elements that are

---

[58] Both of these South American tribes are real, described by Alexander Humboldt in his account of his travels, but the allegation that they live on earth is fanciful.

scarcely numerous, and which are the only ones—I insist on the phrase—that concur usefully in the maintenance of the human body? Let's be precise. Everything that constitutes nourishment is composed of nitrogenous materials mixed with other substances deprived of nitrogen. At that is the point, I venture to say, at which we have veritably crossed, with a single bound, the limit imposed upon us by the stupidity of the impotent...

"Starting from that principle, that nitrogen is the nutrient *par excellence*, we said to ourselves: why has humankind created trouble and innumerable dangers for itself for such a long time, by searching all over the world for substances of various tastes, forms and colors, when it is so simple..."

"To get them from the very elements of nourishment."

"Exactly. And to do that, what do we require?" At this point, Truphemus slowed down, emphasizing each word. "To analyze the elements in the human body, and to establish their proportionate quantities, in order to replace them as they are used up."

"In truth," said Aloysius, "one could not enunciate our ideas more clearly."

"Man," continued Truphemus, visibly flattered by this direct homage, "contains carbon, oxygen, hydrogen, nitrogen, phosphorus and iron. If, by binary or tertiary combination, these elements produce various substances—salts, acids or others—under the influence of life, they produce organic matter, and, as the great Berzelius[59] put it so well, organic compounds are oxides of radicals, which themselves result, some from two elements, carbon and hydrogen or carbon and nitrogen, others from three, carbon hydrogen and nitrogen...but let's pass over these details."

"Yes, let's pass on!" said Aloysius.

---

[59] The Swedish chemist Jean-Jacques Berzelius (1779-1848) devised the conventional system of symbolic notation for chemical elements and compounds and determined the chemical formulas of numerous simple compounds.

"Ought we to accept without question the ridiculous condemnation pronounced by ignorance upon any attempt to synthesize organic compounds? Have not Döbereiner, Hatchett and Wöhler proved that the solution of the problem is close at hand?[60] What did their experiments require in order to become definitive?"

Truphemus looked at his companion shrewdly.

Aloysius smiled. "Yes, what did they require?" he said in his turn.

There was a momentary pause. The two scientists savored their triumph as the conservation renewed it.

Truphemus was the first to recover his gravity. "What those precursors of Aloysius and Truphemus required, was to understand that if the combinations were effected, it was under the influence of a principle that it is not given to man to define, but whose existence he establishes: the principle of life. In consequence, in order for organic matter to be produced, it is necessary that the combinations occur under the influence of that same principle. In brief, and by way of conclusion, it is sufficient to introduce oxygen, carbon, nitrogen and hydrogen into the human body for matter to be synthesized by the action of life."

"And to think," said Aloysius, pensively, "that successive generations have suffered hunger because they could not procure grain, meat or vegetables." Each of these three words was pronounced with an untranslatable disdain, further emphasized by a snigger from Truphemus.

---

[60] Johann Wolfgang Döbereiner, Charles Hatchett and Friedrich Wöhler were all chemists of note; Döbereiner observed patterns of kinship between elements that laid the foundations of the periodic table and Hatchett discovered niobium, but only Wöhler—the first person to synthesize an organic compound (by accident)—offered any "proof" that the solution to the problem in question might be "close at hand."

"And yet," the latter observed, "has not the wisdom of nations been shown the true path by the phrase *living on air?* But let's pass on."

"Let's pass on," Aloysius repeated, once more.

"It was therefore necessary to contrive ingestion into the human organism, and submission to its action, of the primary elements of all nourishment, after having carefully established the proportions of atomic weights. For an analyst such as you, dear master, that was child's play...."

"It was child's play," said Aloysius, flattered in his turn.

"Then, to reduce these elements into a form such that their ingestion would be easy: a form that was obvious, the liquid form. Having succeeded in the liquefaction of nitrogen, previously attempted in vain, and modifying the combined proportions of oxygen and hydrogen in such a manner as to produce various solutions, we then composed these different liqueurs which, for a year now, have served as our nourishment."

"And we've not done at all badly out of it," said Aloysius, whose thinness appeared to delight him.

"I'm doing even better!" said Truphemus, closing is eyes and tapping his round and hollow abdomen with his fingertips.

"It has to be said," Aloysius went on, "that you're a gourmand—a nitrogen gourmand, especially. Damn! What consumption! And you thrive on it..."

"What do you expect? I'm a hearty eater!"

"But what a joy," Aloysius continued, "to feel free of all those ridiculous worries to which humankind has so long been condemned, no longer to have those pretended educated tastes which make one a slave to one's nerve-endings. But why have you reminded me of all this, my dear master?"

"Because, my friend, I'm on the track of a discovery even more astonishing, even more remarkable..."

"Impossible!"

"I assure you of it."

"Tell me! Tell me, quickly!"

"I admit," Truphemus said, "that our conversation has gone on longer than I anticipated. I'm hungry! If you're agreeable, we'll resume after dinner…speaking of which, what's on the menu today?"

"It's egg day…$C_{48}H_{36},N_{16}$.[61]

"Very well—let's eat."

IV

The box that bore the title of dining-room was not the least bizarre place in that eccentric habitation.

When the two scientists went into it, by the described means, the two other inhabitants of the house—Dame Tibby and her daughter, that is—were already there.

In the middle of the room there was a table, which would have been quite unremarkable if its sparkling white tablecloth had not been covered with objects that were hardly fitted to give rise to the idea of a meal. At the four places that were to be occupied by the diners, various strangely-shaped items of apparatus, intermediate between bottles and alembics, were set.

At one end of the table a glass bulb with a slender curved neck was partly submerged in a little bucket filled with iron filings. Above the bulb was an electric lamp with two carbon filaments.

When Aloysius and Truphemus arrived, the woman and child stood up.

Dame Tibby was still young, scarcely 40 years of age. She had undoubtedly been pretty, to judge by the delicacy of her features, but her entire physiognomy was imprinted with such an expression of suffering, and her thin cheeks revealed a fatigue so profound, that she seemed less a woman than a tormented shadow.

---

[61] Lermina adds a footnote here to assert that this is the chemical formula of albumen.

Netty was small; she was five, but had scarcely attained the stature of a two-year-old. Her complexion was so blanched, her forehead so pale, that one hesitated to believe that it was blood that ran in her veins. Her eyes alone were alive; there was a malice in her gaze—or, rather, a diabolical wickedness: not a glimmer of sweetness, but a limitless harshness. If she spoke, her voice was dry and hard; one might have imagined that one were listening to the grinding of an automaton's wheels.

Master Aloysius, her father, went to her and ruffled her hair affectionately; the child did not smile. She turned towards the scientist, her eyes dull and staring, with flashes of blue steel.

Trumphemus greeted Dame Tibby gallantly, saying to her in his reedy voice: "Well, do we have an appetite today?"

Dame Tibby seemed gentle, but it must never be forgotten that appearances are eminently deceptive. She raised her head at this remark like a horse that feels the spur. "An appetite!" she cried. "I'd certainly like to know whether hunger is a chronic illness here!"

"What!" said Aloysius, with a snigger. "Here you are, my love, becoming accustomed to the use of scientific parlance…"

"At least it's better," she said, angrily, "than swallowing your wretched drugs…"

"There, there—let's not get carried away!" Aloysius went on, while Truphemus judged it inopportune to get mixed up in the conversation. "I know that you're attached to the paltry preoccupations of the lives of the ignorant…"

"Certainly, if by that you mean rump steaks and mutton chops…"

Aloysius smiled with an expression of profound pity. "You let yourself be seduced by color, and by taste!" he said, getting up and gazing at the bottles disposed on the table. "Here—look at this pure, clear liquid. It includes all the constituent elements of herbivorous mammals. Nothing is missing. How would it be more agreeable, I ask you, to wear out your teeth tearing and grinding that fibrous flesh? But enough of that. What Saint John Chrystostom said about fasting, I apply to our system: it's the death of vice, the life of virtue; it's the peace of the body and the ornament of life; it's the rampart of chastity and the boudoir of modesty…"

"Bravo!" said Truphemus. "A little more nitrogen, if you please."

"Be careful, my dear friend," Aloysius went on, passing him the tube. "You'll obtain a plethora, and then, watch out for congestion!"

"*Après nous, le deluge!*"

"That *après nous* won't be long coming," murmured the incorrigible Dame Tibby, sipping a combination of hydrogen and carbonic acid in small doses.

"Again!" said Aloysius, impatiently. "My dear Dame Tibby, will we never reach an understanding?"

"No, certainly not, as long as you condemn Netty and me to these accursed nutriments."

"I will point out to you, my love, that our Netty is not complaining about it."

"That doesn't surprise me! She wouldn't have the strength. Well, since we're on the subject, I'll tell you once and for all what I think. For all your scientific pretensions, you and your worthy acolyte Mr. Triphemus, are madmen…"

"Oh!" said Truphemus, personally offended, and interrupted while partaking of a mixture with a hydrocyanic acid base, to facilitate his digestion.

"You've no need to protest, Mr. Truphemus!" cried Dame Tibby, excitedly. "You're madmen and murderers! Yes murderers! And what's even more atrocious, great Doctor Aloysius, is that, not content with killing your wife, here you are poisoning your child!"

"Madame!" Aloysius put in. "Poisonous substances…"

"As to that, you only have to look at her, poor dear! Is that a child? She's nearly five years old—five do you hear? In two months! Well, is that a girl of five? She's too tiny, too weak. Ah! While I had milk—me, her mother—I sustained her, nourished her…during your first experiments, I succeeded in introducing a few scraps of that nourishment you disdain, but which she needed…today, nothing—nothing but your repulsive compounds! And she's dying of your nitrogen and your oxygen—but you're quite content, yourself! She's sickly and rickety, she isn't growing, she isn't alive—death already has her in its grip. And you, shut up in your poisoners' laboratory, you're looking for the quickest way to rid yourself of her, and me!"

Exhausted by this violent effort, Dame Tibby slumped back in her seat.

Aloysius had recovered the calm appropriate to adepts of the true science. He merely murmured: "Woman, as Saint John Chrysostom says, is the cause of evil, the author of sin, the stone of the tomb, the gate of Hell, the fatality of our miseries."

The child looked successively at her mother and the doctor, with expressionless eyes.

Truphemus ate…scientifically.

"Have you finished?" Aloysius asked, eventually. "To whomever has not faith, nothing can be given. Our system is based on positive data, which your whining cannot invalidate. I have spoken."

The doctor was, however, more disturbed than he cared to let on.

Truphemus leaned towards him, and whispered into his ear. Aloysius looked at him, surprised and joyful at the same time.

"Yes, yes," Dame Tibby continued, having noticed this aside. "Plot, plot…but all this can't last."

"Madame," said Truphemus, drawing himself upright to the extent that his rotundity would permit, "let me tell you that you are mistaken as to my character, if you suppose for a single instant that I could give any bad advice to Doctor Aloysius. I am, on the contrary, convinced that you will thank me when you know the result of the conversation that I am presently requesting of Netty's father…"

Dame Tibby shrugged her shoulders. After this irreverent gesture, the meal came to an end.

A few minutes later, the two scientists, thanks to the mechanical combinations of which we have spoken, were in the box known as Dr. Aloysius' study.

"My dear friend," said Aloysius, "don't play games with my impatience. I confess to you that Dame Tibby's words have disturbed me greatly, although I didn't want to let her see…and I'm not without anxiety regarding the fate of our dear Netty…."

"And what did I say to you just now?"

"That you've found a way to give her strength and health."

"And I'll prove it."

The conversation then became so intimate that it would have been impossible for the keenest ear to catch a single word—except that, periodically, Aloysius could not restrain a gesture of astonishment, or shook his head doubtfully.

Then Truphemus became more insistent; he talked incessantly.

Aloysius became motionless again, listening attentively. Suddenly, he cried: "Admirable! Sublime! Dr. Truphemus, you're a genius!"

V

The following morning, there was an unaccustomed bustle in Quiet House. It was evident that a great event had occurred, or was on the verge of realization. At dawn, the door opened and the scientists went out.

Dame Tibby and the child accompanied them to the threshold; it was clear that there had been a reconciliation, for the mother seemed almost joyful. As for Netty, still indifferent, she gazed at the road and the rays of sunlight.

"You see, my dear wife," said Aloysius, "that science always has secrets in reserve for its fervent servants."

"God hears you!" murmured Dame Tibby.

Aloysius and Truphemus did not pause in Hoboken; they hired a carriage there and headed straight for the highway. They were seen passing through Jersey City, Harlem, Yorktown, alongside Central Park, and—more remarkable still—going into Broadway. They continued on their way; when they reached Union Square, they looked around. They seemed as far out of their element as if they had come from the ends of the Earth, but their eyes encountered the sign of a construction company. It was there that they went.

The businessman listened to them with appropriate phlegm, chewing his tobacco and releasing numerous jets of saliva; then he took a pencil, drew up a plan, inscribed dimensions, made his calculations and finally quoted his price.

Truphemus took a gold ingot from his pocket. The merchant looked at it, weighed it, tested it and signed a receipt, which he gave to the two scientists.

"You'll begin work tomorrow?" said Aloysius.

"Tomorrow."

"And it'll take…?"

"A week."

"Good."

And that is why the road going past Quiet House was animated by the comings and goings of workmen; and that is why, three months later, Frank Kerry wrote the following letter to one of his friends.

VI

Frank Kerry to Edward B***, in Baltimore.[62]

Dear friend, you'll finally be satisfied. You've berated me so many times for not being amorous that I expect your most enthusiastic eulogies by return of post. What do you expect? The hour had to chime, and I listened in vain to the days

---

[62] Lermina names the sender of this letter "Franz," but that hardly makes a plausible pairing with "Kerry," so I have taken the liberty of substituting a more likely final letter.

and minutes falling into the past without any sound striking my ears.

You know me: born to an invalid mother, who was driven to despair by my father's positivism, I've sucked the mortal milk of fantasy since birth. Poor woman! Tiny as I was, I still remember seeing her leaning over my crib, her huge blue eyes looking into mine, which had just opened...one might have thought that she was trying to plunge into them, as into an unknown world—and I opened my eyelids very wide, so as to leave her the largest possible field...then, as in a mirror, I saw unknown worlds appear in her dilated pupils, illuminated by sparkling radiance, or landscapes develop, profound and infinite in perspective, disappearing into distant shadows—or, better still, it seemed that beautifully contoured and colored shapes were approaching me, as rapidly as if they had wings.

Those were my first excursions into the land of dreams: that attraction developed—that terrible attraction—which draws you so far, so very far, that no return in possible. Whenever I was alone I closed my eyes and looked...at what? The darkness, the darkness in which I experienced love, for which I sought, for which I yearned.... In that darkness, voluntarily formed for myself alone, I created by means of imagination a world that belonged to me, into which no other penetrated and never will penetrate: an egotistic enjoyment only appreciable by people who have sufficiently mastered themselves to savor it slowly and consciously.

I grew up. I found myself thrown into the external world. How paltry it seemed to me by comparison with my own universe! What you called beautiful was only a deviation from that ideal of which I had the pure notion; your colors were garish, your lines irregular, your monuments grotesque. I searched in vain; if I heard one of you talking eulogistically about some spectacle or building, I immediately went to the indicated spot, but never experienced any other sentiment than profound disillusionment.

Would I be better off contemplating humankind itself than studying its works? Oh, there again beauty left me cold.

Not one forehead on which the thought of Infinity was resplendent! Everywhere, on the contrary, the practical cares of everyday life inscribed in premature wrinkles. On the youngest faces, paltry preoccupations; in the physiognomies of old men, regret for the past—no impulse towards the future, imminent as it might be.

And—need I say it?—*materiality* horrified me. I could not understand why anyone condemned himself to live in that icy environment called society, which is nothing but an immense cemetery, when it was so easy to create an entire existence of ecstasy and reverie.

Adolescence came—what you call the age of passion, as if that impetuosity were not, on the contrary, an effect of matter, tending to dominate and enslave the soul. Within me, the struggle was violent. I was full of vigor, my blood boiled in my veins, my temples pulsed. Little by little, though, true sentiment was liberated; what spoke in me was a new aspiration towards the ideal that is beauty.

It was no longer sufficient for me to contemplate it, to admire it; I wanted to possess it, to identify myself within it, to steep myself in it somehow by bathing in its effluvia. I made one concession to prejudice, however. I admitted *relativity* in perfection—which is to say that I loved a woman. She was admirably beautiful. Oh, upon my word, no more splendid manifestation of life could ever have been encountered. You would all have proclaimed her the masterpiece of masterpieces, and even women turned their heads as she passed by, irritated by the homage that they were obliged to render her.

Ah, I remember…and I laugh about it still; I laugh about it, I tell you. I remember the flood of envy that was directed at me when the beautiful Themia chose me among all her admirers. Poor woman! She loved me…I'm convinced of it. When I talked to her, she tried to understand me and fixed her large velvet eyes upon me as if she wanted to read my thoughts. Poor, poor thing! She was as beautiful as your marble or your diamond: the marble that is the most beautiful striated stone, the diamond that reflects light and cannot retain a single ray of it for itself! One day, I left, cursing her, and never saw her again.

Then I went traveling. It seemed to me that nature, with its superhuman dimensions, would eventually measure up to my creative imagination. Certainly, I am not a layman, and I defy anyone to refuse me the intelligence of the beautiful; I understand *as well as anyone* the enjoyment that a mind circumscribed in its aspirations can feel, particularly in the presence of the Ocean, when one is alone at night in the bow of a sailing ship. The creaking of the masts is a harmony that recalls the weakness of human works by comparison with that corner of the work of creation. There is something in the passing wind like an expiration of the immense All; the horizon is so distant that the eye can scarcely discern its contours...but further on! further on! Columbus, heading for America, had a goal towards which his thought was directed; he could be satisfied—but where is the end for someone who has the consciousness of infinity?

The *non-finite* extends beyond conception, which is itself merely a way-station, a time of rest, thought being nothing but an emanation of the brain, an imperfect organ, since there is something above and beyond everything created: the creative force itself, the thought of which arises from the infirmity of its producer. Who knows of what a stone hurled upwards by a sling might dream? It senses itself climbing the ladder of the sky, it yearns for immeasurable space—but, the force of the sling being x, the forward thrust of the stone will be x. Momentarily, it falls back. Thought itself hooks on to the point that it attains by means of its special power, and from there, its fatigue repaired, hurls itself onwards towards new limits.... O thought! Sole joy of humankind, sole strength, sole power, real essence of humanity, which overleaps your grotesque worlds in a single bound, and finding there not even a point of support, asks itself: Where? How? Why?

No, you'll never understand that torture. You're reasonable; you occupy yourself with your business. I love you! I don't know why. You alone connect me—or, rather, connected me—to humankind. You have a good heart, you're honest, you're loyal. There are also depths in honesty; generosity holds something of infinity; you console me for the narrowness of other hearts.

When I came back, having visited that which men have visited before me, having also, for the sake of pride, scaled peaks reputed to be inaccessible, contemplated sights that no human eye has ever beheld, I consulted my heart. It was empty. No joy had come to satisfy the faculty of expansion that drew my entire being.

It was then that I made you part of my project. I found myself torn between two alternatives: death and study. Death! Why did that word frighten me? Why did I experience in pronouncing it, a sensation similar to glacial cold? Why did my own disintegration seem fearful? Oh, If I had at least been sure that, liberated from the material fibers that enlaced me like a net of steel, my thought would have been able to launch itself freely towards immateriality, to plunge forever into waves incessantly renascent of infinity...but where is the proof of that possibility?

Above all, I wanted to see, to know, to anticipate that future before launching myself into it, as the diver does who tests the sea's depth before throwing himself into it. And then again, could not these faculties, whose existence I observed I myself, procure me the joys I sought by their exercise? Was not the instinct that guided me proof in itself that it could be assuaged? Does not the man who feels the pangs of hunger for the first time find in that very appetite the proof of the existence of aliments? Does he not then go forth to search for what does not come to him?

I resolved to dedicate myself to new studies—and you know, my friend, that, furnished with all the necessary instruments, strong in my ardor and my will, I exiled myself voluntarily from the city to install myself on the little hill that is north of Hoboken. Here, for several months now, far from the world, I no longer look at the ground; my eyes, ceaselessly turned to the sky, interrogate that immense space whose limits are imperceptible. Oh, my dear fellow, if you only knew what splendid intoxication overwhelms my entire being during those long contemplations! The whirlwind of the infinite echoes in my brain...

Who, therefore, needs opium, hashish, and all those poisonous drugs that overexcite the brain to give one a feverish joy of which one does not even have a clear consciousness? For myself, calmly and coldly, I gaze at the sky. Then the hypnotism of the sidereal profundity imposes itself on my organs, and, in a sort of cataleptic immobility, I perceive nameless splendors. My senses are multiplied tenfold. I see in those eternities the lives of worlds that move and perpetuate themselves. And what movements! Vast cascades of light, rotating, falling and rising again in a limitless circle: the tides of the ether brushing the sidereal masses, and sometimes—a frightful reminder of my weakness in the face of that force!—annihilating them like paper balls in a founder's furnace!

Then I fall back, broken and crushed; the intoxication is too violent—the fibers of my being are compressed by the pressure of splendor!—and nature takes back its empire as I faint.

It was during one of these crises, a few days ago, that an event occurred which might have a decisive influence on my existence. It happened one afternoon. The sky was clear, save for a few vaporous clouds floating in the sky, into which the light seemed to sink as in a transparent lake. I gazed, and the splendors I sought soon presented themselves to me.

The horizon appeared to me as an immense iridescent ring, in the middle of which concentric circles in parallel layers formed luminous and ever-changing waves, admirably tinted. These waves multiplied, and the space left free by their circumferences continually diminished in extent. At the central point was a resplendent radiant spray. All of a sudden, in the very heart of that dazzling symphony of light, a creature appeared. I can't describe her; words fail me. She was the synthesis of all beauties, the birth of all gracefulness; she was the angel, the *ideal*, a thought given form, a dream come to life.

She looked at me; her eyes met mine…it was as if I had been struck by lightning!

Naturally, when I recovered consciousness, my first thought was that the apparition had only existed in my imagination. Besides, where could such perfection be living? I was sitting on the terrace of my house, my head in my hands, letting my eyes wander at hazard. I was taking a rest from these emotions by looking at the ground, when a strange spectacle struck my eyes. Would you believe that, throughout my sojourn in that habitation, I had not yet examined the surroundings?

I don't need to insist to make you understand that my eyes, devoted to vision since my earliest childhood, are endowed with a faculty of perception infinitely superior to that which other men's eyes possess. What I perceived distinctly about four miles away, which struck me with astonishment, was a sort of palace of glass, about the size of an Oriental pavilion. There was not a particle of iron or wood to be seen. Curiously enough, the plates of glass upon which the Sun darted its sparkling rays were, without exception, violet in color—a violet that is only found in the crystal named iolite.

The pavilion was situated in the middle of a garden in which, without exception, all the trees, branches and the very leaves were of that same color; the ground, the soil, was also violet.

A door opened, and a young woman appeared, dressed in long violet vestments; these vestments were made of a gauze that allowed the light to circulate around the mot admirable body of which any sculptor ever dreamed. These divine forms owed nothing of their perfection to humanity; it was like a molding of condensed vapors, so pure and soft was its beauty. A veil of the same material and the color shaded the face, whose lines ere ideally ravishing. I cried out. It was her!—the one who, a few minutes before, had appeared to me radiant with splendor and immateriality in the midst of that scintillating sky. It was her!

Ah! I understood then what Love is. I understood that overwhelming sensation that takes possession of all the forces of being, stirs them up and revives them. She! For the first time I could pronounce that word that word with an inexpressible shudder, while it resounded like an echo in all the fibers of my body. That woman, that child—for I did not know, on my honor, the detail escaped me!—was my own thought; she was my infinity…she was my life…

Finally, I existed, I felt, I loved.

She! She!

Since you take a keen interest in that which concerns me, I shall keep you up to date with what happens. Thus far, I have not been able to reach her, but I do not despair of succeeding in that. Despair, when all my vitality is concentrated in that desire! When she is waiting for me, as I am waiting for her, when she calls to me, as I call to her!

Farewell for now, my friend—for now!

VII

Master Aloysius and Master Truphemus are in their laboratory—which is to say, the cellar—but the stoves are extinct, the retorts seem melancholy, and the alembics have a contrite air.

Even more contrite and melancholy than these inert objects, however, are the two animate beings who greet one another mutually with the name of doctor.

They are sitting down, facing one another. Aloysius' thinness in more cadaverous than ever; Truphemus is just as round. Their arms are hanging limply down, in an attitude of discouragement. They look at one another, seemingly hesitant to speak.

"Bother!" says Truphemus, finally.

"Drat!" Aloysius replies.

"That must be…"

"Evidently."

"Human resources have their limits…"

"They have their limits."

"That's indisputable."

"Indisputable…"

"Certain…"

"Sure…"

Then silence falls again. Aloysius is downcast; Truphemus is despondent.

"And yet…"

"However…" Aloysius adds.

"The theory is sound…"

"Indisputable…"

"Indisputable…"

"Certain…"

"Sure…"

A further silence.

Truphemus recovers his presence of mind first; he puts both hands on his abdomen, which he taps.

"There, there!" he says. "We mustn't allow ourselves to be beaten…and above all, we must never lose sight of the scientific method. If you're agreeable, my savant companion, we'll study all the facets of the problem logically."

"Go on," said Aloysius, whose indifference seems to acquiesce in advance with his associate's reasoning.

The latter is not easily troubled; he is the orator of the duo.

"So, let's retrace the chain of our deductions one by one, and see if we might have erred in some essential particular. First, this happened: your daughter Netty seemed to be wasting away, even though we had given her a double dose of nitrogen and albumin. Is that right?"

"True!" replied Aloysius, unable to refuse this first concession.

"The child was puny, her limbs were not developing sufficiently, and I sometimes recollect the anger that Dame Tibby…"

"May God have mercy on her soul!" murmured Aloysius—which informs us incidentally, that Netty's mother is dead. The unfortunate woman had succumbed to a fatal anemia.

"May God have mercy on her soul!" repeated Truphemus. "So I said…." He searched his memory momentarily. The inopportune invocation of the Deity had raised an obstacle to the certainty of his argument. "Ah! I said that the new problem was this: to make the development of the body march in step with its nutrition. That's what I had the honor of revealing to one evening, if you recall, when we were shut up in our laboratory after a succulent meal. Now, here I lay claim, if I may, to a certain originality of invention. I drew your attention to a phenomenon that experience had demonstrated to us…it is the rule, in science, that one can only proceed from the known to the unknown. What was the known? That a plant, a vegetable entity, subject to the action of violet light, grows with an infinitely greater rapidity than a vegetable subject to the action of white light. The fact is known, yes or no?"

To this rather peremptory proposition, Aloysius replied with a nod of his head, the *nutus* of the ancients—which sufficed for the positive Truphemus, who resumed with a new ardor.

"Good! What, then, was the unknown, the X to be discovered or verified? An analogy then suggested itself. This was the unknown: would the same phenomenon be produced if it were no longer a matter of entities placed in the second echelon of nature, but of motile creatures furnished with organs of locomotion—in a word, animals…if it were a matter of human beings? When I communicated this thought to you, which I do not hesitate, in spite of my modesty, to qualify as a stroke of genius, your superior intelligence was immediately struck by all that it presented of the ingenious, and especially by the immense horizon that it opened up to science. Were you struck, yes or no?"

"I was struck," said Aloysius, meekly.

"Now, the ideal opportunity presented itself to carry out a conclusive experiment immediately. I still recall my words: 'Master,' I said to you, 'a scientist has nothing that truly belongs to him; the researcher is neither proprietor, not possessor, nor papa. Your daughter Netty is rickety, sickly, undersized. Let us try on her the experiment that has succeeded so often with plants.' To which you replied by this eminently practical sentence, which proves that sentiment never loses its rights: 'Is a young girl not a flower?' I made the observation that that was exactly the issue at stake, and, with a common accord, we agreed to submit young Netty to the constant action of violet rays. As truly intelligent men, we did not wish to delay the execution of our plan, and within a few days we had the violet pavilion constructed. I had coated the trees with the same color and modified their sap. You prepared a kind of sand designed to change the color of the ground. There remained the matter of costume, and Dame Tibby, who had adopted our idea with enthusiasm…."

"May God have mercy on her soul!"

"May God have mercy on her soul! As I was saying, Dame Tibby ran up the clothes that the child would wear with her own hands. All that is undeniable, undeniable, undeniable…."

"Undeniable," repeated Aloysius.

"Now, three months have gone by. During that entire time, young Netty has been subject to the action of violet rays; she has seen violet, thought violet, eaten violet…she is impregnated by violet, steeped in violet…and it has been clear to us that our deductions had not led us astray for a single instant…for…."

"She has grown," murmured Aloysius.

"Grown! Grown! Say that she had sprouted more rapidly than the liveliest of cryptogams! By the end of a fortnight she had put on half a foot; a month later, she measured three feet three inches. Today,"—here there was a pause—"she stands four feet eight inches, a perfectly normal stature for a woman. In three months, we have turned a child into an admirably-constituted creature who has reached her full height. Science has vanquished nature; it has constrained it to obedience; the result obtained is admirable, exceeding our wildest hopes. However..."

"However...?" said Aloysius, shaking his head.

"As nothing in this world is perfect, there is a shadow upon our perfect satisfaction—a shadow all the more serious, I confess, because it troubles certain previously-held notions..."

Aloysius, who had listened patiently thus far, stood up so suddenly that all his joints cracked at once. One might have thought that 50 knucklebones were rattling against one another. "She's an idiot!" he cried, raising his eyes to the ceiling with an expression of profound despair.

Once again, Truphemus was able to keep calm, and he went on softly: "Idiot, idiot...perhaps it depends on what we mean by the expression, which seems to me improper..."

"Say stupid, silly, foolish...call it what you will," Aloysius went on, "but it's no less true that intelligence is absolutely lacking."

"I said 'what we mean'—but I don't think there's any need to shout. If it's necessary to raise one's voice—which is incompatible with the calmness befitting a wholly scientific discussion—I shall reply in the shrillest tone of which my larynx is capable: 'No, no, and thrice no!' She is not an idiot, nor stupid, nor silly, nor foolish!"

"What is she then?"

"She's five years old in terms of intelligence, but she's 20 years old in body."

"You're talking Hebrew! Explain!"

"Nothing is simpler, though," Truphemus continued, resuming his professorial attitude. "The cerebro-spinal nervous system is the seat of sensibility and the source of voluntary movement; the action of the brain is indispensable to the perception of sensations and the manifestation of will—but where our knowledge stops is when it is necessary to decide whether the encephalic apparatus is the producer of thought or only the activator of faculties originating from a source other than the working of the system. When I told you just now that what happened today threw me a little, it was because until now I had been a partisan of the former hypothesis—which is to say, the production of thought by the cerebral apparatus. In the case that concerns us—that of Netty—the apparatus has developed, but thought has remained stationary. Do you understand?"

"I understand," said Aloysius. "What can we do, then?"

"I've no idea," replied Truphemus. "What about you?"

"No idea," Aloysius said.

At that moment, a loud noise was heard outside, like numerous pieces of glass breaking.

The two scientists raced out of the house into the grounds.

"Where's Netty?" cried Aloysius.

The violet pavilion had been built in the middle of the garden; it was a cage of large dimensions, in which a few indispensable items of furniture had been disposed, all covered in cloth of the same color. It was there that the child on whom the two chemists had tried their serious experiment lived. It was from there that the noise had come. A large pane of glass had broken.

But where was Netty? The two men looked everywhere, in vain. There was no one. They set out to make a careful tour of the garden, each taking one side, bending down to inspect every clump of foliage.

"Here she is!" cried Truphemus.

And from a bush beneath which she was concealed, the scientist drew out Aloysius' daughter Netty by the hand.

Certainly, anyone who had seen her three months earlier would not have believed that he had the same creature before his eyes. Netty, the puny child, had become, under the influence of the Truphemic regime, a sturdy young woman, who appeared to be at least 18 years old. And she was, in fact, an admirably beautiful creature. It was certainly her that the young dreamer had seen from the heights of his open-air observatory, and his enthusiasm was justified. Her body was an assembly of all the physical perfections; she was life in its most complete and symmetrical manifestation.

161

Taken by surprise, the young woman leaned back to resist Truphemus' grip—and, in truth, it seemed that it would only require an abrupt gesture to extract herself therefrom—but under the influence of shame and fear, she began to cry, letting loose piercing cries: "No! No! It wasn't me! It wasn't me!"

Aloysius came running, his legs clicking. "Don't hurt her!" he shouted to Truphemus.

"But I haven't touched her!" replied the fat man, letting go of the young woman's hand.

The latter realizing that she was free, immediately ran to a corner of the pavilion, where she crouched down and curled up. She raised her elbow level with her forehead, and continued whimpering and protesting.

"Let's see! Let's see! My little Netty!" said Aloysius. "There's no need to get upset like this. Oh well! After all, it was an unfortunate accident. No one's going to eat you!" And he teased her blond hair with the crooked tips of his bony fingers.

She raised her steel-blue eyes towards him. "You won't hit me, will you?"

"No, no! Come on, come with me."

Taking her by the arm, Aloysius led her gently into the garden, looking at her and thinking about Truphemus' theories regarding the cerebro-spinal nervous system.

"How did it happen?"

"I don't know, Papa. I wasn't there. I didn't see anything…"

"Don't lie! A girl of your age….that is to say, no, a big girl like you…"

Netty resumed weeping even harder, crying: "I'm not lying. It wasn't me!"

Nothing was more singular than the appearance of her face as she pronounced these words. Its lines, perfect in their regularity, were deformed by the contortions of a despair more apparent than real. It was the grimace of a child on the face of a woman—something that resembled a mask of Madness.

162

Aloysius looked at it with an expression of profound discouragement.

Truphemus came up to him and tapped him on the shoulder. "A word!" he said.

"I'm all yours," murmured the doctor. And, drawing away from the young woman slightly, he came closer to the rotund Truphemus.

"Perhaps," said the latter, "there might be a way."

"Be careful! Be careful!" cried Aloysius with an indescribable expression of terror. Pointing at Netty, who was lying on the ground making little piles of sand with her bare hands, he added: "We've already tempted Nature too far. She'll avenge herself."

"Is it really Doctor Aloysius that I hear?" Trufemus went on. "Is it really that superior intelligence, for which science has no secrets, and who does not admit the insolubility of any problem? Don't you understand that every human work is in need of improvement? Haven't we achieved anything? Isn't that body the most admirable work of art that science has ever produced? I can't pretend that the mind doesn't leave much to be desired, but the fault is evidently reparable. What would you say to a delicate operation, the idea of which struck me only a moment ago? It's evident that the cerebral matter that fills Netty's skull is insufficient or badly-conformed. That's what, in my humble opinion, it's important to determine. It's easy to do: it'll be sufficient to make a circular incision with a sharp instrument, which will detach part of your daughter's skull…"

"Shut up!" howled Aloysius. "Executioner! Torturer!" Losing control of himself, he hurled himself on Truphemus.

The latter, alarmed, took a few steps backwards.

At that moment, someone knocked loudly on the door to the street.

VIII

Frank Kerry to Edward B***, in Baltimore.

My dear friend, I don't know if I'm mad or dreaming, but, in truth, I'm experiencing new sensations, of which nothing in my life until now had gave me the feeblest glimpse. Is it love, then, that has taken possession of me? I leave it to you to give a name to this transformation in me. One single thought absorbs my entire mind. Infinity seems to be nothing next to that *finity* whose name is beloved, dark light next to brightness!

In my last letter, I told you that I had tried in vain to get close to the one who had become my entire life, my entire hope. This is what happened. For the first time since my arrival on the hill in Hoboken, I had emerged from my Thebaïd—and, orientating myself by means of the observations I had made from my terrace. I headed for the Elysian Fields. There, encountering a few passers-by, I asked them for directions—but I forgot, at first, that I was faced with limited natures, incapable of understanding the sensations that were oppressing me. I spoke as if I were writing to you. No one understood. Fortunately, I remembered that science gave me a sure means of determining the exact situation of the glass palace.

I returned home, and with the aid of a sextant. I made a minute calculation, which indicated to me, within a few yards, the point for which I was headed—and then I went back. My calculations had not deceived me. I recognized the walls of the grounds, and the house facing the road. I tell you—I, who had the unprecedented boldness to hurl myself, a lost soul, into the abysms of the whirling ether, felt myself, faced with a simple door, the most timid and feeblest of children.

First, I wanted to know who the inhabitants of the house were. I made enquiries of the few neighbors—rather distant ones, besides—who might be able to give me a little information. It seemed that, in general, I was not very welcome. I could only obtain vague details; I thought at first that people were mocking me.

The house about which I was asking questions had a diabolical reputation in the neighborhood, and it was easy to see, in the attitude of my interlocutors, that they would have much preferred not to talk about it. It was obvious that it inspired an inexpressible terror in everyone. As for its inhabitants, it was impossible for me to obtain any precise information. Two old men, considered to be the demons of that unknown inferno, were described to me as the sole occupants of the property, along with a little girl two or three years old. I spoke in vain, in covert terms—so fearful was I to profane the angel of my dream—of the young woman I had glimpsed. The boldest assured me that there had never been a young woman in the house—unless, he added, some she-devil had come to join the party….

What remained for me beyond doubt was that there was a mysterious shadow overhanging the whole affair, and I became all the more ardent to pierce it.

I resolved, before presenting myself directly at Quiet House—that's the name of the dwelling—to find out everything I could by myself. I slipped around the walls of the grounds. A few strangely-formed trees extended their branches over the top of the wall, which as not I good repair, offering an opportunity to scale it. It was there that I determined to establish my observation-post.

The first time that my hands and feet assisted me in that painful ascent, my heart was beating so violently that I thought I would be unable to attain my goal—but when I raised my head, I thought I saw once again in the celestial azure the adorable form of the One who was calling me, and I redoubled my efforts. Finally, I attained the summit of the wall, and I plunged my avid gaze into the grounds.

I had not been mistaken. The glass palace existed. It really was that violet color, soft and pale at the same time, which glistened in the sunlight. And finally, I saw…her!

But what was she doing? I confess that, at that moment, I thought I was no longer master of my reason, and today I am asking myself again whether what I saw might not have been a trick of my imagination. She was sitting at the foot of a tree, leaning forwards, in such a fashion that her admirable blonde hair was trailing on the ground. She was scraping the sand with her slender fingers, and when she had formed a little heap she took it in her hands and threw into a zinc bucket that she had beside her. Then she overturned the half-full bucket on the ground, lifted it up, stamped on the ground, sat down again and began heaping up the sand and filling the bucket all over again.

An innocent occupation, but one whose strangeness struck me immediately. I stayed there for an hour, hoping that my presence might finally be perceived. Vain illusion! The sand went continually from the ground to the bucket, to fall back from the bucket to the ground. I studied her. Oh, my friend, how much more beautiful she was than anything of which I had dreamed! What purity of form, what diaphanousness there was in that charming creature! The position in which I found myself, however, was becoming extremely uncomfortable. I had perched on the thickest bough of one of the trees touching the wall, and after this long pause, with the wood digging into my flesh, I felt numbness take possession of my entire being. My hands were having trouble holding on to the wood that served me as a point of support. It was necessary to end it! But I as so afraid of frightening her—that dear and perfect creature who was still dreaming as she macerated her dust!

I called out to her once; she did not hear. Then, becoming bolder, I cried: "Angel escaped from Heaven, adorable creature whom humanity does not have the right to count among its imperfect creatures…!"

This time, she had heard. She raised her head—and what a face, my friend! No, although I am a wanderer, as a poet once said, in my starry dreams, although the dazzling perspectives of sidereal space have opened before me, no, never had a beauty more profound, more intoxicating, imposed itself on my being…I was dazzled, mad with admiration and love.

It is evidently that state of overexcitement that disturbed my mind to the point of rendering me prey to the most grotesque hallucination that was every produced. Don't believe what you are about to read. It was not; it could not be.

It seemed to me—I insist on the evident illusion—that, while looking at me with an expression that was both surprised and alarmed, she contracted her face into a comical grimace, and that, putting her hand to her nose in a vulgar gesture that I cannot describe without insulting her…she stuck her tongue out at me!!!

Is it not evident that fatigue had obliterated the faculty of vision? But how can it be that our feeble nature is so far from mastery of itself that it can create such phantoms? I felt faint. I half-closed my eyes, and let myself fall back on the other side of the wall. Then I ran, as fast as my legs could carry me, to shut myself up in my house. I was fearful of mental alienation, whose iron fingers were beginning to dig into my brain. I was in desperate need of rest; I wanted to fall into a momentary oblivion to take the pressure off my nerves.

Sleep came.

When I awoke, I was saved…

I was saved; I had calmed down. And the first effort of my reason proved to me the insanity of what I thought I had seen. She, a grimacer! As well suppose that the sky, the stars and planets might indulge in epileptic convulsions. It was an error, born of an unhealthy brain…and I was so profoundly convinced of it that I got down on my knees, with my arms extended towards the glass pavilion, and begged the pardon of the insulted angel.

Then I was remorseful. By what right had I permitted myself to play the role of spy? Why had I attempted to surprise my beloved? Were my intentions not purer than the heavens of which she is a visible emanation? I had to repair my fault and enter the door of that house into which I had sought to introduce myself like a malefactor. Thus, as soon as the night had refreshed my senses, my resolution as made; I put on my best suit and went to Quiet House.

I knocked violently on the door. It seemed to me that every blow of the knocker echoed dolorously in my soul.[63]

IX

"Someone's at the door!" said Truphemus, scarcely recovered from the fright that Aloysius' abrupt movement had given him.

The latter made no reply. The knocking became louder.

"Someone's at the door!" Truphemus repeated. "Shall I open it?"

"Go to the Devil!" cried Aloysius.

Truphemus had a character so well-conformed that he welcomed these words as consent. It must also be admitted that he was not displeased to find a pretext for breaking of a conversation so badly begun. Hazard favored him in that respect, since Quiet House never had visitors, and he hastened to take advantage of the stroke of luck. He had, however, not taken account of a very particular circumstance. It had been so long since the door had been opened, and the hinges and metal fittings had so completely rusted up, that he strove in vain to pull the batten towards him. The visitor was still knocking.

"Enough! Enough!" cried Truphemus, on a note belonging to an as-yet-undiscovered octave. He had seized the inte-

---

[63] I have resisted a strong temptation to edit this "letter," which—as the reader will shortly discover—could not actually have been written, and if it had been, would not have manifested the particular state of relative ignorance that it does. Merely shifting the last few sentences into the future tense would not, however, solve the problem. It is therefore necessary for the reader to suppose that Frank has been mentally composing this missive as he walks to Quiet House, anticipating a plaint that he will never, in fact, commit to paper.

rior door-knob with both hands, and was pulling hard, with his feet braced on the floor, but in vain.

Meanwhile, Aloysius, recovering from his fit of exasperation, heard the racket. He took it into his head to discover the cause. At the first glance, he divined Truphemus' difficulty. "Hold on!" he shouted to him. And, passing his long and fleshless arms around his companion's waist, he tugged on Truphemus, who was tugging on the door.

"Push!" they shouted at the visitor.

The visitor gave the door a vigorous kick; the batten opened; the hinges turned—but the movement was so abrupt that Truphemus fell backwards on top of Aloysius, who fell down. As they fell, they knocked over two enormous demijohns—fortunately empty—which broke, upsetting a rack of retorts in their turn. There was a rattling sound, and an indescribable confusion of men and shards of glass…upon which Frank Kerry, the blond resident of the Hoboken hill, gazed in profound astonishment.

Falling is easy. Getting up again is more complicated—though less so for Aloysius than his companion. Aloysius succeeded in getting to his feet quite rapidly, but Truphemus, in view of his rotundity, found himself in the situation of a tortoise awkwardly posed on its back. Aloysius took him by the arm, but in vain; the scientist's back slid along the floor, no projection serving as a point of support. He uttered plaintive and desperate squeals.

"Wait," said Frank to Aloysius. "I'll help you." He seized the other arm and placed his foot against one of Truphemus' feet. Aloysius did likewise, and the two of them, releasing a vigorous "Hup!" succeeded in replacing the ball on its axis. It oscillated briefly, then became motionless. It was done.

Then the three individuals looked at one another, without saying a word.

Truphemus was definitely a man of strong character; he was the first to recover his self-possession. Bowing to he young man, he said: "Thank you, sir. Please come in. Would you care to tell us the object of your visit?"

Frank bowed to the man who had addressed him, and followed the two scientists. "I wanted to talk to you." he said, "about a matter of the utmost importance."

"Let's go into my study," said Aloysius.

Chains and pulleys grated, to Frank's great surprise, and a short while afterwards the three men were in Aloysius' private box.

"Go on, sir!" said the scientist.

"I'm not superfluous?" asked Truphemus.

"Oh," said Aloysius, addressing himself to the young man, "I have no secrets from my companion."

Frank was not without a certain feeling of embarrassment. What surprised him most was that his beloved was dependent, by virtue of family ties or some other circumstance, on one of these two scarcely seductive individuals. "One of you," he said, finally, "must be the father of a charming, adorable young woman that lives in this house?"

"That's me," said Aloysius.

"Very well! Sir, I come, as an honest man, to ask for your daughter's hand in marriage. My name is Frank Kerry, I'm rich, my position is independent, and all of my life's happiness is in your hands…"

He would have continued, but he was prevented from doing so by a bizarre occurrence. At the first words of his request, Truphemus had crossed his arms and closed his eyes; then little strident whistling noises had begun to escape from his lips. A sort of dull rumbling had begun in Aloysius' throat. These two sounds had merged, in contrasting tones, and increased in volume. There had been a sudden explosion.

The two scientists were laughing, and laughing. Truphemus' abdomen inflated and deflated like trampoline on which a clown was bouncing; Aloysius' entire body was shaking, its various parts clicking like a multiplicity of castanets…

And Frank looked at them, interrupted, bewildered, asking himself what was so violently funny about a lover of the

170

infinite asking to be united with the most beautiful creation of natural forces…

Patiently, however, he waited. A few words were beginning to escape the breathless lips of the two scientists.

"In marriage!" said Aloysius.

"At her age!" added Truphemus.

"A bride!"

"Five years old!"

While the two chemists recovered from this nervous shock, and Frank braced himself to listen to the necessary explanations, all of a sudden…

X

Events were happening down below of a character that presented a very particular interest.

When Truphemus, hearing knocking at the door, had gone back into the house, followed a few minutes later by Aloysius, Netty, whom they had left weeping profusely and screaming at the top of her voice, had immediately raised her head. Looking through her splayed fingers, she had convinced herself that the affair of the broken windows would have no consequences. Then she started laughing and executing one of those naïve dances—rudiments of the choreographic art—that only children can imagine. Then, placing the index-finger of her right hand on the index finger of her left, extended in the direction of the house, she manifested by that gesture, repeated several times, the scant importance that she attached to paternal wrath, even admitting that it existed.

Afterwards, doubtless to give vent to the exasperation to which she found herself prey, she started running around the garden, plucking flowers, throwing them into the air and then trampling them. Then she returned to the pavilion, where she tore up a few soft furnishings—but these salutary exercises appeared insufficient to repair her lost tranquility. Suddenly, her face took on an indescribable expression of satisfaction; her gaze was turned towards the house at that moment. There, for the first time in three months, the door—by courtesy of a forgetfulness that must be attributed to Aloysius' troubled state of mind—stood open.

Netty approached the door on tiptoe and stretched out her neck. It was at that moment that the pulleys were drawing up the scientists and the young man in the box in question.

The spectacle that the young girl had before her eyes certainly had nothing seductive about it; on seeing her pause hesitantly at the top of the staircase leading down into the cellar, one might have thought her an exile from some celestial world, gazing curiously into the antechamber of an infernal place.

She listened. Not a sound. She was alone. She undoubtedly felt a certain dread, but her curiosity was so powerful! She had so often desired to penetrate these hermetically-sealed rooms! Abruptly she decided...she moved forwards, hesitantly extending one foot, then the other, her ears continually alert. She eventually found herself in the laboratory.

At that moment, Truphemus and Aloysius burst out laughing.

Netty looked around. All these new objects were extremely confusing: nothing but carboys, cylinders, long-necked flasks; the most bizarre mixtures filling glass vessels; then immense stove on which new preparations, amalgams and as-yet-incomplete compounds were simmering....

She ran to the console whose indicator buttons were connected to the motors operating the chains. She put out her hand, then withdrew it, then finally ran her fingers rapidly over the various buttons, as she might have done on the keyboard of a piano...

Immediately, she recoiled uttering a cry of fright.

All the mechanisms were brought into play simultaneously. The chains grated; the pulleys turned madly; the system of counterweights, losing its equilibrium, no longer worked; the boxes were descending with vertiginous rapidity, then rising up again with vigorous leaps, as if they had acquired a new strength.

Netty ran—and, like a bird that has flown into a room through an open window, she bumped into every jutting object and every corner. She stumbled, grabbed hold of something…it was the motor of the large electrical machine…and off went the immense glass disk, gliding between its cushions…!

A torrent of sparks flew into the air like a shower of stars, with an increasingly powerful crackling sound.

Netty was terrified. She wanted to flee; she wanted to get to the door, but she bumped into everything as she went. Retorts, flasks, alembics and carboys shattered. Liquids flooded out; gases regained their liberty.

The most unexpected compounds were realized then. The chemical elements were confronted with one another. It was a conflict of the fundamental forces of nature.

The boxes were still going upon and down, shaking the three unfortunates, one of whom had come to Quiet House in search of happiness.

In a strange glow that was incessantly changing color, Netty was still running…

Asphyxia seized her by the throat and cast her down…

Then there was a frightful explosion…

And everything collapsed.

Thus perished the inhabitants of Quiet House, and that is why Frank Kerry never found the happiness of which he had dreamed.

Rémy de Gourmont: *The Automaton*
(1889)

Rémy de Gourmont (1858-1915) was born into an aristo-cratic family whose fortunes had been much reduced, not so much by the 1789 Revolution as by the depredations of the English during the Napoleonic Wars. In 1876, he went to Caen to study law, but when his father gave him permission, the following year, to continue his studies in Paris, he followed a primrose path very familiar in the annals of French literature, abandoning his studies in order to devote himself to "livres et l'amour" [books and love]. He observed, in a typically me-thodical fashion, that the former would develop his intellect and the latter his sensuality, thus completing his personality in an appropriately holistic fashion. He remained permanently preoccupied with the ideas of self-development and personali-ty and with contrasting dichotomies: male/female; thought/emotion, body/soul, materialism/idealism and so on. His ex-ploration of such complementarities guided him into all man-ner of philosophical and moral heresies, but he retained the aristocratic aloofness communicated by his early upbringing.

In order to make ends meet, de Gourmont applied for a post at the Bibliothèque Nationale in 1881, and many of his early publications were educational works produced in that context, but he gradually built up a successful career in jour-nalism, primarily as a literary critic. He became the principal theorist and chronicler of a movement first labeled "Decadent" and then rechristened "Symbolist," but his first novel, *Merlette* (1886) was undistinguished. In 1887, he met Berthe Courrière, who had formerly been the mistress of Joris-Karl Huysmans and had served as the latter's guide to the occult underworld that was chronicled in such graphic detail in *Là-Bas* (1891). She captivated de Gourmont far more powerfully than she had contrived to do with the misogynistic Huysmans, and he incorporated modified images of her into much of his subsequent work.

Symptoms of the fact that de Goumont's relationship with Berthe soon ran into trouble are probably visible in "L'automate: conte philosophique" (1889), although he subsequently published much more clinical analyses of her character and of the relationship's inevitable breakdown in his first successful novel, *Sixtine* (1890; tr. as *Very Woman*) and the novella *Le fantôme* (1891). De Gourmont never included "L'automate" in any of his collections, presumably because he was dissatisfied with its relative unsubtlety, but it was reprinted in a 1982 omnibus of *Histoires magiques et autres récits*. It is one of the most graphic examples of the *contes cruels* he wrote under the influence of Villiers de l'Isle-Adam, whom he first met in 1888 and with whom he formed a friendship based on their mutual distress at having fallen so far in a world that would not recognize their intrinsic nobility. Like "Quiet House"—but in a very different fashion—the story probably owes something to the example of Villiers' *L'Eve future.*

De Gourmont also formed a friendship with Alfred Vallette, and helped him to found the *Mercure de France* in 1890, which went on to become the primary vehicle of literary Symbolism, and for which he did much of his finest work— although one of his early political articles got him the sack from the Bibliothèque Nationale and forced him to make a living thereafter from his pen. Through Vallette, de Gourmont met the young Alfred Jarry, who ploughed his inheritance into a short-lived *avant-garde* Symbolist periodical *L'Ymagier*, which he and de Gourmont co-edited, but de Gourmont could not follow the literary course towards surrealism followed by the younger writer, his style remaining much more staid and polished. De Goumont's reputation soared—Anatole France described him as "France's greatest living writer"—but his ambitions were rudely undermined when he contracted what was then known as "tubercular lupus," although it is actually an auto-immune disease. Its early effects are often seen in the

175

skin of the face, and de Gourmont was horribly disfigured by that phase of the disease, forcing him to become a recluse. He continued to write voluminously, and successfully, but he endured a painful martyrdom in parallel, which colored his attitudes to life and love deeply.

The forced detachment of his subsequent interest in erotic matters eventually resulted in the production of the remarkable *Physique de l'amour: Essai sur l'instinct sexuel* (1903; tr. as *The Natural Philosophy of Love*, although a more accurate rendition would be "The Physics of Love: An essay on the Sexual instinct"). There is a sense in which that work was the ultimate culmination of the thought-process whose first graphic illustration was "L'automate:" the extensive contemplation of the possibility that we are all automata, especially in respect of our sexual behavior. When he wrote the *conte cruel*, de Gourmont probably knew little about the science that features in the story as a kind of malevolent haunter—he dedicated the tale to "Théodore Ribot"—although the forename of the principal French pioneer of clinical psychology was actually Théodule—but he made up for that lack thereafter, and achieved a dramatic sophistication of the perspective here presented in casually brutal terms.

Like Ulbach's "Story of a Naiad," this story is not a scientific romance in the usual sense of the term, its speculative element taking on no material form, but it supplements such stories as "Perfectibility" and "Quiet House" in providing a particularly graphic example of the philosophical horror that the scientific world-view induced in some of those who reacted against it—and also of the fascination that it exerted upon them simultaneously.

"There you are!" concluded Laube. "Do you understand? Vaguely. Oh well, imagine two clocks; one chimes, the other doesn't. Both keep equally good time. In the one that chimes there are two sets of works: one controls the hands, the other the chimes. Stop the works controlling the chimes, and you have a clock exactly similar to the first, which tells the time just as perfectly; we think them both perfect. The chiming mechanism is, therefore, a superfluity, an embellishment.

"It's the same for consciousness—I mean psychological consciousness.

"In the human clock, consciousness is the chimes. Hold on, I'll extrapolate my comparison. We've supposed that our two clocks work with equal perfection—that's the term we've employed and we are, indeed, dealing with ideal clocks, demonstrative instruments as superior to marine chronometers from Liverpool as those same chronometers are to a trinket-watch from the Rue de la Paix—but it's quite evident that whichever of our two clocks has the simpler mechanism will also be the better one, the less vulnerable to imperceptible derangements, the less sensitive to atmospheric influences. You'll admit, therefore, that the clock without chimes is mathematically superior to the one that's complicated by an extra series of works. If you've followed my reasoning, you'll reach the conclusion yourself: take away man's chimes—which is to say, his consciousness—and you'll have lessened the probability of his going wrong."

"So you're being serious," Mérillon replied, after a pause. "You expect me to believe…"

"Have you understood, yes or no?" Laube resumed, not without impatience.

"It's absurd, my dear chap, completely absurd. So the ideal for man would be to lose his consciousness, to act without knowing he is acting, and, in consequence, no longer to think! Automatism, therefore, would be a superior state for humankind!"

"Precisely. You're an engraver, and in your business you don't just have the hand, you have talent. Here's a *Dante*, after Raphael's *Dispute*,[64] which is proof enough. Well, be sincere: aren't the etchings with which you're most content, in general, those that you've dashed off in a frenzy of inspiration, in a state of mind in which, carried away and overwhelmed by fever, far from calculating each stroke, you've put them together with an unconscious precision?"

Mérillon admitted that, as any artist would have done; there were instances of his work, the best, that he scarcely remembered having executed. "My *Dante* is one of those—but that's not automatism; it's inspiration."

"Yes, artists and poets, the most automatic people on Earth, would be quite astonished if one demonstrated to them, piece by piece, the mechanism that they call Inspiration. Inspire me O Muse! *Sicelides Musae*…!" And Laube, pitilessly, burst out laughing.

"Let's see," he continued. "Let's take a poet. He imagines writing a sonnet to his mistress on this theme: *You're cruel to me, but you'll grow old. When you have white hair, I'll tell you that you made me suffer, and then your regrets—your belated regrets—will ameliorate my pain slightly.* You've identified, haven't you, one of Petrarch's sonnets—it's sufficiently well-known, thanks to the imitations that Ronsard, Voltaire and even Béranger made, the latter two stripping away the mysticism that gave it its charm. The argument crops up again in many verses, many letters from unknown lovers: *You'll be sorry one day, but it will be too late.* That's it, fundamentally. And the poet imagines what he'll suffer: images come into his head, immediately translated by the various verbal representations of *pain*. She'll grow old: *weak eyes, silver hair, dark clothes, faded complexion*. Hence *no feminine pride*; he'll no longer be afraid; she'll be *disarmed*; he'll tell

---

[64] The full title by which this painting is usually known—which is, of course, relevant to the story's dispute—is *The Dispute of the Blessed Sacrament*.

178

all; *the martyrdom* of each moment—and, as an analytical representation of the time elapsed, the words *years, days, hours* surge forth. Here, quite naturally, an association of sad ideas: *it will be too late.* Then the bitter joy of a bitter *revenge: You'll feel it yourself, and I'll suffer less (for you'll have sympathized with me)*—that last thought remains unexpressed, the poet allows his dream to die in an irony.

"All these ideas or images, as you see, link together perfectly, and, after having thought for two or three hours, the poet—who thinks in verse as soon as the thought becomes precise—will sense inspiration and write his sonnet as if under dictation. And take note that all of this preliminary mechanism will have escaped him, all the more so because his mistress is a habitual, if not constant, object of his thought." Laube got up and took up a book, riffling through its pages briefly. "You can verify my analysis, reproduce it yourself. It's the 11th sonnet: *Se la mia vita dell'aspro tormento.*"

"All right," replied Mérillon, stuffing his pipe. "I believe you, but if the analysis applies to me, goodbye graver. My intelligence is in my hands, my muse is my pipe."

"Fool!" Laube cried. "You're giving me arguments against yourself. Just repeat your sentence, which I'll put into my thesis. My intelligence…." He had caught hold of a piece of paper and wrote on it, while tapping his heels feverishly on the ground—one of his characteristic actions. "….is in my hands and my muse…she's a show-off, your muse."

"Don't make fun of Helicon!"

Laube, very cheerful, raised his head again and swept back his long blond hair with a stroke of his hand. His face was lit up, as if he had found a treasure. "Did you have a brainwave? Let's see…and my muse is my pipe. Nice, to be sure, that's nice. My dear chap, if you were only in the Institut or an influential critic, I could use that as your epigraph. Damn! You're a superior being, though—you're making rapid progress towards the ideal, absolute automatism."

"Thanks," said Mérillon, polishing his fine chestnut-colored moustache with his thumb and forefinger, "I think I know what I'm doing, feeling alive. It'll be fun, your automatism!"

"He'll never understand. Neither fun nor depressing—nothing. You'll do what you need to do without knowing it; you'll eat, sleep, walk like a mechanism, without stomachaches, without nightmares, without embarrassing mistakes. You'll love…."

"Mechanically. Thanks again."

Laube shrugged his shoulders. "That's where you are now: love, women…it's bound to happen. It's a phase. After that one goes on to God, the immortality of the soul. Human infirmity always reverts to ratiocination about the only two beings that don't exist: woman and God!"

"I don't know anything about God, but I like to imagine…."

"God is the Unconscious, the Infinite automaton. I'll spare you the arguments. A being without limits had no consciousness of itself, sine there's nothing outside it and, metaphysically speaking, consciousness is the sensation of its own limits. Let's put such lofty subtleties aside. We're on the subject of woman. Well, my dear chap, I've given woman a great deal of thought, and I've suffered in the process—that's the way to get to know her. Having escaped from her influence, I've analyzed her. I've thrown the plumb-line into the well and I've got to the bottom of her. Listen…."

His eyes sparkling, his lips apart, his body leaning forward, his right hand extended in a demonstrative gesture, Laube took on an inspired air that was bordering on the fantastic. A blazing coal fire reddened his thin face, his bulbous forehead, his swept-back hair and his long beard. The light of the fire—for the lamp had gone out—projected the shadow of his straight nose between his two eyebrows. He was clad in a brown dressing-gown, like a Franciscan habit, and in that mansard cell he truly resembled some monk of the time of the philosopher's stone.

Mérillon took his pipe out of his teeth and looked at his friend with an anxiety tined with fear. He was a decent fellow, impressionable and—according to the guidance of his whim—capable of work or idleness, indifference or passion. His hair, which fell in curls to the collar of his velvet waistcoat made the bourgeois in the street think: "Oho, an artist!" He was proud of that, but, at the end of the day, he cared only for his art, Juliette—a beautiful girl who lived with him—and his friend Laube, a Russian with a German name who had been born in Constantinople, brought up in Italy, received a doctorate of philosophy in Heidelberg and now lived in Paris as a student.

"Listen," Laube went on, fire in his gaze, lowering his voice, emphasizing the two significant words in his sentence as if he wanted to unite them into one: "*Woman* is an *automaton.*"

Mérillon submitted meekly to the impression. He went pale, and remained motionless.

Laube went on: "Woman is an automaton. I'm sure of it. I've proved it. It's here." He struck a large pile of papers heaped up on the table with his hand. "It's here. She lives, she speaks, she thinks, she loves—yes, loves—without knowing that she is living, speaking, thinking or loving. You've seen them laugh, cry, faint, scream in pain or pleasure: automata! Ants and bees, which do their work so well, are intelligent creatures that are not conscious of their intelligence, clocks without chimes; many people are the same. Consciousness is only given to a small number, to the degree that we, the others, possess it. There are many steps between the consciousness of a Goethe and that of a shoemaker. You, an artist, have moments of automatism. Among women, one in 100,000 attains consciousness, but the others—all of them—are automata.

"A woman hangs around your neck, she embraces you, speaks softly to you, then, an instant later, in a bad mood, ignores you, speaks harshly to you, tends towards sarcasm. She doesn't know what she's doing. The internal witness is absent. Passion, the all-consuming desire that you see in their eyes, the languor after pleasure that is painted there in such charming colors and subtle tomes, is all unconscious isn't it? But her love itself is nothing but an automatic movement; she loves you as she hates you, without suspecting it. You talk to her, and she replies, without knowing that she is replying.

"Oh, my friend, these creatures for whom we suffer and sometimes die, are dolls, playthings. They don't know that you're happy with them, they don't know that you're suffering, and if you die before the eyes of one who no longer loves you, she won't know that you're dying for her. Do you not see them, always dominated by the present impression, pressing on towards the momentary goal without seeing anything beyond, without prejudging the consequences, like a mount that carries its rider, desire, wherever its whim takes it. They're all desire; the semblance of will that one thinks one sees in them is nothing but the sum of accumulated desires, which advance blindly, like a mass whose weight is its only locomotive mechanism.

"The psychology of woman—what a combination of words! There's no consciousness there, only physical laws. Sensation that is not reasoned is no more interesting to study than the percussion that makes a stick of dynamite explode. What is the soul? It's consciousness. The council of Mâcon, which has been denied but whose existence I have verified, was right at least to raise this suspicion: does a woman have a soul?

"The day when I discovered this, the automatism of woman, I felt the most poignant anguish that a human creature can support: the illusion had become impossible to maintain. It made me weep. Now I can see, and, in the presence of a woman, I experience the curiosity of a technician inspecting the steel works of a new machine. For they don't all resemble one another, in spite of that fact; they have different ways of being unconscious. One can still amuse oneself with that. And what's good about it is that they sometimes conduct themselves as if they had the capacity to watch themselves act; one might think that they were reasoning. That held me up for some time. Oh yes, they reason, but—and this is the long and short of it—without knowing it, as an adding-machine reasons. That's what constitutes their superiority in the accomplishment of the function for which they are born: love. The role of woman is to love, to perpetuate; they carry it out marvelously; nothing distracts them, except the influence of the man to whom attraction points them, necessarily, as the Sun directs a sundial. Thus, *woman* is an *automaton*. Examine your Juliette carefully, my dear chap."

Laube had concluded.

Mérillon got up, his legs a trifle unsteady, and he went out slowly, as if under the dominion of a dream, having said but one word: "Goodnight."

When he got home, he found Juliette asleep in bed. He gazed at her anxiously.

"Automaton!" he sniggered—then shrugged his shoulders, as if to say: "After all, who knows?" But his weak head, disturbed by Laube's strange monologue, filled up with irrationalities, and the word *automaton* suggested to him very clearly the image of those waxwork women that one sees in glass cases in physiological exhibitions at the Barrière du Trône, respiring with a mechanical movement of their breasts and abdomen. In the candlelight, Juliette's face, beneath her black hair took on a very similar tint, shiny and livid. He looked at her interestedly then; she seemed worthy of attention, like a "curious and cleverly fashioned" item.

In the respite granted to him as the hallucination gradually wore off, he decided to go to bed, but not without precaution, fearfully, starting at every contact. When she woke up, putting her arms around his neck to draw him to her, wrapping herself around her, he shivered. Then, rebelliously, he tried to release himself—and having got one of his hands free, he pinched her.

She squealed. "Oh! That's not nice! Swine."

He burst lout laughing. "Hey—an automaton that weeps!"

Afraid in her turn, thinking that he was drunk, abruptly annoyed, she turned to the wall, saying goodnight in a dry tone.

"Perfect! The automaton goes to sleep, the automaton sleeps. Truly, that's *curious and cleverly fashioned*." And after a further snigger, satisfied at no longer feeling so close, he fell silent.

He got up the next morning hardly having slept, starting at every movement Juliette made, with the fear of having of a very complicated and dangerous machine next to him, like a workman sleeping a few inches away from a driving belt.

"What's wrong with you, Jacques?" she asked, waking up in her turn, disturbed by the night's bizarre occurrences.

"Nothing. Leave me alone. I'm going to work. Leave me alone, will you?"

Used to such abruptness, especially in the morning—for Mérillon was grumpy during the early hours of the day, wont to retreat into absolute mutism—she did not persist, falling silent in her turn.

Then, at a loose end, she opened the piano and strummed the keys. This aural distraction did not usually trouble the engraver. Sometimes, when he was in a good mood, he even said that he enjoyed it, finding work easier to the rhythm of the tinkling notes. This morning, the music threw him back into his obsession; raising his head, he watched the fingers go back and forth across the keyboard, full of curiosity, as attentive as a child before Vaucanson's flute-player.

"Excellent, that mechanism." Then, louder: "Very pleasant—go on."

To see her eat was such a great astonishment for him that he forgot to eat himself, leaving his plate full.

"Aren't you hungry, then? Are you feeling ill?"

"It's so amusing, watching you."

He was no longer afraid. Curiosity replaced the initial fear; he was getting used to it. And he said: "Dear little machine, you don't know what you're doing. You go on and on, and you only attain the shadow of pleasure, because you're unaware of it, your pleasure. You aren't like me, a sentient reed, and when all the fires of sensuality overwhelm you...."

He stopped the parody here.

This dissection of love did not take long in coming to seem fastidious. He became disgusted with himself, limiting himself to questions, the answers to which he waited for impatiently, and received with the attention of a physician observing a rare disease. He turned the poor girl's brain around, probed it, dissected it with a scalpel, and squeezed it as children do with an orange, in order to draw out every last one of the banalities swelling that population of cells. And during these operations, abetted by his obsession, he noted down Juliette's words—by which means he learned her entire history, without understanding it.

Believing it to be a profound interest of affection, she let herself go, searching the depths of her memory for recollections and the bottom of her heart for tenderness. As for him, he congratulated himself on his skill in analyzing mechanisms, murmuring internally: "What an admirable machine that woman is!" When she had nothing more to tell him, he grew bored; with no curiosity remaining, he fell prey to a depression, whose weight increased day by day.

When he went out, it was with expressions and precautions like the eccentric of which Zimmermann gave an account, who could not see a woman without feeling sick. He kept as far away as possible from those he met, closed his eyes as they passed by, and came home in despair, with the sensation of having been persecuted by all the automata of Paris.

Laube gave rise to an analogous impression. He had only gone to see him once since the evening when he had thrown him so badly off balance, and which still made him shiver three weeks later. One evening, when he was wandering distractedly through the streets, they found themselves face to face.

"Why, it's Mérillon! What have you been doing?"

"Nothing."

"That's very little for a chap like you."

185

"Nothing. Finished. I'm bored. You know Juliette—well, it was true."

"What? Oh…!" Laube did not dare to go on, thinking of some feminine treason—and Mérillon did, in fact, have the appearance of a rather melancholy victim of love—so he continued: "All the more reason for coming to see me. You know that I never go out in the evenings, on principle, to the homes of friends where there are women. They're such sluts. And during the day, I philosophize."

"How's it going?"

"Slowly. A new subject. I'm short of observations. And when I ask for information, people give me news items or dirty stories. They tell you some obscenity, and add: 'Well, what do you expect? That's feminine psychology for you!' They simply don't understand."

"It was true!" Mérillon continued, who was in no state to comprehend three sentences in succession.

"I'll come to see you, then. Shake you up a little! You're alone yes?"

"Why? No. She's there, always there. She comes, she goes. She horrifies me."

"Go on!"

"It was true. I've made notes, I've written astonishing things—yes, astonishing. You'll have all that, I promise you. It was true. Oh, Laube, it's all your fault. I was happy, why did you tell me that? Why not leave me my deception? Truth, ob-ser-va-tion—I've had enough of them. It'll end badly, badly, badly. Leave me alone. Why are you staring at me like that? I'm not an automaton—not me, sir!"

He turned on his heel and disappeared into the shadows, while Laube, disconcerted, said to himself: "And that's what a girl does to an intelligent man! Another one lost. Loving those creatures! The poor wretch! Automatism always exists in extreme passion: love, despair, etc. That's a chapter I might have forgotten. Ah, a lucky encounter. Unless he goes mad, which will come in the third part—to follow."

Laube went on his way.

Mérillon went home, his excitement diminished, prey to a state of depression that frightened Juliette. Without saying a word, he looked at her with bleak, staring, animal eyes, and—without any philosophical implication, but, on the contrary, with a profound pity—she voiced a thought that haunted her lover.

"One might think him a machine," she murmured. "What is he afraid of? I've never seen him like this. My God! How much he's changed!"

He wandered around the apartment for some time, rummaging in the corners as if, like some dying animal, he were looking for a place to lie down.

The next day, as he seemed more lucid, she questioned him gently, seeking a cause for his black moods, thinking that it might be some annoyance in his work, some frustrated ambition. He listened with eyes in which sad astonishment was readable, making no reply.

He maintained this desolate appearance for a long time, and for days on end Juliette watched him prowling around, looking like a dog begging to be fondled—but at the slightest contact, he shrank back. The repulsion that he had felt at the beginning of the crisis seemed to return, further accentuated: the instinctive movement of a visionary driving back a hideous apparition. Terror invaded his troubled eyes; he fled from Juliette, turning his head at her approach, hesitating to go to bed at night, only yielding to a nervous exhaustion—for he no longer slept.

She trembled; he watched her from the corners of his eyes, like an enemy, with sly glances, collecting himself, ready to pounce.

"I'm definitely dealing with a madman," she said to herself. "My God, what should I do? What will happen? Oh, he'll never dare to touch me. I've heard it said that madmen submit to the authority of people who are dear to them. Oh, that's what he's like!"

Not for an instant did it cross her mind to leave, or to alert Jacques' friends; she wanted to try to save him, at least to spare her lover the shame of a padded cell. She had the justified fear of hospitals that poor people always feel. In spite of her fear and sadness, she smiled more than she had in better days, treating him like a child, scolding him gently, trying to play with him.

As he relaxed, unintentionally, she took heart again, in spite of the suspicion that she always saw in his dull eyes. That would pass.

One morning, on waking up, she found him standing up, his clothing in disarray, the front of his tie hanging over his shoulder, with a shoe on one foot and a slipper on the other. With his arms crossed and his head held high, he was staring at her.

"What a get-up! What are you doing there? Come here!"

She leapt out of bed, seized him in her arms and tried to draw him to her, intending to tame him with her caresses, for his fixed appearance was frightening.

"Don't touch me! Don't touch me!"

He took several steps back. She continued forwards, arms still outstretched. He recoiled further, she followed him.

Suddenly, the expression on his face, which was bordering on ferocity, became fearful, and he fled, going to hide in the kitchen, still crying: "Don't touch me! Don't touch me!"

There, when she joined him, he assumed a defensive attitude, like a timid cornered animal. She caught up with him in a corner. Then releasing himself violently, he seized a carving-knife from the table, and with a single blow, sank it into her breast.

She collapsed.

At the sight of the blood spurted from the wound when the knife was withdrawn, Mérillon became excited. He brandished his weapon, from which blood was dripping, crying: "The automaton bleeds! The automaton bleeds."

He burst out laughing.

"Go on, go on! Bleed, then—bleed! Bleed!"

And he attacked her furiously, stabbing her randomly with the bloody blade.

"Bleed, bleed, automaton!"

He released a deep sigh, and, as if relieved, said: "*The automaton's dead!*"

Putting the carving-knife back on the table, he calmly went out of the kitchen and, without even darting a backward glance at his crime, went to sit down at his work-desk.

The boards, the papers, the tools, everything was stained with blood, for he had red hands and his sleeves were soaked.

He worked, hacking the wax randomly with disorderly strokes. He worked for a long time, and then he went out.

The streets, at mid-day, were fully of people in a hurry: workers and clerks, running to hasty meals. They looked, astonished, at his bloody hands and clothes, his incoherent costume, but as he was quite calm, after glancing at him, they mostly continued on their way. Little by little, though, more attention was directed towards him. Then, seeing that he was being observed, he stopped in the middle of the road, struck a pose, and cried: "Well! Yes, I've killed an automaton!"

"A madman!" they cried. "Arrest him."

"An automaton. A thing like this!" And he advanced towards a woman who was trotting along, with a little basket on her arm.

The woman screamed; they threw themselves upon him.

He was dragged to the guard-post, still shouting, to the great delight of the crowd that was escorting him: "*I've killed an automaton!*"

They could get nothing else out of him. In the padded cell where he was locked up, he retained his obsession, and seemed very proud of having committed an act that he doubtless considered very difficult and very rare.

Laube went to see him, without being able to make himself recognized.

"Poor fellow, weak in the head," the philosopher said. "That's what transcendent philosophy can do to an imbecile! When I've finished my thesis, I'll write an article on him for the *Archives of Comparative Psychopathy*."

Marcel Schwob: *The Future Terror*
(1891)

Marcel Schwob (1867-1905) came from a family with
strong literary connections; his father had been at school with
Gustave Flaubert, was a friend of Théophile Gautier and
Théodore de Banville, and had once collaborated with Jules
Verne when the latter was still a struggling playwright and
diehard Romantic. His maternal uncle, Léon Cahun, was a
successful writer of historical fiction, mostly for younger
readers. Schwob established his own literary reputation within
the Decadent Movement with the Poesque short stories in
Coeur double [Duplicitous Heart] (1891) and the more varied
Decadent tales in *Le Roi au masque d'or* (1892; partly translated, along with items from other collectons, as *The King in
the Golden Mask*) before going on to greater success with the
lachrymose novel *Le livre de Monelle* [The Book of Monelle]
(1894), the collection *Vies imaginaries* [Imaginary Lives]
(1896)—a series of imaginary biographies of medieval characters about whose actual lives little or nothing is known—and a
fictionalized study of *Les croisade des enfants* [The Children's
Crusade] (1896), before ill-health put an end to his productivi-
ty and then his life.

Schwob was held in the highest possible esteem by his
contemporaries. Oscar Wilde dedicated "The Sphinx" to him
and entrusted the task of polishing the prose of *Salomé* to him
and Pierre Louÿs. Alfred Jarry dedicated *Ubu roi* to him, and
consented to don mourning-dress for his funeral (having earlier caused a tremendous scandal by turning up to Stéphane
Mallarmé's funeral in a pair of yellow shoes borrowed from
Rachilde). He would doubtless have gone on to spectacular
further achievements had his career not been but short, and his
intense interest in Medieval history might not have prevented
him from undertaking further excursions into scientific romance. "La Terreur future" is the only example in *Coeur
double*, but *Le Roi au masque d'or* includes a prehistoric rom-

ance in the vein popularized by J.-H. Rosny *aîné*. Both stories are marginal to the genre, and the particular item of automated machinery featured in this futuristic tale is incidental to the thrust of the Symbolist allegory, but it nevertheless provides an interesting example of the nightmarish imagery to which the Frankenstein syndrome can give rise.

The organizers of the Revolution had pale faces and eyes of steel. Their vestments were black and close-fitted, their speech curt and arid. They had become this way, having once been different—for they had preached to crowds, invoking the names of love and pity. They had traveled the streets of capitals with belief in their mouths, proclaiming the union of populations and universal liberty. They had inundated dwellings with proclamations full of charity; they had announced the new religion that would conquer the world; they had gathered initiates enthusiastic for the nascent faith.

Then, in the dusk of the night of its execution, their manner changed. They disappeared into a town hall where their secret headquarters were. Bands of shadows ran along the streets, overseen by strict inspectors. A murmur was heard, full of deathly presentiments. The environs of banks and rich houses trembled with new, subterranean life. Sudden outbursts of clattering voices were heard in distant quarters. A buzz of machines in motion, a trepidation of the ground, terrible sounds of ripping cloth; then a stifling silence, similar to the calm before a storm—and all of a sudden, the tempest was unleashed, bloody and enflamed.

It burst in response to the signal of a flamboyant rocket launched into the black sky from the Town Hall. A general cry was released from the breasts of the rebels, and there was a surge that shook the city. Large buildings were trembling, broken from beneath; a rumble that had never been heard before passed over the Earth in a single wave. Flames rose up like bloody pitchforks along the instantly-darkened streets, with furious projections of girders, gables, slates, chimneys, iron T-beams and ashlars. Window-glass flew everywhere, multicolored by firework sprays. Jets of steam burst out of pipes, gushing out from various floors. Balconies exploded, twisted out of shape. Bed-linen reddened capriciously, like dying furnaces, behind distended windows. Everything was full of horrid light, trails of sparks, black smoke and clamor.

Buildings, falling apart, were reduced to jagged fragments, their shadows covered with a red cloth; behind the buildings that collapsed on every side the fireballs spread. The crumbling masses seemed to be enormous heaps of red-hot iron. The city was nothing but a curtain of flames, bright in places, somber blue in others, with points of profound intensity, in which passing black shapes could be seen gesticulating.

The portals of churches were inflated by the terrified crowd, which flowed everywhere in long black ribbons. Faces were turned, anxiously, towards the sky, mute with fear, eyes staring in horror. There were eyes that were wide open, by dint of stupid astonishment, and eyes hardened by the black rays they short forth, and eyes red with fury, mirroring the reflections of the conflagration, and eyes shining and pleading with anguish, and eyes that were wanly resigned, whose tears had ceased to flow, and eyes tremulously agitated, whose pupils roamed incessantly over every part of the scene, and eyes that were looking inwards. In the procession of livid faces, the only visible differences were in the eyes—and the streets, amid the shafts of sinister light hollowed out in the gutters, seemed braided by moving eyes.

Enveloped by a continual fusillade, human hedgerows retreated into the squares, pursue by other human hedgerows that advanced implacably, the fleeing company agitating its strangely-illuminated arms tumultuously, while the company on the march was tightly-packed, dense, orderly and resolute, its members moving in step, without hesitation, following silent orders. The barrels of rifles formed single rows of murderous mouths, from which extended long, thin lines of fire, irradiating the night with their mortal stenography. Above the continuous roar, amid the frightful pauses, a singular and uninterrupted crackling sound was audible.

There were also knots of people, grouped in threes, four and fives, interlinked and obscure, above which whirled the flash of straight cavalry sabers and sharpened axes stolen from the arsenals. Thin individuals were brandishing these weapons, furiously cleaving heads furiously, joyfully puncturing breasts, sensuously slashing bellies and trampling the viscera.

And through the avenues, like scintillating meteors, long cylinders of polished steel rolled at high speed, drawn by fearful galloping horses with flowing manes. They looked like cannon whose barrel and breech were the same diameter: at the back, there was a sheet-metal cage manned by two busy men tending a furnace, with a boiler and a pipe from which smoke emerged; at the front, there was a large, shiny and trenchant indented disk mounted at an angle, rotating vertiginously in front of the muzzle of the central tube.[65] Every time an indentation encountered the black hole, a clicking sound was heard.

These galloping machines paused outside the door of each house; vague forms were detached from them, and went in. They came out two by two, charged with bound and moaning parcels. The stokers fed these long human bundles into each steel tube, regularly and methodically. For a second, jutting out to shoulder-level, a discolored and contorted face was visible; then the indentation of the eccentrically-turning disk threw out a head in the course of its revolution. The steel plate remained immutably polished, the rapidity of its movement launching a circle of blood which marked the vacillating walls with geometric figures. A body fell on the roadway, between the machine's large wheels; its bonds broke in the fall and, as a reflex movement of the elbows propped it up on the flagstones, the still-living cadaver ejaculated a red jet.

---

[65] The word I have translated here as "central tube" is *âme*, which is used here in a specific sense to refer to the central element, or axis, of a mechanical assembly, but also retains the more general meaning of "soul" or "heart." The resultant wordplay is sometimes carried over into knowing English references to "the soul of a machine," but does not translate. A few weaker puns of the same stripe have, alas, been lost in this translation, which cannot retain all the sly ambiguity of the original.

Then the rearing horses, their flanks pitilessly lashed by a whip, drew the steel tubes onwards. There was a metallic shriek, a profoundly shrill note in the sonority of the tube, two lines of flame reflected in their periphery, and an abrupt halt in front of a new door.

Save for the lunatics killing in isolation, with naked blades, there was no evident hate or fury—nothing but destruction and orderly massacre, a progressive annihilation, like a continuously rising tide of death, inexorable and inevitable. The men who were giving the orders, proud of their work, surveyed the action with rigid faces, perfectly fixed.

At the corner of one dark street, the clattering hooves of horse encountered a barricade of headless corpses, a heap of trunks. The battery of steel tubes paused amid the flesh; above confusedly contracted arms a forest of fingers was raised towards the sky, pointing in every direction, like the colored spearheads of a future revolt.

Stopping the guillotine-guns, the whinnying horses refused to mount an assault, their nostrils steaming, crushing the backwash of green entrails beneath their iron-shod hooves. Amid the palpitating flesh, between the branch-work of inanimate hands, desperately stiffened, there were spurts of flowing blood.

The priests of the massacre climbed up on the human barricade, into which their feet sank, taking the horses by the head, dragging them by the bridle, while they snorted, and forced the wheels to pass over the scattered limbs whose bones cracked. Standing in the midst of their butchery, faces lit up from within by the Idea and from without by the conflagration, the apostles of annihilation gazed attentively into the depths of the darkness, at the horizon, as if they were expecting to see an unknown star.

Before them they saw an accumulation of broken facades, randomly distributed stone steps and smoking rafters, with bricks, splinters of wood, pieces of paper, scraps of cloth and sandstone paving-blocks in vast numbers, jumbled up in heaps as if hurled by some prodigious hand.

There was also a half-ruined poor-house, in which the chimneys, cut vertically, had released a long band of soot, with branches at different heights. The lower part of the wooden staircase had collapsed, broken half-way on the first floor, with the result that the shaky steps led nowhere in particular, towards rampant flames and contorted cadavers, like a frail footbridge descending from the heavens.

All the interior life of these wretched rooms was visible, exposed to the light of day: the grate of a coal fire; a patched-up peat-burning stove; a brown clay fire-pot; dented black saucepans; rags heaped in corners; a rusty cage from which a few green sprigs still protruded, in which a little grey bird was lying on its back, its feet withdrawn into its belly plumage; scattered medicine-bottles; a camp-bed stood against a wall; torn mattresses from which tufts of seaweed were protruding; pots of withered flowers, mingled with soil and plant debris—and, sitting amid polished floor-tiles, torn away from the grey cement, a little boy face to face with a little girl, triumphantly showing her the brass spindle of a rocket that had fallen there.

The little girl had a spoon stuck in her mouth and was looking at him with a curious expression. The little boy clenched his fingers, whose tender skin was already wrinkled, about a movable lock-nut and, rotating the screw, lost himself in contemplation of the device. They stamped their thin feet in turn, taking their shoes off, profoundly absorbed, not in the least astonished by the air that was coming in or the horrible light that was flooding them—until the little girl, drawing out the spoon that was swelling her cheek, said in a whisper: "That's funny—mama and papa have gone, along with their room. There are big red lights in the streets, and the staircase has fallen."

All this the organizers of the Revolution saw, and the new Sun whose dawn they awaited did not rise—but the idea that they had in their heads suddenly flared up, they experience a sort of glimmer; they vaguely understood a life superior to universal death; the children's smiles broadened, and brought about a revelation; pity descended upon them.

And, with their hands over their eyes, so as not to see all the terrified eyes of the dead—all the eyes that eyelids could no longer cover—they staggered down from the rampart of slaughtered human beings that surrounded the new city, and fled recklessly into the red shadows, amid the racket of galloping machines.

Louis Mullem: *A Rival of Edison*
(1909)

In his youth, Louis Mullem (1836-1908) was a composer of music as well as an author, but he gave up both vocations in order to concentrate on his career as a sober political journalist, which extended from the heyday Second Empire almost to the eve of the Great War. He is still remembered for a notable collection of *Contes d'Amérique* [American Tales], which exhibits the influence of James Fenimore Cooper, but is otherwise almost forgotten in the fields of literature and music. He was sufficiently successful in his subsequent endeavors, however, for the statesman Georges Clemenceau—who was later to negotiate the Treaty of Versailles—to attend his funeral.

"Un Rival d'Edison" is taken from *Contes ondoyants et divers* (1909), a posthumous collection assembled as a memorial by Mullem's friends. The collection is conscientiously dedicated to Clemenceau, but Gustave Geffroy, who wrote the preface, did not bother to stress the author's political achievements, preferring to remember such distant occasions as their chance meeting in a café with Mullem's literary hero, Villiers de l'Isle-Adam, and a Christmas Eve when Mullem played the organ to accompany Maurice Rollinat's carol-singing.

The collection contains two other speculative conversation-pieces, "Le Progrès supreme" [Ultimate Progress] and "L'Éternité chimique" [Chemical Eternity]; like them, "Un Rival d'Edison" was probably written some time before its publication, although its representation of Edison in middle age implies a date no earlier than the late 1880s, and—like other items in this anthology, but again in very different fashion—the story might well have been inspired by Villiers de l'Isle-Adam's publication of *L'Ève future*. This was not the earliest fictional anticipation of television broadcasting, even if one allows for a substantial time-lag before its publication, but it is interesting as a study of technological disenchantment whose gentle tone stands in stark stylistic contrast to "The Future Terror."

Monsieur Jonathan Dubourg had invited a number of the most famous scientists to his native town. Dinner had just finished and they were enjoying coffee in the drawing-room. Learning and expertise of every sort, speculative and practical, was represented by a local elite of professors, engineers and industrial bigwigs. This harmonious gathering would have had everything required to found a veritable provincial *Institut*, had it not been fearful of that bothersome ostentation.

The scientists in question each reserved for himself an admiration strictly limited to his particular specialism. With regard to Jonathan Dubourg, they were of one accord in holding in high esteem his considerable wealth, his comfortable and hospitable house, and the luxurious feast laid on by his venerable housekeeper, a *cordon bleu* cook of the first order. They also appreciated the beautiful lawn edged with trees that was attached to the dwelling. Finally, they enjoyed the uninterrupted flow of the ever-exquisite beer and the excellent cigars that the admirable householder distributed to his guests in that shady arena.

As for certain ultra-scientific opinions too stubbornly maintained by Monsieur Dubourg, his continual claims to be engaged in researches similar to those of the famous Edison and his ill-concealed bouts of bad temper when the illustrious Yankee beat him to the solution of some important problem— all of that drew nothing from these distinguished friends but an exchange of discreet smiles, emphasized by a furtive tapping of index fingers against foreheads. By this means, they surreptitiously indicated to one another an inoffensive mania attributable to old age.

Today, though, despite the indulgence consequent upon a good meal, they judged that Monsieur Dubourg had overstepped the normal bounds of moderate infatuation, and even went so far as to dread that the amateur enthusiasm of their honorable host might now be verging on pure and simple madness. He had, in fact, written a postscript to his letter of invitation: "Finally! Finally, I have arrived first at a discovery that the glorious American has attempted in vain until now: the transmission of visual images over long distances—that's what I've achieved! This is the extraordinary marvel that I shall have the honor, after dinner, of displaying to your eyes!"

Such a boast! Such a proclamation of victory over impossibility! His aberration must certainly have become extreme, and the guests, exaggerating their usual signals, seemed to be acknowledging the urgency of subjecting Monsieur Dubourg's increasing excitement to restorative medication.

With a contained cheerfulness, however, they followed Monsieur Dubourg on to the large lawn, where the promised magic was to be produced in the radiance of the summer evening. There, the assembly was suddenly plunged into a limitless amazement by the strange arrangements that the inventor had made.

At the far end of the garden a stage had been set up, with a dozen steps, surmounted by a vast mirror framed—not inelegantly—by multicolored drapery and attached laterally to the trees. Two clock-faces suspended in the foliage to the right and the left marked incomprehensibly different times. Beyond these decorations was open countryside bounded by a hill, about which wound a mysterious network of telegraphic wires supported at the tips of poles.

The almost mortuary calm of the distant town was magnified hereabouts into an august depth of silence—in which Jonathan Dubourg began to speak, after having shown the assembly the waiting chairs arranged in a semicircle around a table amply supplied with the famous beer and the incomparable cigars mentioned above.

"Don't worry," he said, "about being bored by a long speech. I'll get straight to the point, Gentlemen, after a few indispensable but very brief explanations."

The reassuring promises of this opening encouraged the listeners to plunge themselves into the attentive impassivity induced by smoking choice Havanas. Monsieur Dubourg climbed the steps of his stage. He manifested a noble intellectual bearing by virtue of his lofty presence, his fine white hair elevated by the frissons of the breeze. As a gleam of enthusiasm lit up his eyes, Jonathan Dubourg also had a sort of vengefully ironic twist to his lips. In truth, he was not unaware of the fact that his beloved fellow townsfolk suspected him of a slight cerebral deficiency. He had, in consequence, the fine attitude of an innovator who was no less disdainful of anticipated criticism than he was confident of the future of his work.

"For the moment," he continued, "what you see is a simple pane of glass backed by a tinted metal plate. Thus far, nothing new—it's merely a somewhat sketchily-improvised mirror. But this, Gentlemen, is where my work becomes more specific: the sheet of metal is composed of a special substance, totally unknown to science as yet, whose formula, I take pride in informing you, is known only to me. Take note, I beg you, that this substance, defying analysis before employment, leaves no trace after one has made use of it, Now, submit this layer of metal to the effect of a powerful electric current. Immediately, its surface liquefies into an infinite number of microscopic globules, whose iridescent oscillation exactly reproduces the image and movement of all objects present in the field of light in which the electrical transmitter—whose disposition, composed of a sequence of graduated lenses, is also my secret—receives its initial influence..."

The audience jeered. "Pooh! Is that all!" the puffs of cigar-smoke seemed to murmur.

"I sense your objections," said Monsieur Jonathan, with some slight annoyance. "You're saying to yourselves that this is the usual effect of any mirror, and proves nothing except that the electricity plays some role in this most banal repetition of reflective phenomena. But wait—oh, wait! The spectacle that is, I hope, about to be displayed to your eyes in this mirror will be the instantaneous reproduction of a scene from which we are separated by thousands of leagues. The people, their actions, and the objects that surround them will be represented in all their exactitude, in motion and in color. The colored transmission of reflection, Gentlemen—that is the miraculous and natural experiment to which you will bear witness!"

A few complaisant *bravos* emerged from the clouds of smoke. They wanted to push the implausible Jonathan to the limits of supreme madness.

"The living image of which I speak," the imperturbable Monsieur Dubourg continued, can be multiplied in any quantity of reflectors, thanks to the perfect homogeneity of metallic layers and the absolute parallelism of fluid effects. Unfortunately limited by my personal resources, I could only carry out this first attempt with two mirrors, which will relay their images reciprocally, but they are linked to on another by the transatlantic cable. That's already quite long, as distance goes. And I flatter myself that your surprise will not be small, in witnessing the appearance of the spectral image of the eminent person who has deigned to assist me—and who, for his part, will have the similar advantage of perceiving you.

"I now appeal for your most intense attention. These projections, for the present, do not last long. After a few seconds, the metal being molten, the globules evaporate, like spherical droplets on a red-hot iron, and the picture dissipates into a thick mist. Later on, we shall avoid this inconvenience by means of a prompt succession of plates. Later still, capitalists on the lookout for millions will hasten to generalize my process. Before multiple mirrors the theater of the universe will display its beauties, its festivals and its disasters. Even ships, in continuous communication by means of cables, will be visible throughout their perilous journeys, until the tragic moment of their explosion. Thanks to me, I tell you, the viewing public will be able to contemplate sights, living creatures and things—the sum of all luminous and moving life! Isn't that magnificent? Isn't it sublime?"

The invited learned men put on a show of ecstatic enthusiasm. "Quickly! Quickly! The formula, the launch, the shareholders, the millions, the billions!" they clamored, madly.

Monsieur Dubourg drew himself up to his full height, superb in his scorn, with fire in his eyes, shaking his fists.

"Are you talking already about vile publicity and filthy lucre?" he said, indignantly. "Is anyone thinking about the triumph of science? Does no one share the anguish that is oppressing me, at the moment of verifying the exactitude of my calculations with my first experiment?" The orator paused, then continued: "But I have confidence. That's all I have to say. The two clocks, linked across the ocean, are marking the precise Franco-American moment fixed for the experiment. Come what may, let's see…"

Standing to the left of the vast frame, Monsieur Dubourg activated a rotating disk—doubtless the communicator—inserted in the drapery.

All of a sudden, marvelously, it was as if the reflective surface tore like silver paper, revealing the décor of a office: a table heaped with papers, next to which was the exact silhouette, the indubitable outline, of a human being: yes, a perfectly ordinary, rather stout, gentleman in a frock coat, his coarsely-featured face emitting the smoke of an enormous cigar, his keen gaze sketching out superlative astonishment and indecision…

The prominent people present were no less alarmed. Phantom or chimera, science or magic, hallucination or mirage, the bewildered spectators' hearts beat faster.

At first, Monsieur Dubourg only risked a single glance from the corner of the apparatus. An exclamation of joy erupted from his throat.

"Victory! Victory, my friends!" he proclaimed. "I have the honor of presenting to you my illustrious correspondent, the incomparable and generous Monsieur Edison. He is hesitant; he still does not see anything distinct in the luminous waves of the mirror placed in front of him. Like you, just now, he believed himself to be in the presence of a vulgar mirror. Let us hasten to enlighten him."

He took a stride towards the middle of the glass. The two reflections confronted one another. Monsieur Edison, his arms upraised and his mouth wide open, such was his confusion before the prodigy, expressed all that with a pathetic gesture summarizing extreme delight.

Monsieur Dubourg bowed respectfully; their hands, reaching out to one another, simulated a friendly contact. That pantomime between the living man and the apparition was delightful.

"My dear Monsieur Edison," said Jonathan, "My future French renown salutes your former Yankee glory."

"But I can't understand you at all, my dear Monsieur Dubourg!" was the reply they believed they could read on Edison's moving lips. "But wait!" he mimed, extending his left hand and seizing a fountain pen with his right, which came down on a piece of blue paper.

"A congratulatory telegram, no doubt," the delighted Dubourg inferred.

A magical product of improbably reality, a charming jest of the unknown, the huge spectral Edison simply continued writing while, as Jonathan had predicted, a thick mist covered the glass, eventually dissipating to reveal the metal plate, as bare and grey as before.

The guests, similarly emerging from their clouds of to-bacco-smoke, walked incredulously towards the stage. Their analytical minds demanded the support of rigorous scientific certainty. It was necessary for them to examine in detail the incredible "transmitter;" they needed, above all, to verify a certain hypothesis, irreverently based on the extent of the space contained in the interior of the instrument.

These mistrustful investigations were, however, inter-rupted by the arrival of the chambermaid carrying the ex-pected dispatch.

The radiant Monsieur Dubourg unsealed it and started reading. "Admirable! Perfect! Conclusive! Here, my friends, is what the memorable Monsieur Edison, my noble and loyal colleague, has sent me...but what's this?"

Jonanthan's features were suddenly overtaken by a frightful sadness.

"Alas, gentlemen, like you, just now, he too says to me: *Quickly, quickly, shareholders, send the formula, the materials. Quickly! Quickly!*"

Everyone held their breath, disconcerted.

"What! No!" Dubourg protested, proudly. "Begone, gold! Respect for genius! Glory, without vile partnership with the inventor whose sole name will be attached to the work—if that justice is refused to me, the experiment that you have just witnessed will not be repeated, and the impenetrable secret of my discovery will go with me to the grave. On that point, feel free, my dear fellow citizens, to continue to accuse me of madness, or to commiserate with me, a great man misunderstood…"

Alas, the dear fellow citizens inclined, as always, to the supposition that he was "a little touched in the head" and persisted in their annoying hypothesis regarding the possible maneuvers of an unknown person behind Monsieur Dubourg's mirror.

"Who knows, though," a few of them said to themselves, looking beyond the network of telegraphic wires, "how many voices will extend across space in the future…?"

Alphonse Allais: *Erebium*
(1904)

Alphonse Allais (1854-1905) was a prolific contributor to popular periodicals of the late 19th and early 20th centuries, renowned for his humor. His enormous output included a small but fairly numerous minority of satirical speculative vignettes responding to contemporary scientific discoveries and technological developments. Although his entire works have now been assembled in a series of omnibuses, only a third of which consist of articles collected in book form during his lifetime, no one has taken the trouble to go through them and abstract the speculative items for separate publication, although a specialized volume of that sort would make an interesting illustration of the concerns of *fin-de-siècle* scientific reportage, and thus help to illuminate the more selective concerns of the period's scientific romance.

The following item first appeared in two parts in the June 5 and 9 1904 issues of *Le Journal*, the second part under the separate title "Où la science s'arrêtera-t-elle" [Where will science stop], Allais had already addressed the notion of "lumière noire" [black light]"—as invisible radiations were initially christened by such pioneering French experimenters as Gustave Le Bon—in two previous pieces in the same periodical, "Un peu de science" [A Little Science] (February 28 1896) and "Révolution dans la pyrotechnie" [A Revolution in Pyrotechnics] (July 16 1897).

Allais' satirical pieces poking fun at science and technological progress undoubtedly helped to inspire Gaston de Pawlowski's comic vignettes describing imaginary inventions and the parodic accounts of the Scientific Era included in *Voyage au pays de la quatrième dimension* (1912; tr. in a

Black Coat Press edition as *Journey to the Land of the Fourth Dimension*).[66]

    This double item was reprinted in the fourth issue of Philippe Gontier's *Le Boudoir des Gorgones* (October 2002).

---

[66] ISBN 978-1-934543-37-5.

1.

Like everyone else, I had heard mention of Erebium[67]
and the amazing property possessed by the new element: that
of projecting a globe of darkness around it. I admit, however,
that like everyone else—the inventor being a chemist in San
Francisco—I considered it as an item of American bluff, hoax
or humbug pending further information. This W. K. Goldcock
was obviously a shameless self-publicist, or a skillful practical
joker. Just as the discovery of radium was slightly surprising,[68] so the advertisement of this paradoxical substance took
all of us—my friends in the great laboratories and your humble servant—aback.

Erebium! A material body as large as the head of a pin
able to produce darkness over a radius of three or four meters.
What a joke!

Henry Becquerel, d'Arsonval and Lippmann, not to mention the likeable new director of the Pseudotechnical Institute,
Max de Nansouty, and a few other well-respected scientists,

---

[67] Although Allais spells it Érébium rather than Érèbium, the
name of the imaginary element is undoubtedly derived from
Érèbe [Erebus], the name given to a mythical region of subterranean darkness overlying the classical land of the dead.

[68] Allais inserts a footnote here: "Radium, in fact, only amazed
simpletons. Radium emits light; all metals emit light. The only
difference between radium and other metals is the low heat
necessary to its incandescence. In the same way, mercury is
content to melt at what we call ordinary temperature—which
only serves to prove that mercury is an extreme case among
metals. The story of radium is the greatest hoax of the 19th
century; I shall soon demonstrate this, irrefutably, in a lecture
whose memory will not soon be effaced."

were unanimous in shrugging their shoulders in response to the news.[69]

The young Pierre Trébucheau, already reputed as a genius, was an exception. "Why not?" he said. "We have the means of producing heat and cold at will; why should we not produce darkness with the same ease with which we already produce light?"

As we all protested against such perfectly antiscientific simple-mindedness, however, there was an even more unanimous shrugging of shoulders around Trébucheau, with which all of ours, for once, joined in.

"But, unfortunate collection of idiots that you are," he persisted, "light and darkness are just words, like heat and cold—words vaguely expressing phenomena intermediate between the states that set limits upon our vestigial perceptions."

We had just respectfully made the observation to Trébucheau that we knew that when a laboratory assistant came to tell us that the gentleman whose card he held out to us was asking to be admitted.

The card bore the name *W. K. Goldcock.*

Professor d'Arsonval was the first to recover from his stupor.

"Bring him in!" he said, wanly.

---

[69] Allais gives Becquerel's forename (which is more frequently rendered as Henri) to distinguish him from his father, who was also a noted physicist. The other names cited here are also those of real contemporary scientists; Jacques-Arsène d'Arsonval was a significant pioneer of electrophysiology, Gabriel Lippmann a Nobel prize-winning physicist best known for his work on the development of color photography and Max de Nansouty a well-known popularizer of science who helped compile guidebooks to the *expositions* of 1889 and 1900.

The laboratory door, which faces south, opens on to a vast and admirable well-lit courtyard. As soon as it is opened, a flood of light overwhelms you, especially when—as was the case in this instance—it is about midday and the weather is fine.

The laboratory door opened.

As I have just said, it was about midday and the weather was fine—but the laboratory door opened into the most intense darkness.

Some old Arab or other claims that the perception of God is able to distinguish the blackest of ants wandering around on the blackest of marble surfaces on the blackest of nights. Perhaps that's true—but what can mere men do when they suddenly find themselves confronted by an unaccustomed Limbo?

Speaking in strongly-accented French, a voice emerged from that darkness: "I'm not disturbing you, then, gentlemen?"

But how can one relate something as sensational in so few lines? Make your way, therefore, ladies and gentlemen, to one of the impending performances.

2.

Have you ever found yourself in the bizarre situation, when opening your door to some visitor, of seeing something coming into your house like an immense sack of coal that is not content merely to be intensely black, but takes pleasure in radiating around itself a dense twilight.

Such was the spectacle to which we—Messieurs Henry Becquerel, d'Arsonval, Lippmann, Max de Nansouty and yours truly—were witness: a spectacle hardly banal, of which the last-named has recently traced a brief preliminary sketch in these very pages.

A voice was heard, seeming to emerge from the upper part of the coal-sack: "I'm not disturbing you, then gentlemen?"

There was no longer any doubt about it; we had before us W. K. Goldcock, the inventor of Erebium—and Erebium was not a mystery, nor a confidence-trick, nor a hoax, nor a bit of fun, nor an item of humbug. Erebium really did have that amazing property of emitting darkness, or at least of obliterating daylight, within a certain radius.

The block of shadow moved, seemingly gliding around us—and every time the block reached one of us, one of us disappeared, as if absorbed by a mobile night.

The voice resumed, mockingly this time: "Well, gentlemen of science, don't you recognize me? Is it because you're seeing me for the first time?"

"If one can call this seeing a man," Monsieur de Nansouty observed.

"Or is it because I've covered myself with a simple dust-sheet impregnated with erebium permanganate? Ah! Erebium, which surprises you as much as radium!"

Suddenly, there was a violent shaking inside the coal-sack; then we saw it collapse on to the ground, occupying a much more restricted volume than it had a moment before. Emerging from the patch of obscurity, after greeting us with a smile, a middle-aged man bent down and performed the gestures folding an item of clothing. As these movements progressed, the patch of darkness diminished to negligibility, finally disappearing into a satchel that the man had slung over his shoulder.

"W. K. Goldcock," the gentlemen said, introducing himself.

Professor d'Arsonval hastened to introduce all the individuals present at that unforgettable scene to our visitor.

"W. K. Goldcock," continued the latter, "or, more accurately, Guillaume Charles Vidor, former first-class pharmacist in France, forced by an ungrateful magistrate to expatriate himself, in consequence of some petty matter of selling abortifacient materials during a time of prohibition."

"We are happy," Monsieur Becquerel declared, "to see, yet again, such a beautiful discovery made by a Frenchman."

"Would it be indiscreet...?" the good Monsieur Lippmann murmured, timidly.

"Not at all, not at all, my dear professor. Here: just as fish exist that are endowed with what Doctor Raphael Dubois calls biophotogenesis—which is to say, the faculty of emitting light originated by their own physiology—so the opposite also exists—which is to say, fish that are capable, in certain circumstances, of producing darkness and surrounding themselves with it."

"Like a squid..."

"You said it. Nansouty..."

Everyone burst out laughing.

"With a very small quantity of substance," our friend continued, "a squid can darken a considerable volume of water, virtually instantaneously. Was that operation anything other than a vulgar and material muddying of the waters by the addition of foreign substances? That is what I suspected. After a month's work, I succeeded in isolating *Erebine*, which I thought at first to be an organic substance, but soon perceived, to my amazement, to be erebium oxide."

What will the consequences of this discovery be? Immense, undoubtedly, but of an order difficult to specify, for the moment.

In the wrong hands, erebium might, alas, become a weapon injurious to the orderly functioning of society in general, particularly where brave process-severs and poor creditors are concerned!

André Mas: *The Germans on Venus*
(1913)

Very little is known about André Mas, whose dates of birth and death are unrecorded; the by-line may well be a pseudonym. *Les Allemands sur Vénus*, here translated as "The Germans on Venus," was initially published as a booklet by the *Revue des Independants* in 1913. The timing was unfortunate; the Kaiser's forces invaded France within a year because his Empire's sense that "its share of this world [was] not large enough"—as Mas' preface puts it—had given rise to actions quite different from those described in the story. After the war, the by-line appeared on two further works of speculative fiction in booklet form, the first formulated as a long poem, "Sous leur double soleil des Dryméennes chantent" [Beneath their double Sun, Drymeans sing] (1921), and the second as a prose romance set in the same locale, "Drymea, monde des vierges" [Drymea, world of virgins] (1923). Both of the prose works were reprinted in 2004 by Apex.

The Apex edition of *Les Allemands sur Vénus*, from which this translation is taken, is photographically reproduced from the original booklet; it includes a reproduction of the cover, which bears two quotations from German writers; one of them, attributed to "Léo Stahl," translates as "The future of Germany is in the stars;" the other, from Heinrich Heine translates as "To the English, the sea; to the French, the land, to the Germans, the kingdom of the Heavens." The Apex edition also reproduces a dedication to "My master and friend, Henry Beuchat of the Canadian Arctic Expedition." (Beuchat was a noted anthropologist based in Paris.)

In addition to these embellishments, the text has two further supplements of interest. The first is a bibliography, divided between previous works of fiction dealing with interplanetary travel and scientific works consulted with respect to the technology of space travel and the design of a hypothetical Venusian ecology; this is particularly interesting for the clear indication it gives of the consciousness that an international genre of "space fiction" was firmly established in 1913, comprising both classic and popular works. The bibliography is followed by a parody of a "bill of lading" applicable to future interplanetary transport, which neatly rounds off the satirical component of the text, emphasizing the manner in which seriousness and comedy were routinely combined in texts of this sort.

Although modern references to *Les Allemands sur Vénus* sometimes dismiss it as a slightly distasteful item of nationalistic propaganda, the narrative is sufficiently ironic to defy that charge, and is historically interesting in two other ways. Firstly, it takes more care in its description of a hypothetical means of space travel than any previous work, with the arguable exception of Jules Verne's two-part account of a lunar voyage; it features one of the earliest fictional "space walks"—undertaken to clear a blockage in the spaceship's waste-disposal system!—and includes some original speculations about the possible effects of weightlessness. Secondly, it takes more care in its attempt to design a hypothetical biosphere for another planetary surface than any previous work, especially in terms of that biosphere's evolutionary dynamics. By modern standards, both these attempts are inevitably primitive and grossly mistaken, but they were remarkable for their time.

Although Mas' propagandistic endeavor had been anticipated in Russia by Nikolai Fyodorov and his protégé Konstatin Tsiolkovsky, Mas cannot have been aware of their work, or he would certainly have acknowledged it. Tsiolkovsky did not manage to complete his science fiction novel *Vne zemli* (tr. as *Beyond the Planet Earth* and *Outside the Earth*) until 1916, although he had begun it in 1896, and it did not appear in book form until 1920; this means that "The Germans on Venus" was the first-published item in a remarkable series of propagandistic works of fiction by rocket enthusiasts, which was to

215

be continued in Germany by Otto Willi Gail's *Der Schuss ins All* (1925; tr. as *The Shot into Infinity*) and in America by Laurence Manning's "The Voyage of the Asteroid" (1932).

Preface

"For the progress of Man will always be limited if he has
no other horizon than his narrow terrestrial horizon, and one
may suppose that a moment will come when the only progress
that remains to him will be an astronomical progress."
Charles Richet [70]

"When the cooling of the Sun has rendered this world
uninhabitable, it might be that life will continue
on its sister planet. Shall we be able to conquer it?
Obscure and prodigious is the vision that I evoke…"
H. G. Wells

The scientific bases of this novel are taken from *Vers les
autres Mondes*, one of the first attempts to resolve the most
important question after that of death: do other humankinds
exist, and can we contact them? Professor Hauchet's discourse
is a reproduction, in its entirety, of my article in the 15 Janu-
ary 1913 issue of *L'Avion*.[71]

Some will accuse me of anti-patriotism, but this study is
objective. I have worked from nature. Léo Stahl is not a myth,
any more than his words are. We always think of "old" Germany, but the Empire is only as old as a human adult; in the
full pride of youth, it finds that its share of this world is not
large enough—and German's self-confidence is formidable,

---

[70] Charles Richet (1850-1935) was best known as a physiolo-
gist, in which capacity he was appointed a professor at the
Sorbonne and won a 1913 Nobel prize, but he was also a pioneer of aviation, a novelist and poet; his literary works include
three scientific romances published in 1887-92, two of them
under the pseudonym Charles Epheyre, which he used on
much of his early work.

[71] Mas adds a footnote here giving the following reference:
"*L'Avion*, Dr. Loisel publ., 8 Rue du Faubourg Montmartre."

served by a proverbial systematization and perseverance. "It is to the Empire of the World that the German genius aspires," an imperial voice has said. Now, the world expands according to our power and our will; it may be the world of Augustus, bounded by England, the Baltic and the Sahara, or boundless space—and the empire of another world will cost him a thousand time less in money and blood than a single league of Champagne!

We, the French, can forget our internal struggles briefly. It is by showing how others believe in their fatherland, and what destinies it promises them, that we shall learn to cherish our own.

Part One: The Push Towards The Stars

I. The Ideas of Doctor Hauchet

Heinrich von Reinhardt resumed the work of his old master, Graf von Zeppelin, and completed it. The monsters that he launched into the submissive air crossed the Atlantic in a single bound, and he was covered at the age of 37 with honors and gold. In the Empire, his name was a fanfare; the shadow of his work extended over Europe. His friends called him, jokingly, "a barbarian of genius." His build was massive, his strength inexhaustible. But he realized what he had dreamed in the flame of inspiration, with the dogged perseverance of his race. Neither he, nor Otto Rosenwald, nor Hauchet understood, to begin with, the significance of the moment that brought them together one fine morning in Heidelberg.

Rosenwald was still at the age of joyful devotion, and to him von Reinhardt took on a godlike stature. Rich and independent, however, he welcomed a man equally used to risking his life, hard work and making merry—and von Reinhardt liked him, recognizing him as a man of sound constitution, which rang true.

Hauchet, with his keen eyes beneath his bald forehead and his tall, sturdy body, was also not unknown to Reinhardt. Their lives intersected at the Congress of Aviation and meetings of similar Associations, enough for them to look forward to seeing one another again. As for Rosenwald, Hauchet had known him and won him over two years before, at the International Conference of the Franco-German League.[72]

They talked about the latest aerial successes, and Otto, the youngest of the three, joked: "What is there to do now? Go

---

[72] Mas inserts a footnote giving the address of this organization as "4 Rue Greffule, Paris."

to the Moon? Listen to the Doctor—he'll explain the method to you."

"Really?" said von Reinhardt. "I'm at your disposal, Doctor." He never neglected any idea, crazy as it might seem, but was vigilant and always on the lookout. *There's an ounce of truth in every ton of error* was a proverb created for his use.

Hauchet paused for thought, then, in a calm voice that gradually became more animated, said: "It's a common idea nowadays, and almost everyone says, 'After aviation will come something else; man was not made to crawl upon the Earth forever; his destiny must be higher.' Every dream that man has conceived must ultimately be realized, when it arrives in its scientific phase. Let's review the facts.

"The terrible dream of rising into the sky, overcoming the Earth's gravitational attraction and crossing the gulf of space to penetrate the virgin atmospheres of other worlds comes down to a question of speed. Flammarion and Moreux[73] have demonstrated that it only requires a moving object to be launched from our Earth with a relatively limited speed—11,309 meters in the first second—to attain a practically infinite end. For if that speed diminishes, the attraction of the Earth diminishes with the square of the distance. At ten terrestrial radii—63,660 kilometers—the attraction will have fallen to 1/100th; a kilogram would weight ten grams. At 100 radii, that weight falls to 1/10,000th. And at a relatively small distance of two radii, weight relative to our world is already a fourth of that which oppresses us thereon. These figures are proved by all our science, without wearying the reader with mathematical explanations.

"The problem thus comes down to imparting to a mass of a several tons—travelers, provisions, etc.—a velocity of 14 or 15 kilometers per second, because it's necessary to take into account the frightful resistance of the air at such speeds and

---

[73] Camille Flammarion and the Abbé Théophile Moreux were France's leading popularizers of astronomical science.

it's necessary that the speed is more than 11 kilometers per second at the moment of emergence from our atmosphere.

"One thinks of Jules Verne's cannon, but present explosives are insufficient, and besides, the frightful recoil would annihilate its passengers on departure despite all shock-absorbers, brakes and so on. It's necessary to depart with a gradually accelerated speed. Industrial mechanics permits that. We shall, therefore, utilize centrifugal force; its application to the launch of projectiles has already been studied several times since 1880.

"Let us imagine a wheel of large diameter, and a profile such that its thickness increases from the circumference to the center, the heaviest mass being around the axle—exactly the contrary of industrial flywheels. This wheel is made of the finest steel, with perfectly smooth faces. The axle is flexible, turning in liquid oil—under pressure, if necessary. We start the wheel turning by means of an alternating motor, in the fashion of a turbine. The latter can achieve a speed of several 100 rotations per second.

"At the periphery of the wheel, a hollow is fabricated containing a vehicle retained, either by some sort of clamp or by metallic blocks forming a locking-mechanism at the two extremities—an apparatus, at any rate, enabling the vehicle to be detached in a given orientation within a fraction of a second. We can do that by means of a catch within the lock, for example, or some other mechanism.

"One can hardly imagine the enormous initial velocities that can be imparted by a wheel of an almost current diameter: ten meters. Its circumference will be 31,40 meters, and it is not unreasonable to suppose 200 rotations per second with a Laval turbine equipped with an alternating motor. Now, we already have a velocity of 6.280 meters per second, by which means our projectile could easily travel several thousand kilometers.

"An apparatus of this type, which I shall call an 'explorer,' installed on the equator and aimed towards the sky, given appropriate measuring-devices, would already permit hyper-atmospheric probes of practical interest—for we are utterly ignorant of what happens only 60 kilometers above our heads. These projectile probes would be capable of going up hundreds of kilometers. Falling back into the sea, they could be gathered up following a fall that some mechanical device—a parachute with rocket-flares, for example—could slow down and signal.

"After experiments of this sort, we would enter into the phase of interplanetary voyages, which would evidently demand a titanic launch-engine that could only be constructed by a Nation—and there is an extraordinary analogy there with the beginnings of aviation. The Wright brothers' apparatus had to be *launched* by means of a special apparatus, then to be sustained in the air by its own means.

"Now, we have at our disposal *presently*—Esnault-Pelterie[74] has demonstrated it, among others—a motor adequate for an apparatus isolated in space and separated to some degree from the heavy gravitation of the Earth to displace itself at will. This is the reaction-motor. The principle dates from the time of Hieron of Syracuse,[75] and all our engineers know it. In brief, any apparatus that can project in space or in the atmosphere a high-speed jet of gas, will recoil therefrom.

Now, we make use of powerful explosives such as panclastite, transportable in the form of two separate liquids that are only mixed at the moment of their explosion. Panclastite burns with an enormous production of temperature. Its fall, in

---

[74] Robert Esnault-Pelterie (1881-1957) was well-known in 1913 as a pioneer of aviation, but his endeavors as a propagandist for space travel by means of rockets were then at a very early stage; his book on the subject, *L'Astronautique*, was not published until 1930, following a lecture series launched in 1927.

[75] Hieron II of Syracuse was the patron of the ingenious Archimedes, to whom discovery of the principle in question, in the 5th century B.C., is generally attributed

the presence of the absolute cold of space (-273°) would therefore be considerable, and the energy produced maximized.[76]

"We therefore have a vehicle in space provided with a reaction-motor—or rather two, one at each end. These motors would, in effect, be cannon-barrels of the finest metal, long enough to use all the energy produced. The panclastite will be detonated therein in measured doses by means of a conceivable apparatus. The gas is precipitated outside and the vehicle recoils. Its weight, in space, is equivalent to a few kilograms at most. The mass of the expelled gases similarly diminishes with gravitation, but their speed remains the same—the chemical energy of explosive mixtures does not change in the void.[77] We are, therefore—at the cost of a few risks, admittedly—masters of our movements in open space, the motors being displaced along with the vehicle.

"But a reaction motor, however powerful it might be, can only raise a vehicle that is initially at rest from the ground at the cost of a vast expenditure of explosive that none would remain for the rest of the voyage—for beyond the Moon, interplanetary distances are measured in millions of kilometers. That is why we must bring centrifugal force into lay for the launch.

"We envisage a wheel of very large diameter, in the form already indicated, decreasing from the center to the perimeter. An 80-meter diameter, corresponding to a circumference of

---

[76] Mas' assumption that the temperate of interplanetary space is absolute zero is mistaken, but the rate at which the temperature of the exploding gas falls is, in any case, quite irrelevant to the impulse imparted to the rocket. Panclastite was a liquid explosive made by mixing dinitrogen tetroxide with a fuel such as carbon disulfide at the appropriate moment; it was swiftly superseded during the Great War.

[77] Mas confuses mass and weight here, again mangling his argument unnecessarily, but it remains fundamentally sound, as the deployment of rockets in modern spacecraft demonstrates.

251 meters, would give, at only 30 turns per second, an initial speed of 7530 meters per second. Now, there is no need for us to hurry. One could easily take 12, 24 or 48 hours to bring the wheel up to its maximum speed, and present-day motors would be largely adequate to the task.

"Half of the wheel will be buried in a ditch; the axle will be directly activated by an alternating motor and a steam turbine. It will be flexible, to avoid any displacement. The projectile in its hollow will be launched instantaneously at a given moment by an electrical apparatus; it will depart towards the Zenith.

"The vehicle will affect the classical form of a dirigible attacking the air thick end first. It will have two steel hulls with a void between them, in order that its internal heat will not escape into the void of space, and double windows, engineered so that they can be opened from the inside or outside— if the projectile falls back, the voyagers will be unconscious. Liquid air and caustic soda—with a device for passing gas through it—will be provided for respiration. Canned food, water, coffee, etc., will not represent an enormous weight, allowing for three voyagers—the minimum, from the scientific and human viewpoints. The observation apparatus will be located at the front of the projectile; provisions of all sorts will be placed at the rear, to lower the center of gravity. A laboratory will be in communication with the void for all imaginable experiments, and we shall design a direct-to-space system for the evacuation of wastes. The projectile will also be fitted with wireless telegraph.

"The air resistance on departure is one of the greatest difficulties. We shall depend, in that respect, on coating the projectile with a layer of fusible metal, which heat will change into liquid or gas, protecting the steel. Besides, at 8 kilometers per second, the trajectory through a slightly resistant atmosphere will last 10 or 12 seconds at the most, and the next 20 kilometers of the atmosphere is rarefied.

"It is, moreover, not necessary to imagine that we, as masters of the wheel, shall send the projectile and its passengers with the speed at which they will go through space to another world. Although there is a limiting velocity—11,309 meters per second—that will launch a projectile into the deserts of space permanently, a lesser and more practical speed of at least 8 kilometers per second will permit it to describe an enormous ellipse whose focal point will be the terrestrial orbit.

"Departing thus, our projectile will become an independent celestial body, capable of describing a closed arc that will allow it to come close enough to the target planet—probably Mars—for telescopic examination to be fruitful, and even to deliver material messages by sending miniature projectiles to the planet via the direct-to-space apparatus.

"Then, having satisfied their curiosity, our projectile would complete the arc that it is describing and return to Earth with increasing velocity. It is necessary not to forget that the reaction-motor constitutes a chance of indisputable security, for space is large and the Earth is small. In space, however, where bodies weigh very little, the least effort of the motor can transport the projectile thousands of leagues, for there is neither air nor weight there—nothing but void.

"To sum up, if we depart with a velocity of less than 8 kilometers per second, we shall describe a relatively short ellipse. At 8 kps, we shall orbit the Earth. Above 8 kps, the described ellipse will gradually increase. At 10 kps, we shall reach the Moon. At 11,309 kps, our goal is, in fact, infinity.

"This is neither fantasy nor fable. It is evident that many people will consider this titanic journey, and this projectile traversing space with its reaction motor, carrying several men, with a stern eye. It is also evident that the great adventure of which we speak involves unknown risks. We do not know how men might be affected by weightlessness. Perhaps there are gases unknown to our science in space, invisible to our eyes but capable of killing us. Perhaps enormous bolides will crash into us, consigning us to incandescent death. Perhaps… The Universe is infinite and Man is very tiny.

"We are attempting here, however, the first scientific solution of the problem of interplanetary communication. In all that we have read on the subject, with the exception of Jules Verne's cannon, Wells' Cavorite—a substance impenetrable to gravitation—would be the most practical method, but we know of no such substance as yet.

"Even outside the viewpoint of science, the occupation by humans of another world would be the greatest feat in our history. No one can foresee what unknown wealth it would bring us. Perhaps the planet Venus is nothing but an immense mass of radium! And the red planet, Mars, might be able to inform us of an epoch-making science.

"A poet has said: *The time has come to conquer the planets and mount an assault on the stars.*"

The doctor fell silent, still vibrant with excitement. Rosenwald's eyes shone with a flame similar to his, although these theories were entirely new to him, and he murmured: "What an idea! What a grandiose idea!"

"Yes," von Reinhardt added, pensively. "It's an idea worthy of the grandeur of Germany and its mission in the world." His large body drew itself upright forcefully.

They looked at one another in silence, but the winged words had taken flight. Their thoughts were in accord now, beyond words.

Rosenwald almost shouted: "Hauchet, you have faith! I shall put my life in the balance with you. And you, my friend, who know the Earth, the deep sea, the frozen sky up there among the stars…you're sated with the world. It has fulfilled your dreams. Forge a higher dream, for yourself and for our Fatherland…"

As he fell silent, a band struck up *Deutschland, Deutschland über alles*. A vivid blush rose up in Heinrich von Reinhardt's face—and all three of them left for Paris by the first train, bound for Hauchet's house.

II. Germany's Future is in the Stars

When they came back, von Reinhardt was full of exultant energy, and Rosenwald's intoxication equaled that of joyful wine. As soon as he returned to his workshops in Mannheim, von Reinhardt summoned two dozen specialist experts by telegraph, put the question to them, and set things in motion. His incontestable authority was, it must be admitted, an important counterweight to their initial incredulity. Then they thought about it and, sheltered from indiscretions, on tranquil evenings beneath placid stars, around savory platters in the familiar light of soft lamps, those men made plans to conquer another world—or all of them—by choice. It required no more for human history to be cut in two, before and after.

Already, though, they were specializing. "They're preparing a manual," said Ronenwald, one evening.

Hauchet lit a cigar, smiled and replied: "I'll tell you a story about a Dane, a German and a Manual.[78] It's so good that it's true. I knew the three characters, for the Dane was on the Sund border with the German. The weather was good and the sea, seen from the cliff, was calm.

" 'I'd love to take a trip on the Sund,' said the Dane, 'but I don't know how to operate a sailing-boat.'

" 'Me neither,' said the German, 'but don't worry. I have my navigation manual in my pocket.'

"On the strength of that book, they embarked, and, as long as they were in the shelter of the cliffs, everything went perfectly well. When their boat went out into the open sea, though, it began to dance around. The Dane became uneasy.

---

[78] There is an untranslatable play on words here. The French *manuel* becomes "manual" in English, so the name Manuel—which doubles as a slang term for "Spaniard"—is only phonetically and not orthographically ambiguous.

" 'I'll see what the manual says,' his companion offered—and without further ado, he tied up the sail, took out the book and began to riffle through it—but the wind turned abruptly in the tied-up sail and, a moment later, the manual, the Dane, the German and the boat were at the bottom of the Sund. They'd be there still but for the opportune arrival of fishermen who, having no manual…"

"And the moral is…?" asked Rosenwald, laughing.

"There isn't one—that's the best thing about it," Hauchet concluded.

And they held other joyful conversations that evening, for the preparatory work was finished. Now the talk, for weeks or months, would be of hammers and lifting-tackle.

The next day, von Reinhardt had a communiqué sent to the German press, and the loquacious newspapers transmitted the rumor to everyone who could read.

The French newspapers approved of the audacity of the idea, partly because of Hauchet, and, for the most part, did not think the endeavor beyond the industrial strength of Germany. *Le Matin* fretted in vain about an "ambition no longer pan-Germanist but, so to speak, pan-uranist."[79]

Spain protested timidly. Was it not encroaching upon the rights of God to go to these worlds, doubtless placed so far away by design? The Italians composed many sonnets. The intellectual fraction of Russia took a great interest in the question, as did the United States, which only regretted that there was no America in the story. In Austria, opinions were divided, mainly because no one was listening, as usual. The smaller states bordering Germany were very pleased that she was thinking about the stars rather than them. All England, however, burst out in a gale of laughter, which resounded eve-

_____

[79] So-called because Urania is the muse of astronomy—a reference easily construed by literate Frenchmen of the era, familiar with Camille Flammarion's best-selling scientific romance *Uranie*.

rywhere the leopard and the unicorn reigned.[80] Let Heinrich have his way! It would not lead to worldly hegemony—that was the main thing. *Punch* mocked—but Germany took no notice. No one was in doubt, no one asked the opinion of a neighbor; a unanimous pride dilated the heart of Deutschdom.

"We have found our way," proclaimed all the newspapers, "the way dimly foreseen for so many centuries! Not the vanished dream of eastward or westward, northwards or southward expansion! No, expansion into the skies, expansion towards the stars, where no one shall bar our route! The founders of our national unity are dead, alas, else they would have brought us this idea, with God's aid! We Germans have always succeeded in doing what we desired to do. In this too we shall succeed!"

At that time, the formidable confusion of interests, even more than the rising tide of socialism and the actions of trades unions, Sovietized pacifists and Freemasonry, had forced a Franco-German *entente*. The Empire would not lose by it, said its financiers, and at least Heinrich and Jacques Bonhomme would keep some of their cash, instead of seeing it spent on cannons and other trinkets.

Voltaire, prince of mockers, wrote: "The art of government consists of taking as much money as possible from the many in order to give it to the few." The definition rang true once, but once is not always. This explains how a liberal vote of the Reichstag and a national subscription by an enriched populace warmed to white heat by enthusiasm—in addition to the Emperor's personal gift—brought the millions of marks that were necessary, and more. It was a one-time expense. The apparatus and engines constructed would last 200 years and more, and the kilometric tonnage of the interplanetary journey

---

[80] The substitution of a leopard for the British heraldic lion is presumably deliberate. In the following sentence and elsewhere I have used "Heinrich" as a generic German name rather than the "Michel" that Mas employs.

would descend to a price inferior to that of cargo boats, according to the calculations of Professor Reuler.

It was then that an unknown poet, in a single hour, incarnated the soul of a race and produced a famous hymn, the most formidable affirmation of a man and a people that the world had ever known:

> *The future of Germany is in the stars.*
> *O Germany extend thy hand*
> *And dress yourself in a crown of Suns!*
> *Tenebrous worlds roll in endless space*
> *Waiting for you to impose on them*
> *The good and just law of loyal man and God Himself.*
> *Germany, reign over the Ether*
> *And conquer the very stars*
> *And break out on this petty Earth*
> *Which is no more than a footstool*
> *Of your thought and your will,*
> *In a colossal and joyful burst of laughter,*
> *For man must surpass himself.*
> *A sage has said:*
> *Aspire to renew the work,*
> *That God has set himself*
> *For His love is with us.*

Thousands and thousands of men had these verses of Ludwig Mayer's on their lips.[81]

---

[81] The verses attributed to this "unknown poet" are presumably the author's, giving rise to the suspicion that Ludwig Mayer might have been the real name of the person who adopted "André Mas" as a pseudonym.

III. The City of Stars

Far away, near the equator, beneath the torrid Sun and deluges of rain, the Wheel grew, day by day and hour by hour. The effort and the will of a people were forged in its titanic structure of steel, looming up into the clear sky where the stars scintillated. Neither gold nor sweat, nor even good human blood—the finest cement for anything higher than ourselves— was lacking in its birth.

Now it was raised above the town and men, beneath its framework, raised their heads, full of pride in the work that was finally complete. Out to sea, steamers with breathless engines were proceeding slowly towards the violet horizon, with the mountains of Cameroon in the distance.

First, there was the arrival of a swarm of workmen and their supervisors, whose invincible discipline changed the appearance of the region for miles around within a month. The tall ships, sounding their sirens, unloaded enormous quantities of steel, manufactured under other skies by other men. Great electric spotlights then lit up like nocturnal hawk-moths, the arms of cranes were extended and the screech of machinery became never-ending. Then a flock of fast-moving wagons began their whining course beneath their loads, and the dream became slid, rivet by rivet, piece by piece, in such sturdy metal that the storm-winds blew at it in vain. One morning, the huge scaffolding, the thousand arms of chains, the far-reaching electric cables, the stiff shafts of elevators and the whirling pulleys all felt the fatigue and tiredness of the workers bearing them, for the Wheel, the Port of the Zenith, the Emporium of Interplanetary Exchange, reflected the glory of the rising Sun—and when evening came, it threatened the sky and its multitude of stars.

The town had grown up around it: a new town, clean and tidy, in which the effort of a century was concentrated. That too sprang from the ground, with its houses cast from molds, its rapid tramways, its verdant parks and its running streams—for years, science had subjugated the obscure force of great rivers, and the docile energy of cataracts ran through slender steel wires across the dark continent. The white man's burden is as heavy as the planet, but he accepts it, bears it and molds it, now that he is no longer divided against himself, brother against brother, mouth against mouth, hand against hand. The great illusion of peoples has been swept away by the force of gold, and their hatreds have become weaker as their interests have become confused, to the extent that any blow struck at the heart of one stabs all the others.

The people of the town gravitated around the three men who launched this dream into the world. They tasted the powerful joy of the hard work that leaves its mark more profoundly with every passing day. Now they had earned their reward, they gathered beneath the impassive stars in the sky, peacefully awaiting the passages of the planets through the shoreless seas of the void, fixed since time immemorial.

Of the experiments they have undertaken, of the days of passion when, for the first time, the steel spindle that emerged solely from the hands of men, will penetrate the inaccessible ether, there is no need to tell the story, for it belongs to the history of science. No more shall I describe the East African airfield that Heinrich von Reinhardt built, on which the German airfleet, an immense eagle, sank down at every point; or even Doctor Hauchet's "by-product," the astonishing Aeracs: aeroplanes with massive hulls propelled at 300 kilometers an hour by the furious expulsion of their reaction-gases, capable with their variable wings of flying higher than condors soar above the Andes. I shall say no more, for this history is only concerned with the conquest of another world.

It was a great day when the Congress of Charlottenburg opened, for it was a simple matter of choosing a world for humankind's first step. The monstrous range of the Wheel embraced an almost-unlimited expanse of space, but it was necessary not only to reign over the dark black desert where even the stars are dust. Our bodies are made of flesh, although we wish to be gods. We can, however, only believe with diffi-culty in other humankinds higher than ourselves, across that extent, and—if they are there—the magnificent opportunities of a new science and perhaps other intelligences than intelli-gence.

Three worlds were under discussion: the Moon, Mars and Venus. Earth's satellite was set aside straight away, good for fantastic voyages, but certainly insufficient for a nation like Germany, narrowly confined on its own world. Water, air and aliments, if they were not entirely lacking there, would only be sufficient for the most sober of nations. Vegetation there seemed limited, the conditions of life hardly tenable.

Nevertheless, Professor Heimar defended the Moon on five counts:

Firstly, the astronomical: no air or troublesome vapor; a night of 354 hours, during which one might study the sky with the maximum magnification, employing a spectroscope with-out atmospheric intrusion—in brief, the ideal observatory.

Secondly, the meteorological: from there, with our large telescopes, we can follow the descent of icebergs and the movement of clouds, reporting them by wireless telegraph.

Thirdly, that of military exploration: every 24 hours the Earth turns before a telescope installed on the Moon; one can see and signal the progress of an ironclad battleship or a large body of troops—and from an armchair, one could set up a global map at one's ease.

Fourthly, the industrial: daughter of the Earth, the Moon contains the same minerals, hence ores, soda, potash, pumice-stone, lava etc.—and a Lunar cubic meter is six times lighter to shift. After all, there is the surface area of two Americas up there: more than a hectare for every inhabitant of Earth.

Fifthly, the colonial. There is no air, but it can be manu-factured! Then, again, to return to our planet from up there only requires an initial velocity of 2600 meters per second. Timorous people hesitant to entrust themselves to the Wheel of the City of Stars will go up there; the limiting velocity is

3000 mps instead of 12,000! It will be the Hamburg of Space, the way-station of the stars, the *Sterndeutscher Lloyd.*

The jurist Zuben, for his part, put forward the idea of an industrial and penal colony of the Prussian state. The difficulty of escape militated in its favor—and he proposed that the Moon should initially be used to lodge the victims of article 175 of the German penal code. This suggestion was received with the seriousness that it merited, and white Phoebe was held in reserve, solely in order to demand compensation if anyone else wanted to go there.[82]

Mars, the enigma of our solar system, better known than Venus, had serious partisans, but it too seemed too small, with a diminished atmosphere and narrow seas. The interested public was nevertheless deluged with statistics and documents relating to the red planet, and mouths from Bavaria or Brandenburg gravely discussed the pros and cons over beer-glasses and succulent meal—but the *Simplicissimus* rallied all the votes, saying, quite accurately: "Since we can, for once, choose at our ease from the Heavens, without anyone snatching from our mouths what we thought we had, as has happened before, let us take the fattest." These wise comments were illustrated by a cheerful cartoon, *The Modern Judgment of Paris*, and although presented in a slightly mocking manner, it was well-received.

Jupiter was colossal, but distant; it seemed to offer nothing for an extended sojourn, but water boiling under gases at 300 atmospheres of pressure, and only an Empire of Tritons or Sirens could be founded there until further notice.

There remained Venus, the morning star, the star of love, our sister world. These appellations, and others just as sweet,

---

[82] Article 175 of the German penal code was a proscription of homosexuality. Phoebe is one of the less popular synonyms for the Moon, although the goddess in question had received a boost to her popularity when she was represented in Georges Méliès' most famous silent movie, known in English as *A Trip to the Moon.*

234

distributed in the newspapers and magazines, won the hearts of all sentimental Germans to her cause. It is something, in any land, to have women behind you; Venus, goddess and planet alike, knew that.

At the Congress, Hauchet pleaded her cause, soberly, clearly and justly. "Venus is similar to the Earth, with snowy Himalayas, overflowing Amazons, titanic plateaus, storm-tossed oceans, beneath a hotter Sun. Life must be abundant there, swarming. Oppositions occur every 19 months, as opposed to 26 for Mars. Although the calculation of the trajectory is more delicate because of the increasing attraction of the Sun, there is no danger from any wandering planet like Eros. And, in the case of conquest, note this: if current theories regarding the life and death of elements are true, there is more radium and other similar substances on Venus than on Earth—and perhaps other, unknown, elements."

The chemists and physicists felt their hearts flutter at these words. Of 500 votes, 458 guaranteed Venus an interplanetary flight at the earliest possible opportunity. As usual, the Congress was concluded by a banquet, for a satisfied stomach communicates to be brain a love for what is to come, and forgetfulness of even courteous disputes.

IV. The Departure

The final months separating von Reinhardt and his companions from the flight to Venus were magnificently calm. It was a matter of arriving at the great adventure with clean minds and unperturbed muscles—and, according to Hauchet's advice, they ought not to regret anything left behind on Earth. He talked about that easily, the Doctor. Having filled their eyes filled with the multiple beauties of this world, measured its extent and found it insufficient, they would be able to attempt such a risk, a leap into the unknown.

The Devil took a hand, however, and stirred up two blue eyes and blonde hair for the desolation of Rosenwald—"for love is a malicious archer, who strikes at an even greater range than the Wheel itself," as a French reporter dispatched by *Le Journal* wrote, somewhat satirically. Otto swore to leave even so, however. Fraulein Hilda Liebfen agreed, despite everything. After their engagement, time passed for them six times faster than it should have.

The great day arrived, in glorious sunlight.

That morning, the Wheel was set in motion, with an acceleration no greater than a meter per second. The mist disappeared, and an anxious crowd—thousand of eyes, vast, dense, profound, come from all over the world—covered the camp, the surrounding fields and the roofs of the town. The ironclads of the Atlantic squadron lined upon out to sea, surrounded by other warships, fully manned. Yet, more men were heaped up in a prodigious crescent of sailing ships, steamships and huge barges. The breath of that crowd created a vapor in the warm air; its murmur was like the sound of the sea.

The flags of 20 nations flapped in the wind, and chimneys rising up into the sky discharged steam. The monumental Wheel inclined slowly, and one foot of shining steel took the place of another. The most distant ranks of the crowd saw nothing at first. Then, after two hours, the noise of the alternating motor extended into the distance, immediately expelling turbulent clouds of steam.

Suddenly, the racket of the pistons ceased, for the Wheel now seemed like a shield against the fiery sky. A murmur of anxiety ran through the crowd, and in the silence the whistling of the Wheel was audible. A crown of steam surrounded it, a tremulous white aureole, scattered with sparks.

Brunschweig, the chief engineer, thought for a second that the life of the travelers was a feeble little thing amid that chaos of flame and noise. He leaned over the telephone that linked him to the projectile, but reassuring words replied to his call. And the hours went by. The clear day proclaimed the joy of life. The spectators thought of the men who, within the shell of steel, sensed that their projectile was ready to take fight. One sole man on the ground, the engineer at the mechanism triggering their departure, was the master of their destiny.

Then, lamps lit up in the dusk, and the air filled with the buzz of the crowd and the machine, for the turbine was working almost at top speed. A few more minutes passed by. Astronomers and engineers huddled around items of apparatus. Everyone's hearts beat a little faster.

In the distance, the squadron's cannons thundered a last salute. Everyone took off their hats. The town's orchestras had been playing heroic marches all day, but now there was silence. Brunschweig raised his eyes towards the starry shy, put his finger on the control-button, and pressed it. A bell rang. A detachment mechanism was activated. Twenty seconds more—and suddenly a streak of light streaked the sky, at a stroke, in the direction of the dark zenith.

They were on their way.

V. The Heavenly Road

Novels of space travel imagine a feverish activity among the travelers at the moment of departure: the intoxication of velocity; a rush to the windows; rapidly-beating hearts; cries of enthusiasm. In reality, it was not like that. When the hatchway had been sealed over their heads, the voyagers heard the workmen's hammers for another minute applying fusible cladding to the last few square centimeters left uncovered for their entry. Then there was calm.

The projectile, visited 20 times before, no longer had the attraction of novelty. They sat in their recreation-room, beneath the observatory, and Rosenwald uncorked a bottle of good Rhenish whine. They honored it according to its merits, and immediately afterwards von Reinhardt observed that it was time to go back to the gyroscopic cabin—for it will not have escaped the intelligent reader that, in the course of their regular rotation, the voyager would find themselves upside-down at every turn, not to mention that the frightful development of the centrifugal force would crush them against the walls. This had been averted by mounting a central cabin in a gyroscope. This heavy ring of steel launched at great speed maintained a constant position for itself and its occupants. Similar items of apparatus have been developed for other purposes, for the direction of submarines and the automatic equilibration of torpedoes and aircraft, and have not similar seats, immobile during the worst turbulence, been envisaged for protection against sea-sickness?

The cabin was small and padded, almost cramped. As soon as they were there, the gyroscope commenced its rotation. Various ingenious mechanisms prevented them from being inconvenienced. Rosenwald switched on the little electric lamp and aid; "Let's eat"—which they did, to get their breath back. The gyroscope hummed.

After coffee and cigars, they chatted. The cheerful Otto and Hauchet, rich in talk of science or mockery, made the time pass agreeably. Von Reinhardt listened, which was easy for him. He saw himself on his way, piloting his projectile—his *Sirius*, as it had been baptized—with an almost imperial hand.

They departed thus without being aware of it; the rotation of the gyroscope accelerated with that of the Wheel. The tremors of the hull could not reach them, only the noises of the gigantic machine in operation.

Suddenly, von Reinhardt said: "We're moving—there's nothing audible."

They looked at the chronometers. They were still turning in the little cabin, and it was necessary to wait. They could stop the gyroscope from their position, but that would be dangerous at top speed. Now that external energy was lacking, it would slow down gradually. Time passed while they advanced with planetary velocity into unlimited space.

After a further three quarters of an hour. Hauchet activated the Silber brakes. Within a minute, the rotation, already very slow, was conclusively arrested, and the three men emerged into the *Sirius*.

Rosenwald activated the inferior porthole, and sunlight suddenly invaded the projectile. Groping blindly, he closed it again and opened a second, which revealed the Earth amid the stars. They were already 20,000 kilometers away; with the aid of large telescopes they could examine at their leisure the green seas, the vast rivers and the stains of cities. The white pole shrank slowly beneath their eyes.

They began to make themselves comfortable. As their emotions were still working away inside them, Rosenwald got out his planner and they dined magnificently. When they had immolated a few bottles, they went to the waste disposal unit, but it was not working. The tube did not refuse its service, but the door to the void was obstinate.

"The fusible metal has not completely melted directly outside it!" said Hauchet.

The other two looked at him, without laughing—for the idea of conserving three months' detritus and excretions was far from pleasant.

"I anticipated this," said the Doctor, smiling.

He went to his bed, lifted the sheets and triumphantly brought out a sort of black suit of armor. He set it upright.

"What the Devil...?" Reinhardt began.

"To go outside, if the weather's good," replied the joyful Rosenwald. "Great idea, Hauchet."

And the Doctor set about getting into the suit of armor. Jointed to perfection, the hands very well articulated, it comprised a double layer of ebonite rubber with a reservoir of liquid air sufficient for an hour. Evidently, a man enclosed within it could defy the most intense cold, even that of absolute zero.

"I've tried it out ten or a dozen times in the course of my studies on the physiology of extreme cold but I didn't want to mention it to you until the occasion arose," said the smiling Doctor. "The occasion arrived very quickly."

The other two sealed him in perfectly, and he went slowly down to the laboratory, one of whose doors communicated with the void. His companions waited. A few moments later, they were surprised to see feet through the porthole, the wrong way up. They ran to it, looked out and whistled. The doctor was floating upside-down, suspended between the nadir and the zenith, motionless and unsupported. A short while later, he returned to the projectile, guiding himself along a rope unrolled from his waist, and set to work.

Ten minutes later, he reappeared.

"A word of advice for you, Rosenwald, if you want to frolic in space. It's charming; you're as light as a feather—but beware of the escape velocity. Remember that you're on a very singular planet, and that the least effort will send you beyond the gravitational attraction of the projectile into space. You'll become a planet yourself and your own sole inhabitant—which is a glorious prospect, but beware of asphyxiation!"

240

Rosenwald looked out of the porthole, and no longer had any inclination to try it. Beyond the vicinity of the flamboyant Sun, from which furious protuberances sprang forth, the stars—points of light set against the ebon sky—seemed disquietingly bright.

Von Reinhardt and his friend were not professional astronomers, and they limited themselves at first to operating the recording apparatus that had to replace human observers for the occasion: photography; measurements of light intensity; the composition of exterior space; views of the Earth; monitoring the conditions of life in the projectile itself—the absorption of oxygen in conditions of minima weight and 1000 other problems posed by the new conditions. Then they went up to the observatory, searched for white Venus and began to study it with their narrow-focus telescope. That kept them occupied until it was time for bed, after a dinner worthy of the circumstances.

But they could not sleep. Weight diminished slowly with every inch they advanced—and it is the sole force that we and nature have been unable to modify in the history of the Earth. The human organism continued to function regularly, but the conditions were modified to a considerable degree. The first symptom was an increasing overexcitement, a feverish activity of speech and gesture. The blood, less heavy, flooded the brain under the constant pressure of the heart, which did not change itself. Read clouds were passing before their eyes and it seemed to them that a vice was gripping their heads.

From the very outset of the voyage, they would have succumbed to an intellectual delirium, like excessively wise gods, if Hauchet had not anticipated the circumstance. They immediately took drugs to diminish the activity of the heart and relax their blood pressure considerably, their muscular activity being minimal.

That is a point that the explorers of other worlds have never envisaged. Man's resistance to all possible forces, serums and radiations has been tested, but no one has ever been

241

able to ascertain how his body will stand up to an increase or diminution of weight.

The three men waited, immobile in their camp-beds, each one next to a porthole. It was necessary, in large measure, to trust their own resistance and take the chance. Whatever they did, their brains were working at high tension and they soon resembled hashish-eaters, laughing without any reason, their speech disordered, gesturing madly, and yet understanding everything perfectly.

Then fatigue overwhelmed them, crushingly. For hours, the liquid air apparatus released the vivifying gas; the gas-recycler rotated in its corner; the ventilator hummed, forcing the air charged with human exhalations through the tubes irrigated with calcium chloride. The mechanical life of the all the complex and precise recording devices continued without human intervention.

Finally, Rosenwald woke up. He made a gesture and suddenly found himself carried into the air, outside is bunk. Then he looked at the ship's clock. It marked hours, days and moths and he saw that he had slept for two full days after the cerebral excess and enormous expense of their first hours.

He shook his comrades. Although they felt very weak, their primitive torpor was succeeded by a joyful animation. Simply lifting a finger, in that extraordinary weightlessness, now set the entire body in motion. Without losing any time, they made four cups of excellent coffee in the solar oven; then effervescent beer washed down the excellent meal that Hauchet prepared for them. Afterwards, they went to the laboratory.

Rapidly, regularly, imperceptibly, minute by minute and hour by hour, they were advancing towards Venus. From the tenth day onwards, they could see the snowy peaks of its high mountains through its telescope, and the new world's disk became appreciable to the naked eye.

The days went by, measurable only by the chronometers, monotonous but rich in sensations and discoveries. They watched their planet increase in size slowly; they calculated the moment of greatest proximity before *Sirius* would close its arc towards the Earth. The dazzling glory of the Sun increased. At his calculating machine, Hauchet probed the enigma: a tiny, pensive creature before the high stars, who was nevertheless measuring some of them in a few in a few grams of grey matter.

Humankind was waiting for them in the little spark lost in the Heavens that was our world.

VI. The Unexpected

It was time for the trajectory of the *Sirius* to curve back towards Earth. The space explorers had gathered more information regarding the sublime Heavens and the Morning Star than previous centuries had accumulated. There were about to bring this booty back to us. Their long voyage through the gulf of the void had certainly not been futile; they also had pictures of the far side of the Moon.

Their velocity needed to decrease as they drew nearer to Venus, then increase gradually as they returned towards the Earth. But had it actually decreased? They had no point of reference among the cold stars. The titanic distances rendered the movement of the *Sirius* infinitesimal. The observations they made with a micrometer of the gradually diminishing increase in the diameter of Venus' disk were their only means of obtaining an approximation of the distance they had traversed.

The truth became manifest. The arc was not closing. The simultaneous attraction of Venus and the Sun had countered the antigravitational effect of their velocity, and the *Sirius* was following a new route through space, dependent on three causes, and probably others still. Hauchet attempted to calculate them, and a council of war was held in the observatory.

"We have to induce some reaction against the course of the *Sirius*," Rosenwald opined.

"In which case the projectile would evaporate in flames," said Hauchet, "its movement converted into heat. No, either we go on too quickly, missing Venus, and then must beware of the Sun—we'd be drawn to it like moths—or we try to reach Venus, or we attempt to return to the Earth. There are chances of success; there are more of failure. In the last case, the *Sirius* would describe a new ellipse in space, which would be very interesting but might be far too prolonged, for we can't possibly cross 20 million kilometers with nothing but the reaction

244

motor. We'd remain on our course. Providing the impulse is easy—but then we'd become an independent celestial body and the movements are so complex they'd become unpredictable. Besides, as a scientist, I vote for the voyage to Venus. If both of you opt for the return to Earth, I'll obey—but don't forget that the Wheel is still in place and that wireless telegraphy is possible, from world to world, with the energies we'll create."

Imagine those men, in that narrow room, beneath the indifferent gaze of the stars, between two infinities, those champions of our race, deliberating upon the great adventure. When Hauchet fell silent, the others looked at him, palely.

"Do you think we'd be able to carve out a niche for ourselves up there?" asked Rosenwald.

The Frenchman's eyes slowly filled with an unsustainable gleam. He simply replied: "There's a song that goes: *We are a race of gods.*"

"Well said!" cried von Reinhardt. "It's a dream worthy of our race. Set a course for Venus!" He laughed loudly. He drew his large body up to its full height, and bounded like a lion in the overly narrow space.

"Now," said Hauchet, "let's send some postcards. You Germans…"

"What?" said Rosenwald.

But the Doctor brought out a packet of cards from his desk, marked a position on each one, signed it, and then held them out. "You're forgetting our messengers," he said.

His journal was briefly printed, in ten copies, on the ship's writing-machine. The "messengers" consisted of aluminum sheets with little pieces of steel lowering their centers of gravity. After being launched into the void towards a world, so as to fall upon it, the aluminum sheet acted as a parachute, while a whistle attracted attention, and the whole was designed to float on water.

"It's a great pity," Rosenwald joked, "that Ariel, or Urania, or a Venusian can't sign with us."

With heroic precision, they filled out their postcards. Inserted in ten messengers, sealed at the bottom, Hauchet took possession of them, and, clad in an ebonite suit, he left the *Sirius*. He looked back momentarily. The distant Earth was shining, peaceful and foreign. A rapid shiver ran down Hauchet's spine. Then he took the first of the messengers, flexed his robust arm, and hurled it into the void. The device disappeared in a trice, more rapidly than a bullet. The man, confronting the void, repeated his action. He seemed to be sowing the field of stars for a strange harvest—and a thought, perhaps a farewell, flew away, free, into space.

A few days later, they saw Venus invade their nadir, its attraction making itself felt. It was a world, another world—and the three men, the first from our Earth to visit another planet, were playing the great game of Life and Death in all its beauty.

Venus the white extended itself. The peaks of its mountains, set against the flaming Sun, were like lace. The destiny of a conquering humankind and of a future humankind was about to be decided on the chessboard of the worlds.

END OF PART ONE

Part Two: Venus, German Colony
(Otto Rosenwald's Journal)

I. The Arrival

Our velocity began to increase so quickly that we were afraid that we might pass Venus by and meet an incandescent death in the Sun a month later, in an unprecedented impact. For Hauchet, it was a period of hectic activity; for us, of anxious idleness. There was no sound, no flame, nothing but abrupt tremors to testify to the activation of the reaction-motor. There were two long days of maneuvers. We passed behind the planet, using its gravitational attraction as a brake, then began to describe a complex arc to which Hauchet alone could put a name. For hours, we flew parallel to the planet. Then we began our descent. The greatest danger was past. We belonged to this world, and our *Sirius* was flying at a distance of 50,000 leagues, drawing closer to its rapid rotation by the minute.

Our hearts leapt at the sight of the horizon that seemed to be revealing itself to us. "A little lower than the angels," we had traced out route through space, but the thought of the Empire was within us.

At the end, the stars darkened. We entered the atmosphere. A tube and a system of balloons permitted the analysis of the external environment. First, we went through a layer of rare gases. The noise of the reaction-motor became perceptible, while we rocked from one side to the other, for the velocity of our fall was reduced to about 2000 meters per second by virtue of tacking, and the double work of the motors attempted to make us advance horizontally through the thick atmosphere. For a terribly long minute, we were swallowed up by enormous clouds, without knowing whether we were going to crash into one of those mountains with which Venus bristles, especially in the southern hemisphere. Then, a grey daylight reappeared. We were now flying almost level, progressing by leaps and bounds, and our motors were exhaling without respite— but the air, almost twice as dense as ours—saved us, opposing a slid resistance to the extreme rapidity of the gas flooding from our apparatus.

For a second, I glimpsed a snowy layer of clouds through the porthole before disappearing into it. We were bouncing off the padding and the detonations of the motors were rolling like a cannonade. Then, there was a heart-rending stop and the sensation of a steep fall. Weight reasserted its rights upon us, brutally.

We struck a mass of water diagonally. Suddenly, turbulent foam rose up around us. There was sudden darkness, one bounce, then two, and a regular swaying began. We were at rest, after that immense voyage across space.

I ran to the observatory, but I could see nothing through the porthole by the living fluidity of waves. Distant horizons revealed themselves; then, in the far distance, formidable mountain summits. They glowed in the Sun like silver cupolas, partly disappearing into the second layer of the white clouds that protected this world from the extreme proximity of the Sun.

"It's the sea," said von Reinhardt.

Hauchet began an analysis with the aid of the aforementioned tubes. First he established the nature and composition of the air, then its chemical and biological innocuousness, attempting to identify microbes. Afterwards, he took a sample of the water; a drop flamed in front of his spectroscope.

"Yes, we've come down in the southern hemisphere."

That was the better of our options. Now, it was a matter of reaching land.

We had made provisions for the eventuality that, on returning to Earth, we would come down in the ocean or a desert, and we possessed two aircraft propellers. We opened a porthole; the first draught of new air, the air of another world, filled my mouth with a fresh and sweet taste. We burst into joyful laughter, while Hauchet deployed the propeller outside and connected it to the motor.

The *Sirius*, two-thirds submerged, obeyed; it began slowly to displace itself as we desired. A 100 kilos on Earth only weighs 80 on Venus, while the denser air suited our propellers very well.

Eventually, the shore appeared before our eyes. We focused our attention. Strange and multitudinous plants were entangled on the emerald rocks. The *Sirius* scraped on the sandy seabed, stopping 100 meters away, and we navigated by guesswork, approaching as close as possible. Finally, we found an inlet, at the mouth of a fast-flowing river hollowed out in the rock. We moved slowly against the current.

That swift water welcomed us. Its depth was adequate for us to advance without encumbrance. The width attained 200 meters, and when we had come through a sort of gully, we then found ourselves in a plain, behind the cliffs. Our first concern was to anchor the projectile to the bank, then to inspect the surroundings of the *Sirius*, marvelously calm beneath the ardent Sun.

II. On the Ground

Usually, in all the literature that I have read, immediately after arriving on a new world, people set off adventuring, with their hands in their pockets, nothing being safer than an unknown planet—but we were too wise for that. We examined the plain, bristling with sumptuous vegetation and extending as far as the black mass of the distant cliffs. Other, higher, cliffs barred the river for ten or 12 miles, and there was nothing within 100 paces but a seemingly-inoffensive grayish block.

The result was that, taking my stout rifle, I took the chance of getting down. The heat outside the *Sirius* was truly Saharan. I yearned for fresh air and shady forests. My companions joined me.

"A veritable monastery," said von Reinhardt. "Venusian game must not come here."

As he was speaking, the block I mentioned suddenly got up: a massive, solid, weighty form. There was an immediate dull roar; then the creature's panting respiration revealed a formidable organism, which as coming towards us. With one accord, we stepped back, lowering our heavy rifles.

"To the *Sirius*!" cried Hauchet. "We need to take a look at this. Run!"

We leapt forward; he covered our retreat. The porthole and the ladder were still there, fortunately, and there was no oscillation to fear, given our firm anchorage. We were inside in a second, and the Doctor climbed up unhurriedly. The creature arrived at top speed.

I didn't recognize the horror, and Hauchet said that it had never existed on Earth. We named it *Tridens ferox*, and the species is rare. At any rate, the creature stood up, as big as an elephant standing on its hind legs, its shapeless limbs hanging down like a squamous robe. It had no muzzle, only a sort of whitish triangle that opened and closed rhythmically. It came forward deliberately, like a creature unfamiliar with its enemy, and the ground shook at each step. Twenty paces from the *Sirius*, it slowly crouched down.

Then the sound of an elephant-gun rang out. The Doctor stifled a curse, but the explosive bullet—two to the pound!—had struck the mass full on. The flame burst forth and the brute began coughing with the power of a motorized drill, rolling around in the convulsions of a furious agony.

Finally, death came. The terrible structure became still.

"Stay up here with your rifles. I'll go take a look," said Hauchet.

We inspected the surroundings and the Doctor went forward. Scientific interest soon made him forget the danger. Suddenly, with a shiver, I saw another form loom up behind the rocks. This one also descended rapidly towards us. Less burly than the *Tridens ferox*, it reminded me of vaguely familiar forms. At any rate, it took no notice of us, and, suddenly pivoting upon itself, threw itself towards the doctor like lightning. I fired and missed. Von Reinhardt dispatched five cartridges from his repeating rifle, but in vain.

The Doctor raised his head. No man was ever so prompt. With one bound he threw himself to his right, behind the corpse of the *Tridens*. With another, he found himself almost in contact with the new enemy, and discharged a round carrying an explosive bullet into its skull. The creature collapsed.

Thus we made contact with the fauna of Venus. We learned subsequently that our bad luck had brought us into the only plain 300,000 meters round whose gorges and slopes accommodated all these giant creatures.

While we dined, very animated, trying valiantly—but in vain—to cope with a slice of *Tridens*, the exultant Hauchet crowed: "My friends, we have arrived at the most interesting moment. This world, with its hot Sun, seems expressly made for reptiles. They have reigned here. Some people on Earth think that they still reign—but my ongoing studies of the *Tridens* and the other animal, which I have baptized *Rhinoformis Reinhardtii* imply that…"

He paused, took the piece of *Tridens* out of his mouth and put it on the table, despairingly.

"...Imply that," he resumed, "these charming animals are no longer reptiles and not mammals. Are they intermediaries? No. Why? Do you want the same things to appear everywhere, invariably? Boring! They belong to an inferior class of a new order that I have just created: the Pseudosaurs, or false reptiles."

I inscribed that in my *Venus Yearbook*.

"We have fallen into a very interesting world," he continued. "These Pseudosaurs, especially the *Tridens ferox*, were worth the trip on their own. A pearl, a true pearl. No bones, cartilage; scales worthy of a cubist; an unknown jaw; a marvelously powerful organism, of course—I wouldn't give a *sou* for a tiger who faced up to one. Nor, by Jupiter, a rhinoceros!"

"It would be nice," said von Reinhardt, smiling, "to explore Venus from a distance and study these pearls from a safe height. For my part, I don't like eating *Tridens*, and I'll be annoyed if it tries to do the same to me."

"Very true," said Hauchet. "We'll set up the aerac[83] shortly, and start by killing a few of the cousins of our defunct friends if they try to get in our say."

When dusk came, we put together the aerac, at the cost of some hard work, borrowing materials carelessly from the *Sirius*—but we reserved the test flights for the following day.

There was a delightful sensation of security after days of anguish. Behind our steel walls we certainly had nothing to fear from men or beasts—only from earthquakes. And we dined like gods. Afterwards, we observed the night through the portholes. There was no moonlight or starlight beneath that heavy vault of leaden cloud, but the formidable solar radiation gave rise to a very faint twilight, and formidable jaws were

---

[83] The aerac—Hauchet's own invention—was earlier described as a jet plane with variable wings, but the one the travelers use on Venus seems more like a helicopter; I have, however, retained the improvised term.

lurking in the darkness. Eventually, something advanced to-wards us, and we used our electric searchlight to unmask an immense, swift creature with a soft tread. It stopped short, petrified by the sudden light, and von Reinhardt's rifle rang out. Turning its back, the creature decamped so quickly that it was impossible for us to fire again. The night was tranquil after that.

It rained heavily throughout the next day, and the clouds were dark and low. Then, on the third day, the Sun swept them all away, and Hauchet, balanced on the aerac, took to the air at a height of 30 feet.

We decided that we would all embark, for we had to live or die together. Hauchet took the lead; we had hours of rapid travel before us.

We climbed slowly towards the cliffs, aiming for the highest summits. We passed over vast creatures, asleep or moving slowly. A labyrinth of rocks extended beneath us, then a valley filled with lush brightly-colored vegetation, in which orange and yellow were dominant, then granite hills and fur-ther valleys—a complex network that we would not have been able to penetrate on foot. At regular intervals, we rose up above the spurs of mountains. The winds buffeted us briefly, while we searched for a shelter. Slowly, the summit at which we ere aiming loomed up in the sky, and we decided to set down on a rocky terrace above an enormous mist-filled valley. The aerac set down a few paces from the edge.

"We ought to be high enough," said von Reinhardt.

As he spoke, the wind chased the clouds away and we contemplated a Venusian landscape of wild grandeur: titanic mountains in a starlit chain formed a distant background to immense valleys filled with the roar of cascades. The flaming Sun had melted the glaciers, but its glare illuminated monstr-ous cones erected on the surrounding plateaus—undoubtedly ancient volcanoes. And that chaos of granite, lava, darkening air and ravines extended for league upon league, repetitive, immense and terrible.

For a moment we remained open-mouthed before that otherworldly beauty, magical in its enormity, its light and its noise, set against the red sky. Then von Reinhardt ran back to the aerac. A stone column rose up into the sky. A second later, the black white and red flag stood out against the sky, and Heinrich took possession of Venus in the name of His Majesty the Emperor. He stood up tall and proud, like a god, and the colors of the Empire floated around him. My heart leapt with enthusiasm and I cried "Hurrah!"—but Hauchet stood up in his turn, very gravely.

"It's good, Monsieur, to have thought of your fatherland. Allow me not to forget mine. Without me, would you have dreamed of what we have accomplished? I ask, on behalf of France, at least for a foothold—and I would like to see my colors displayed, without infringing your rights."

"That does you honor," said von Reinhardt, seriously.

Hauchet advanced to the rock. From his pocket, he took a silken cloth, and the blue, white and red played in the lively air, cut across by a gold triangle surrounding the motto: "Science; Humanity; Fatherland."

"Higher even than your nation and ours," Hauchet said then, "you see here the badge of the Future when the nations will be absorbed into one, and which, with me, sets its foot upon this new world."

"You dream immense dreams," murmured von Reinhardt, "and you have already brought one dream to a marvelous realization."

And we soared like eagles over mountains and valleys, beneath the immense Sun, amid livid clouds pushed by the strong winds.

III. Explorations

We had described circles around the *Sirius*, within a 100-mile radius, and apart from the wild Pseudosaurs, no higher life-forms had become manifest. The Pseudosaurs were only manifest on the high plateaus. Their valleys must have condensed the world's temperate life: rustling steams fed by the eternal clouds undoubtedly ran there. In our plain, enclosed by rocks, only brutal and formidable presences were concentrated, doubtless originating from other places on the planet, to which the dense vegetation assured abundant pasture.

There was also the matter of discovering the mineral riches of the world, masked here by the mantle of tangled plants: radium-containing springs, saline or thermal; future energy-sources that could be utilized at will—for our panclastite was diminishing even more rapidly than our provisions.

"With sufficient energy, I could telegraph Earth," Hauchet said.

We could only see our planet in brief periods of clarity on rare nights, between the clouds, but that hope sustained us, and we decided to explore the marshes. Hauchet spent a week fabricating explosives with metallic peroxides and sulfur discovered by the ton along the cliffs, in the lairs of three or four Rhinoforms that we took care to exterminate. And we entrusted our destiny to the aerac.

After rocky beaches, there were gaping precipices, steep paths and finally lush shiny plains, swarming with plants. Then lakes, extensive waters disturbed by the twisting of immense creatures, from which infinite reed-beds sprang. From these clumps rose giant dragonflies with iridescent wings, and gigantic cockroaches—nightmarish vermin. There were monstrous leeches, hideous fish—an entirely unknown and malevolent fauna swarmed there, supporting voracious predators of formidable size, near relatives of the phytonomorphs that once reigned over our lagoons. One of them, extended beneath the aerac, suddenly reared up, and the long body, erect above the miry waves, darted jaws of steel towards us. Our engine lifted us up almost immediately, and we continued our course towards the sea. Its immense and monotonous mass beat the rocky coast with an eternal swell, while Pseudosaurs galloped and frightful birds flew over the shore. A few of them dared to give chase to us, our size seeming inferior to them—but our rifles spoke to them, their argument carrying so much weight over such a range that they did not continue.

Ascending to the plateaus again, we found a forest. It extended into the distance, dark and dense, devoid of the cries of beasts and the flutter of birds, and an irrational fear took hold of us. We avoided going down.

"I don't know what's there, but I'm afraid of it," said von Reinhardt.

"Carnivorous plants?" I suggested.

"No," said Hauchet. "Worse, perhaps…"

As we hovered, something moved. It was a huge, massive animal with a thick skull. It advanced towards the forest and went into it. There was no movement or sound below. Suddenly, the creature leapt up, howled and became stiff, 20 meters beneath our feet—and there were other bones there.

"Electricity! Lightning bolts!" cried Hauchet. "Radioactive tissues!"

It would doubtless be better to describe struggles and battles, but the fact is that, with our aerac and the prudence we brought to our explorations, if we did not get too close to anything, we were not in any great danger. We drew up a map of the region, as best we could, from Reinhardt's mountain, and cleared the ground around the *Sirius*, with some difficulty. The plants, full of moisture, refused to burn; the heat was frightful and such was the saturation of the air that sweat could not evaporate—but we arrived at our goal with the aid of Hauchet's explosives, and the carcasses of the monsters distributed around us created a barrier of terror.

Then we discovered, further away, a zone of dismal, heavy, lukewarm eternal rain. There, the Venusian plants are practically incombustible and fire is never seen. The dominant creatures are large semi-terrestrial mollusks, inhabitants of limitless pools of the intermediary region. Bolder flights carried us to high plateaus above ravines gleaming with strange fires in the tenebrous night, lakes of ice dormant between the crags, torrent bounding in joyous spray. There we dared to descend and camp, for the Pseudosaurs were as unknown there as the lightning-plants. Immense metallic masses confused our compasses. There were numerous smaller creatures, agile and fugitive—but one evening, we felt the wind of death pass by.

We had parked the aerac close to a peaceful lake, lit a fire of grass that we had cut and dried in the Sun—there was less rain at these heights—and we were chatting gaily, waiting for dinner, when Hauchet murmured: "Have you noticed that the air is getting thicker?"

A fog was, indeed, flowing out of a gorge towards us, getting nearer by the minute—something like a slow inundation. Our friend looked again, then suddenly cried: "To the aerac!"

We obeyed. The docile apparatus took off. An instant after, everything disappeared, while we set down on a firm terrace higher up, and the somber mass passed on. Our fire as still burning, but when the cloud reached the lake there was a sputtering sound and the fog suddenly vanished. The familiar flame of the fire invited us to go back down but Hauchet stopped us.

Finally, he allowed us to resume our position down below and our hearts leapt when we saw the discolored plants drooping.

"It's a form of cyanogen," our friend said. "It's necessary to be wary of the mineral."

I learned that to my cost the next day. We were near to another lake, whose water was dark but marvelously transparent; that excited my curiosity. The water was quite shallow and my companions were paddling in it a short distance away. I took off my sturdy boots and did likewise. It was very pleasant. Everything seemed secure when Hauchet saw me going forwards.

"Come back!" he cried.

I was one step from the edge, when there was a gust of cold wind and the lake suddenly solidified. The pressure on my bare legs was so horrible that I cried out in pain. Reinhardt leapt forward with a pickaxe and attacked the ice—was it ice?—with a giant's strength. Hauchet arrived with fire.

They got me free and managed to carry me to the aerac.

"It's a phenomenon of supercongelation," the Doctor explained, later, "caused by an inopportune wind. Otto, you would have been struck dead for the sake of a bath!"

Be that as it may, we ascertained the lie of the land in its entirety: marshes, high plateaus, shores, completing the map, gaining a better knowledge of its goods and evils, and made preparations for the winter for two months.

IV. Those Who Might Have Been....

One morning, Hauchet showed us shining clouds in the south. It was the gentle fall of mortal snow. It scarcely reached the ground, but others came. Fortunately, we had taken our precautions. The *Sirius* was overflowing with provisions: fish caught with lines of steel, turtles, edible plants, and alcoholic liquors extracted from mosses or mushrooms. We woke up to a dark sky, the clouds racing under the last of storms. Then we went back to sleep.

The river did not freeze, but it was impossible to go out on those days. There was a deluge of rain. Wind and hail competed in battering out steel walls, so furiously that it was sometimes necessary to close the hatches. I was at a loss to understand that black winter, in such close proximity to the Sun, but Hauchet explained it to me. The inclination of the planet's axis was the cause; cold water inundated us while other parts of the planet became infernos.[84]

"Console yourself," he said. "The seasons are brief—and goodbye Sun, goodbye heat. It will be back soon enough, though."

We smoked, read, and drew up our programs. Through the windows we watched the deserted plain on which the cold rain crashed down frightfully. Hauchet cheered us upon with his stories and multiple talents. By turns, he was editor of a facetious handwritten newspaper, a violinist, a lecturer with slides—he was a great help to us.

And a day dear to our hearts was drawing near: Christmas. It was the first feast-day on Venusian soil and we wanted

---

[84] In fact, Venus' orbital inclination is only slightly more than three degrees, but that was extremely difficult to determine by distant telescopic observation because the thick cloud did not permit any surface features to be seen, so Mas was free to speculate in 1913.

it to be as beautiful as possible, so we looked forward to Christmas Eve, and everyone prepared surprises.

We had done well to bring a little fir-tree, for there are none on Venus. We stood it up in the drawing-room, decorated with fish-grease candles. By its familiar light we distributed a few small gifts. Our hearts became sad as we thought of the distant fatherland and our loved ones there—but Hauchet played, and the cares were lifted from our hearts by the joyful music. An unfamiliar champagne sparkled in our cups. Crayfish appeared, followed by many other triumphant dishes. At the sight of so many good things, we recovered our courage. Hauchet surpassed himself in everything, even the cooking!

On departure, we had received letters and many postcards. That day, I re-read my Hilda's welcome handwriting. She was waiting for me up there, on Earth, where people were rejoicing—and we could hear nothing but the wind in the mountains. Would she have to wait for me forever? She would rather cross the immensity of space to join me. I also found forget-me-not seeds in the letter, so I gathered them up in order to sow them with the utmost care. My companions thought it a very poetic idea.

In this regard, I ought to say that Hauchet had brought a fine collection of various seeds for his experiments, and that we intended to plant them in favorable spots.

And the winter passed. One morning, it was no more than a dream. The Sun resumed its majesty. The fresh air filled us with a new zest for life, and we were preparing for an excursion when something unexpected happened.

First, there were distant flights. Closer to us, Pseudosaurs passed by, crushing the thickets. They were extending their necks, running southwards. Other monsters followed rapidly, a veritable dread urging their herd onwards. There was even a group of *Tridens ferox* galloping with the others.

We looked at one another. Such panic had to signify a cyclone or an earthquake, for what other enemy would be able to frighten these creatures? Then the fleeing creatures thinned out. Finally, a distant line appeared on the rain-dimmed horizon—a single mass at first, then separate shapes. We extended out telescopes avidly.

What was advancing towards us in serried ranks belonged to no known class of living creatures. They were five or six feet tall, with bare, smooth skin, large batrachian mouths, and massive, enormous and awkward hands—but a frontal projection jutted out from each face and the eyes were small, clear and keen.

There were thousands of them. Many, grotesquely, were carrying objects of various sorts in their hands; others were running back and forth. There was an orderliness about them. The unexpected had come into play. If the planet produced these robust and disciplined beings in multitudes, our very existence became problematic, full of dangers.

They were still coming closer, and the multiplicity of plants was flattened beneath their mass. The sunlight glinted on our projectile without appearing to disturb them—and the troop reached the river, heavy, massive and formidable. Dense dispositions hastened towards us.

In their rudimentary brains, they doubtless thought of us as a rock more regular than the others; they passed by, minute after minute, piling up on the river bank. Then the entire mass precipitated itself into the water, with a unanimous surge. Their bodies, suddenly agile, acquired a new, unsuspected vigor, and the monstrous herd reached the other bank, scaled it, and continued on its way. A sonorous bellowing rent the air.

When they had disappeared, we came out and advanced towards the river. A pool extended its shining waters. They suddenly became troubled, and forms reared up: a band of monsters! Laggards!

We hesitated momentarily. We could have exterminated a dozen in an instant, but that would bring back the furious horde. A unanimous assault on the *Sirius* would exhaust our ammunition, and if other herds were wandering around the planet, innumerable and watchful, it would be war!

But the creatures did not seem hostile. They came forward awkwardly. Golden eyes glistened in the moist flesh, while their thick hands beat the air. Then they squatted down on their palmate feet and began bellowing like bulls. Afterwards, they fell silent, but one continued in isolation. Hauchet replied, bellowing as the other did.

The scene was as comical as it was distressing. Abruptly, our friend, continuing his cries and gestures, retreated towards the *Sirius*. We did likewise, slowly. Suddenly, he began to sing. His loud voice took flight into the heavy air. The silent and motionless creatures seemed to be listening. He fell silent. They croaked noisily. He started again. They closed their wide mouths. And he dared to do what no man would have believed. He advanced towards the great brute who seemed to be the leader of the horde, met the gaze of the golden eyes, and took a viscous paw in his strong hand, still singing. And he held out a handful of thick grass.

The monsters crowded around him, open-mouthed, their gestures parodying his, attentive and suddenly mute. Then he came back, slowly. And the creature came forward, fearlessly. He thought we were similar to him, sons of his race. And that, undoubtedly, is why they did not attack us.

At close range, his body-structure was initially reminiscent of that of a frog, but the gaze was different and the skull was that of a cat. Between the soft lips, to either side, a sharp canine tooth projected. His enormous hand, gold and sticky, touched ours. Fearlessly, he waited.

We climbed up into the *Sirius*. He waited for us at the bottom of the ladder.

"We'll have to tie him up to keep him," said von Reinhardt.

"No," said Hauchet. "I'll give him a drink in this cup."

That was what he did. The creature howled in delight, his eyes shining—and he assembled his kin with raucous cries. From their gaping mouths and their cavernous breasts rose a horrible hymn. Then they went away.

"Gentlemen," said Hauchet, "we have studied the future human being of the planet, which would have given Venus a master if our humankind had not dreamed my Dream! If the batrachians lost their chance on our Earth, it was because of their feeble stature, but the marshes here permitted them to grow.

"Their race has multiplied vastly in the temperate regions as well as the equatorial and the great reptiles of yesteryear as well as the Pseudosaurians have done them the service of forcing their association. Besides, they are not limited, as fishes are, to a homogenous watery environment. They can and must be familiar with the shore, pouring over the hills and the edges of woods as well as the soft mud of lagoons. Did you see their teeth? There's no doubt in my mind. By claw and by jaw they distribute poison, perhaps extracting it from the putrid mud. Are they viviparous, oviparous or asexual? We don't know. At any rate, they're carnivores. That will permit them to compete successfully against the Rhinoforms and *Tridens*, and eliminate them one by one. Once the herbivores have disappeared, goodbye carnivores.

"They have hands, Gentleman—that hand that seems so indispensable, with which Huyghens endowed all the inhabitants of all the planets! And this changing planet constrains them to change. The Pseudosaurs are better than the Reptiles, but they count too much on themselves to unite and are adapted to a solitary existence. The birds seem unsociable and voracious here, very far from the African weaver-birds for example. You have seen that they have taught the lesson of terror to everything else and have forgotten it themselves. We have not seen them in our excursions. I presume that their hordes are based near the equator and along neighboring terrains, in the forests of the deep, warm valleys.

"These are lost children. I think the plateaus and the mountains are too dry for these…" He paused. "…Batracanthropes. In any case, they'll need a million years to reach our level. When we are here…" Laughing, he added:

"If communications are established with the Earth, what a task for the Prussian administration!"

"What?" I asked.

"To Germanize them!"

"French frivolity!" said Reinhardt, with a smile.

"It's because I'm frivolous that I flew here," said the Doctor.

We drank a toast to everyone.

V. The Valley of Peace

That day, a dense fog enveloped the aerac and the heavy clouds were still thick when a dark form appeared above us. It was gigantic, further magnified by the refraction of the air. I extended my rifle out of a window, but I did not have to make use of it for the creature came down just far enough to be reached and struck by a rotor-blade. It recoiled and fall like a stone, but the aerac spun around and made an abrupt descent; half of the rotor blade ad been broken off.

There were a few fearful moments, and that fall through darkness remains the worst of my memories. Then the motor started spitting out gases and we danced furiously in mid-air. The descent continued, in 30 or 40 meter spasms. Emerging from the fog, we saw bushes heaped up in verdant waves coming to meet us. We bounced, rebounding like a rubber ball, and came to rest 30 feet above the ground.

"You've saved us, Hauchet," said von Reinhardt.

"It was simple enough," the latter said, smiling, "to remove the tube from the gas turbine and make the reaction work against the fall."

"It was necessary to think of it," I said.

We got out the spare rotor-blade and surveyed the undergrowth. Down below, on ground covered with black humus, saturated with carbonic acid, the heat had to be frightful. I thought about the rubber-hunters of Brazil, and then felt a sudden surge of fear, because something was climbing up the tree, more smoothly than growing moss: something large, viscous, powerful and voracious. I took aim at the creature at a range of 20 paces and fired. It immediately became motionless, then flowed into the shadows and disappeared. I kept watch anyway, and there was a slow movement in the darkness. But the rotor-blade was mounted. Hauchet looked down too. He did not say a word. Clenching his teeth, he pulled the lever and we took off.

"I think there are colonies of insects and giant spiders down there," he said, "with jaws dripping with poison and sharp stings a-plenty in the darkness. We'll have to make a collection some day."

The dark selvedge of the undergrowth retreated before us, bordered by cliffs and a savannah extending beyond our horizon: a sea of ground-hugging plants beneath the Sun, replete with fecund vitality, swarming with life.

All of this was constructed on a titanic scale. That peaceful plain extended for leagues. The animals that ran fearlessly beneath the aerac's flight-path had a different character, closer to familiar types. Here was the reservation of the Future; in this vast space, away from the sheer mountains, unknown species were in competition. The sunlight glinted on a lazy river.

"It's the Valley of Peace," said Hauchet. "There was a time on Earth, at the beginning of the Tertiary, which lasted longer than the entirety of human history, in which only herbivores existed on the face of the Earth. The brutal reptiles had disappeared; the carnivores had not yet been born. Fear was forgotten. Then the carnivores came, terribly: lions, tigers, blood-drinking machairodonts, giant bears. Fear increased, increased further—then Man appeared, worse still. Imagine if the evolution of carnivores had stopped with the marsupials. The human grass-eater and gatherer of nuts might have disdained fresh meat and red blood, remained ignorant of war and hatred! But an obscure mammal, the Cain of his race, killed in order to live—and the Earth was changed forever. But we are bringing peace to this world, the law and justice of humankind supported by the blade of his strength. We are changing the course of evolution, destroying the devourers—fitting out the planet, in brief."[85]

---

[85] The word I have translated as "fitting out" is "*équiper*;" as deployed here and in the final chapter, it might pass for an early anticipation of the notion of terraforming. Although Hauchet is probably mistaken in the supposition that there was ever an interval in Earthly evolution in which carnivores were

I thought about that as we hovered over the river. The very air seemed alive. On and above the ground, in the water, everything was vibrant with invisible or manifest life. The next few hours were exultant for us. We drew nearer to a capricious tributary of the river.

From the bank we saw scintillating waves, in which 1000 iridescent creatures sparkled. These creatures were not confined in the prison of shape. They were changing, ramifying at will—but the phenomena we observed did not stop there. A feverish activity ran through our bloodstreams, flames filled our eyes and the intoxication of their air was like an excessively strong wine. Lichens were growing on the aerac's runners, while enormous mushrooms burst forth here and there, whose spores immediately began to increase. A thousand creatures, visible and invisible, intoned an immense hymn around us. The transparent water flowed, and our dreams flowed with it, and life in torrents.

Our overexcitement alarmed Hauchet. The aerac took us further away. Plants of a savory appearance grew everywhere, and in the first steam where we stopped we found excellent fish. So many good things put us in a joyful mood and we decided to make camp for a few days. We set down on dry firm ground.

Evening came, the fire burned placidly; there seemed to be nothing to fear, and my poetic soul drew me towards the stars, which came out that night.

Then we discovered a lake bubbling amid gold-splashed marble. The precious metal was glittering in the bed of a

---

absent—although the notion was presumably borrowed from one or more of the three books on palaeontology that Mas cites in his bibliography—and the logic of the subsequent extrapolation of that premise is decidedly dubious, the sensitivity Mas shows to evolutionary theory in his description of Venusian life is very unusual for its time, as is the striking notion of colonization as a crucial evolutionary diversion amenable to planning and control.

dried-up river—but that useless wealth was less important to us than the oil-wells in Hauchet Valley, 100 miles from the *Sirius*. With the warm water and the masses of gold we made a gigantic Voltaic pile, and our endless call for help rose up into the sky, and beyond.

VI. The Arrival of the Conquerors

The months went by, and the Plain of Sirius was subjected to human law. No creature existed except by our permission. By means of traps and the rifles, we exterminated the *Tridens* and the Rhinoforms, and we used landslides to seal off the valleys open to the marshes, for Man is strongest when he is only limited by himself. Slowly, we gave that part of the other world a familiar appearance. The deluges of rain and the furious winds became no more than auxiliary incidents. Our recording devices, vigilant sentinels, kept watch on the Heavens, the land and the waters. And one morning, on the sheet of paper on which the radiotelegraph was set, I read the signal emerging from the void. My heart ceased to beat.

Across the immensity of space, our brothers were coming. That minute was the greatest of my life. My friends came running, seeing me so pale, and I showed them the signal, unable to speak. We embraced one another in silence, and we aimed our electric searchlight towards the sky. Our post continued to function, ever vigilant—and we waited.

The recorder stopped in the night. The hours passed. An entire day went by before we received further news. When it came, it intoxicated us like a full-bodied wine, for, beyond the mountains the marshes and the valleys, other men were waiting for us.

How we ran to the aerac! And the hour that followed was decisive, for suddenly, blinded by the enormous Sun, we perceived five projectiles standing up in the masses of soft mud and reeds into which they had sunk on landing. We swooped down like an eagle, and out of an open hatch came the biologist Vornheim, His eyes were shining behind his gold-rimmed spectacles, and our cries rose up to the leaden sky. And there was Hilda, in my arms, exiled from the Earth for my sake. She was the first woman to set foot of the soil of the Star of Love!

When the projectiles, with their powerful engines, had been extracted from the grip of the hospitable marsh, the aeracs deployed their wings. Evening found us back at the Sirius, beneath flapping flags, in the joy of triumph: we modern Teuton knights, conquerors of boundless space.

Here Otto Rosenwald's journal concludes.

VII. The Washington Conference
and the Division of Space

When the allotted time elapsed without bringing back the *Sirius*, Germany's anxiety spread to the entire world. No one knows what hypotheses might have been put forth if the Prince of Monaco had not found one of the messengers a month later, with the three's dispatch. Then sadness took swing like a breath of wind, and there was no question that a relief mission had to be organized. Was the Wheel not there?

But the Yankees were aroused. One of old Europe's peoples surpassing young America! Well, if the Germans were investing 100 men and 100,000 marks, they would invest 100,000 dollars and 300 workers—and their own Wheel would be established like a dream in Panama, the center of the world.

Almost simultaneously, Carnegie, d'Estourelles de Constant and Flammarion proposed an international conference.[86]

---

[86] Although it not cited in the bibliography, Camille Flammarion's *La Fin du monde* (1895), whose first part describes an international conference to discuss possible courses of action in the face of an impending comet strike, seems to be a significant influence on this chapter. The other two named individuals are the American philanthropist Andrew Carnegie (1835-1919) and Baron Paul-Henri d'Estournelles de Constant de Rebeque (1852-1954), who had won the Nobel Peace prize in 1909 for his tireless work organizing peace conferences and ententes and attempting to further the cause of European Union. Charles Richet, who provided the novella with one of its head-quotes, was also famous for his pacifist beliefs as well as his scientific achievements. Although Mas' characters make very free use of their hunting-rifles, it is worth noting that the underlying philosophy of the novella is a pacifist one; in effect, Mas is proposing the colonization of space as a glorious

271

Washington was chosen. It was the first diplomatic gathering to carry the full stamp of the Scientific Era, for it required, behind the delegates' speeches, industrial strength, scintillating gold and the forceful will of crowds.

White and yellow races initially looked at one another in silence. Japan, at least, although tested by a recent financial crisis, conceived limitless hopes. It claimed its place in the Cosmos ardently.

It was necessary not to lose sight of the fact that humankind had taken 100,000 years to secure its domination of the world. How long would it take for other planets? Agreement was absolutely compulsory.

Unlike many conferences, however, the Congress was not long in getting under way, for the Americans were already at work in Panama. Germany's shipyards started a series of interplanetary vessels with the *Adler* and the *Himmelsgeier*, furnished with the latest improvements and machines specially designed for the atmosphere of Venus. Agreement was necessary.

Italy laid claim to a part of Mars, on the basis of the work of Schiaparelli, the great observer of the red planet. She obtained the equatorial zone. Naturally, Germany retained Venus, occupied by its nationals, but in answer to their request, she granted the Yankees preferential tariffs and mining options. Enormous Russia was granted the Moon. She asked for no more than that, estimating its terrestrial power as adequate, but she obtained compensations in Persia and the Far East, and then took advantage of the opportunity of a loan guaranteed by the new colony—at 4½% interest.

Austro-Hungary got her share, not much, on Mars, without anyone knowing why; but the Austrians were secretly

---

alternative to the Great War that was very obviously impending in Earth, and the nationalist views expressed in the story are undercut by an irony that actual history only served to re-emphasize.

thinking of deporting the Hungarians—who were thinking about the Poles, who were remembering the Croats, who...

To silence the weaker states, they were awarded the asteroids between Mars and Jupiter, *en bloc*. They were probably not content, but they bore it as best they could. The industrious Swiss, however, obtained Eros, a planetoid more than 200 kilometers in diameter, whose orbit passes between Mars and Earth; they were already planning an interplanetary hotel.

For the first time since she had joined a conference, England got nothing. The British were never able to take the matter seriously, *because there was no precedent!* After Germany and America, Belgium swept up that which remained—mines on the Moon, the Martian poles, various planetoids—reserving the privilege of taking part, at least in the matter of railways.

The French government was unable to proceed with the wise slowness that it cherished. A public outcry and the personal intervention of the Head of State obtained us the concession of the continent Herschel and other Martian territories, an observatory on the Moon and two more on Venus—and a Ministry of Planetary Relations was created without delay. It needed an astronomer; it was therefore given to a lawyer. Besides which, the Martian territory—the most important—was put under military rule and attached to the Colonial Office; in consequence, the Hyperavions were attributed to the Ministry of Marine and 7477 speeches were made, only 7473 of which were on secular defense.

Japan was given potential rights to Jupiter, the giant planet equal to 1300 Earths. The Yankee appetite could only be assuaged by annexing to the stars and stripes the distant planets of "Saturn, Uranus, Neptune and those beyond not yet discovered." But German diplomacy had its compensation: all the satellites of these enormous worlds, with those of Mars, and rectifications of frontiers on each of these immense globes, comprising ten million square kilometers—18,000 times the size of the Empire, almost 20 times the size of the entire Earth—which even contented the Pangermanists.

With Mercury, a minuscule world beneath a flaming Sun, no one seemed concerned at first. Then the Greeks annexed it—which discontented the Italians. The latter wrote everywhere that Mercury had been the god of thieves.

Thus Humanity set to work.

The second expedition was that of Michel de Lursac, to Mars, and if it did not reach the red planet, by design, it resolved nearly all the mysteries of that world.

The occupation and industrial conquest of the Moon was the work of the years that followed.

Another expedition, ten years later, reached Mars, and the improvement of wireless telegraphy in the interim was already sufficient to permit constant communication across the gulf of space.

On Venus, the human race spread out amid a powerful and terrible nature, hostile and favorable by turns. It would be a refuge when our Earth died, in a future still countless millennia distant, devoid of its fluid mantle of sea and air.

Interplanetary crossings to Venus, Mars and the Moon became rapid and continuous, easy to make by the middle of the 20th century. An ambitious, energetic and hard-working humankind had the immense and joyful task before it of fitting out three worlds to its needs and desires. And it found no enemy, no other humankind, for on Venus no such race had yet come into existence, on the Moon it no longer existed, and on Mars it was extinct.

Our readers have all read Jorge Raubier-Brown's poignant book *The Brains that Died: A Humankind Departing*—an immortal work dedicated to the dying Martians. The time was ripe, propitiously, for the Humankind of Earth. The Divinity had determined that in His gigantic plan.

Before the poet Mayer, whose famous song excited the generations that preceded the era of Venusian control, this formidable tableau slowly unfolded. Under his very eyes, the City of Stars extended, an immense buzzing multitude of active and happy men. His giant statue confronted it, pointing at the heavens. He gazed upon that new beauty, made of order, youth and ceaseless energy, a beauty that the Ancients would have admired. And with his already-failing hand he wrote the final words of the Imperial Hymn, his last work, which had the most colossal success everywhere his language resonated, for it encapsulated, better than anything sung before, the limitless ambition of Germany, her self-confidence and her immense pride:

We are the race of the sons of the god of the Hammer,
And we have the will to conquer the Empire of Stars
And to become the people of the Lords of Infinity.

THE END

Selected Bibliography

LITERATURE

Latin:

 Cicero, *De natura deorum* (Voyage in spirit)

Greek:

 Lucian, *Voyage to the Moon* (A storm)

German:

 Kepler, *Somnium* (Voyage in spirit)

Swedish:

 Swedenborg *Voyage to the Celestial Earths* (Voyage in spirit)

Italian:

 Dante, *Divine Comedy* (Voyage in spirit)

French:

 P. G. Daniel, *Voyage du monde de Descartes* (Voyage in spirit)

 Cyrano de Bergerac, *Histoire comique des Etats et Empires de la Lune et du Soleil* (Magnetism, rockets, expansion of fluids by heat)

 Jules Verne, *De la Terre à la Lune* (Giant cannon)

  ---   *Autour de la Lune* (ditto)

  ---   *Hector Servadac* (Collision with a comet)

 Voltaire, *Micromégas* (Knowledge of the laws of the universe)

 Pierre Boitard, *Voyage dans les planètes* (Assistance of a spirit)

 Arnould Galopin, *Le Docteur Oméga* (Cavorite, common term for substances impervious to gravitation)

 Henri de Graffigny & George Le Faure, *Les Aventures extraordionaires d'un savant russe* (Atomic bombardment, comet, giant cannon)

 George Le Faure, *Les Robinsons lunaire* (Hypothesis of a very extensive terrestrial atmosphere.)

 Gustave Le Rouge, *Le Prisonnier de la planète Mars* (Levitation)

--- *La Guerre des vampires* (Volcanic eruption on Mars)

Jean de La Hire, *Le Mystère des XV* (Radioplanes)

André Laurie, *Séléné Co. Ltd.* (Augmentation of the attractive force of the Earth, bringing the Moon closer)

--- *Les naufragés de l'Espace*

Lectures pour tous (1912), "Au XXe siècle" (Radioplanes)

Auguste Blanqui, *L'Eternité par les astres* (Nature is repetitive; the Earth is multiplied in time and space by the million)

English:

George Griffith, *Stories of Other Worlds* (Antigravitational force)[87]

John Jacob Astor, *A Journey in Other Worlds* (ditto)

Edgar Allan Poe, *Eureka* (Origin and end of worlds, God)

--- "Hans Pfaal" (Gas lighter than hydrogen and greatly extended atmosphere)

H.-G. Wells, *The War of the Worlds* (Martian giant cannon)

--- *The First Men in the Moon* (Cavorite)

--- "The Crystal Egg" (Communication between two similar crystals and intervision)

Roy Norton, *The Vanishing Fleets* (Cavorite)

Mortimer Collins, *The King* (Incarnation)[88]

George Du Maurier, *The Martian* (Incarnation)

---

[87] I have translated the English titles that Mas cites in French back into English; in this particular instance, I have retained the title Mas cites, which was that of the serial version of Griffith's work; it was reprinted in book form as *A Honeymoon in Space*.

[88] I have translated the title that Mas gives, although I presume that the reference is to Collins' *Transmigration* (1874); it might have been retitled in French translation.

SCIENCE

Camille Flammarion, *Astronomie populaire* (The Principle of Limiting Velocity in "Les Aérolithes")

Théophile Moreux, *Quelques heures dans le ciel* (Mention of limiting velocity. Impossibility of giant cannon)

--- *Les Phénomènes de l'Atmosphère* (Air and atmospheric layers)

S. Herrera, *Etudes comparatives des moyens employés pour aller dans les planètes* (The author concludes in favor of Cavorite)

Sciencia (1904), "À Mexico"

A. Perrett, *Les Explosifs* (Panclastite)

L'Année Scientifique (1884) (ditto)

Thèse d'Esnault-Pelterie in *Revue de Physique* (On reaction and the reaction motor)

A. Le Mée, *Revue des Revues* (1903-1905), "Communications avec les planètes" (Theoretical possibility)

Charles Cros, "Communicatons avec les planètes" in *Excursions dans le ciel* (Luminous signals)

Edmond Perrier. *La Vie dans les planets: Vénus* (Editions de la *Revue des Revues*)

Camille Flammarion, *Les Terres du Ciel* (Venus)

L'Année Scientifique (1887) (The reaction motor. The principle of reaction. Accident to the Buisson-Ciurcu motor.)

La Nature (1887) (ditto)

L'Année Industrielle (1897) (Undetailed mention of Thayer balloon moved by the reaction of compressed air. Dickinson centrifugal force cannon)

Revue Scientifique (1889) (Use of centrifugal force to launch projectiles (Hicks). Mention.)

Emile Gautier, *Les Étapes de la Science* (Undetailed menton of an American ship powered by reaction of dynamite)

Félix Bernard, *Précis de Paléontologie*

Von Zittel, *Grundzuge der Paleontologie*

H.F. Osborne, *Outline of Paleontology*

L'Année Scientifique (1886) (Ship moved by the explosion of a gaseous mixture and its reaction against the water)

   ---   (1891) (Motor for aerial navigation using both explosion and reaction)

René Lorin, "Le moteur à reaction" in *L'Aérophile* (1908-09)

A Bill of Lading for Venus:
Mars-Venus-Mail Planetship Company

Herbert Line Venustadt
Direct Service from the Earth
to Mars and Venus via the Moon
Routh & Co Bank, Agents.

Loaded in good order and condition by .... of Venustadt on .... and on the good Planetship called
.... of which .... is commander for
the present voyage, or (whoever else might be commander)
lodged in the port of Venustadt, destination Venus. The merchandise will be delivered in good order and condition, as will
the passengers, to the abovementioned port of Venus (except-
ing Acts of God, the enemies of the Emperor, planetary or
interplanetary pirates, theft, barratry, acts of terrestrial or other
populations or princes, insufficiency of packaging or of the
Wheel, gyroscopes or any other machinery, impacts, rains of
bolides or other objects occurring in space or worlds, the cold
of space, the heat of the Sun, errors committed by the captain,
the crew or the engineers of the Wheel, breakage, explosion,
fire, collision on arrival on any world, planetoid or bolide, and
any other hazard of space, planet or intermondial navigation of
any nature or sort whatsoever, or any other peril that might
develop if the said Planetship returns to Venusdtadt or any
other port and is obliged by any cause to end its voyage and
transfer the goods and persons to any other Planetship in
space, with the liberty to go with or without pilots, to guide
and assist the Planetship in any situation).

In consequence, the Mars-Venus-Mail Planetship Co.
engages to deliver the said passengers and cargo (under these
terms and conditions, at the risk of the sender and at the expense of the owner of the Planetship) to the abovementioned
port of Venus. In respect of which the freight is payable in
advance, at the current rate of exchange applicable to the Earth

and Venus, in bank-notes presentable on the day of the Planet-ship's arrival.

Any damage for which the ship-owner will be responsible must be reclaimed by the party in possession of the goods when the damage occurred. Customs duties (planetary or otherwise) are the responsibility of the sender. The owner of the Planetship is not responsible for money, gold, documents, coins, jewelry, paintings, statuary and other goods of value, except by special arrangement. The passengers are responsible for damage caused by them to the Wheel, the gyroscope and any other item of equipment throughout the planetary transit from port to port.

In the case of blockage or interdiction of the port of destination (or for any other cause if it is deemed that safe arrival cannot be guaranteed) the captain can disembark elsewhere,

The responsibility of the ship-owner is limited to 50 francs a ton in payments, saving any contrary agreement.

Any claim against the captain or the ship-owners, for any cause whatsoever, must be made at the port of destination on Venus.

Venustadt, on ……………………..

By:

The Agent

Théo Varlet: *Telepathy*
(1921)

Théo Varlet (1878-1938) was the son of a lawyer based in Lille, but his family was unusually well-off, having property and business interests in Russia. He grew up feeling that there was no need for him to make a living and decided to dedicate himself to a literary vocation. He contributed poetry and criticism to a wide range of literary periodicals, and published four collections of poetry before the outbreak of the Great War, beginning with *Heures et rêves* in 1898. Although he arrived on the scene too late to participate in the Decadent Movement, Charles Baudelaire was one of the more obvious influences on his work. He claimed to have attempted to follow up Baudelaire's "research" in the use of drugs to attain "artificial paradises," reporting extensively on his own supposed experiments with hashish, opium and—most dangerously—ether, although it is not clear how seriously those reports ought to be taken. In *Au paradis du haschisch; suite à Baudelaire* (1930) he catalogued more than 100 such experiments allegedly conducted between 1908 and 1914, including illusory out-of-body experiences that took him into remote regions of outer space and illusions of existing in another person's body, but it is impossible to be certain whether such short stories as "Télépathie" are based on actual experience, or whether the ostensible documentary is actually a fictional endeavor in disguise.

The Russian Revolution of 1917 wiped out the family fortune that had provided Varlet's living expenses while he made little or no money as a writer; like many other initially-vocational writers before him, he was abruptly confronted by the necessity of making a living from his pen. His primary source of income thereafter was translation; he translated most of Robert Louis Stevenson's works, John Buchan's *The Thir-*

ty-Nine Steps and Jerome K. Jerome's *Three Men in a Boat,* among many others. He became a writer of scientific romance almost by accident, when his publisher, Edgar Malfère, hired him to revise some highly imaginative, but somewhat rough-hewn, works by Octave Joncquel, two of which were published the two halves of *L'Epopée martienne* (1921-22; tr. in a Black Coat Press edition as *The Martian Epic* [89]).

The only volume of prose fiction that Varlet had published in advance of the Martian epic was a collection of short stories, *La Bella Venere* (1920) [the tile is the name of a boat], some of whose contents were recycled in *Le Dernier satyre* [The Last Satyr] (1922). He went on to collaborate with André Blandin on the timeslip romance, *La belle Valence* [Valencia the Beautiful] (1923) and subsequently published three solo novels, including two scientific romances: the Vernian *Le Roc d'or* [The Golden Rock] (1927) and the disaster story *La Grande panne* [The Great Breakdown] (1930). A further scientific romance, *Aurore Lescure, pilote d'astronef* [Aurore Lescure, Spaceship Pilot] was issued posthumously in 1940. At least some of these will hopefully be featured in future Black Coat Press publications.

"Télépathie" was one of the items added to *Le Dernier satyre*, although that does not necessarily mean that it was written in 1921. It is followed in that collection by "Autres notes de Haschisch" [Further Notes on Hashish], which is similar in its style and visionary content. Although it is on the very margins of scientific romance, it is interesting in the context of that genre's evolution and eventual supersession by science fiction because of its conscientious attempt to imagine what the experience of telepathy (a term then in its literary infancy, although it had been bandied about for some time in the field of "psychical research") might actually feel like, and what its existential consequences might be. Previous literary representations of "thought reading" had been decidedly primitive, and Varlet's attempt to sophisticate the notion was

---

[89] ISBN 978-1-934543-41-2.

several years ahead of Muriel Jaeger's *The Man with Six Senses* (1927), the first British scientific romance to undertake such a project; it is also much neater in its deployment of *conte cruel* irony.

Hashish—I never take it.

Not that I affect a naïve magnanimity of a Balzacian stripe and refuse to "think involuntarily." On the contrary, I envisage such poisonings as a kind of sport, and I find the new glimpses that they offer into the world of the mind seductive, in the same fashion as a trip in an automobile, a voyage in a balloon or a submarine dive.

I discovered my path too soon. It was only at the beginning of my research that I could have hesitated, eclectically, between various "artificial paradises." I certainly had a passing curiosity with regard to hashish then, but that oriental drug seemed so difficult to obtain that I kept putting the matter off, and eventually no longer thought about it. An old initiate of the good poison, I acquired a touch of the exclusivism that makes toxicomanes like us as sectarian as priests of different religions. The morphinist treats the opium smoker like a Moorish Turk and brutes drunk on alcohol have only insults for drinkers of ether like us—and we give them as good as we get. For myself, without going so far as to suspect Baudelaire, I've always held his hashish in very scant regard.

Now, I know; it's worse than I suspected, and I won't be taking it again.

With ether, at least one knows what to expect. One can establish the formula of one's folly, the percentage of its dreams. Given a particular dosage in decigrams, I know in advance the result of each etherization.

Taking opium is still possible, despite the sinful sophistication of apothecaries and the tiresome lacunae of its efficacy, but if you have a mind with a somewhat mathematical bent, if you want to conserve in dementia that lucidity of analysis which produces the finest sensuality for aestheticians—to observe one's own intoxication—if you delight in launching your dream like an obedient airplane into the sky of pure madness, beware of hashish, tenebrous and perfidious hashish.

When you've absorbed hashish, that's it—nothing more to be done. You've embarked, with your hands and feet bound, on an uncontrollable machine, which has taken off for an unknown flight.

I had no suspicion of that when, one afternoon, I accepted Albert Chaylas' offer. He was astonished to find out that I, fervent for artificial paradises as I am, was unfamiliar with it. How to obtain it? Quite simple: any druggist will furnish anyone with indeterminate quantities of *Cannabis indica*. Pharmacists use it themselves, albeit for rather grotesque purposes, such as soothing corns and calluses.

Having, like many an *habitué* of a single poison, an enthusiasm to recruit acolytes, Chaylas was happy to initiate me in the use of his favorite drug, perhaps cherishing the hope of making me abjure ether.

According to his scrupulous rites, he made some very strong and very hot coffee, took two unequal measures of hashish from a little Delft pot, dissolved the larger in his own cup and offered me the other on a spoon. It was a sort of dark green glue, with a penetrating odor of marsh-grass and a bitter taste like that of excessively-concentrated *souchong* tea. Mixed with coffee, the stuff was drinkable, and a second cup took the taste away temporarily.

To pass the preliminary hour of waiting, when no effect is manifest, I proposed that we re-read *Les paradis artificiels*, as a tourist guide to the marvelous land in which I was about to venture. Chaylas dissuaded me. To suggest impressions thus was contrary to spontaneity; one ought to let the effects emerge as they will. And, well used to hashish, he began to talk about trivial things, without the slightest allusion to the drug.

Despite my efforts, I was distracted. The enigmatic result disturbed me. That provisional inefficacy, the poison's silence, threw my experiment off course. What would happen next? Would there be, as with ether, an ineffable beatitude leading up to the sequence of dreams? Or opium's ocean of images, iridescent and agile ideas?

Sprawling in an armchair, next to the fire, I examined the large room, lit from above by a single electric lamp, attentively. I peered into the dark corners that the phantoms of hashish must haunt every evening—in vain. Chaylas, stretched out on the other side of the table—where I could only see his head, among the books and knick-knacks—nonchalantly smoked his long Dutch pipe and chatted with a placidity that redoubled my impatience.

In the intervals of the conversation, I held my breath to assure myself that the clock was still ticking.

I observed myself minutely. The annoying taste of marsh-grass was prowling under my palate again. My throat was dry, but I had no desire to stretch out my arm towards my coffee-cup to drain the last remaining drops. The heat of the coke fire filled me with an irresistible somnolence that was not at all disagreeable. My legs became heavy, as at the commencement of opium's effect…but nothing else. It was very little, 45 minutes after the absorption!

The high bookshelves stuffed with volumes, the paintings with gilded frames, a panoply of daggers and arrows, rifles and revolvers mounted on the walls—all loaded, in accordance with Chalyas' eccentricity—remained close at hand and stable, quite real and tangible, without the slightest appearance of the fluctuation that, after a few sips of ether, transfigures the external world into a décor devoid of relief or perspective, slack and vacillating.

"Are you sure," I asked, point-blank, "that your hashish isn't a huge hoax?"

"A huge hoax?" Chaylas riposted, slowly, in a bizarre nasal tone. "A huge hoax?" And he began to laugh—soft, dry, jerky laughter. He deposited his long pipe on the table in order to laugh more comfortably, and more wholeheartedly, his head thrown back behind the cushions of his divan. He was literally writhing with laughter. "A hoax! Hashish a hoax! I'm sure of it! A huge hoax! Fernand, old chap, you'll be the death of me!"

I found this overly familiar hilarity incongruous and disproportionate. I was offended. I let him see it.

"You're laughing? My supposition isn't so stupid, though—since I don't feel anything."

"You don't feel anything? That's true, my poor friend! You can't, any more—but you shall see, you shall see!"

That sort-of-apology softened me up. I didn't want to upset him. My question might, indeed, have seemed absurd to him. And I smiled myself.

I resumed my observations. The walls retreated, as if the room had visibly expanded. My torpor increased. It seemed that a subtle emanation was rising up from the carpet, soon bathing me up neck-deep: an emanation from which only my head emerged, in which I was about to be drowned—and I experienced a bizarre sensation of inhabiting a foreign body, of never having noticed how alien my body was.

I examined Chaylas' head. I had never looked at him either! The brass-bound edge of the table was presently adjacent to a shelf unit whose upper part was filled with books. In the glass-fronted lower part, amid the scattered knick-knacks, that strange Chaylas was a radiantly beaming Japanese mask! He made me laugh: an inconvenient dry and jerky laugh, then an outburst of broad laughter; and an absurd exclamation sprang from my lips: "An ape! My dear Albert, you have the head of an ape!"

The head formed a grotesque grimace of hilarity, the eyes squinting, the mouth twisted.

"An ape! Yes, Fernand, an ape! You too! You've got one too, haven't you?"

Indeed, I had. Everything—my own words, Chaylas' head, that Japanese showcase, the entire room, including the caricaturish hands of the clock, had taken on an irresistibly clownish appearance. I stood up, and stood on the divan in order to take a panoramic view of things, and I improvised a burlesque performance of a particularly humorous character.

The jokes were flowing through me with such abundance that I had no time to develop them. I could only mark their passage by quintessential allusions—but Chaylas half-understood, even seeming to divine with an extraordinary perspicacity what I was about to say, and replying to my gibes before I had enunciated them with sparkling, and no less elliptical, pleasantries.

For those ten minutes, we held the most extravagant synod of laughter that it is possible to imagine.

Little by little, the topic was exhausted. The last volleys faded away. I sat down again.

"It's nothing," Chaylas affirmed. "It's starting."

And I realized—it was a parenthetical thought—that we were now fully under the influence of hashish.

How does one describe the inexpressible? That room seemed to me to be isolated in space, 100,000 leagues from the Earth; we had transmigrated to another planet; my body harbored an exceedingly agile and subtle soul; and brief flashes of consciousness were the only memory of my previous self…

An exquisite and disturbing prodigy, to have transgressed the fastidious bounds of my individuality, to have rejected the old envelope of quotidian appearances, to see things with new senses, and perhaps—who knows?—*in depth*, in their essential aspect!

Yes, breaking through the membrane of reality, here is the fullness of hashish. No hallucination, to tell the truth. My ideas, prompt and jerky, pass by sequentially, unrolling cinematographically, as voluble as the mechanism of a watch whose escapement has just broken…

At the same time, deep inside me, in the utmost depths, an indiscernible thought, as enigmatic as a beam of light rising from a mine-shaft, rises gradually towards consciousness.

Chaylas was smiling. What was he dreaming? Why, as he looked at me that smile of complicity? Why was I, too, smiling with a secret disquiet?

We look at one another, motionless.

He would have liked to speak too, but he dared not, any more than I did. That is so embarrassing to day, so dubious still! Which of us would give voice to the idea, the suspicion of which was oppressing me, setting a chill in my heart?

He's said "All right?" and I've replied "Yes, fine"—to gain time, obviously. He gets up, inspects the walls, goes to lie down on another divan on the other side of the fire, facing me…that's normal. No, there's no mystery there.

Another heavy silence. Again that ambiguous and constrained smile. More and more embarrassed, that ominous smile. For the secret, the terrible secret, will get out; it seethes in our brains like vapor under pressure; it expands around us, saturating the room with an atmosphere more revelatory than explicit speech. The mystery reveals itself, communicates itself without anyone having said a word. He knows too! We both know! And yet—for it is necessary at all costs that the other does not know that the other knows—we each persist in smiling, smiling with a fixed and cataleptic grimace.

And I remember. Intermittently, I recollect the series of my previous meetings with Caylas. I analyze successively his somber character, his bouts of pessimism, his perverse taste for flirting with death. One day, he mixed with his opium pills a pill of the same appearance containing a lethal dose of strychnine, and, inviting me to imitate him, swallowed one selected at random. He was mad when, having put a live cartridge in his revolver, he made me spin the magazine blindly, then cried: "Three!" Three times, with the barrel of the gun in his mouth, he pressed the trigger, without releasing the bullet—which came fourth. And that other day when he said to me, with a strange expression, as he pointed to his mistress: "If she pleases you…"

I had my eyes open, though, and when these images vanished—as a face reflected in an unsilvered glass melts into things placed behind it as they become clearer—I see Chaylas in front of me, on the divan on the other side of the fire, studying me curiously.

We were young then—it was two years ago! The poison's premature old age had not yet injected such scorn for life into our veins—but me, me! I am not so detached, am I?

"Evidently."

He has replied, aloud, to my psychic interrogation. It's clear. He knows. He is penetrating my thoughts as I am penetrating his! Our thoughts, absolutely synchronous, are progressing as one, within two brains.

Absolutely synchronous?

I see by the character of his smile, in which I read *our* ideas, that the coincidence is not complete. There is, here and there, a *temporal displacement* in the transmission.

But he must know whether it is really true, whether this prodigy of telepathy, by a mysterious effect of the drug, effectively links our cerebral cells, whether our psychic dynamisms have really entered into communication, whether the thought is circulating between us as if between vessels linked by a U-tube.

Is it true? And I say: "Oh—that would be wonderful!"

"Wonderful, yes, isn't it?" replies Chaylas, whose gaze never leaves me. "You too?"

No more doubt.

As motionless as a statue, I do not manifest my emotion. And this is how our occult duality proceeds within me, alternating my own thoughts with others, of a somber and haggard character, which I do not recognize, undoubtedly furnished by Chaylas. An influx of comic sadness and mortal disgust—the flagrant uselessness of our life—strange ideas that I adopt, that I *have to* adopt, as Chaylas, by virtue of the reciprocal flow, *has to* admit my thoughts into him.

Independent asides slip into the interstices of this psychic conversation: parcels of myself, protected from the contagion, reflecting in flashes on the horror of the phenomenon. An ultra-determinist, accustomed by other poisons to see my lucid consciousness as nothing but an inactive witness of fatal energies that take control of my pseudo-will, I rebel, this time, against finding myself under the direct influence of another human brain, subject to another's ideas—even with the assured revenge of the same empire over him.

And from time to time, assuming the materiality of speech, the expected replies formulate themselves at their precise moment. This is what confirms the sorcery; he replies to my mental question.

"Oh, that's right!"

"No doubt."

But I'm deceitful, at present; taking refuge in a strictly personal islet of lucidity set apart from the currents and eddies of our duplicate thought, I entrench myself there, to test whether we are indissolubly linked.

Sometimes, I have the upper hand; I feel my thought running into him, like a river into the sea; sometimes, it is his that flows back into me, irresistible, as the tide fills an estuary.

Let's go! Stronger! No? But who is in command of our psychic couple—you or me? Reply! Reply out loud, I demand it!

He says nothing. He is still looking at me. But an internal voice cries: *Me! Who thought that? Him or me?*

And I strive with all my might: Ah! for this, I employ free will! I stand up, bracing myself with all my strength, in order to vanquish that antagonistic will. Interlocked like wrestlers in the ideal space that separates us, seemingly indifferent witnesses, our wills engaging in a duel with wild moves. Somersaults of triumph go through me. His shoulders are about to touch! And I press down, oh, I press down! But my hold is broken without his having acknowledged defeat, and I must defend myself in my turn, terribly.

It's a duel to the death. To the death, because the oscillatory, intoxicated, whirling-dervish double thought is vertiginously interlocked in a spiral of alternate litanies descending towards suicide.

He wants to kill himself—he's mad: I should certainly have realized that—and that old obsession will be realized today. He is thinking, I know, about the weapons hanging on the wall behind him—those loaded revolvers that he sees, as I see them, without looking at them...ho! Isn't it me who has just suggested it to him? Did he really think it?—And then you'll kill me (for he has the proselytism of suicide, he wants me to deliver myself from life, in spite of myself), you'll kill me, and then yourself; we'll kill on another, with revolvers over there. Oh, don't come any closer! I forbid it! See, I'm staying still (to maintain him in his place too, for if I try to forestall him, he'll perceive my intention immediately, and I can't—very quiet, this, very quiet!—kill him before he can do the same to me). Enough, I forbid it! Let's think of something else for a moment, so that I can get some respite in our hand-to-hand combat, to gather strength, to tame your impulses; so that I have the time to vanquish you; let's go on to something else, let's go on! (But I don't find anything, and in the void of my suggestion, it's his mortal thought that will hold sway, filling me too....) Listen, I remember... (No, not that! I don't want to! I've said nothing! A shadow! A shadow over that!) ...that your mistress... (Am I mad, then, to tell him about that? Me, I don't want to. Me? Who's me?) That day we... (No! Nothing! Nothing! Ah, Victory! Nothing.) Listen. I'll tell you...

And our black gazes, our pupils enormous sound one another out. Our faces are terrible, oracular.

"Come on! Come on! Let's go! Yes, these are our synchronous thoughts. Let's go! A mysterious communal force, overwhelming, our Destiny, springs forth from the duplicate utmost depths of our being. Come on! We're going to die!

Traitor! You lied! It's your insanity that you want to pass off as our Destiny. Me, I want to live! I will live. My strength is coming back. I will! I will!—Victory! I've taken command of the couple. (For a brief instant, perhaps? No matter, it's enough.) Stay there—I order you to stay there! Twenty seconds! Twenty seconds! I want you to stay, madman!

Ah! I've leapt up! I was able to leap up!—ahead of him—to open the door, close it from the outside, lock it, and run away, free, run away into the darkness, to my home, to shut myself in too, to lock the door...

The connection between us is broken. A few fragments of his thought are still floating around me. Vanquished, he

tried to turn the drama into a joke, to excuse himself prosaical-
ly...

After an hour on watch, revolver in hand, I sensed that he
was going to sleep.

Saved! I had reconquered my individuality, my precious
individuality, submissive only to the play of eternal forces,
and not to an unbearable conjunction with another human
brain!

I dared to go to sleep.

When I woke up from a slumber swarming with horrid
dreams, the memory of the adventure disturbed me again. I
had recovered my normal consciousness and my full lucidity,
but, in contrast to the aftermath of the phantasmagorias of
ether, I was unable to see the telepathy of the previous evening
as a simple illusion. The drug's effect had ceased; I was reasoning with my everyday brain—that brain which systemati-
cally denies the possibility of supernatural force—and yet I
did not believe that those stranger phenomena were purely
subjective in nature.

Even if they were only an illusion due to the hashish, had
they not drawn from the depths of my organism, revealed and
given birth to the consciousness of a crazy inclination—latent
until then—to suicide?

And what if it were true? What if it had been true?

Should I interrogate Chaylas? But today, returned to a
civilized lucidity, would he not deny those savage impulses,
that wild scene in which he had conducted himself like a
caveman? And what about me? Had not my own role been
grotesque and odious?

So I avoided him. I had him sent away from my door—
after all, he might have come to ask me why I had locked him
in his room!

It was necessary, however, to bite the bullet when we
bumped into one another a week later on the boulevard. He
was, as always, taciturn and closed off. He did not raise the
question. Devoured by one of those fatal curiosities that de-

mand the illumination of something that should forever remain in shadow, I wanted to know.

We were silent. A slight vertigo, like an after-effect of hashish, was communicated between us despite the positive atmosphere of the boulevard.

At the precise moment when I was about to speak, I saw a hesitation on his face identical to mine: a dread that I might reveal to him the reality of the adventure—and the least allusion, by him or by me, would be irrefutable proof!

Simultaneously, we turned our eyes away. Simultaneously, we voiced the same commonplace.

BLACK COAT PRESS

Gaston Leroux. *Chéri-Bibi*
Gaston Leroux. *The Phantom of the Opera*
Jean-Marc Lofficier. *The Katrina Protocol*
Jean-Marc & Randy Lofficier. *Edgar Allan Poe on Mars*
Jean-Marc & Randy Lofficier. *Robonocchio*
J.-M. & R. Lofficier (eds.). *Tales of the Shadowmen 1: The Modern Babylon*
J.-M. & R. Lofficier (eds.). *Tales of the Shadowmen 2: Gentlemen of the Night*
J.-M. & R. Lofficier (eds.). *Tales of the Shadowmen 3: Danse Macabre*
J.-M. & R. Lofficier (eds.). *Tales of the Shadowmen 4: Lords of Terror*
J.-M. & R. Lofficier (eds.). *Tales of the Shadowmen 5: The Vampires of Paris*
Xavier Mauméjean. *The League of Heroes*
Frank J. Morlock. *Sherlock Holmes: The Grand Horizontals*
Marie Nizet. *Captain Vampire*
C. Nodier, Beraud & Toussaint-Merle. *Frankenstein*
Charles Nodier. *Lord Ruthven the Vampire*
Henri de Parville. *An Inhabitant of the Planet Mars*
John William Polidori. *Lord Ruthven the Vampire*
P.-A. Ponson du Terrail. *The Vampire and the Devil's Son*
Albert Robida. *The Clock of the Centuries*
Eugène Scribe. *Lord Ruthven the Vampire*
Brian Stableford. *The New Faust at the Tragicomique*
Brian Stableford. *Sherlock Holmes and the Vampires of Eternity*
Brian Stableford. *The Stones of Camelot*
Brian Stableford. *The Wayward Muse*
Brian Stableford (ed.). *News from the Moon*
Villiers de l'Isle-Adam. *The Scaffold*
Villiers de l'Isle-Adam. *The Vampire Soul*
Philippe Ward. *Artahe: The Legacy of Jules de Grandin*
P. de Wattyne & Y. Walter. *Sherlock Holmes vs. Fantômas*
David White: *Fantômas in America*

www.ingramcontent.com/pod-product-compliance
Lightning Source LLC
Chambersburg PA
CBHW030347020726
47493CB00003B/722